The Good Shepherd
and the Last Perfect

The
Good Shepherd
and the
Last Perfect

By Susan E. Kaberry

The Book Guild Ltd

First published in Great Britain in 2022 by
The Book Guild Ltd
Unit E2 Airfield Business Park,
Harrison Road, Market Harborough,
Leicestershire. LE16 7UL
Tel: 0116 2792299
www.bookguild.co.uk
Email: info@bookguild.co.uk
Twitter: @bookguild

Copyright © 2022 Susan E. Kaberry

The right of Susan E. Kaberry to be identified as the author of this
work has been asserted by her in accordance with the
Copyright, Design and Patents Act 1988.

All rights reserved. No part of this publication may be
reproduced, transmitted, or stored in a retrieval system, in any form or by any means,
without permission in writing from the publisher, nor be otherwise circulated in
any form of binding or cover other than that in which it is published and without
a similar condition being imposed on the subsequent purchaser.

This work is entirely fictitious and bears no resemblance to any persons living or dead.

Typeset in 11pt Minion Pro

Printed and bound by CPI Group (UK) Ltd, Croydon, CR0 4YY

ISBN 978 1915122 148

British Library Cataloguing in Publication Data.
A catalogue record for this book is available from the British Library.

To David, as always.

Preface

In the Middle Ages, the County of Foix (now part of present-day Languedoc) was an independent fief of France. It was governed by the counts of Foix and the minor nobility or Lords who were subordinate to the count, but who had some influence on the government of the region. The ordinary people or peasants were not subjected to the ancient regime as it existed in the Kingdom of France and were free to own land and property themselves. As a result, some of them were as wealthy as the minor nobility of the area, if not more so.

It was in the County of Foix in the first half of the thirteenth century that a group of Christian dissidents flourished. They believed that the church in Rome had lost sight of God's teachings and become worldly, materialistic and corrupt, the work of the devil. They eschewed many of the teachings of Roman Catholicism, believing that the devil made the physical world and our bodies, and that God created our souls. They did not believe in the transubstantiation of bread and wine at the altar into the body and blood of Christ. These dissidents were the Cathars, the Good Christians or Good Men as their followers called them.

The Cathars revered their holy men and women, known as Perfects, so called due to the simple lives they led, renouncing the pleasures of the flesh, and eating only fish and vegetables. They believed that through undertaking the ritual of the *consolamentum* just prior to death, that the dying person could be absolved of their sins and their soul would be saved. This ritual involved the laying on of hands by a Perfect, questions about the dying person's beliefs and readings from the Gospels. The moribund Believer then embarked upon the *endura*, a fast until death.

The Cathars were regarded as heretics by the established church in Rome, and a brutal and persecutory campaign was mounted against them in the first half of the thirteenth century with the intention of eradicating them. The Albigensian crusades (so called as many Cathars had lived in the town of Albi) acting on orders from the Pope, committed a series of atrocities against the Cathars. Many thousands were killed, imprisoned and tortured throughout the area. By far the worst of the carnage took place at Béziers, in 1209, on the feast of St Mary Magdalene, 22nd July. It was estimated that 15,000 to 20,000 innocent people were butchered by an army of crusaders and French mercenaries under the command of a Papal legate named Arnaud Amaury. The legate and his troops arrived at the gates of Béziers demanding the release of the 220 Cathars thought to be living there. They were refused, fighting broke out and Béziers became the scene of a bloody massacre. When asked how his men should know which people were heretics, Amaury's notorious reply was, "Kill them all; God will know his own." The streets, littered with severed limbs and dead bodies, ran red with blood.

At the hilltop Cathar stronghold of Montségur there were further scenes of mass killings. A ten-month long siege resulted in 200 Perfects and Believers being marched down the steep rockside to their deaths on the Catholic bonfire which lay below. As well as these large-scale killing sprees, the homes of individual Cathars were torched, turned into dung heaps and their land was confiscated. Many people were interrogated and imprisoned in the notorious prison named The Wall, at Carcassonne. Prisoners could be subjected to horrific torture until they confessed. Less persecutory punishments were pilgrimages and prayer. One of the most common punishments was to be condemned to wear large yellow crosses attached to the outer garments of the condemned person. The wearer was shunned and found it difficult to obtain work. Many became beggars and lived on the fringes of society. As a result of this persecution the Cathars were left with no Perfects to lead them, and the Believers went underground.

By the end of the thirteenth century Catharism had been almost erased. But by remaining out of sight a few die-hards had retained a foothold ready to embrace a revival if it came along. And come along it did, in the shape of the Authier brothers of Ax (now Ax-les-Thermes), who spearheaded a campaign which fanned the flames of a Cathar revival towards the end of the thirteenth century and into the early years of the fourteenth century. After studying for four years in Lombardy, the Authier brothers became the new Perfects. Their ministry was centred in the Sabarthès, the area in which the mountain villages of Montaillou and Prades lay, or the Pays d'Aillou, as it was also called.

Becoming aware of this heretical activity, the Church appointed Jacques Fournier as Bishop of Pamiers in 1317. Bishop Fournier formed his own Episcopal Inquisition and systematically hunted the Cathars. He arrested suspects and subjected them to questioning, imprisonment and punishments if they were found guilty of heresy. Bishop Fournier was known for his rigor, for his penetrative questioning and for his meticulous recording of the interrogations he undertook. It is because of his methods that we know so much about the final revival of Catharism, and about the daily lives of the ordinary people who lived in the area 700 years ago.

The people spoke Occitan, the 'langue d'Oc', which gave its name to the area. As a native of the region, Bishop Fournier spoke Occitan. The written records were made at the time of the interrogations and subsequently translated into Latin. They were stored in the Vatican archives until the middle of the twentieth century, when they were released into the public domain. A number of these records have since been translated into French and English. Pierre Maury's deposition was the longest of all the records. He was the shepherd upon whom this book is based. There are no records of Guillaume Belibaste's interrogations.

Bishop Jacques Fournier's careful record-keeping has ensured that the ghosts of all the players in the drama of the last Cathars of the Languedoc remain to haunt the world forever. In the documents the shepherds, the churchmen, the noblemen and the peasants are revealed in all their human weaknesses, as well as in their moments of glory. They were men and women with lives both ordinary and extraordinary. Their voices were silent for 700 years. It is time they were heard.

Susan E. Kaberry

PART 1

1299–1305

CHAPTER 1

Guy Belibaste, 1299, Cubières

Guy strode out at speed along the track between the rows of vines. Anger drove his pace. How could his father treat him so? He had been sent away as if he were a child, to deal with some thieving shepherds, when two Cathar Perfects – the Good Men – whom they'd waited weeks to meet, were in their home. It was one of many such occasions that had occurred over the years; each time Guy thought it would be the last. It never was. This time his father had taken advantage of the Perfects' presence knowing Guy would not dispute in front of them. So, Guy was on his way to confront three shepherds who had been seen selling meat and sheepskins in the local tavern. It would take him all day to walk to the pastures and back again, and by that time the Perfects would have left. *He had no idea that he was walking towards events which would change his life forever.*

He was soon out of breath (his usual walk being a kind of meander), and as his pace slowed, he calmed down. He looked at the neat rows of vines on either side. They stretched into the distance towards the surrounding mountains, whose snowy peaks glistened in the sun. How enduring and strong they were – God's creation – as he himself was. If it was the right path God would help him in his quest to meet the Perfects. He should ask God to help him. He stopped to kneel on the grassy verge. *Dear Lord, show me the way to salvation and give me strength to follow it. Amen.* He remembered something. *And forgive me my sins, Amen.* He felt calmer. God would know he had no time for a longer prayer. And he had a feeling that God was listening to him and that soon he would meet the Perfects for himself.

Guy's fascination with the Cathars started in childhood at his mother's knee. His mother told her sons stories of the bravery of the Cathar Perfects in the past, when they faced persecution by the Inquisition. Guy's great uncle had been a Perfect and, along with all the other Perfects, he was hounded, persecuted and burned alive. The remaining Cathar Believers, including his parents, with no-one to lead them, had gone underground. But three years ago, two brothers from Ax, Guillaume and Pierre Authier, had given up their law practice and left their families to go to Lombardy, where they studied and became Perfects. They had recently returned to the area and were preaching in the homes of Believers. At this moment, Pierre Authier and another Perfect, Philippe d'Aylarac, were in his father's house. How sure they must be about the way to salvation, sure enough to leave so much behind. Guy had hoped that his father would be pleased about their shared interest in the Cathars and that this would connect them. Now it seemed unlikely. His father did not want him there. He should stop expecting his father to change. He would find a way by himself to meet the Good Men. He was passionate about this alternative faith in a way that he had never been about anything else. He was desperate to meet the Good Men and hear what they had to say.

As he came closer to the valley where the sheep were grazing, his thoughts turned to the thieving shepherds he must confront.

How he hated confrontations. He rounded a hill, and the valley came into view. There before him lay an amorphous mass of grey sheep. The animals' bleating drifted up to him. At the edge of the flock were two of the shepherds he must confront. One looked up and glimpsed Guy. He turned to the other shepherd and pointed towards Guy. They both shielded their eyes and watched as Guy approached. They looked more like wild animals than men with their tangled hair and shaggy beards. Guy took a deep breath as he walked towards them.

"Good day, Jacques, Barthélemy," said Guy. "How fares the flock?"

"All's well," said Barthélemy, looking Guy straight in the eye. Was there a hint of challenge in the look? Jacques looked down and scuffed his leather-booted foot in the dust. Guy followed his gaze. The boots looked to be new and made of good-quality leather.

"That's a fine pair of boots, Jacques," said Guy. "Where'd you get them?"

"In Cubières," said Jacques. "The shoemaker made them for me." Jacques looked up at Guy.

"They must have cost a lot of money," said Guy. Jacques shrugged.

"When did you go to Cubières?" said Guy.

"Last week," said Jacques, glancing at Barthélemy, who nodded agreement. "We went together, and left Jean and the dogs guarding the flock. We weren't gone long."

The dogs. Guy looked around. He saw only one dog lying near the barn. "Where's Chief? My dog?"

"He died," said Barthélemy. "When we were in Cubières."

"Where did you bury him?"

"We haven't got round to that."

"Where is he? What have you done with him?"

"He's over there, behind the rocks." Barthélemy pointed to an area where a few bushes surrounded a rocky outcrop.

Guy swallowed. Tears pricked his eyes. Chief had been his favourite dog. He shook himself; he mustn't cry in front of these rough men.

"You should have let us know," said Guy. His voice cracked. He cleared his throat. "How long were you in Cubières? I heard you were in the tavern."

"We didn't go to the tavern. We bought cheese and bread from the market; Jacques collected his boots, and we came back. When we returned the dog was dead. He was old, you know, and he'd been off his food for a few days and lying around a lot, not his usual self."

"Where was Jean?" said Guy. He cleared his throat again.

"He was in the barn," said Jacques.

"Where is he now?" said Guy.

"In the barn," said Barthélemy.

"Doesn't he ever come out of there?" said Guy. His voice had gained some strength. "Go and fetch him Jacques, then count the sheep."

"We might be one or two down," said Barthélemy.

"Get Jean out here," said Guy.

Guy watched as Jacques went to the barn. He came out with Jean, the third shepherd. They went to the side of the barn to pick up hurdles. Guy went to look for Chief. A cloud of black flies swarmed up as he approached the rock, behind which lay the body of Chief. It was wriggling. He edged closer. Urgh. The body was seething with maggots. A sickening stench emanated from Chief. Guy covered his nose and mouth and turned away. He watched the men as they sorted through the hurdles. Many were broken.

"There aren't enough to pen the sheep and count them," said Barthélemy.

A wave of despair coursed through Guy. He started a rough count of the animals. There should be at least two hundred sheep. But without pens and hurdles and all of them working together, it was an impossible task. The sheep milled round, bleating loudly as if they knew there was something wrong. Guy gave up counting, enraged with himself for even trying. Barthélemy turned his face away to hide a smirk. Jacques laughed.

"You should have maintained those hurdles – you should have erected decent pens. I know there are sheep missing," Guy shouted.

"We always lose one or two to wolves and bears," said Jacques.

"No, no," shouted Guy. "It's down to you three – you've been seen in the tavern in Cubières selling meat and sheepskins."

Guy stepped forward, grabbed Barthélemy, who was nearest, by his tunic, and shook him. Their faces were close. Eye to eye, nose to nose. Phew, Barthélemy stank like a filthy old animal. Guy let go of Barthélemy and turned to the other two.

"What about you, Jacques? And Jean?" Guy shouted. Jacques stared blankly. Jean backed away. "You stinking, bastard sheep thieves!" Infuriated, Guy grabbed Barthélemy again and shook him. They struggled together as Barthélemy attempted to push Guy away.

"What about the Good Men and your family?" shouted Jacques.

With a sudden upward thrust, Barthélemy pushed Guy's arms off him and shoved Guy away. Guy staggered back, lost his balance, righted himself and ran towards Barthélemy, who took a step back. Guy tripped. The momentum caused him to fall onto Barthélemy, who hit the ground with Guy's weight upon him. Guy flailed, then pushed himself up and off Barthélemy. Breathing heavily, Guy made a fist and stood, legs apart, looming over Barthélemy, ready to knock him to the ground if he rose. Barthélemy did not move. Jacques sidled over, looked at Barthélemy and knelt beside him. Jacques touched Barthélemy's face.

"Barthélemy!" Jacques gave Barthélemy's cheek a small slap. There was no response. Barthélemy's eyes were open. Blood was seeping from under his head, forming a thick crimson patch on the ground.

Guy knelt and fumbled through Barthélemy's ragged clothing to find a heartbeat. He couldn't feel anything. He moved his hand over Barthélemy's chest. No heartbeat? Surely not. He couldn't be... Barthélemy's eyes, fixed and unmoving, stared at Guy in accusation. Guy looked away. He could not close those eyes.

Jacques, still kneeling, shook Barthélemy's body. "Barthélemy!" He turned and fixed his eyes on Guy. "He's dead! You've killed him!"

Guy stood and moved back a pace, still staring at Barthélemy. "No... no..."

"He's not breathing," said Jacques.

Jean came closer and they all stared at the thin, spare body, wrapped in its filthy rags. Barthélemy's face was waxy pale. His lips were blue. The blood was spreading.

"It was an accident," said Guy. "I tripped..."

"You killed him," said Jacques. He stood.

Jean nodded his head. "We'll report you to the Bailiff," said Jean.

"And there's the heretics..."

Guy looked from one to the other. "This was an accident." The shepherds shook their heads.

Guy staggered back and stared at the scene. Barthélemy on the ground, bleeding – the other two shepherds watching him accusingly. Think... he must think... but he couldn't think, and his instincts screamed go – just go. So, he turned and ran faster than he'd ever run before. He must go to warn his father and the Good Men that the shepherds threatened to report them. He tripped and stumbled over a rock. A sharp pain shot up his leg. But he didn't stop. He focused his attention on avoiding more obstacles. He ran on, concentrating on the track in front of him and pushing the image of the dead shepherd out of his mind as it threatened to overwhelm him.

When he reached the track that led to his father's farmhouse, he was gasping for air, and his head was spinning. He stopped, slipped his soaking tunic over his head and attempted to dry the sweat off himself. He threw the tunic to the ground and stumbled to the shady side of the track, where he sank to his knees and collapsed full-length, face down. The grass felt cool and soft under his cheek – if only he could lie there in the shade and sleep. But as his breathing calmed, the vision he had fought to suppress slid into his mind. Barthélemy, the dead shepherd – lying on his back on the ground, his eyes open and staring, blood seeping from under his head. Guy stood and, steadying himself against the tree, he heaved up his guts. Bitter fluid gushed from his mouth until there was nothing left in him. He wiped his mouth with his hand, moved away from the mess and slumped against another tree. He must find the courage to face his father.

He looked across the track at the rows of vines stretched out into the distance. This was his father's land, and his father's land before him and so on for as long as anyone could remember. One day it would belong to Guy and his two brothers. It was what he was born to and what was expected of him. He was in his mid-twenties, with a wife and two children, working as a farmer alongside his brothers and his father. But he had no feeling for the land and the animals like his brothers. They knew what to do naturally but he… well, he was useless. Now this.

Guy stood. He must face his father about… Barthélemy, but most of all he must warn him that the shepherds knew of his family's connection to the Good Men, the Perfects. The longer he delayed, the more danger both the Good Men and his family would be in. He hardly dared to think about what all this would mean for his wife, Estelle, and their two babies.

He was shaking as he approached the farmhouse. He stood for a moment outside. *God help me – give me strength.* He crossed himself before going through the front door and into the large hall, where his father was sitting at one end of the long table with the two Good Men. It was a relief to find the Good Men still there. Their presence would temper his father's response. They were deep in conversation, but they stopped and looked at Guy as he entered the room. The looks of astonishment on their faces reminded Guy that he was partially naked and filthy.

"Guy," said his father. "I didn't expect you… what's wrong? You look—"

"I killed him." Tears welled up in Guy's eyes. He brushed them away and sank down on the bench next to his father. He put his head in his hands. A sob escaped from him. He took a deep breath. "I killed him. He's dead."

"Who?" His father glanced from Guy to the Perfects and back to Guy. "Guy, whatever do you mean?"

"I didn't mean to… it all happened so quickly – I tripped and fell on him. It was an accident… he fell back… and he's dead…"

"Slow down, Guy." His father poured water for him. "Here, drink this, try to calm yourself and tell me exactly what has happened."

Guy gulped the water and looked at the three men seated around the table. His father looked aghast; the Good Men looked concerned. After another sip of water and a deep breath, Guy began.

"They said wolves had taken some sheep, but we've never had trouble with wolves there before, so I said the two of them had been seen in the tavern in Cubières, selling meat and sheepskins. Jacques laughed. I got hold of Barthélemy and shook him. He broke my hold – I staggered back. He shouted that he knew about our family and the Good Men. I moved towards him, and… I don't know what happened… I must have tripped…" He stopped for a moment and caught his breath as the scene replayed in his mind. "I fell on top of him… he was on the ground… his eyes were open, staring at me." Guy took another deep breath. "And… blood, blood, there was blood coming from under his head…" He looked at his father and the two Perfects. "He's dead. I killed him."

CHAPTER 2

Pedro Maury, 1299, Montaillou

It was early morning. The mountain village of Montaillou lay sleeping under a thick blanket of mist. Inside a house on the edge of the square, Pedro Maury was slowly tiptoeing towards the front entrance. Pedro, tall and slim with big feet, was terrified of tripping up and waking his family. His father would try to stop him, and his mother would be distraught if they knew he was leaving. Pedro held his breath – no-one stirred. He closed the door behind him and exhaled into the thick mist. He had to get away from this village of thugs and heretics and make a new life for himself. If only he could have left with his father's blessing, but that wasn't possible. He shivered and pulled his cloak close as he walked down the track through the sleeping village. God, that mountain mist had already seeped into his blood and bones.

When he was clear of the last house, he stopped to look back at the village. Through the mist he saw a flame flickering at the corner of one of the houses and heard the crackle and swoosh of fire. Was that his aunt's house? He should raise the alarm. But he blinked and it stopped. His imagination was playing tricks. He licked his lips and swallowed. Was this a warning of things to come, or a vision from the past? Either way, it disturbed him.

Pedro had been thinking of leaving home for the past two years. It was after the last visit to his cousin's farm in Arques, where he'd gone with his father to buy a couple of lambs, that the idea had formed in his mind. Pedro Maury and his cousin Raymond Maulen were friends as well as relatives, and now Pedro hoped that when he turned up at Raymond's farm later that day, Raymond would let him stay and help him find work. Otherwise, he would be on his own. He would be seen as young and inexperienced by potential employers, although he had worked with his father's sheep since he was a child. At least he felt sure that Raymond would allow him to stay overnight.

It was Pedro's love for his family that had kept him in Montaillou, but the last disagreement with his father, and a recent encounter with one of the village thugs, forced him to make a decision. It was the end of summer 1299; the new year and a new century was in front of him. As far as anyone could recall he had turned eighteen that year. It was time to leave. He had a long day's walk ahead of him, and he must look forward to the future. The surrounding mountains were emerging from the mist, leaving lingering wisps around their rocky summits. His heart lifted with the mist.

The sun rose and the day heated up; Pedro took off his brown woollen cloak and carried it with his small bundle of clothing and food. He passed bleached fields of yellow straw stubble as the land flattened out on either side of the track. A few farmhouses dotted the landscape and he saw men in the distance, working on their strips of land, harvesting oats and barley. At midday he noticed a pale green stream beside the track, gurgling over its stony bed. He bent down to slurp a few handfuls of water. This would be a good place to eat his bread and cheese. He sat under the branches of a sweet chestnut tree and leant against its trunk; the gentle running of the water in the background was restful.

He opened his eyes. There was a sound... hooves clopping on the rocky track. He turned his head... something... was emerging from a bend in the road. An apparition in white was moving towards him leading a pure white mule. Holy Father, was this a spirit from another world? Had it come to punish him for leaving home like this? He leapt up and crossed himself. His heart banged so deep and strong in his chest, it almost hurt him. But it was a man with a mule laden with bulging sacks of flour. At every step the animal took, puffs of white flour rose up from the sacks. Man and mule were covered in it.

"You gave me a fright," said Pedro.

The man laughed. "I went to the mill with some grain early this morning," he said. "I'm always covered in the stuff when I come back." He leant on the stick he carried and breathed heavily. "These mountain tracks don't get any easier as you get older." He knelt beside the stream with a groan and drank the cold water from his cupped hands. He sighed as he sat down. "My old knees ache," he said as he brought forth a small leather flask from the folds of his tunic and took a sip. "This keeps me going." He raised the flask. "Good health to you."

"And to you," said Pedro.

"Where are you going?" said the man.

"To Arques," said Pedro. "I've walked from Montaillou this morning."

"You've made good progress then." He offered his flask to Pedro, who shook his head. "Montaillou, eh?" The man wiped his mouth with the back of his hand and fixed his rheumy eyes on Pedro. "There's a lot going on there, I hear," he said.

Pedro caught his breath. What did he mean? Surely, he wouldn't risk...

"You look a sensible young man, I'm sure you can hold your tongue when necessary? Besides, there's only you and me to hear it." He paused. "You may know, the talk in Ax is all about the return of the Authier brothers, the Perfects. They're back from Lombardy, ready to start their ministry." Pedro could feel the man's eyes piercing him. He lowered his head. "And there's plenty in Montaillou ready to follow them. It will lead to trouble, you know, as it did before."

Pedro swallowed hard. This was dangerous talk; best to stay quiet. They sat together in an uncomfortable silence for a moment or two until Pedro stood up and asked the man how far it was to Arques.

"It's some way yet. I reckon it'll take you the rest of the day – just follow the track."

Pedro picked up his cloak and bundle and set off along the track. That was a difficult moment with the old man. Ever since the time three years back, when everyone in Montaillou was talking about the Authier brothers who had gone to Lombardy to become Perfects, there had been rumours of spies. Now the Authiers were back, and it was said the Inquisition in Carcassonne had increased the numbers of spies. Pedro didn't relish being suspicious but it was best to be cautious.

It was the Perfects or Good Men who had caused the most recent disagreement between Pedro and his father. In the spring of that same year, Pedro had just finished shearing his father's sheep. He had leant against the fence, satisfied to see the neat pile of sheepskins and happy because he knew his father would be pleased too. Then he looked up and saw Bernard Belot making his way across the meadow from the nearby wood. Bernard was a great bear of a man with a big red face and no teeth at the front of his mouth, having had them knocked out in various brawls. His face usually had a frown on it, but he waved and sauntered up to Pedro, grinning. His gaze slid over to the pile of fleeces.

"Best quality fleeces, eh, Pedro?"

"Not bad."

"Have you heard?" said Bernard, looking around as if there was someone nearby who might hear them. "The Authier brothers are back; they need support whilst they spread the word. You should give something, Pedro."

"I've nothing to give," said Pedro.

"A couple of those fleeces will do."

"They're my father's."

"Your father helped the Good Men in the past," said Bernard. "He'll understand. He knows they're not like our Roman priests." He spat on the ground. "And they're the only ones who can save our souls." He put his face close to Pedro's. "You want your soul to be saved, don't you, Pedro? So, give them two fleeces."

Pedro knew that if he didn't do as Bernard told him, Bernard would punch him there and then, or, more likely, he would get someone to do the job for him, and Pedro would be assaulted one dark evening and beaten up. Pedro gave Bernard two fleeces. His father was furious when they counted them out later.

"Pedro, I can't afford to give away fleeces to anyone," he said. "And you've given them for the Good Men. If Bernard Belot takes against you, and we must trust no-one, especially a man like Bernard, who would betray you to the Inquisition on a whim, do you know what they would do to you?"

"If I hadn't given the fleeces to Bernard, he would have been angry and you might have found me up on the plateau next to the château one morning, beaten senseless or worse."

"That's the problem," said his father. "People sway in the breeze depending on who they're talking to. We won't know who to trust any more."

"We're a long way from Carcassonne – surely the Inquisition won't bother with us up here in Montaillou," said Pedro.

"Pedro, never, ever underestimate them." His father shook his head. His face looked drawn. "I shall stay clear of the Good Men this time and so should you."

"I'll stay well away from Bernard Belot," said Pedro, though how he could possibly do that in such a small village as Montaillou, he did not know.

But Bernard's words – "They are the only ones who can save our souls" – had stayed in Pedro's mind. How could they promise salvation? What made them so certain that theirs was the right way to achieve salvation? Anyone who followed the wrong path would end up in Hell. How could he find out enough to choose for himself? To speak to the Good Men was a great risk. The Inquisition would imprison you for less. He shivered at that thought. That would be the worst of all punishments. He would rather be burned at the stake, although that was usually reserved for the Perfects.

The stories about the past were part of the fabric of life in Montaillou – absorbed from the trees whispering in the wind, drifting down from mothers to children clinging on to their skirts – stories that seeped into everyone's flesh and bones. Relatives, friends and neighbours had perished when thousands were slaughtered at Béziers. The streets, littered with severed limbs and heads, ran red with blood. And there had been a year-long siege at the Cathar stronghold of Montségur, atop a mountain peak a stone's throw from Montaillou, when two hundred Perfects and Believers were burned alive on a Roman bonfire when they surrendered and walked down the mountain. All this was done in the name of God. How could this bloodshed be what God wanted? And how could anyone know which is the right path to follow? He couldn't ask a Roman priest. Even thinking these thoughts was a sin in their eyes. No, it had to be the Good Men who answered these questions.

Only a few days after promising to stay away from Bernard, Pedro was walking past the Belots' house early one morning when Bernard came out. He ran up to Pedro.

"Come here," said Bernard. He pulled Pedro around the corner of the house and pinned him back against the wall. His arm pushed painfully onto Pedro's chest, his face was close, his foul breath –

stale alcohol – wafted up Pedro's nose. "The Good Men are coming here next week," he said. "They'll preach in our house – come and hear them." Bernard gave a violent push into Pedro's chest before backing off. "Don't forget."

Pedro nodded weakly. He was winded. He leant forward with his hands on his thighs, trying to catch his breath. As his breathing settled, the pain eased enough to allow him to straighten up and move away from the Belots' house. He walked down the steep track through the village towards the meadows below, where the church was situated. The church was a special place, a place of pilgrimage, and he always felt at ease there. Two centuries before, a child had a vision in that meadow, of the Virgin Mary surrounded by animals. When the vision had disappeared, the animals' footprints were left on a rock where they had been standing. The footprints were still visible. Pedro crossed himself as he walked past the rock to the far side of the church, which overlooked the graveyard and the meadows beyond. There was no-one about. He sat down on the dry grass at the base of the wall and put his head in his hands. He felt pushed and pulled in all directions. He loved his family and his loyalty to them was strong, but his father disapproved of his ambition to be a shepherd. They were a band of ruffians, his father said, a law unto themselves, low in status. But he wanted – no, *needed* – the freedom. It would kill him to be a weaver like his father, cooped up all day indoors. Then there were the tensions that were starting with the revival of the Good Men. It brought out the worst in Bernard Belot, and there were many others like him in Montaillou, ready to take advantage of the need for secrecy. Everyone was steeped in the Roman church and its doctrines – but many harboured deep resentments against the church. The taxes they took were extortionate, they even took animals off those who had no money, and the priests, well, their behaviour was not always as it should be. But how could he reconcile his love for, and belief in, the God of the Roman church, when he could not deny his wish to discover more about the Good Men? It was time to make his own way in life, to make his own choices and decisions. And to do that, he would have to leave the village.

It was late evening when Pedro arrived at Cousin Raymond's stone farmhouse on the edge of the village of Arques, tired and footsore. He was assailed by doubts as he stood at the farmhouse door. Had he done the right thing coming here? How would they receive him? Would he be welcomed? He felt sure that Raymond would help him if he could, and if not, well… he would have to go to nearby farms to see if anyone would give him work. He raised his hand and knocked on the door.

"Pedro," said Raymond when he opened the door. "Are you alone?" He peered into the darkness. "Come in, Cousin."

Raymond ushered Pedro through the entrance and into the large hall, the main living area of the house where Eglantyne, his wife, sat beside the fire. This room was the centre of their home. Food was cooked and eaten here, and it was where the entire household gathered. As big as it was, the furnishings were homely and simple, a great wooden table with benches around it. The benches next to the fire had sheepskins on them. He felt comforted to see it all as it had been for as long as he could remember.

"Pedro." Eglantyne stood and embraced him. "What a surprise, how are you? Would you like something to eat? There's cold chicken and bread."

She disappeared through a door which led to the storerooms at the back of the house. Raymond followed her. Pedro sat beside the fire and watched as they placed bread, meat and wine on the table. Raymond was about ten years older than Pedro, stocky and strong-looking, with a touch of white in his dark beard and hair. He worked hard even though he had inherited this prosperous farm and land from his father a few years ago. He had married Eglantyne shortly afterwards. She was the youngest daughter of a family of minor nobles from a neighbouring village and not considered a beauty and unlikely to make a good match. Her family had status and a crumbling château, but not much money. It was a marriage arranged to suit everyone, and it could have been merely that, but it seemed to Pedro to be much more. He noticed the affection between them – Raymond touched Eglantyne as he passed; she gave Raymond warm smiles. They both wore working clothes; Raymond a wool tunic and Eglantyne a kirtle with a tabard over the top. Her long dark hair was tied back under her simple head-dress. Her facial features were strong and gave her a look of strength and warmth. This was a busy household. They had three young children and Eglantyne's mother, Bérengère, had lived with them since her husband died and her eldest son had taken over the château. There were household servants and farmworkers too.

"Come and eat," said Eglantyne.

Raymond asked Pedro about his family as he ate.

"They're well," said Pedro. "But worn out. My father spends all day weaving and my mother and brothers never stop, so many chores…" He hesitated for a moment. "I might as well tell you, I left without my father's permission or knowledge."

"Ah," said Raymond. "I wondered what brought you here."

"Father would never agree to me leaving, so it was the only way I could go. I left without saying goodbye."

"They'll soon find out that you're here," said Raymond.

"I know, that's why I came here. I want them to know I'm safe."

Raymond laughed. "So there was no disagreement between you?"

"We were always disagreeing. Father wanted me to stay and be a weaver like him, but I couldn't bear that. I want to be a shepherd; I like being outside all day with the animals. My father disapproves of shepherds."

"They can be a wild bunch at times," said Raymond. "Won't your father come to get you?"

"No, he's too busy. I think he will be angry with me, but he'll come around to the idea. He can manage without me; as you know there are plenty more brothers at home: Jean, Grégoire, Guillaume are growing fast, and even little Arnaud is handy around the house. Guillemette can help Mother with the women's work until she marries and leaves like Raymonde did at eighteen." He hesitated. "But I see it may put you in a difficult position."

"As long as you understand that if anyone comes looking for you, I will not lie."

"That's fair enough," said Pedro. "I need to find work; do you know if any of the farmers around here need a shepherd?"

"We're a man down. One of the shepherds injured his leg a week ago and he can't walk far. So, if that will suit you, I'll take you down to the valley tomorrow and you can join the shepherds there."

"Are you sure, Raymond?" said Pedro. "You know I don't want any favours."

"Do you want the job or not?" Raymond laughed.

"Well, yes, very much so—"

"No more to be said then," said Raymond.

How fortunate Pedro felt. Not only had he managed to leave Montaillou, but now he had a job doing exactly what he wanted. Raymond and Eglantyne were the best of cousins. He ate and drank happily, whilst telling them all the news from Montaillou – except he did not mention the Good Men. That was something he would have to be quiet about until he was sure it was a suitable topic here. That night he slept, for the first time in his life, in a bed, alone. Usually, he shared a room and a bed with one of his four younger brothers. He fell asleep thinking of walking over the mountains with the other shepherds and a large flock of sheep.

The next day, Raymond took Pedro to the rich pastures in the valley where the sheep stayed over winter. Raymond told him as they walked that some of the shepherds had left the previous month with the sheep belonging to other stockbreeders, south over the mountain passes to Aragon, where there was plenty of rich grass for the animals. Pedro's body tingled and his feet itched as he listened; this was what he had wanted to do since childhood when he first knew about the transhumance – it was almost within reach. First, he must learn more and gain experience.

Raymond left him in the valley with the other shepherds and told him to return each week to his house to collect food and supplies for the men. The six men welcomed him. Two of them, the Maurs brothers, were from Montaillou, and already knew Pedro. Another was a dark-skinned Saracen, called Mofferet, from a land much further south. He spoke with a different accent. The others were local men. Mofferet, who was head shepherd, asked him if he could put up fences. Pedro nodded.

"Good – this afternoon I want you to help Jean and Martin make a new enclosure for the sheep with the wood we chopped yesterday," said Mofferet.

Pedro set to work with the men and the day passed quickly. At night, the men slept in a stone barn, lying on sheepskins and covering themselves with their cloaks. In the evenings, they lit a fire for cooking and sat wrapped in their cloaks, eating their supper, enjoying the warmth from the flames and talking. Pedro often sat up late beside the fire after the others had retired. He watched the embers as the fire died down, and if it was a clear night he looked up at the stars in the heavens and wondered… Sometimes one of the large, white mountain dogs that guarded the sheep from wolves and the occasional bear would saunter towards him and keep him company.

CHAPTER 3

Guy Belibaste

Guy's father paced the room. "It was an accident – surely the law must be lenient?" Guy's father looked at Pierre Authier. The two Perfects exchanged glances.

"I must tell you the truth," said Pierre Authier. "It's Guy's word against the other two. Guy is likely to be found guilty."

"Surely not," said his father, standing still. "The Public Prosectutor knows us – we are a family of good standing in the community… and those shepherds – they're rogues, untrustworthy. I'll go and speak to the Public Prosecutor myself and explain what's happened."

"They're accusing Guy of murder," said Pierre Authier quietly. "A man is dead – two witnesses say so, and two against one…"

There was a silence. Guy's father paced again. "Are you sure?" He stopped and looked at Pierre Authier.

"I was a lawyer…" said Pierre Authier.

"Yes, yes, of course," said Guy's father. He sighed. "If that's so, Guy will have to hide until it all blows over."

"There are plenty of places I could hide on the farm," said Guy.

"The loft of the barn would be a good place; no-one will think of looking there."

"The first thing they'll do is search the farmhouse and the outbuildings, when they realise Guy's missing," said Pierre Authier.

"I should never have employed those three shepherds; I knew they were no good, but there was no-one else at the time," said his father. "But we must think—"

"They mentioned the Perfects," said Guy.

"Do they know we're here?" said Philippe d'Aylarac, looking hard at Guy.

"They said they knew about you and… and us," said Guy. "How could they know you're here now?"

"Someone could have betrayed us," said Philippe d'Aylarac. "I think we should leave."

"Is that possible?" said his father. "That you have been betrayed?" He shook his head. "Then, you must leave… but darkness will soon fall… can you hide somewhere? And what about Guy? Guy, where can you go?" His father stopped pacing. "I know… you could enter a monastery, a closed order where no-one knows who you are."

"A place where I can pray for forgiveness," said Guy, his voice shaking. "Somewhere I can ask God for his help; God knows I would never kill anyone on purpose." Tears welled up and rolled down his face.

"There is one such place I know of," said his father. "An abbey higher up in the mountains, remote…"

The two Perfects were talking together in low voices. Pierre Authier looked up and spoke.

"We must leave now. Guy can come with us to our safe house, where he can stay until he is ready to move on. We're used to travelling at night under cover of darkness. But we must move quickly. If those shepherds have reported us as being here… well… we should all make haste."

"What do you want to do, Guy?" said Philippe d'Aylarac.

Guy was speechless. Sweat dripped off his forehead. He wiped it away with the back of his hand. How could this be? For months now, since he'd first heard about the revival of the heresy, he had wanted to be with the Good Men and learn their ways, but for it to happen like this... And what about Estelle, and the children?

"You will have to leave just as you are... leave everything behind, your wife and family. It will be dark soon, we'll walk through the night, it won't be easy, you must decide... and quickly," said Philippe d'Aylarac.

"That will put you in more danger," said Guy's father to the Perfects.

"We are always in danger," said Pierre Authier.

"And we're always ready to move," said Philippe d'Aylarac. "Guy, if you want to come with us, we must leave now."

"Guy, I fear they're right," said his father. "You must go with them."

CHAPTER 4

Pedro Maury

It was Friday. It had been a good week. Pedro had fallen into the work easily. He relished being outside with the animals, the comradeship of the men and the talk around the campfire in the evenings as they ate their meal. Now he was to eat supper with Raymond and his family, stay the night in the farmhouse and return to the pastures the next day. On Sunday, he would look after the sheep with another shepherd whilst the others went to the church at Arques. The shepherds took turns to attend church and the priest accepted that arrangement. In all the years he had attended church with his family in Montaillou, he had only missed a service if he was ill, and that had been a rare occurrence. How were his family? Had they heard where he was? Shepherds walked between Arques and Montaillou regularly and they would pass on news of him. It was likely his father had worked out why he had left, if not where he was. His mother – always a loving mother, he hated to upset her – but he knew they would understand in time.

Raymond opened the door when Pedro knocked.

"Come in, Pedro, there's no need to knock, you're part of the family – just walk in, make yourself at home."

The smell of bread baking and meat cooking pervaded the room. Bérengère, Eglantyne's mother, was sitting at the table along with two others.

"Pedro," said Raymond. "Meet Ricard and Sybille Peyre, our neighbours, and their baby, Marquèse."

The couple, who smiled at Pedro, were much the same age as Raymond and Eglantyne. They wore working clothes. The baby was in her mother's arms. She smiled and gurgled as Pedro approached the table. He stroked the baby's soft cheek. With five younger siblings, he was not much interested in babies, but baby Marquese was a particularly beautiful child, smiling all the time, her sweet little face framed with dark curls.

"Take a seat, Pedro," said Eglantyne, who entered at that moment carrying food on platters. "You're just in time for supper, it's lamb tonight." She gestured to the platters. "I'll bring bread now."

"Guy Belibaste should have been here tonight," said Raymond. "He's the son of a farmer friend of ours from Cubières – we have a lot of dealings with each other, but he's not arrived, something must have happened to prevent him from coming."

"Maybe he'll join us later," said Eglantyne.

Eglantyne brought in more food and baby Marquese was put into a wooden cradle next to the fire, where she cooed and gurgled until she nodded off. Everyone helped themselves to the meat and the bread, and no-one spoke much for a while. Eglantyne brought out cheese, figs, sweet grapes and nuts.

"That was quite a feast," said Pedro.

"We meet with friends here most Friday evenings," said Raymond.

"What brought you to Arques, Pedro?" said Ricard Peyre, as he dabbed up some crumbs of cheese with a piece of bread. Pedro explained, leaving out the Good Men and Bernard Belot.

"If you're a good shepherd," said Ricard, "you will never be short of work. There are plenty of untrustworthy shepherds about, not so many good ones."

After the meal, Ricard and Sybille left with baby Marquese wrapped up in a wool blanket. They had a short walk to their farm at the other end of the village. Guy Belibaste had not arrived, and everyone was tired. It was time for bed. As Pedro lay in his bed, full of wine and food, and feeling sleepy, Ricard's words played over again in his mind. More than anything he wanted to be a good shepherd.

The weeks passed quickly, and the weather changed. It was windy, cold and rainy. Just before Christmas, the shepherds asked Pedro to go back to the farmhouse for flour for breadmaking a day earlier than usual. He headed off over the foothills in good spirits. There was snow on the higher peaks in the distance and the sun was shining. Over the weeks, Pedro had met more of Eglantyne and Raymond's friends and neighbours. He was at home with them all. The last time he was there, Raymond had asked him if he would go to Cubières, to the Belibastes' farmhouse, when the weather improved. To explore further afield and to know the mountain routes was just what he wanted. It was a privilege to be trusted with the task of taking the money that Guy Belibaste should have collected when he failed to arrive that time; no-one had heard anything about Guy since. Pedro hadn't had any news from Montaillou, either; maybe Raymond would have heard from his family this week.

It was early evening when Pedro let himself into the farmhouse. He was momentarily confused. Had he entered the wrong house? No, this was the same large hall that he was used to, but now it was full of people, sitting at the table, eating and talking. This didn't look like the usual group of friends and neighbours dusty from the fields, who had called in for supper and a gossip. The men were attired in tunics of fine wool and the women were wearing kirtles of brocade fabric and crisp, laundered head-dresses. He looked again. There was silence as all heads turned to look at him. There was Sybille, Ricard… other neighbours… he knew them all. Eglantyne jumped to her feet. Sybille put her hand over her mouth. He'd walked into a celebration of some kind – one that he had not been invited to. Eglantyne took a deep breath in, physically pulling herself together.

"Oh, Pedro, we weren't expecting you tonight, we… erm…" She gave him a tight smile. "Well, well." She moved her platter to one side then back to its original place, then drummed her fingers on it. "Why don't you find a seat, Pedro? I'll bring a platter for you. Make room for Pedro over there." She gestured with her hand across the table.

As she turned to go, she almost bumped into Raymond, who was coming through the door carrying a platter with fish on it.

"They have sent some of their fish—" said Raymond.

"Pedro's here," said Sybille. Raymond stopped in his tracks and looked around. His eyes alighted on Pedro and widened in what for a moment looked like fear. He cleared his throat.

"Pedro, I didn't know you were coming… so… now then…" Raymond straightened up, physically pulling himself together like his wife. "Here's some extra fish, what a good job we had some extra, there's plenty for everyone."

He placed the platter on the table and followed Eglantyne, who had left the room. The others remained silent. Pedro sat down in a space next to Ricard Peyre. Fish? Fish wasn't usually served in the evening, and who had sent it?

"So, how's life on the pastures?" said Ricard in a hearty tone, clapping Pedro on the back. The others started murmuring together until the usual atmosphere of talking and laughing prevailed. There were only two servants working that evening and Raymond dismissed them early. Raymond seemed unable to sit still and was in and out of the hall regularly. What was going on here? Pedro knew the layout of the house, which was one of the larger houses in Arques, being on the edge of the village. It had been added to over the years, and he knew there were several rooms upstairs. There were two sets of stairs, one leading out of the main hall where the guests were all dining and another at the back of the house where storerooms and barns were attached. Pedro was sure he heard someone moving about upstairs throughout the evening. There must be other guests in the house who were dining elsewhere. Raymond had said "they have sent some of their fish". It was not the time to ask questions and the others did not comment. Perhaps he would bump into them or even share a room when he went to bed. But as time went on, Raymond whispered in Pedro's ear. Would he sleep in the hayloft of the barn next to the house that night as he thought some of their guests would stay the night in the house? And would Pedro leave early the next day as they had some business to discuss with a couple of their guests?

When Pedro rose early in the morning, only Raymond was up. Raymond had assembled the flour that the shepherds required, and he sent Pedro on his way. And Pedro, whilst he puzzled over it again once or twice, had another interest occupying his thoughts.

Pedro went to church in Arques when he wasn't minding the sheep. He listened to the preaching, although he questioned some of it in his own mind. It was even more important to be seen at church now. There were said to be spies and priests who would report poor attenders to the Inquisition. Away from church, amongst people they trusted, some of the congregation had thoughts and questions about the Roman faith, and its priests. Now it would be foolish at the least and could be dangerous to indulge in sharing these ideas. Maybe one day he would have an opportunity to speak to the Good Men. In the meantime, he went to church and remained quiet.

He noticed a girl who attended each week with her family. He glimpsed her standing on the other side of the church, a few rows in front. She was a petite figure with chestnut brown hair falling over her mantle. His eyes kept sliding back to that sight – he longed to see her face. Her parents were with her, and her younger brothers and sisters. They ranged down in size from another girl nearly as tall as her to a little one in her mother's arms, who was restless. The girl entertained this little one, making him laugh by pulling grotesque faces at him. She squinted her eyes and pulled her lips out with her fingers. Pedro felt a laugh rising from his stomach and he tried to stifle it by pretending to cough. Next time he looked, he saw her pretty profile altered by her tongue coming out and wiggling at the baby, who giggled with delight. A flicker of desire stirred in him and he shifted about. Next, this fascinating girl tickled the baby's ribs, which brought on a loud screech of delight and a stern face from the mother, who passed the child over to his father. From time to time, the little one and his sister exchanged a grin. She needed only to wave her fingers towards him, and he collapsed in his father's arms with a giggle. When the service was over and the congregation filed out, Pedro lost sight of her. He pushed through the crowd of people that lingered under the elms. Surely he hadn't missed her. There she was, bending down, her mantle slipping from her shoulders to minister to the little one again, who was now standing on two sturdy legs, rubbing his eyes and looking cross. Pedro stood entranced. She looked up. She gave him a small, wary smile before she turned back to her little brother. Her features were dainty, and he'd caught a glimpse of a slim figure. For the rest of the week, whenever he was unoccupied, he saw that chestnut hair tumbling around her shoulders. He wanted to see more.

It was the Sunday following the celebratory meal at Raymond's that Pedro stood with Raymond and his family in church. There she was in the same place. Could he speak to her? Was she already betrothed? She could be; she was of marriageable age. He pushed his way outside as soon as Mass ended; he must find her amongst all the people milling about under the elms. The late autumn sunshine warmed the air and the dry yellow leaves scrunched under their feet as they enquired after each other's health, their children's health and how their sick aunt in Carcassonne was doing. Where on earth was she? She couldn't have left already, but, then again, what should he say to her?

His height meant he could scan above the crowd, but he couldn't see her. Just then there was a commotion, the crowd parted and her little brother came running through, chased by his sister. Pedro jumped into action, waylaid the little one, picked him up and held him up high.

"Where are you going?" said Pedro. The child looked around and broke into a howl. His sister was on his heels. She smiled as Pedro placed him in her arms.

"My little brother, Arnaud – Arnie," she said. "He's such a handful whenever we come to church; he doesn't like to be still and quiet."

"I've got a little brother called Arnaud too," said Pedro as he handed the child over to her. They exchanged smiles.

Raymond caught up with him. "We wondered where you were," he said. "Are you off to the pastures now?"

Pedro waved to Eglantyne and the rest of the family at the corner of the church and made his way to join the other shepherds. She'd smiled at him. Did this mean she was as interested in him as he was in her? He thought so. This thought made him smile again.

"You're very quiet this morning," said Jean Maurs. "Are you all right?"

"Judging by the smile on his face, I'd say everything was very much all right," said Martin Maurs.

"Yes, I'm just remembering… it's nothing." He laughed. The others exchanged glances and laughed too.

All that week, his feelings alternated between the heights of elation, believing she was interested in him, and plunging into the depths of despair at the thought that she was betrothed already. It was possible. Many families made alliances between their offspring at early ages to consolidate their property and goods. He dreamt about her, dreams of removing that mantle and kirtle, stroking her skin, kissing those pink lips, possessing her. He woke up hard every morning even though there was already a damp patch beneath him where he had spilled over in these heated dreams.

The following Sunday his eyes lingered on her back during the Mass. She turned again and smiled at him. He was sure now that she was feeling the same about him as he her. They were attuned to each other. After Mass and encouraged by this, he made his way through the milling crowd over to her family group, trying to look casual.

"I see little Arnie was behaving himself this week," he said.

"Yes, he's a bit quieter today," she said.

Pedro looked at Arnie, who was in his father's arms. "Hello, Arnie," he said. Arnie frowned and turned away, hiding his face in his father's cloak.

"But grumpier," she said.

"He's tired," said her mother.

"Best get him home soon," said her father. "Bernadette." He gestured in her direction and looked around. "Where are the others? We must round them up and get back now."

"I expect we'll see you next week?" said her mother, smiling at him, her voice warm and friendly.

Pedro nodded and said goodbye. Bernadette and her family were farming folk. They reminded him of his parents in their simple working garments and their large family of children. Although Pedro's father was a weaver, he could not make a living by weaving alone and his parents had a smallholding with a pig, a few sheep and chickens to feed the family. He wondered what Bernadette's home was like. Bernadette, such a pretty name, and her mother so friendly. Should he have tried to say more? He would have to wait another whole week of wondering whether she was interested in him, whether she was betrothed, then feeling certain she was. Later in the barn, lying on sheepskins, warm and relaxed, in his imagination and dreams, he undressed and caressed her, entered her, gently at first, then urgently as he woke up with a moan of pleasure.

Later that week, he was with the shepherds huddling around the campfire, which glowed warm and bright against the cold, dark evening. They ate their supper of bread and cheese, when one of the others asked Mofferet when he would next go south to see his wife and family.

"When I've earned enough money to go back and stay there for a while again," Mofferet said. "Maybe in spring next year."

"Are any of you others married?" Pedro asked.

"Most shepherds don't marry; it's not the life for a married man," said one. "Look at Mofferet, he hardly ever sees his wife. Women don't like that." He grinned. "But that doesn't mean you can't have a woman."

Pedro noticed one or two of the others smiling and sniggering. He felt the blood rush to his face as he looked around at the group of eight shepherds. Thank God for the darkness and the campfire's heat to disguise it.

"There are women," said another shepherd. "By the thermal pool at Ax, and if you catch the clap you can bathe in the pool for a cure." There was more sniggering and laughing.

"Or if that doesn't cure it – then the hospital's only next door."

More laughter. Pedro wished he hadn't asked. Jean Maurs, sitting beside him, patted him on the back.

"Take no notice of that lot, Pedro," he said. "Maybe you've got someone in mind, eh, a nice girl?"

The shepherds loved to talk and gave their opinions on every subject when they sat down together round the fire in the evenings. But Pedro was shocked when one of them spoke of the heresy one evening. Maybe most people can't keep their mouths shut when there's a secret to keep.

"You three are from Montaillou," said this shepherd, glancing at Pedro and the Maurs brothers. "I heard in the town tavern about the Authier brothers – that they're back and living in Montaillou?"

Both Maurs brothers shrugged. Everyone turned to look at Pedro as the last person to have come from Montaillou. He caught his breath but could only shake his head and shrug his shoulders. He looked down.

Jean Maurs spoke. "I don't want to hear about them. My father was ruined by them."

"Our mother is very bitter," said Martin Maurs. "She says that none of them can be trusted, neither Roman priests nor the Good Men."

"What happened, Martin?" asked Mofferet as Jean Maurs stood and walked off to the barn.

"The Inquisition took most of my father's land. He had to wear the yellow crosses," said Martin. "He died too soon because of it. My mother won't have anything to do with the heresy and neither will I."

He got up and followed Jean into the barn. Pedro wished the others goodnight and went after Jean and Martin. He fell asleep thinking of pretty Bernadette.

It was another two weeks before Pedro was able to attend church again. A boy had arrived at the pastures with a message for one of the other shepherds telling him his father was seriously ill and he needed to go home. Being a man down meant Pedro had to stay behind when the others attended church. Not seeing Bernadette for two weeks gave him some distance. He recognised the truth of what the shepherds had said during the conversation about marriage. Marriage was not compatible with the shepherd's way of life. And yet shepherds did marry. Some women must accept that way of life. He did not relish the idea of the women who waited to service shepherds and other men with rootless lifestyles. He wanted a loving relationship, but was he expecting too much of any woman? And still in the back of his mind there were the Good Men – he wanted to find out more. How could that be part of his life unless any woman he married or became betrothed to was also a supporter? But overriding these concerns was the thought that he must take things a step further with Bernadette, spend time alone with her and get to know her better. Perhaps then he would find it easier to understand what he wanted and where he was going.

Bernadette was standing in church as usual with her family. She looked around – she was looking for him. She spotted him and gave him her warm smile. Raymond whispered in Pedro's ear.

"Someone's pleased to see you, Pedro," he said. "You've kept that quiet."

"There's nothing to say," said Pedro. "Not yet."

She was under the elms after Mass, standing with her family in their usual place. Pedro went over and was greeted by her parents.

"We've missed you these last two weeks," said her mother.

"I had to stay on the pastures," said Pedro. "I had to mind the sheep."

"You're a shepherd?" said her father. "Good shepherds aren't always easy to find. That reminds me, I've some work waiting for me, why don't you walk along with us?"

Her father positioned himself alongside Pedro, as the family group gathered and moved off along the track.

"You're not from Arques," he said. "What brought you here?"

"I came from Montaillou to work at Raymond Maulen's farm," said Pedro.

"Raymond Maulen's farm, eh?" said her father. "That's a big farm, he's a stockbreeder. I believe he does well."

"He's my cousin," said Pedro.

"Is he now? And where is your family? Montaillou?"

"Yes, my father's a weaver, but we have a few animals and I've always looked after them."

"You didn't want to be a weaver like your father?"

"No, I couldn't stand being cooped up indoors all day."

"Here we are," said Bernadette's mother. They stopped where a narrow track led off from the main one.

"We live down here," said Bernadette.

"I should take my leave," said Pedro.

"Come with us, and Bernadette can show you our animals," said her father.

A small farmhouse came into view as they rounded a bend in the track. Cultivated land lay on the far side of it, and a couple of pens and ramshackle sheds stood near the farmhouse. Chickens and goats wandered around as they approached. It was like his parents' smallholding, the same way of life, and he sensed the same struggle for survival. For his parents, it had become even harder since the Inquisition had confiscated a portion of their land.

The family went indoors whilst Bernadette showed Pedro around. In between the pigs and the sheep, she asked him more about where he came from, and why he'd left home. He explained to her; she listened. His gaze met hers, and her warm chestnut eyes, which matched her hair, were shining. She was young and lovely. But when there was a lull in their conversation, and as they leaned on a wooden gate and watched two pigs snuffling in the dirt, he felt a sudden urge to leave.

"Let's go in," said Bernadette. "Stay and have a drink with us."

He accepted; it would be rude if he didn't. He sat eating bread and drinking milk with her family round the table. The children argued and teased each other, and baby Arnaud cried. It was all so familiar. He left with an invitation to stay for a meal after church the following week. But a vision of another life hovered at the edge of his mind.

Christmas was on the horizon, and in the days running up to Christmas Eve, the shepherds brought the ewes that were to be first-time mothers into the sheepfold next to Raymond's house. Raymond, Ricard Peyre and Pedro had been cleaning the muck off the ewe's tails, examining their feet, trimming the ones that needed it and feeling their bellies for evidence of lambs. The ewes didn't care for this and were milling around bleating loudly. Even using wooden hurdles, it was hard work to separate them, as the animals seemed to object to being moved around. The stench of the animals and their droppings was strong despite regular cleaning, but the three were used to it. They stood in the middle of the animals for a moment, weighing up the situation, making sure they'd examined them all.

"She's big, maybe twins?" Pedro pointed to one of the ewes whose large belly protruded out either side of her body.

"We'll keep an eye on her," said Raymond. "Well, I think that's it for now."

They moved to lean against the outer side of the pen and stood watching the ewes as they quietened and settled.

"You're learning fast, Pedro," said Raymond. "And… I think you like work here. Do you want to stay?"

"Yes, I like it here."

"You're a natural," said Raymond. He glanced at Ricard. "There is something… I want to say… to tell you what we, that is, Eglantyne and I, and Ricard and some of our friends and neighbours… have been talking about…"

"Oh?" said Pedro, looking from one to the other.

"Yes." Another glance at Ricard. "We think… we all think… there is something missing from your life."

"What do you mean?" said Pedro.

"Well, you remember a week or two back you came to the farmhouse one evening a day earlier than usual?" said Raymond.

Pedro nodded. "Yes."

"I don't think you miss much, Pedro, and I'm sure you noticed… something," said Raymond.

"Well…" said Pedro.

"In fact, we had some visitors who were eating upstairs."

"Oh? Really?" The sheep were still and quiet as if they too wanted to hear what Raymond was saying.

"For God's sake, tell him," said Ricard. "I can't stand the suspense."

"All right, all right," said Raymond. "In fact, it was the two Perfects, Pierre Authier and Philippe d'Aylarac."

"Ah," said Pedro. "That fish, they don't eat meat, do they?"

"That's right, they stayed the night, and they talked to us for most of the next day. You know, well, I don't know what you know, but the Authier brothers have ordained more Perfects – Philippe d'Aylarac is one of them."

"We've been talking about it ever since they came back from Lombardy," said Ricard. His face was flushed and animated. "There are others in Arques, our friends and neighbours – who want to know more, like us, and the Good Men are travelling – preaching and explaining the faith to those who want to know."

"What are they like, these two Good Men?" said Pedro. "I've been wondering what kind of men could give up everything for their beliefs."

"They're men like any others; their flesh, their bones, their shape, their faces are all like those of other men," said Raymond. "But they are the only ones who walk in the ways of justice and truth like the Apostles. They never lie and they don't take what belongs to others – even if they found gold or silver lying in their path, they would not take it unless someone made them a present of it, unlike our Roman priests. And, best of all, they can show us the way to salvation. What do you think of that, Pedro? That the way to salvation is through these men whom the Roman church calls heretics?"

"But how do you know that theirs is the right way?" said Pedro. "I've heard some good sermons recently from the Minorites."

"Look at this way, Pedro," said Raymond. "There are two churches: one which forgives and understands, and the other that punishes and wants to possess people. Which do you believe to be the better one?"

"I think the one that forgives has to be better than the one which punishes," said Pedro. "I don't know which one that is, but I believe in God and the Holy Apostles."

"And so do we," said Raymond, looking at Ricard. "Why don't you come and judge for yourself? Next time the Perfects are staying with us, you could come to hear them speak."

Ricard moved to stand in front of Pedro. He placed his hands on Pedro's shoulders. "I know it's a big step," he said. "But the only way is to meet them and judge for yourself."

"What about the Inquisition?" said Pedro. "Isn't it dangerous to have the Good Men in your home?"

"That's why you must remember not speak to anyone about this, not the Maurs brothers, not the other shepherds; trust no-one," said Raymond.

"Well, what do you say?" said Ricard. "Do you want to hear them?"

He knew what he wanted to do, but he said, "Let me think about it."

Christmas Day was busy as a couple of the ewes were lambing early. Pedro stayed in the sheep pen whilst Raymond and his family went to church. To celebrate Christmas, Eglantyne and her mother had cooked a special meal of wild boar, which Pedro ate later than the others, so that Raymond and Ricard could eat their meal together with their families. He didn't mind this, nor the cold and lack of sleep, as lambing was the best of times for him. To see healthy lambs born was a joy, to lose a lamb or ewe was the saddest thing. He loved to see a newborn lamb licked by its mother, taking its first steps and nuzzling her to find her teats. It never ceased to amaze and delight him. That year, they were lucky, none of them died in the sheep pen and the ewe with the big belly had twins. Sitting in the sheep pen alone apart from the animals, he thought again of his family. How were they? Were they eating wild boar like they usually did at Christmas? Maybe his father had managed to get hold of one through a friend who owed him a favour; that was how it usually worked – a good length of woven cloth for half a boar. His parents were old before their time with overwork and too many children. It was not possible for them to visit him. He should try to find time to visit them. He'd never been away from them at Christmas before. He'd been busy with his own concerns and his new life, but in the new year, after the lambing, he resolved to visit them.

But after Christmas, news from Montaillou arrived in the shape of Grégoire, Pedro's brother. He brought a message from his father to Raymond and Eglantyne about saving one the best rams for him for later. His family had discovered where he was a few weeks earlier. The ram was simply an excuse to send Grégoire over to find out how he was, as the rams were far too young to be judged. Grégoire brought family news. Guillemette, their younger sister, was betrothed to Bertrand Piquier, a cooper, and Jean, the brother two years younger than Pedro, and two years older than Grégoire, who also wanted to be a shepherd, was disagreeing with Father, just as Pedro did. Everyone was well, although Mother was tired and Father had been angry when he first discovered that Pedro had left, but he had forgiven him now. In the village the Benet family, as well as the Belots, had been building lofts onto their houses. Pedro knew these were for the Perfects to stay in, so he flashed Grégoire a look as he spoke of this, which he hoped Grégoire would understand as "be careful what you say". Grégoire was too excited about these things. He didn't seem to understand the dangers. However, it did seem that Grégoire was being sensible about this, because it was only when they went to their shared bed for the night that Grégoire, who was fit to burst with the news that their father had relented about the Good Men, let it out.

"I thought he was determined not to be involved this time," said Pedro.

"He's changed his mind," said Grégoire. "He said his head told him not to get involved again, but his heart told him otherwise."

"So, what's he doing?"

"He went to hear them speak at the Belots' house one evening; they're always there," said Grégoire. "And they came to our house the next day and talked to Father. Mother gave them food for their journey, and now Aunt Gaillarde, and Aunt Mersende, and their families are following the Good Men too."

"I hope they know what they're doing," said Pedro.

"There's no threat from the Inquisition in Montaillou," said Grégoire. "Everyone knows that Father Clergue and his family are Cathars. He protects us."

"Father Clergue? How can that be? He's a Roman priest," said Pedro.

"Don't you see? He tells the church authorities that all's well in Montaillou, that there are no heretics there." Grégoire laughed. Pedro didn't join in.

"They've got the whole thing sewn up then, haven't they, the Clergues?" said Pedro.

Grégoire gave Pedro an enquiring look. "What do you mean?"

"Bernard Clergue is the Bailiff of Montaillou, with the power to arrest people and throw them into the dungeon of the château, and his brother Pierre is Priest… it seems to me those two brothers have control of most things in Montaillou – be careful not to cross them, Greg," said Pedro.

"You always think too much and question things," said Grégoire. "I'd say it's the other way round – they protect us."

"What about those in Montaillou who don't support the Cathars? Can they be trusted? Suppose they decide to speak out against their neighbours?"

"They wouldn't do that," said Grégoire.

When Grégoire left the next morning, Pedro returned to the Arques valley and the other shepherds. There were newly born lambs in the pastures now too, although they had lost one or two that were stillborn. Pedro took food for the shepherds, but he only stayed two nights as Raymond wanted him back at the farmhouse. He strode out on his way back. The healthy new lambs gambolling and butting their mothers for milk had made him happy. The snow on the mountains gleaming in the sun, with the rich blue sky behind them, pleased him too. He shook his head in disbelief that he was doing what he had always wanted to do. Even on a dull, cold day, he was usually happy and contented in his new life, but at that moment he felt exhilarated.

When he arrived at Raymond's house and entered the kitchen, he was jolted out of his good mood. Eglantyne and her mother were sitting at the table holding hands and crying. They looked up as he entered, their faces stricken with pain.

"What is it?" he said. "What's happened?"

"Oh, Pedro, it's baby Marquèse," said Eglantyne.

"What?" Pedro sank down on the bench beside them as an ice-cold shiver shot through him.

"She's dead, Pedro," whispered Eglantyne. "The poor little thing died."

That beautiful child, who was always smiling, was dead. How could this have happened? There must be some mistake. He looked at Eglantyne and Bérengère, and he knew they were not mistaken. God had taken that beautiful child.

"May God rest her soul." Pedro crossed himself.

"Ricard and Sybille are utterly distraught," said Eglantyne, patting at her tears with a kitchen cloth. "No-one knows how to comfort them, especially Sybille, who found Marquèse... in her cradle."

"God is cruel," said Bérengère. "To take a pure little soul like that."

"When did this happen?" It seemed unreal to him.

"Two days ago. Sybille can't eat or sleep; she is out of her mind with grief. Ricard has gone to Ax, to bring Marquèse Botohl here. She is... was the baby's godmother and Sybille's sister-in-law. They're very close. They hope she can comfort Sybille and help look after Montaigne, their other little girl. Sybille's mother is with her, but she won't see anyone else."

"What about the priest?" said Pedro.

"Sybille won't have him near her," said Eglantyne. "She says God has forsaken her and she has no faith in the priest."

They looked at each other; no-one spoke. Pedro looked down; he was overwhelmed by sadness. This terrible news made no sense.

There was nothing any of them could say. It was beyond words. They sat in silence until, after some time, Eglantyne rose to prepare food for the household. Bérengère followed her. Pedro sat alone at the table. How could God allow this to happen?

Early in the evening a few days later, Raymond came to the sheep pen where Pedro was keeping watch over a couple of sheep that hadn't yet lambed. Raymond looked at the two sheep lying on the straw.

"All quiet here?" he said.

"Yes," said Pedro.

"I've been over to see Ricard and Sybille," said Raymond.

"How are they?"

"I spoke to Ricard – Sybille was resting. Ricard went to Ax with Marquèse Botohl; he brought the Perfect back with him," said Raymond. "Pierre Authier."

"To his house?" said Pedro.

"Yes, Pierre Authier came to help Sybille. Ricard says he helped them both," said Raymond. "He stayed for two nights and days, talking and praying with them. He promised that he would come back to preach to their friends and neighbours – us. He said to tell everyone, they are the only ones who can save our souls."

"That's what everyone says."

"He's going to bring another Perfect with him," said Raymond. "We can all go to hear them preach at Ricard's house. You will come, won't you, Pedro?"

A month later, Pedro was on his way to Ricard's house where the Good Men were to preach that evening. The thrill of anticipation and risk about meeting the Perfects made him feel more alive. The evening light over the distant mountains seemed clearer and sharper. The smell of wood smoke seemed richer, his limbs felt stronger, and his heart beat deeper and firmer than usual. Pierre

Authier himself, Ricard had said, and another Perfect, not yet named. Pierre and his brother, Guillaume Authier, were the most revered Perfects of all. Pedro had wanted to know from the first moment he'd heard they were back what it was that made people so willing to follow them when the risks were so high. Even his own father, usually a cautious man, who had already lost so much because of his belief in the heresy, was willing to risk it all again. They must have something special about them and what they say – when the Roman church has forbidden the people to meet them, to help them in any way, to talk about them and even to *think* about them. The Roman church must feel the heresy could weaken the powers they have over ordinary people, the power to take animals and land off people as taxes, and the ability to ignore the vow-breaking behaviour of certain priests. It was no wonder the heresy appealed to people. The Good Men, the Perfects, seemed to practise what they preached. Now Pedro was about to meet them and listen to them preach. This was an irrevocable step, especially if there were witnesses. His father's words, "trust no-one", came back to him. But it was hard to believe that anyone he knew in Arques could be a spy. The Inquisition surely didn't even know about the Authier brothers yet; it must be safe enough.

And then there was Bernadette. Since the last time he'd seen her, doubts had been floating in and out of his mind. The same questions arose many times. Was he ready for marriage? Was marriage for him at all? He had just gained his freedom and here he was contemplating tying himself down into a situation just like his father's. He had no doubts at all about being a shepherd. He was learning so much now and, in the future, he would be able to walk over the mountains and find work in other places. This was what he had always wanted. To marry now would restrict him. There would soon be children, and money would be tight; making a living, feeding and clothing a growing family would take all his strength and energy. Take care, Pedro. And did he know Bernadette? *Really* know her? He had only spent a few hours with her. She seemed a lovely girl, but it wasn't enough time to judge. Perhaps what he felt was just desire? He did desire her, but above all else his heart's desire was for freedom. Freedom to walk the mountains whenever he wanted to, freedom to work wherever he wanted, freedom to love whomever he wanted and freedom to believe in what his heart told him was right. Bernadette was the kind of girl from the kind of family that would require him to make a commitment to marry in the Roman church. As far as he could tell there was no whiff of the heresy around Bernadette's family. Marrying Bernadette would mean not seeing the Good Men, either that or deceiving her, and he would want to be honest with any woman he loved and intended to marry. Now he was about to take an irrevocable step into the world of the Perfects and their faith, something he could never talk about to Bernadette, or anyone else who wasn't involved. What did he want to do? The answers were becoming clearer.

It was early evening when he arrived at Ricard's farmhouse. His hand shook as he raised it to knock on the door.

"Ah, Pedro, good to see you," said Ricard, welcoming him with an embrace.

"Are they here?" said Pedro.

Ricard nodded and ushered Pedro into the entrance of the house. He whispered in Pedro's ear as he took him through the great door facing them and into the hall. "Pierre Authier has brought his son, Jacques," he said.

Ricard and Sybille's home was like Raymond and Eglantyne's. Although a substantial farmhouse, it was simply furnished with a great table and benches, sheepskin rugs on the stone floor and a fire in the corner. A few people were gathered there, most of whom Pedro recognised, including Raymond and Eglantyne. Sybille, who he hadn't seen since baby Marquèse had died, was sitting next to the fire. She looked thin and pale. She gave Pedro a small, strained smile when he caught her eye. Sybille's mother was beside her daughter. Marquèse Botohl was there with her brother, Guillaume Escaunier, and Ricard also introduced Pedro to Raymond Gayraud, the Bailiff of Arques, and Gilet de Voisins, who was the Squire. The Squire and the Bailiff – Raymond must be sure of their trustworthiness to have them present.

Everyone was sitting on benches arranged near the fire. The bench facing Sybille and her mother was empty – where the Perfects would probably be seated. Pedro sat down where there was a space next to Guillaume Escaunier towards the back of the group. He didn't feel he should be at the front. It seemed to him a great privilege to be there, waiting for Pierre Authier himself and his son, Jacques. Everyone was quiet and still, the atmosphere taut with the expectation of meeting the Perfects.

Guillaume Escaunier whispered into Pedro's ear. "Have you seen the loft space that Ricard and Sybille have prepared for the Perfects?" Pedro shook his head. Guillaume lifted his hand and made a sign with his thumb and fingertips together to mean what he mouthed at the same time. "Beautiful."

The door opened and Ricard entered with the Authiers. Pierre Authier was a slightly built man. His son was a little taller and resembled him. They were both fine-featured, good-looking men with alert, blue eyes. They had a refined and learned air about them. They both wore blue tunics made of fine wool. Pedro remembered Raymond's words: "They are men like any other men." Of course they were, but there was an aura around them… they were special. The others all fell to their knees, so Pedro did the same.

"God's blessing and ours," said the two Perfects, and sat down. Pierre Authier asked everyone to sit and the two of them looked around at the group and smiled, as everyone arranged themselves back on the benches.

"My friends," said Pierre. "It is such a great pleasure for my son, Jacques, and I to be here with you all this evening and to be welcomed at the home of Ricard and Sybille – first of all, before we speak of our faith, I must ask you all to remember to be careful when you leave here. After this evening, you will be full of joy because tonight you will hear how to achieve true salvation. Naturally, you will want to encourage others to do the same, but we must all be cautious – our enemies are brutal and ruthless, and will stop at nothing to destroy us. You must always be on your guard because you never know who is listening. Always remember my warning. Now, I will start by explaining some of the beliefs that underpin our faith, but first Jacques will read from the Gospel of Saint John."

Jacques stood up and looked around with a serious expression on his face. He held a book in his hands, which he said was a copy of the Gospels. He read from it in Latin. It reminded Pedro that Pierre Authier had been a notary, and that the Authiers were learned, well-educated men. The room was warm, and with Jacques reading in Latin, Pedro felt his eyes closing. He hoped it wouldn't all be like this. Fortunately, it was a short reading and Jacques soon sat down. Pierre Authier began to speak. He remained seated and spoke in a friendly way as ordinary people might speak to each other. He managed to combine warmth with dignity.

Pierre told the story of the fall of the souls from Heaven, and how the Devil managed to sneak into paradise and seduce the heavenly souls into leaving by offering them property, fields and vineyards, gold and silver, and other material gifts. Pierre said the souls had fallen through a hole in Heaven until the Father noticed and put his foot over the hole. The Father said to them, "Go for now," meaning that the souls could be saved in the future and return to Heaven. Pierre said that everyone could be saved, even the Bishops and Priests whose souls were Satan's counsellors, but their souls would have the hardest journey. The souls who were on earth realised their plight and were sad. The Devil offered them the tunics, which are our bodies, to give them comfort. The bodies could not move, so the Devil asked the Heavenly Father to breathe life into them, and this

He did. This was how people's bodies became the Devil's, and how people's souls became God's creation. But the most important thing – said Pierre Authier – was that no-one could be saved and returned to Heaven without the offices of the Good Men, the Perfects, who alone could perform the deathbed ritual of the *consolamentum*. After this ritual, the person must fast until death – and while the fasting or *endura* may hasten their death, that doesn't matter because their soul will be saved. However, said Pierre, if the *consolamentum* does not happen at the right time – which is when the dying person is able to coherently answer questions about their faith – the soul will pass into another earthly body, either human or animal, until such time as it receives the *consolamentum*. This transmigration of the soul could happen up to nine times, after which it is lost if it does not receive the *consolamentum*, the deathbed ritual.

The people sat still and quiet, spellbound by Pierre Authier's words and his warm, easy way of telling the story, which was like nothing they had heard before. Pierre Authier continued, saying that Christ was not of woman born. This was an unthinkable idea. Christ would not have passed through a woman's body. Pierre said that the word "mother" as used of Mary should be thought of in a broader sense as part of the family of Christians, brothers and sisters, mothers and fathers. Pierre said that the cross should not be revered because Christ suffered on it, nor should the saints be revered, as they are idols.

Pedro and all the company were quiet, sometimes turning to look at each other and express the shock and amazement on their faces at these ideas, which challenged much of what they had all been taught as they grew up in the Roman faith. Pierre Authier went on to say that the idea that the Good Men felt no pain when they were burned alive is a myth, and that people should believe the evidence of their own eyes. He derided the baptism of babies and children as not appropriate until they could make up their own minds about their beliefs and speak on their own behalf. Pierre spoke about the transubstantiation of bread and wine into the body and blood of Christ – he said, as it is commonly said, and as they had all heard said many times before, that the body of Christ, even if it were the size of the huge Pic de Bugarach rock in the mountains, would have been devoured long ago by the greedy priests. Pierre told them he knew that many people already thought that there is no magic at the altar. The bread and wine are not changed into the body and blood of Christ – after all, why would Christ want his body to pass through other people's bodies? There were nods and murmurings of agreement when he said this, but everyone was quiet when he said that the union of men and women was always sinful, even more so in marriage as it happened more frequently in that case, and without a sense of shame. He said that Holy days should not be observed as idleness is a sin, as is eating meat. He finished by reaffirming that only those who receive the ritual of the *consolamentum* at the end of their lives will achieve salvation. But he said they should not concern themselves as some of these sins they could not help but commit, and they would all be forgiven when they received the *consolamentum*.

"This," said Pierre Authier, "is the most important part of our faith; this is how your soul will be saved."

Pedro wanted to ask questions, but as soon as Pierre finished speaking, Ricard said that Pierre and Jacques needed to rest as they had been travelling all through the previous night and hadn't slept much that day. The whole atmosphere of the evening, the presence of these two Perfects, the stories they told and the way they told them with such simplicity and sincerity, he couldn't stop thinking about all of that. There was none of the pomp and ceremony of the Roman church, no threats of punishment, just advice to follow the Good Men, and at the end of your life your sins will be forgiven, and your soul will be saved. It made such sense and felt so right. The Perfects themselves, although commanding of respect, had no airs and graces. He was beginning to think they were right.

CHAPTER 5

Guy Belibaste

His wife was behind him, carrying the baby and holding the hand of their small son as Guy and the Perfects left the farmhouse. His father was behind his wife.

"Estelle, come back…" he heard his father say. "Stay here, I'll explain."

"Guy, what's happening? Where are you going? What's the hurry?" Estelle was crying. "Please… Guy." She sounded frantic.

Guy stopped at the large front doors. He looked back at her. Their eyes met. He shook his head. Leaving like this… it felt wrong. Philippe took hold of Guy's arm and guided him forward.

"Come, Guy," said Philippe. "There is no time to spare, we are all in grave danger."

Guy turned again. Pierre took Guy's other arm; together the Perfects took him into the deepening darkness. There was little moonlight. How would they find the way? A hammer began to bang behind his eyes, his chest was tight and sore, his breathing shallow. A feverish sweat erupted all over his body. He tried to turn again to look at his wife, to explain… to tell her…

"Don't look back," said Pierre. "Follow me. Quickly."

Now Pierre and Philippe were in front of him part way down the track, moving towards the vines. He followed, his heart breaking… behind him was Estelle weeping… and his children, his father and the rest of his family. What was he doing? What life was he going to that they would no longer be part of? God help me and forgive me, he prayed, the miserable sinner that I am.

With his wife's sobs assailing his ears, he tried to concentrate on keeping up with Pierre and Philippe, who moved ahead at speed through the rows of vines. He stumbled and fell on the stony, uneven ground and scrabbled amongst the earth and stones searching for a place to put his hands and push his aching body up. He was hot and sore everywhere now. He picked himself up and that sharp pain shot up his leg again. But he must keep going. Where were Pierre and Philippe? He stared into the darkness, the hammering in his head blurred his vision – then a wraith-like movement at the end of a row of vines caught his eye. They were ghosts gliding between the vines and he was caught in a nightmare where his legs wouldn't move, and he would be left behind. He pushed on, his legs heavy and thick, with needles of pain shooting up his injured leg with every step. At last, he was through the vines and at the edge of the wood. But where were they? He stood helpless and lost, his mind a dense, hot fog. A long moment passed – but they were beside him.

"Can we rest here?" said Guy, feeling so weak that another step seemed impossible.

"No, we must press on and get as far away from the farmhouse as we can before daylight," said Pierre. "We'll find a hiding place to sleep during the day."

"I can't go any further," said Guy.

"Pray," said Pierre. "God will give you strength."

Pierre and Philippe were accustomed to this night walking. They pressed on. Guy, exhausted from running earlier in the day, and with the bang, bang, banging behind his eyes, and his injured leg screaming at every step – he couldn't go on. His chest was tight, and a burning fever enveloped him. But somehow, he followed, faltering, not knowing where he'd placed his feet, knowing only that he must stay behind them and not cause them any more trouble. At times, they stopped, took his arms and with words of encouragement they helped him forward.

Pray, Pierre said, pray... God forgive me and give me strength... he found a rhythm: one foot, then the other; one foot, then the other; one foot, then the other; on and on. He forgot the pain in his ankle and the banging in his head. He moved forward and onward, and he stumbled no more. On and on he went, floating behind the Good Men as if in a dream, and as he gave himself up to God... he knew that God had chosen this for him and that, guided by the hand of God, he could keep going for ever.

CHAPTER 6

Pedro Maury

After the meeting with the Good Men, Pedro felt as if he'd been disturbed whilst sleeping and gently shaken until his eyes had been opened. Listen, they'd said, this is the truth, and you know it. And he did. At last, someone was daring to speak the truth. He had *never* believed that magic took place at the altar, that the bread and wine became the body and blood of Christ. Him and many others besides. The idea of changing bread and wine into the body and blood of Christ – why would Christ want you to eat his body anyway? It stretched people's credulity, and he'd laughed with others as they'd joked that even if the body of Christ was as big as the highest mountain in the vicinity, it would have been eaten already by greedy priests. But people knew better than to speak in that way before the clergy. If the church in Rome treated them like fools and took advantage of its power, the people had to retaliate somehow. Feckless priests, and the taxes and goods they took from people, all this had played its part in breeding resentment, in some people hatred even, and a scepticism about the faith. The Good Men and their gentler, kinder, more tolerant faith with the promise of salvation at the end of life were very attractive.

But to follow the Good Men would be more than fighting back at the church by complaining and making jokes with friends and neighbours. Much, much more. Becoming a Believer would mean a life of subterfuge and danger, life-*threatening* danger. Pedro had shivered when Pierre Authier talked about burning and feeling the pain. The Inquisition usually burned only the Good Men. For him, it could be a pilgrimage, wearing yellow crosses on clothing, prayers or imprisonment. He could not endure imprisonment. The loss of freedom to walk the mountain tracks and be outside in the fresh air would surely kill him. But these Good Men were haunting him, becoming more and more important. What should he choose? At this moment he could walk away and forget about the Good Men, and Bernadette too. She was part of his struggle. He could find a job as a shepherd well away from Arques and start afresh. But his usually itchy feet did not want to walk away; they wanted to stay. Raymond would be waiting for him to speak and must be sensing his prevarication.

It was another conversation in the sheep pen with Raymond that moved things on. They, along with Ricard, who was helping out, had just finished cleaning the pen and were taking a break, leaning against the gate, quietly watching the animals.

"Pedro, I was wondering...?" said Raymond. "You've been quiet since we were at Ricard's..."

"I've been thinking," said Pedro.

"Hmm," said Raymond. "What is it? Bernadette?"

"Well, that's one thing..."

"Are you betrothed?"

"Oh no, nothing like that... I barely even know her."

"Eglantyne and I are very fond of you, Pedro, we think of you as a son and, well... to be honest, I wouldn't like to see you make any decisions you might live to regret. Bernadette is a lovely girl, but she's Roman through and through."

"I know," said Pedro.

"It's a big decision," said Raymond. "But I think you would

be making the biggest mistake of your life if you carry on with Bernadette, because it will lead to marriage. That's what girls want, and her parents will see you as a pair of strong hands to work on their farm. That would be your life and that may be what you want, but I don't think it is. I think you want a different life, Pedro. So, think about this: if you want to marry, you can come to that in a few years' time – first you need to decide what you believe in."

"I know, but I'm not clear in my mind – when I heard the Good Men speak, I believed in what they said, they speak so well, but when I've heard a good sermon in church, I'm pulled in that direction, and then there are the dangers…"

"You must hear the Good Men again," said Raymond. "Then, if you decide to follow them, you should marry a girl who is a Believer. A Catholic girl wouldn't have the 'understanding of good'; she would only make you miserable. You would have to keep secrets from her and after the first few months you would grow to hate each other."

"You could be right."

"In fact." Raymond looked over at Ricard. "Ricard and I have an idea that would solve these problems for you – that is, if you choose to follow the Good Men."

Ricard nodded and continued. "You know, Pedro, I have only one daughter since baby Marquèse… and the truth is I need a son to inherit my farm. Someone to marry my Montaigne."

"Your Montaigne?" said Pedro.

"Yes, my Montaigne."

"But she's only a little girl," said Pedro.

"You know that many little girls are betrothed at an early age for reasons such as this. You would become my son-in-law, Pedro."

"But how do I know that she will believe in the Good Men?" said Pedro.

"My little Montaigne will be brought up in the ways of the Good Men. You would live together on the farm and everyone would be happy."

Pedro was speechless. He looked at Raymond and then at Ricard. He had half expected they would start laughing, that it was a joke, but no, they meant it. They looked at him with serious faces.

"I know this is a shock for you, Pedro," said Ricard. "But it might be a good idea to come and work for me anyway. That way you can get to know us, and it will help you to make your mind up. You can move over to our farm next week."

"What about you, Raymond?" said Pedro. "What do you think about this?"

"I shall be sorry to see you go, but I think it's for the best. It's a good offer, you won't get a better one – think carefully about it."

During the following week, Raymond asked Pedro to go to Cubières to take the money that Guy Belibaste should have collected. Pedro had done other jobs like this for Raymond, collecting money, paying bills, buying goods and animals on his behalf. He enjoyed the change of routine.

So, Pedro was on his way to Cubières. The air felt cold and crisp. The snow-covered mountains gleamed brilliant white in the bright sunlight. Bernadette, Montaigne, the Good Men, and Raymond and Ricard's plan for him all circled around in his head as he strode out. But he reached no conclusion. Best to let it lie fallow for a while. He would be staying at the Belibastes' home that night; he must pray before sleeping and ask God to show him the way.

It was early evening when he arrived in Cubières. Dusk was falling and he saw through the half-light a cluster of buildings in the distance. The scent of wood smoke hung in the still evening air as he approached the village. The first building on the edge of the village was a stone farmhouse. It appeared to have substantial farm buildings at the back, and rows of vines and land stretching behind and on each side of it. This was the Belibastes' farmhouse, just as Raymond had described it to him – a well-maintained and prosperous-looking place.

A short track leading up to the farm widened out in front of the house. A group of people milled around at the doorway to the farmhouse. A well-built man in his late forties stood at the entrance. He was shaking hands with people, embracing others and exchanging a few words with everyone. That must be Guillaume Belibaste. Pedro walked up and introduced himself.

"Ah, Pedro," said Guillaume. "It's good to see you. We've been expecting someone from Raymond's to come over. You've come on a good night. An important guest, the Public Prosecutor for the area, Maître Girard, will be joining us any moment – ah, here are my sons, Bernard and Raymond – Bernard, take Pedro through."

Bernard ushered Pedro into a large hall, the walls of which were painted in a rich red and deep blue pattern. A great table stood in the centre with benches all round it. A few people were already inside, taking off their cloaks and mantles, giving them to a manservant, and talking and settling themselves at the table. In one corner, wood burned in a great fireplace, where a side of mutton and a whole boar were roasting. The rich smell of the meat, the flames of the fire and the decorated walls felt warm and welcoming. This place was more like a château than a farmhouse. Pedro was hungry after his walk. He sat down at the table where he had been shown. Gradually, all the people settled into their places. Bernard Belibaste sat next to Pedro but was drawn into conversation with the man on his other side. Pedro looked around. Most of the people were well-dressed, their clothes of good-quality wool and their boots of fine leather. A few were wearing working clothes like Pedro, whose shepherd's tunic and cloak were the only clothes he possessed. Both Bernard and Raymond Belibaste were wearing shepherds' clothes, so he didn't feel out of place.

Guillaume hurried off and returned with another man – stout and well dressed in a brocade tunic, he looked to be in his fifties. Everyone clapped when they saw him – he must be the guest of honour, Maître Girard. Maître Girard looked around at everyone, nodded and smiled, acknowledging all who were there. When he was seated and settled, they began to serve the food. There was wild boar, which must have been roasted beforehand, and this was carved by Guillaume. The mutton was taken off the spit and left to rest whilst the first platter of meat was served and eaten. Turnips and cabbages came next, and more meat, followed by mature cheese from last year's making. It was the usual food served at the gatherings of local folk, except that this was exceptionally delicious. Pedro, having only eaten bread and cheese on his journey, savoured each mouthful. Bernard Belibaste told him that the fine red wine was from their vineyard. Pedro looked around for Guy, the third brother, and asked Bernard where Guy was seated. Bernard's face clouded and he looked around as if he feared someone might be watching.

"He's not here," he said in a low voice. "He… he had to go away, his wife is here – she's helping my wife to serve the food."

Pedro followed his eyes to the two young women who had just entered. They placed dishes of vegetables on the table before they took their places at the table. Something was wrong, he'd touched on a subject that Bernard did not want to speak of. Guy Belibaste wasn't mentioned again that evening.

Pedro noticed a servant entering with a platter with trout on it. The servant placed it in front of Guillaume Belibaste. Guillaume stood up, looking angry. He spoke to the servant, picked up the platter, looked around at the guests and walked off with the platter, the servant creeping behind him. Pedro looked around the table, but everyone was engrossed in eating or talking – was he the only one to have noticed the little drama? He smiled to himself. It was like the occasion at Raymond's when he had stumbled into a similar situation. But what to make of this? Especially as Maître Girard, the Public Prosecutor, was there. It could be that the others did not understand the significance of the fish. The more likely truth was that they all wondered or knew who was there – another guest, perhaps? Somewhere, hidden behind the scenes.

When dinner was over, Maître Girard mingled with the guests who were preparing to leave. He shook hands with some, embraced others, until there was just Pedro, Bernard and Raymond left. Guillaume brought Maître Girard to meet Pedro.

"I want you to meet Pedro Maury, cousin of Raymond Maulen from Arques," said Guillaume to Maître Girard.

"Good to meet you, Pedro," said Maître Girard. "I've heard good things about you. Have you had a good evening?"

"Yes, thank you, I have," said Pedro.

"I expect our paths will cross again," said Maître Girard, as Guillaume took him away, saying they had some business to attend to.

"Look after Pedro," Guillaume said to Bernard and Raymond.

Bernard looked at Pedro. "There's someone else who wishes to meet you," he said.

"Who's that?" said Pedro.

"We have another important guest who has heard about you – follow me and I'll take you to him," said Bernard. Bernard and Raymond took Pedro through the back work area of the house, and across the farmyard to a barn where they stopped at a locked door. Bernard had the key which he waved in front of Pedro. "Prepare yourself, Pedro, there are two men in here who want to meet you," he said. "I think you may have an idea as to who they are." Pedro nodded. "Just follow me and everything will be *good*," said Bernard.

Bernard unlocked the door. Two men were seated on bales of straw, wearing blue wool tunics. Even though these tunics were covered in dust and scraps of straw, the men looked dignified. They both looked warmly at Pedro and the other two as they entered. The two Belibaste brothers knelt before them and asked for a blessing.

"God's blessing and ours," said the older of the two Perfects.

Pedro was uncertain for a moment, then knelt in front of the Perfects. "Can I… can *I* ask for your blessing?"

"God's blessing and ours," said the older one as he put his hand, warm and firm, on Pedro's shoulder. "You may rise, Pedro, take a seat." He gestured to a bale of straw next to him. "It's the best seat we can offer at the moment." He smiled at Pedro. "I am Amiel de Perles, and this is Raymond Faure. We are Good Men and we're pleased to meet you. We've heard many good things about you, including that you would make a fine Believer. Tonight, we have time only to give the blessing to those we meet; we're not preaching because there are others who wish to talk privately with us." He took hold of Pedro's hand in his. "But there will be other opportunities to hear Good Men preach. We're praying for you, Pedro, praying that you will come to the 'understanding of good'. Salvation is within your grasp. Salvation can be yours."

They both stood and signalled Pedro to stand. They each took hold of one of his hands, looked at him intently but kindly, and Bernard led him out. Pedro followed Bernard, wondering if that had really happened. It was so unexpected and was over so quickly that it did not seem real. But he remembered the straw and dust on the Perfects' blue tunics and the cold hardness of the stone floor when he knelt, and the warm firmness of Amiel de Perles' hand on his shoulder as he gave him the blessing. And as he walked across the farmyard with Bernard, he was sure he felt the presence of someone, or maybe more than one person, lurking in the shadows, maybe waiting for their turn to receive a blessing from the Good Men.

The next day, Pedro left early and returned to the pastures. His mind was slowly filtering through his recent experiences, the encounter with the Good Men, and the conversation in the sheep pen with Ricard and Raymond. Now, he had met four Perfects. There was no denying his regard for them, their gentle, informal ways, and their ideas fascinated him, but when Thursday night came and the week was nearly over, he felt no nearer a decision. He had prayed many times, asking God to guide him, to show him what He wanted him to do. Which path was God's path? Whatever the risks and dangers were, he wanted to follow the right path, God's path. He prayed silently before he settled down to sleep in the barn with the other shepherds, asking God to show him the way. He was warm and comfortable lying on sheepskins and covered by his wool cloak, but he could not sleep, the same thoughts plaguing him.

He woke up with a start. Where was he? Of course, he was in the barn with the other shepherds. As he peered through the gloom, he could make out the forms of the other men lying nearby. There was no sound apart from the soft noises of breathing and stirring that the men made as they slept. It was the middle of the night. He rose as quietly as he could and opened the barn door just wide enough to slip through the gap. The door scraped and groaned as he opened it, and he stopped and peered through the darkness to where the men lay, but no-one stirred. He slipped outside. The air felt cool and fresh. He stood and looked around. There was light from a nearly full moon and the heavens were full of shining stars. The sight entranced him; his eyes roamed over the mass of winking lights above him and he stared, wondering what he might see up there. But nothing emerged; the stars merely twinkled at him. He walked towards the sheep pen at the far side of the barn and sat down on a rocky outcrop. There was some movement on the other side of the pen – one of the white sheep dogs was stretching his front paws out. The dog yawned, shook himself and padded over to Pedro, wagging his tail.

"Hello, boy." Pedro stroked the dog's velvet ears. "Are your old joints a bit stiff?"

When Pedro stopped, the dog nudged his hand with his nose and Pedro stroked him again. The dog looked up at him with his soft eyes.

"What shall I do?" said Pedro. "The Good Men are everywhere I look. Should I follow them? Is theirs the path to salvation?"

A clear image of the old man covered in flour he met on his journey from Montaillou to Arques came into his mind, and how he spoke of the Good Men; he thought of his parents receiving the Good Men in their home, and about being introduced to the Perfects by Ricard and Raymond, and the evening at the Belibastes. Wherever he turned, he saw them – the Good Men, the Good Christians, the Perfects. He remembered what Guillaume and Pierre Authier had given up for their faith. He sat there in the moonlight stroking the dog, and a new thought sharpened and clarified until he saw it perfectly. At that moment he felt God was within him and without, showing him the path to salvation. Everything and everyone, his friends, his family, all pointed towards the same pathway. God *had* shown him the way; he just hadn't seen it until now.

He looked up into the heavens at the shining stars. What more beautiful sight could there be, stars shining more brightly than he had ever seen them before, the moon almost blinding him, so strong was its radiance. The stars, the moon were part of his new awareness, and he was part of the splendour; peace was within him. The ground, firm beneath his feet, the form of the dog standing there looking at him and the cool hardness of the rock beneath his hand – he was meeting God. He fell to his knees, closed his eyes and put his hands together.

"Thank you," he said.

He arrived at Ricard's house the following week with his small bundle of possessions in time for the supper gathering. A small group of friends and neighbours, including his cousin Raymond and the local Bailiff, were already there when Pedro walked in. It was as it had been at the Belibastes' and at Raymond's home previously, with someone or some others eating in another room. A cousin of Ricard's, whom Pedro had met a few times before, Gérard Peyre, was fussing around backwards and forwards all evening, in and out of another door leading from the hall, presumably making sure whoever was in there had what they needed and bringing out empty platters. No-one remarked on this, and Pedro waited to see what would happen. When the meal was over, Gérard Peyre disappeared for a few minutes, then re-entered the room bringing with him two other men. He introduced them as Martin Frances and Pierre Authier, whom Pedro recognised. Everyone knelt with their heads bowed.

"God bless you all," said Pierre Authier. "I must leave you for a few minutes, but I shall return shortly." He left the room with Gérard Peyre. Ricard touched Pedro on his shoulder.

"Pedro, come."

Ricard took Pedro into a small storeroom. Bags of flour and other dry goods were piled up in one corner, and benches had been arranged, one opposite the other. Pierre Authier and Gérard Peyre were seated. They both stood. Pierre took hold of Pedro's hand and asked him to sit beside him. Ricard left the room. Pierre Authier began to talk to Pedro using the familiar and friendly forms of language that Pedro used with his friends and family, although Pedro replied in the formal mode of address to show his respect for the Perfect. Aware of the awe in which Pierre Authier and his brother were held, Pedro marvelled how, despite that, he felt at ease with Pierre Authier.

"Pedro," said Pierre Authier. "I am told that you will be a good Believer, an asset to our growing band of Believers, and, if it is God's will, I will show you the way to salvation. You know we are called heretics and are hated and persecuted like our Lord Jesus and the Apostles. But we are as strong as they were – if we fall into the hands of our enemies, we do not betray one word of our faith; we never lie, nor do we ever betray our fellow Believers."

He asked Pedro the same question that Raymond asked him about the two churches and which he thought was the right church. Pedro gave him the same answer that he gave Raymond, that the right church must be the one that forgives and understands.

"It is we who follow the way of truth," said Pierre Authier, nodding. "We are the ones who forgive and understand."

"So," said Pedro, "if you follow the way of truth and of the Apostles, can I ask why you don't preach as the parish priests do in the church?"

"If we preached in the churches, we would be burnt at the stake by the Roman Catholic church, which has a great hatred for us."

"Why does the Roman church hate you in this way?" said Pedro.

"Because when the people hear us speak, they prefer our faith as we speak only the truth, whereas the Roman church speaks lies."

"I heard a Filius Minor preach in church recently; I thought he said a lot of good things," said Pedro.

"Pedro, you must leave behind what the Filius Minor said, and be sure to put what I will tell you into your heart, because I will show you how the Roman church has told the people lies," said Pierre Authier. "We find in the Gospel that no-one other than Christians will be saved according to the Law. There are many differences between the Roman church and ours. When children are born, the Roman church expects the godparents to bring the child to the church door when the child is just a few days old to be baptised in the faith. The godparents promise that this child will be a good and faithful Christian, yet subsequently he will be wicked and deceitful. This baptism is of no value, because it is not the child who promises to be a good and faithful Christian, but someone else on the child's behalf. We want a child to have reached at least twelve years of age, preferably eighteen, and be able to distinguish between good and evil before he is accepted into our faith. He can therefore promise to bring us good and not evil, to be faithful, and to do all he can to bring others into our church. You are a young man, Pedro, able to make your own mind up. Do you think you are ready to promise these things?"

"I believe that God has guided me to this point," said Pedro.

"I was shown the way by God just as He has shown you, Pedro," said Pierre Authier. "I prayed to Him and asked for help, I examined my own life and my conscience, and I read the Gospels – Saint John's Gospel is the one we follow – and I prayed again. I came to see that my life was too concerned with material things – I was not leading the life that God wanted me to. I had to leave my family and my old life behind, and I went with my brother to Lombardy, where the Good Men can live openly without suffering persecution by the church in Rome. My brother and I studied the Gospels and were taught by the Good Men until we were ready to be accepted into the faith. We were there for nearly four years. Now we have returned, we are spreading the faith and soon there will be many more Believers in our land. You must be happy, Pedro, because the blessing of being a Believer and follower of the Good Men can be yours if you wish."

"If God wishes it, then so do I," said Pedro.

At this point, Gérard Peyre rose and left the room, closing the door behind him. Pierre Authier put a cushion on the floor and asked Pedro to kneel in front of him.

"Pedro," he said, looking intently at him, "God has brought you to my side and if He wills it and you wish it, I will put you on the road to salvation. It gives me great pleasure to help you in this way. But I warn you this is not an easy path; we are hated by the rest of the world, who call us heretics. We must be strong and stalwart like Christ and the Apostles, who were crucified and stoned by their enemies. I ask you now, Pedro, do you want to join us in our faith?"

"Yes, I do," said Pedro.

"You know I am a Perfect and I must lead a Holy life. I must never tell a lie; if I do, I must fast for three days; if I touch a woman then I will fast for nine days on bread and water," said Pierre. "And now I will teach you how to show reverence to me, which is how all Believers revere the Perfects."

"What must I do?" said Pedro.

"You must kneel and bow your head and ask me to bless you using the words, 'Good Christian, God's blessing and yours.' Do this three times and each time I will reply, 'I give you God's blessings and mine.' This is called the *melioramentum*, which you must perform when meeting or taking leave of a Perfect."

Pedro did as he was asked. Then Pierre asked Pedro to stand. He embraced him, kissed him three times and each time spoke these words: "God bless you; God will lead you to a good end and God will make you a good Christian."

"Why is it necessary to do this ritual?" asked Pedro.

"Because of this, you are now a Believer and, when you are dying, I will reach out my hand to receive you. If I find that your soul is in your body, I will, with God's help, save your soul by performing the deathbed ritual, the *consolamentum*." Pierre smiled. "It's nothing to concern yourself with, Pedro. When the time comes, I will talk to you, and lay my hands and the Gospels on you. Through this, your soul will be saved."

So, this was it. He could expect to receive the *consolamentum* at the end of his life; his soul would be saved. More thoughts and questions were bubbling in his mind, but Pierre took his hand and helped him rise.

"Come, Pedro," said Pierre. "We must go and join the others, who are waiting to congratulate you for doing this."

Pierre led him back into the room where Martin Frances and the others were waiting. They stood and clapped their hands when they saw him. They crowded round him, embracing him and patting his back.

"Well done, Pedro."

"Welcome."

"Sit here by the fire."

Raymond brought out a wineskin and gave each of them a drink. "We must congratulate Pedro and wish him a long and good life." He raised his goblet and they all joined in.

"Our numbers are growing," said Pierre Authier. "We have reason to be hopeful for the future and thankful to God for bringing more into our fold."

"We'll rest here tomorrow," said Martin Frances. "And we must leave for Cassaignes tomorrow evening, where one of our safe houses is situated. One of the services you can do for the Good Men, Pedro, is to accompany them as they travel overnight in pairs to go to the homes of the dying, where they perform the deathbed ritual. They then stay in one of the safe houses – there are several, all run and prepared by Believers to receive us. Tomorrow we will go together – you, me and Pierre. We'll leave just after dusk."

"The way ahead might be dark and dangerous at times, Pedro," said Pierre Authier, "but with the support of the Believers, who always help each other, we will get through. Because this is God's way. The right way."

"I vow to always help and support the other Believers," said Pedro.

There were five men assembled in Ricard's entrance hall late the following evening. Ricard and Raymond were to accompany Pedro and the Perfects to the edge of the village and then return to their homes. They all wore shepherd's cloaks and looked the same as any other shepherd or farmer. They glanced at each other. It was time to leave. Pedro was concerned that it might seem odd if anyone saw them – why would a group of shepherds be on the move at night-time? But he reckoned the others were more experienced in these matters than he was, so he kept quiet. They set off along the main track from Ricard's farmhouse, past the mill at Arques, and as they rounded a bend, they came upon the owner of the château, the Châtelain, Gilet de Voisins and the Bailiff, Raymond Gayraud, who had been with them the previous evening, along with a couple of his workers. Pedro's mouth dried. Now what? Gilet de Voisins had been a regular attendant at Ricard and Raymond's soirees, when the Perfects preached – there really was nothing to fear – nevertheless his heart was thumping hard; sweat trickled down his back.

"What are you all doing out and about at this time?" said Gilet de Voisins, who, without waiting for an answer, continued, "I'm missing some animals, four pigs; someone's been stealing them, I'm sure. If you see anything, let me know." And with that, Pedro and the others moved away.

Pedro caught the Bailiff's eye and breathed out. The Châtelain appeared to be so caught up with the loss of his animals that he'd hadn't taken any notice of the two strangers with the group. Either that or he was happy to let them all pass. After this, Ricard and Raymond left Pedro and the Perfects to continue their journey through the night. The going was hard and slow as there was little moonlight, and it was difficult to see where they were treading. They met no other travellers and arrived at Cassaignes early the next morning, exhausted but safe.

Pedro was surprised that the safe house was so ordinary-looking, and set only a short distance away from the village. No-one would suspect anything unusual happened there. Of course, that was how it had to be, an unremarkable place which drew no attention to itself and where no-one would observe the comings and goings. A man who told them his name was Arnaud, and who was dressed in work clothes, greeted them at the door and took Pedro upstairs into a large loft room where he was to sleep. The Perfects were shown into a separate room. Arnaud told them there would be refreshments for them downstairs whenever they wished. His wife would be on hand to serve them. Pedro and the others rested for a few hours before going down to eat. As they ate their fish, Pierre Authier and Martin Frances explained that the network of safe houses had been set up and prepared whilst Pierre and Guillaume Authier were in Lombardy. The Believers had accumulated money between themselves and some had volunteered their homes to be made ready. If Pedro was willing to guide the Perfects as they walked, always together, either to preach in the homes of Believers or to perform the *consolamentum* at a deathbed, he would be invaluable.

"I will be honoured," said Pedro. "I like nothing better than walking the mountains and I believe Ricard will spare me from the pastures."

"It will be dangerous and difficult at times," said Martin Frances. "Walking through the night is safer, but, as you saw last night, it's harder. And you must always be prepared to encounter curious and sometimes dangerous people, and you must never trust anyone."

"I'm beginning to see the risks," said Pedro. "But I want to help."

When he was about to leave, Pierre Authier spoke to him.

"I wish you well, Pedro. You will be an asset to our band of Believers, but I must ask you not to embarrass any Perfects you may encounter with difficult questions. You have been able to question me but remember if a Perfect makes an error in his response he will have to fast for three days. So be discreet always," he said. "I will pray for you, Pedro."

"I too will pray," said Pedro.

"There is no need for you to pray, Pedro. I pray for all the Believers," said Pierre Authier.

"Should I not pray to God?" said Pedro. "Surely I must pray? If I can't pray, I will be… like an animal."

"You can pray if you wish," said Pierre. "The Pater Noster is our prayer, as that was the prayer of our Lord Jesus. But, when you must get up from your bed, get dressed, eat or do some work you could say, 'Benedicte, Lord God, Father of the Good Spirits, help us in everything that we want to do.'"

Pierre walked back over the same ground he had trodden the night before. How honoured he felt that Pierre Authier trusted him enough to ask him to be a guide to the Perfects as they travelled. He had no doubts now. He had found the place and the people he wanted to be with. The faith made sense to him, his friends and family were Believers, and his loyalty, henceforth, was with the Good Men. But it meant making some adjustments. He could no longer see Bernadette. But how to extricate himself without causing too much distress? He regretted going along with the whole situation when he'd had stirrings of doubts and uncertainties all along. He'd been driven by desire and lust, if he was honest. But they had only met a few times and he had made no promises, though he guessed she had no doubts and was expecting him to carry on meeting with her and her family, and that it would lead to marriage. The only way was to make a clean break. The worst part was that he would have to lie to her and tell her he was moving away. She would be hurt and puzzled, and he was sorry it had to be like that. And he must avoid the church in Arques after telling her he was leaving, although that was no hardship. No priest kept track of the shepherds as they moved around so much. His absence would not be remarkable. A new, authentic way of life lay in front of him. He had wanted a different life, and it was beginning.

Over the following year, Pedro continued to work for Ricard. By day he worked as a shepherd. But he was often absent as he accompanied the Good Men on their night-time journeys over the mountains. The other shepherds accepted that Pedro, as Ricard's future son-in-law, would undertake other duties for him and that he needed to travel. The faith was thriving – there was a buoyancy to it, a rightness in the air. Yes, there were dangers, but it was God's path and the Cathars of Arques were uplifted as the group of Believers grew and the numbers of Good Men increased. Several Perfects came to Ricard's or Raymond's houses to preach during this time. There were more secret dinners when neighbours and friends, all Believers, shared food and stories of the new Good Men that were taught by the Authiers. A man Pedro knew from childhood in Montaillou, Prades Tavernier, was a regular visitor at both houses. Prades had been a weaver but became one of the Authier brothers' first new Perfects. When he visited, he often stayed in the cellar at Ricard's. Anyone who entered the cellar might be surprised to see a man in a blue tunic come out from behind a barrel, once he knew who was there. Pedro and Prades exchanged a few words when they met in this way. Prades returned to his spot behind the barrel when Pedro left him. At Raymond's, the Perfects stayed in the loft, sleeping in a bed between beautiful linen sheets specially prepared for them. It was a special honour to have the Authier brothers, as they were the most revered of all the Perfects.

It was towards the end of the following year, that Pedro came out of the barn early one morning and almost bumped into Ricard. Ricard's face looked drawn and tired.

"Ricard, what are you doing here so early?" said Pedro. "It's barely light yet."

"Oh, Pedro," said Ricard, putting his arms around Pedro. He sobbed, holding on to Pedro for a few moments. He let go and stood back a little. He took a deep breath. "Sybille and the baby are very ill... I had to send for a Perfect..."

Pedro knew that Sybille had given birth to another baby girl a few weeks before. He was dreading what Ricard had come to tell him.

"Come and sit beside the campfire," he said, taking Ricard's arm. "The others are still asleep in the barn – we won't be disturbed."

He threw a handful of twigs and small logs onto the embers of the fire and they sat down together, both wrapped in their cloaks as the twigs crackled and burst into flames.

"Sybille and the baby became very ill two days ago," said Ricard. "Vomiting and purging, copious amounts, the baby is only two months old, and I couldn't bear..." He paused as he struggled to control himself. His jaw quivered, and a tear ran down his cheek. "I sent for a Perfect to come quickly – Prades Tavernier arrived yesterday morning. He saw how weak they were, and Sybille begged him to give them both the *consolamentum*. He said he would give Sybille the *consolamentum*, but he couldn't give it to a baby. Sybille was distraught, out of her mind." Ricard paused to compose himself. "Sybille pleaded with him, and in the end Prades relented and gave them both the *consolamentum*. He left them quickly afterwards with instructions to fast until death to achieve salvation. Sybille seemed to be more content after this and fell asleep, but I couldn't rest. I went downstairs and paced around the house, then went into the barn and paced around in there, until finally I sat down amongst the hay." He stopped and looked at Pedro. "The next thing I knew was that I woke up and I could hear the baby crying, so, I ran back into the house, up to the room where Sybille and the baby were. I realised as I entered the room that the baby had stopped crying. And what I saw next shocked me to my core." He took a deep breath. "Sybille was sitting up in bed, suckling the baby. Her mother was there beside her with bread and water on a tray." He looked at Pedro.

"Oh, thank God," said Pedro. "They've recovered."

"But…" Ricard frowned and shook his head.

"But what?" said Pedro. "What's the matter?"

"Sybille broke the *endura*," said Ricard. "And your soul can only go to Heaven if you remain in a pure state after receiving the *consolamentum*, and that means fasting."

"But Raymond, they would die if they fasted – they've survived, haven't they? They're going to continue to recover, aren't they?" Oh God, let me be right. He silently prayed and, on reflex, crossed himself.

"Yes, I know, and they're both much better again this morning – whatever it was has left them. Sybille said she couldn't bear to hear the baby cry and not suckle her. She hadn't much milk, but when her mother came up with the water and bread, she took it and put the baby to suckle, so…" He put his head in his hands. "I don't know what to think, Pedro. Of course, I am relieved and happy they're both alive and, well, I couldn't bear to lose any more… but I can't help thinking that Sybille and the baby will be damned."

"Well, I don't know about that, Ricard. Surely it must be that it wasn't time for them to go, God allowed them to recover, and if either of them is ill again, God forbid, surely, they can receive the *consolamentum* again, can't they?"

"I don't know," said Ricard.

"You must ask the Perfects; this must happen all the time when people send for a Perfect, and it turns out to be a false alarm. I'm sure it's nothing to be concerned about. Ricard, go home to them and be happy that you still have your wife and daughter."

Pedro prayed again as he watched him go, hoping that he had not made a grave error.

In early summer Pedro was head shepherd up on the high pastures of the Rabassoles. It was the time when the shepherds made cheese from the ewes' milk as the lambs were weaned from their mothers. Pedro made bread as well as looking after the sheep and organising the eight shepherds who formed the group, and who would stay with him all summer. It was during that summer that Pedro started to go regularly to Ax, usually to rest after leading one or two of the Perfects' overnight journeys along the mountain pathways to another deathbed. The first time he went was with Prades Tavernier, who took him to a safe house that belonged to a woman called Sybille Baille. Pedro had escorted Guillaume Authier and Prades Tavernier to and from a *consolamentum*, and then to Jacques Authier's safe house just outside Ax, where they left Guillaume Authier. Prades Tavernier and Pedro carried on to Ax, and Sybille Baille's house. Her house was in the centre of the town in a quiet lane in the middle of a warren of alleyways and lanes. Its situation meant that prying eyes could not easily see who was coming and going from the house. Prades knocked on the tall front door. They heard footsteps approaching and one side of the double door was opened by a woman who looked to be a few years older than Pedro. She greeted Prades warmly.

"Welcome, Prades, I heard you would be coming… step inside." She checked the lane both ways and closed the door. They were standing in a short alleyway which was open to a large courtyard. There was no-one around. Sybille faced Prades, bowed her head and said the words of the *melioramentum* to him. She turned her gaze to Pedro. Her dark eyes caught the light from the high opening above the door and gleamed with life as she smiled warmly at him. Strands of dark brown hair escaped from her head-dress, which was half falling off her thick hair. She wore a kirtle of plain fabric underneath a tabard, which had smears of what looked like flour all over it. She noticed Pedro was looking her up and down. She laughed.

"Pedro Maury, I believe," she said. "I've heard about you – all good, I might add."

"I'm pleased to meet you, Madame," said Pedro. His face burned red hot for no apparent reason.

"Oh, Sybille, please, call me Sybille," she said. "You're just in time for breakfast, so come upstairs. Everyone tends to congregate in the large room where the oven keeps it cosy."

They followed her through the courtyard and upstairs to the living room at the back of the house, overlooking the same courtyard they had just been in. The aroma of baking bread filled the room.

"Sit down and make yourselves comfortable," she said, gesturing to the large table in the centre of the room. "What would you like to drink? I have some good wine from the Fenouillèdes, and water, of course."

"Wine sounds good," said Prades as they seated themselves at the table in the centre of the room. "We've been walking all night so I'm ready for a drink."

"I've got some fish for you, Prades, and there's eggs for you, Pedro."

Pedro looked around the spacious room. It was much the same as all the living rooms he went to. There was an arrangement of a bread oven and a fire for cooking in one corner. Shelves and cupboards lined the walls. He watched Sybille as she busied herself cutting bread from a freshly baked loaf and brought a wineskin out of a store cupboard. He liked the look of her; in fact, he couldn't take his eyes off her. She was tall and strong-looking with a liveliness and grace to her. Her hair had all but fallen out of her head-dress. Most women would have been fussing about covering their heads and hair, as it was regarded as immodest not to do so, but she just pulled the head-dress off and tossed it to one side. It made him smile.

"I hate wearing head-dresses; they always fall off," she said, laughing. "I hope you don't mind."

The door into the kitchen opened and two children entered with a young woman. There was a little girl who looked about four, and a boy of about twelve. They both resembled Sybille.

"This is Jacquemette, my daughter," said Sybille. "Arnaud, my son, and Rixende, their nursemaid. It's breakfast time for them."

"I don't need a nursemaid," said Arnaud.

"No, of course you don't, Naudy," said Sybille. "You're growing up fast like your older brothers."

"You've got brothers?" said Pedro. "I've got lots of brothers, I miss them, I miss all my family."

"I'm going to live with them soon," said Arnaud.

"Where do they live?" said Pedro.

"They're in Tarascon, where my father's a notary," said Arnaud.

"Come and sit down, the food is ready," said Sybille.

She gave fried fish to Prades, and fried eggs to Pedro, the children and their nursemaid. Sybille opened the oven and brought out two more loaves of bread.

"Plenty for everyone," she said.

When they had all eaten their fill, the children went out with Rixende. Sybille showed Prades and Pedro to their room, which looked out onto the courtyard at the back. Pedro saw that the house surrounded the courtyard on three sides. The fourth side was a wall with the entrance gate in the middle of it. It was clearly a substantial and well-built house, in a desirable position.

"I'm not ready to sleep just yet," said Pedro.

"Come and keep me company in the kitchen," said Sybille. "I've more cooking to do."

"I'm going to sleep, I'm exhausted," said Prades. "Don't wake me when you come to bed."

Sybille and Pedro went back to the kitchen. He sat at the table whilst she worked. He found he was staring at her and quickly looked away.

"It's a fine house you have here," he said.

"It was my father's house – when he died, I inherited it. I've no brothers or sisters, so it came to me."

"Oh, I see."

"Did Prades tell you about my circumstances?"

"A little, but not much."

"I live here with my servants, who've all been here a long time. My husband told me he couldn't live here if I was following the Good Men and allowing the Good Men to stay, so he left. It was a sad time for all of us but… well, that's how it has to be. My two eldest boys live with Arnaud, my husband, and we think it's better for Naudy and Jacquemette to spend more time with their father, in a more conventional household. I know I'm the subject of gossip in Ax, although I try to keep my life private. I don't want the younger children to see the comings and goings of the Good Men – there are too many secrets for them to have to keep, so it's for the best that they go there."

Pedro watched her again as she busied herself tidying the kitchen, regularly pushing stray locks of hair off her face. She looked at him.

"In case you're wondering," she said, "I changed my name when my husband left. My married name was Sicre. He is Arnaud Sicre. I'm Baille, my father's name." She put more logs on the fire and swept the hearth. "There are more visitors coming tonight," she said. "I cook every day because there are often many people sitting down to meals here."

"It must be hard work," said Pedro. "On your own."

"It's what I want to do," she said. "And I have the servants to help me. I think it must be hard for you and the others who travel around at night with the Perfects."

"It's not so bad when you can come to a place like this," he said.

Sybille went over and put her hand on Pedro's shoulder. "You will be welcome here anytime, Pedro Maury," she said. "If you need somewhere to stay, whether you've escorted one of the Good Men or not, you can always come here."

He touched her hand with his. There was something between them that he had not experienced before.

It felt like coming home.

CHAPTER 7

Guy Belibaste

Guy opened his eyes and blinked. Bright light was streaming in above his head. He was emerging from a deep, dark place. He pushed through the thick fog in his mind and tried to focus on his situation. He was lying on his back in a warm, comfortable bed with soft bedlinen. He took a deep breath in, ouch… tight, raw pain stabbed all over his chest. He tentatively took another, shallower breath, careful… careful… He licked his lips; they were dry, and he had a foul taste in his mouth. He lifted his head up a little to look around. Pain thrummed through his skull.

But he saw enough to know he was in a small, plain room. A table stood next to his bed and a bench sat against the opposite wall. A high window opening in the wall above his head let in light and air. Where on earth was he and how did he come to be here? His mind began to crank up. He remembered that he arrived at this place with the Good Men. How long ago was that? A scene flashed into his mind… he was in the pastures with the shepherds, there was an argument, a fight… was there a struggle? Barthélemy, the shepherd… fell… and he, Guy, had left his father's house with the

Perfects... He tried again to sit up, but his head and chest hurt too much; he was too weak. He sank back onto the pillow and closed his eyes. The faces of his wife and children swam in front of him.

The door opened. A man entered and came over to his bedside. His rugged features had a pleasant set to them. He wore a Perfect's blue tunic.

"Ah, Guy," he said. "You're awake, welcome back." His voice was low and gentle.

"Where am I?" said Guy.

"You're at Rabastens, in a Perfects' safe house," he said. "You came here with Pierre Authier and Philippe d'Aylarac. You've been very sick since you arrived; you've been in and out of delirium. I don't expect you'll remember much."

"Rabastens... how long have I been here?"

"A few weeks," he said.

"A few weeks. I must get up." Guy moved again, forgetting the pain for a moment. "My chest... my head..." he said as he lay back into the pillows.

"Guy, don't try to move, you're too weak," the man said. "You're over the worst now, but you'll need to rest for some time. I need to put poultices on your chest to loosen and soothe it, and I'll give you a herbal remedy for your headache. And, very importantly, you need to drink as much water as you can."

"I'm thirsty, my mouth tastes like a cesspit," said Guy, licking his dry lips.

"I'll get something to clean your mouth, I'll be back in a minute." As he turned to go, he said, "You're lucky to be alive."

"Who are you?"

"I'm Raymond de Toulouse."

After a while, Raymond returned carrying a tray. He cleaned Guy's mouth using a fresh-tasting liquid and with a thin piece of cheesecloth wrapped around his finger. He worked gently and carefully, taking his time to clean Guy's mouth. It felt so good as the sweet cleanness suffused Guy's mouth. He licked his lips; that was much better. Raymond held Guy's head as Guy took sips of cool water.

"I'm going to help you sit up, Guy," said Raymond. "We'll take it slowly."

Raymond carefully helped Guy to manoeuvre his body so he was sitting on the edge of the bed. Raymond encouraged Guy to breathe in as deeply as he could. Guy cautiously took a breath in. A piercing pain engulfed him.

"Oh, Jesus Christ, that hurts."

"It will at first, but you must keep trying; it will help to clear your chest. I'll bring balsam for you to inhale, poultices and linctus, all that will help," said Raymond. "By the way, no taking the Lord's name in vain, please."

"Oh, yes, of course," said Guy, embarrassed about his thoughtlessness. "Forgive me."

Guy looked down at his body. His legs and body were thin and wasted. There was a bandage wrapped around his right ankle. Raymond gently sponged soap and water all over Guy's body. He patted Guy's skin dry with linen cloths and slipped a clean cotton garment over Guy's head. Raymond skilfully changed the sheets by rolling up the dirty ones and rolling clean ones in their place hardly disturbing Guy, before helping him lie back in bed.

"Is that better?" said Raymond.

"Yes, that feels good, but I'm exhausted."

"Rest for a while, then I'll bring you some gruel."

"Before you go, Raymond, can you tell me, is either Philippe d'Aylarac or Pierre Authier here?"

"I'm not sure, they may be out," said Raymond. "Would you like to see them?"

Guy nodded and closed his eyes.

It was a few days later when Philippe visited Guy in his room. Guy was still weak and resting for the greater part of each day, but his chest was less painful and tight with Raymond's ministrations, and his appetite was returning. He ate mainly gruel and bread; the gruel was tasty, but thoughts of chicken cooked over a fire with crispy, golden skin and succulent, wild boar chops and his father's wine – last year's red was the best – entered his mind so vividly that he could almost smell their aroma. And as the fog in his mind lifted further, more thoughts, memories and images came to him. A recurring dream of Barthélemy, the shepherd, lying dead, but his eyes following Guy as Guy moved away, the pool of blood under Barthélemy's head growing larger. Barthélemy the shepherd standing, resurrected but bleeding, his filthy garments flying wildly around him – then Guy trying to run but unable to move his legs. Guy would wake screaming, lying in a pool of sweat. During the day he began to piece together the memories of leaving his father's house that fateful morning, recalling the anger and humiliation he'd felt. Suddenly he saw Barthélemy again. Go away, I can't… leave me alone…

There was a knock on the door and Philippe entered. He came over to Guy and took his hand.

"Dear Guy," he said, "what is it? Are you in pain?"

"No, I mean, yes, less bodily pain now, it's more mental pain. Dreams and memories…" Guy shook his head. "I can't say."

"When you are ready, it may help to speak to one of us. You are recovering physically so well. But mental pain can impede recovery – try not to torture yourself; you are safe here for as long as it takes."

"I owe you all a great debt of gratitude," said Guy.

"We did what was necessary, and our reward is your continued recovery," said Philippe. "Raymond tells me you're gaining strength every day."

"I could just eat a joint of wild boar," said Guy. "I've had enough of gruel."

"I'm afraid there won't be any of that here," he said. "We could find some river trout, I expect." Philippe's eyes were laughing. A small smile passed over his lips.

"Oh, yes, of course."

"In any case we must be guided by Raymond, who is a physician as well as a Perfect. Apart from wild boar, is there anything else I can get for you?"

"I don't know... I can't stop the thoughts... the images... about everything... about what brought me here," said Guy. "The dreams are terrifying."

"A great deal has happened; you need time to come to terms with it, accept the situation and to think about your future..." said Philippe. "And, of course, to pray – I can help you pray if you wish."

Guy grasped Philippe's hand with both of his.

"I'm worried," said Guy. "About my family, and about... what happened... and what I must do..."

"Remember always to pray when those feelings of worry and distress threaten to overwhelm you. You cannot change what has happened, but you can ask God for his help, and God will show you the way. I will come regularly to pray with you and guide you through this. It will take time, but when you're ready I will listen."

"I will pray, Philippe," said Guy. "The memories and images are so real and overwhelming when they come that I can forget to pray."

"God always helps those who ask. It may not be the help you expect but it will be God showing you the way." Philippe stood. "I'll ask Raymond to come and make you comfortable."

Guy lay back. Perhaps after all there would be a way through all this.

CHAPTER 8

Pedro Maury

It was early September, around the time of the Nativity of the Virgin Mary, when Ricard sent a boy to fetch Pedro from the pastures.

"Tell him it's urgent," Ricard had told the boy.

Pedro walked quickly. What was so urgent? Was someone ill? Had the Inquisition arrested someone? He found Ricard pacing around the kitchen, hardly able to speak. As Pedro looked at him, Ricard hit himself on the face. Pedro grabbed Ricard's arm, seeing he was about to do it again.

"Ricard, stop," said Pedro. He held Ricard firmly in his arms to help Ricard gain control. "What is the matter?"

Ricard struggled briefly then broke down and sobbed. "Jacques Authier and Prades Tavernier have been arrested in Limoux," he sobbed.

"Ricard, they will escape or be rescued, I know," said Pedro. "We must stay calm to help them."

"Worst of all," said Ricard, "they were trapped by my cousin. My cousin."

"Your cousin?"

"Gérard Peyre, the very one who has supported the Good Men all along, who has helped them in their mission – *Gérard, my cousin*."

"It was he who took me into meet Pierre Authier," said Pedro. "Why in God's name would he betray them? What's happened?"

"Gérard was arrested in Carcassonne and flung into the Wall, the prison. I didn't know he'd been arrested – they let him out after a week because he did a deal with them – *he did a deal, Pedro – with the Inquisition*. He felt let down by the Good Men who didn't rescue him immediately from the Wall," said Ricard. "And after a week – *after just one week* – he promised to give Jacques Authier and Prades Tavernier to the Inquisition. He asked them to go to Carcassonne to perform a *consolamentum*. He lured them right into the hands of the Inquisition."

"I can't believe Gérard Peyre would do this," said Pedro, just as his father's words, "trust no-one", came back to him. "I trusted him as I trust you."

"They will interrogate Jacques and Prades, and, as you know, their vows mean they cannot tell a lie, so we are all in immediate danger," said Ricard.

The door to the back storerooms burst open just then and Ricard's wife Sybille appeared. She was laughing and crying at the same time. "Praise God, they've escaped! Prades and Jacques have escaped," she said. "Thanks be to God." She put her hands together. "Praise God."

Behind Sybille came the Châtelain, Gilet de Voisins.

"They bribed the gaolers before they even arrived at Carcassonne. They are on their way north to the safe house at Le Born," said Gilet de Voisins. "But it was a close call, and if your cousin opens his mouth and tells the Inquisition more, well… we are still not safe." He shook his head. "I could kill him for this betrayal, but we must think of how we can protect ourselves."

"He's been to all our homes, he knows us all," said Sybille. "And he's met many of the Good Men."

"We should bring everyone together," said Ricard. "We must agree a coherent story that will exonerate us and show Gérard Peyre to be lying."

"I can't stay now, I must return to the pastures; we're two men down," said Pedro. "The Maurs brothers have gone to Montaillou, but they'll be back tomorrow, so I'll come back then. You won't gather everyone together until tomorrow at the earliest."

Ricard looked at Pedro, his face blank as if his mind was far away. He nodded agreement. Sybille moved towards Pedro.

"Be back as soon as you can," she said, worry etched on her face, her voice shaking. "We may not have much time."

Pedro set off walking quickly. It was hard to believe that Gérard Peyre, Ricard's cousin – his *cousin*, of all people – had betrayed the Good Men. Pedro would have trusted him with his life. In fact, he had done just that. The consequences of this betrayal could be a matter of life or death. But perhaps Gérard Peyre had been tortured – or threatened. He could have done this to save himself. And if Gérard Peyre was now free, he might not betray anyone else. On the other hand, he might still be beholden to the Inquisition, under threat to help them find more Perfects and Believers. All Ricard and his friends and neighbours could do would be to deny the charges. But they would have to be very sure of their story if they were questioned.

As for himself, this was too close a call to ignore. He must think about what to do next. He was just as likely to be betrayed as the other Believers. He could find work elsewhere; that was what he had always wanted to do. But could he desert the other Believers in their time of need, abandon them to their fate? But there was little he could do to help them. They had their farms, their animals, their families; they could only stay and brave it out. Surely, they would not begrudge Pedro his ability to up sticks and move on. Someone must have betrayed Gérard Peyre. Otherwise, how did the Inquisition know about him? Should Pedro stay in Arques or move on?

As he approached the pastures, he planned to finish repairing the fences of the sheep pen he had been working on and be ready to leave early the next day. He worked alongside the other shepherds without speaking about his worries. He told them there was a family crisis and he must leave for Montaillou the following day. They accepted his story. He spent a restless night worrying about the other Believers.

When he set off early to walk back to Ricard's farmhouse, he was still undecided about what he must do. He wanted to hear what all the Believers themselves thought. They must be terrified. They could have their homes and farms confiscated. That was one of the penalties the Inquisition used. Raymond and Ricard both had farms that had been in their families for generations, and they would want to protect them at all costs. His own instincts were to leave. He could go to Montaillou to see his parents and look for work.

Pedro arrived at the farmhouse to find many of Ricard and Sybille's neighbours already there. As Pedro entered, they hardly acknowledged him. One or two nodded to him; others just stared. Most of the Believers of Arques were congregated in the hall, sitting around the table where they had gathered so many times before. This time there was no jolly banter, just an eerie silence and a tense atmosphere of fear. Cousin Raymond had his arm round Eglantyne's shoulders. Raymond Marty, a Believer from Junac who had regularly been to Raymond and Sybille's home, sat alone at one end of the table with his head in his hands. Guillaume Escaunier and his sister Marquèse Botohl were whispering together. Two more men followed Pedro in.

Ricard stood up. "I think that's everyone," he said. "You know why—"

Guillaume Escaunier stood up straight away and interrupted Ricard. "Never mind all that, let's get straight to it, because I tell you, Marquèse and I are so desperate, so frantic with worry that the

Inquisition will come and seize our home, that we think the only way is for us all to give ourselves up and go to the Pope to ask for a pardon – that way any punishment would be mitigated."

"No, no," said Raymond Marty. "That's madness, I'm not walking towards the Inquisition, they would still punish us—"

"But the punishment will be much worse if we don't give ourselves up and they come to find us," said Guillaume Escaunier. "They'll be on us and our properties like a pack of wolves."

"Surely Gérard Peyre won't talk any more," said Pedro. "Why would he talk now? He's free and the Perfects have escaped."

"We don't know that. He was here many times with the Good Men," said Ricard.

"And at ours too," said Cousin Raymond.

People began to murmur to each other.

"Guillaume and Jacques Authier came to our home earlier this year, and Gérard Peyre was present," said Raymond Marty.

"We can't take the risk," said Guillaume Escaunier. "He knows everything about us."

Pedro was silent, listening. Marquèse began to cry. No-one thought they could lie persuasively and consistently enough to convince an Inquisitor that they had had nothing to do with the Good Men. There might be other witnesses who knew them and who might speak out against them. They all had a lot to lose. They were thinking of their homes and farms, their animals. There was no other way; they should ask for pardon. But Pedro did not want to go with them. What about their faith – how could they just discard it? Ricard asked for a show of hands. Only Raymond Marty and Pedro did not raise their hands in agreement.

"Well, that's clear, there's a great deal to do in preparation for this, so we should think how we will go about it," said Ricard. "I will go and talk to our priest."

"No-one has mentioned our faith," said Pedro. "Our shared belief in the Good Men as the only way to save our souls. You're too hasty with this decision. I believe this is the devil's work. Satan is behind this."

They all stared at him for a moment. Raymond and Eglantyne exchanged glances. The others seemed lost in thought, looking down at their hands or into their drinking cups. There was a long silence.

Finally, Eglantyne spoke. "No-one, not even the Pope, knows what you think and believe in your heart." She had tears in her eyes. "I will lie if I have to, to save my home and family; I will do whatever I have to do to save them. May God forgive me." Tears fell down her face.

"We have to think of our families and our livelihoods," said Ricard. "They could take our homes and our land; we could be left with nothing. Many of our farms have been in our families for years; we must protect all that. To ask for pardon is the only way."

"I can see that, and if I was in your position, I would probably do the same," said Pedro. "But as I don't have a house, land and a family here like you, I can go anywhere and find work."

"You will put yourself in grave danger if you don't come with us," said Cousin Raymond.

"How's that?" Pedro said. "I can avoid the Inquisition, I have no ties, I don't want to do… what you're planning. I want to continue to support the Good Men."

"I think everyone else is in agreement that we must ask for pardon," said Ricard. "But you must do as you think fit, Pedro." He stared hard at Pedro. There was a silence, everyone avoiding Pedro's eye.

Then Cousin Raymond spoke. "I have an idea, I was wondering who would look after our land and animals if we go away, but if you won't come with us, Pedro, you could look after our animals for us whilst we are gone."

"If I stay here that would put me in danger," said Pedro. "The Inquisition will be after me as soon as they know—"

"It's the least you can do," said Ricard, frowning. "We've looked after you well."

"Things have changed now," said Pedro. "I'll leave when you leave."

Ricard stared at Pedro with desperate eyes. His voice was cold. "You will be safe enough here until we return. We won't tell them you're here; when we return you can leave and go wherever you wish…" Ricard threw Pedro a look – anger, jealousy, probably both; Pedro wasn't sure. "You can go to Ax and stay with Sybille Baille – I've heard all about what goes on there."

"What do you mean?"

"You know what I mean," said Ricard.

Eglantyne and Sybille were crying, and Pedro looked from one to the other. It was true they had been good to him; he began to feel sorry for them… perhaps he should try to help them.

"As long as you promise not to betray me, I'll stay and look after the animals, but I'll need some money; you owe me for the work I've done, Ricard, and I need some more to keep me going whilst you are away."

"How can you think about money at a time like this?" said Ricard, an angry sneer on his face. "I'll pay you when I come back, and I can see what's left of my life and belongings. I'll have no further discussion on the matter."

The Believers organised themselves into groups. Raymond and Ricard were going to travel with their wives. They planned to take their children to stay with relatives in Ax. They all agreed to tell a story about a pilgrimage. First they went to their village priest to take advice from him. They wanted to go directly to the Pope but he told them to go to the Bishop. The morning after they left, Gilet de Voisins, the Châtelain, and Raymond Gayraud, the Bailiff of Arques, who had also stayed behind, came to see Pedro at Ricard's farmhouse.

"Pedro," said Gilet, "I'm staying here – you know I have supported the Good Men in the past, but now I'm claiming no knowledge of them, so that means I have to take certain measures to protect my home and family too. I'm impounding the property and livestock of those who have left to see the Pope. If I do nothing, the Inquisition will become suspicious of us both. I must be seen to be taking action against them as I haven't gone with them," he said. "I'm not turning against them, but I can't ignore what's happening. It won't make any difference to you; stay here and look after the farm and the animals as you said you would. This is just an official way of protecting myself. I'm doing the right thing, and if anyone asks about you, I'll tell them you're in my custody. I think it's unlikely anyone will come to check up on us – they'll take my word for it."

"I understand," said Pedro. "I'll stay here. I'll look after this farm and Raymond's, make sure things are being done properly and the animals are treated well, but when Ricard and the others return, I'll leave."

"I'll revoke the order when they return, if they have their pardon."

Raymond, Ricard and the other Believers were gone for ten weeks. At first, Pedro was racked with worry about whether he'd done the right thing by staying. He slept badly. He had dreams of being chased and unable to move, or of hearing the Inquisition banging on the door early in the morning – come to arrest him – waking up in a sweat, thankful when he realised it was a dream. When he was out on the pastures, he scoured the hills looking for horsemen riding to arrest him and shackle him in chains. He kept himself separate from the men as far he could; he must avoid questions. But the men knew that some of the farmers were gone, and Pedro had to use the pilgrimage story to explain their absence. He was sure they didn't believe him. There were many times when he felt like leaving – just disappearing – but he could not abandon their farms and animals. He had made a promise; he had to keep it. Gradually as the weeks passed and no-one appeared over the horizon to arrest him, he began to feel safer. He still believed that Raymond and Ricard had been too hasty and acted out of fear. The Good Men were only at the start of their ministry and he wanted to be part of that and see how it would unfold. He was not ready to give up on them.

It was the week before Christmas, late one evening, and Pedro was busy in the sheep pen near the house with the ewes, who were due to lamb soon, when he heard movement and voices outside. He knew it was Raymond and Ricard back, in time for Christmas; things must have turned out well enough for them to come home. What a celebration they could have now. He went to greet them. Ricard and Sybille, Raymond and Eglantyne were standing together near the front door. His welcoming smile faded as he looked at each of them. Ricard's face was set in a frown, hard and serious. Raymond looked equally stony. Even Eglantyne's usually warm, friendly face was unsmiling. She looked away when he caught her eye. Sybille began to cry and glanced down when he turned to her.

"Ricard, Raymond," he said, searching their faces. "I'm glad to see you back. What's the news?" No-one spoke. "What's happened? What's wrong?" said Pedro. "Did you see the Pope?"

Eglantyne put her arm around Sybille, sobbing now, whilst tears ran down her own face.

"Let's get this over with quickly." Ricard looked around at the others. "We're very tired and we must go to collect the children tomorrow."

"What do you mean?" said Pedro. He felt a sudden rush of blood to his face.

"We were sent by the priest to confess to the Bishop of Béziers," said Raymond. "We were granted absolution and we have had to undertake penances, prayers. In the future, we must make pilgrimages. Gilet de Voisins will formally restore our property to us tomorrow but – well, Pedro, to tell you the truth, you should have gone with us—"

"And as you didn't confess, you must leave," said Ricard. He stared defiantly at Pedro. His voice was cold.

"I planned on going after Christmas," said Pedro. He looked around at them all. "There are things to tell you about the animals and the farm, and I wanted to hear all your news."

"No," said Ricard. "You must go now, or we will have to arrest you."

"What?" said Pedro, stunned.

There was silence as he searched their faces and stared at them. Was this a game? Both women looked away, wiping tears, but Ricard and Raymond stared back with cold eyes and stern faces. This was no game.

"I've been looking after your animals, your property, your land, never knowing whether the Inquisition were going to come for me. Now you want to arrest me?"

"It was made clear to us that we would be committing a crime if we didn't arrest you," said Ricard. "We're giving you a chance, can't you see? Now get out."

"You betrayed me? What did you tell them?" His shock was turning to rage.

"Nothing... well, not much..." said Ricard. "We underwent intensive questioning; they got it out of us that you were looking after the farms—"

"They may have got the idea that you were a guide for the Good Men," said Raymond, looking away.

Pedro shook his head; he could hardly breathe. "Not much," he repeated. "Only that I helped the Good Men. Don't worry – I'm not staying here with you, I'm going, but you owe me some money."

"Never mind about that, just get out of here," said Ricard.

Pedro stood for a moment looking at them all for a sign that they might… What? Thank him? Sybille lifted her head and looked at Ricard.

"Ricard," said Sybille. "Let him stay, just overnight at least—"

"No, Sybille, be quiet, he must go," said Ricard. He heard Ricard's voice catch as he spoke, but Pedro turned and walked out of the room. He went upstairs to collect the few belongings he had. When he came down, they were all still standing beside the front doors. He stopped before them, standing straight and looking directly at them all one by one. The men glanced at him then slid their eyes away. The women turned away, wiping their tears.

"I've looked after your farms and animals," said Pedro. "It's been no easy task – and this is all the thanks I get for it – I don't want to be with you. You're not the people I thought you were."

He turned and left, slamming the front door behind him. He headed off at speed down the dark track from the farmhouse. How could they be so cruel? They could have allowed him to stay one more night and could at least have paid him the money that was owed to him. He understood that they saw him as a liability, but they could have been civil and shown some gratitude. He was nearly running as he moved along the track, overwhelmed by shock and rage. He rounded a bend and almost bumped into his brothers Jean and Grégoire, who were walking towards Ricard's house.

"Grégoire, Jean!" he said. "What are you doing here?"

"We've come to find you," said Jean. "Is it true that the Believers were betrayed? We've been very worried. Mother and Father sent us to see what had happened to you. We heard you had stayed here. We've been walking all day."

"They're back now; they will arrest me if I don't leave now."

"Why? What's happened?" said Jean.

"Where are you going?" said Grégoire.

"I don't know… this has just happened; I haven't thought any further…"

"Come to Montaillou, spend Christmas with us – Mother and Father, all of us will be happy if you do. And you'll be safe there," said Jean.

"Let's stay overnight at the tavern in Arques," said Pedro. "And we'll set off in the morning."

Pedro told his brothers about what had happened as they ate

their meal at the tavern. They were two of the few people he could tell this story to.

"I should have asked more about what they told the Bishop of Béziers about me," said Pedro.

"They must have said something – they wouldn't have told you to go if the Bishop hadn't told them to arrest you," said Jean.

"I'm sure it will all turn out well," said Grégoire.

"Let's hope so," said Jean.

"I shall have to stay out of the Inquisition's way," said Pedro. "But I'm not going to give up my beliefs. Sybille said that no-one can change what's in your heart and that's true."

"What does that mean?" said Grégoire.

"It means," said Pedro, "that your heart is your own and you can follow it wherever you want and no-one else need know what's in it."

He smiled at Grégoire. He hadn't seen his family all together since he left five years ago. Jean had visited him at Ricard's only a couple of times. It would be good to see all of them and to spend Christmas in Montaillou, in his parents' home where he felt safe. He could look for work after Christmas.

The next morning, Pedro and his brothers retraced their footsteps back along the route he had taken five years previously. He concentrated on walking. It had snowed overnight, and the track was icy. It was freezing cold, and the sky was a thick, heavy grey. They made slow progress. By early evening they still had a few hours of journeying ahead of them. They must continue until they reached Montaillou. It would be so easy to curl up inside their cloaks, but even the most sheltered spot would be deadly cold. It could be fatal. They continued to trudge forward. It was difficult to see as the moon was waning and there was little moonlight. The whiteness of the snow lightened the way a little and there were many stars in the heavens. They pushed on, hardly speaking. It was exhausting and they needed all their strength to keep moving one foot in front of the other, slipping and sliding at times, collapsing onto the snow, where it would be so easy to stay, but forcing themselves upwards and onwards.

It was almost dawn when they arrived in Montaillou. The familiar smell of wood smoke hung in the air as they walked up the main track through the sleeping village towards their parents' house on the edge of the square. They let themselves in to the place where they had all been born. The home where they had played and squabbled with their siblings, where the food they had eaten together had been cooked by their mother, where they slept together, sharing beds and blankets, and where their father worked day in and day out at his weaving in a small space at the back of the house. Pedro looked around; nothing had changed. The room was furnished as it always had been, with sheepskins on the floor, a table and benches. This was not as spacious a house as the farmhouses in Arques, but at least they still had it. The family were asleep when they arrived, but their parents soon rose when they heard them moving around. Jean, Grégoire and Pedro huddled themselves round the fire and took off their steaming cloaks and boots. Their mother came over to Pedro first. She had to wipe away tears in between embracing Pedro and kissing him.

"You're safe and well, and home for Christmas, just look at him," she said to his father, who was embracing him now. "He's a man now. His shoulders have broadened, he's filled out – and he's taller than you by a head."

His father was paler and heavier, and his mother looked thinner, her face lined. His father patted his back and embraced him.

"Welcome, son," he said. "It's good to see you."

"It's good to be here," said Pedro, feeling himself relaxing. At least his family didn't reject him.

Pedro sat at the table with his brothers and sister, Guillemette, who'd followed quickly behind their parents to greet and embrace him. Whilst they ate a breakfast of eggs and bread, they spoke only of the animals and his father's weaving business, and they spoke about their neighbours in lighthearted terms. No-one wanted to speak of the Good Men in front of the youngest children, whose tongues may inadvertently give away dangerous secrets.

When they had finished eating and the younger members of the family had left them to help Mother with the chores, Pedro told his father what had happened at Arques with Cousin Raymond.

"That's the last time I'll have anything to do with Cousin Raymond," said his father. "To turn you out like that is shocking."

"They told the Bishop of Béziers I was a Believer," said Pedro.

"You must be very careful from now on," said his father. "You could go south – I've heard that's what some Believers are doing now. Aunt Gaillarde has been talking of it since her husband died. She could just sell up and go; with her sons to help her, she would thrive, I'm sure."

"I'll think about it," said Pedro.

"Montaillou is in turmoil too," said Father, shaking his head. "It's a strange situation. Everyone knows that the priest and the rest of the Clergue family are Cathars, although it's never openly acknowledged."

"How does he get away with it?" said Pedro.

"He is the church's representative. No-one comes here from Carcassonne; they take his word for it that there are no Cathars in Montaillou. But I've even seen Guillaume Authier coming out of the Clergues' house. He stays there sometimes. Others too. Everyone knows. It's tense – we all know who is Cathar and who is anti-Cathar. And Father Clergue uses his power to coerce any woman he wants into his bed with threats and promises, which they're powerless to resist. He even seduced Fabrisse Rives' young daughter, then married her in the church to Bernard. He continues to have his way with her even though she's married."

"This cannot be what God wants," said Pedro. "Surely the reckoning will come to Father Clergue in the end."

"In the meantime, Montaillou is not a safe place to be," said his father. "I try to keep away from all that, but we have to go to church and live a life of lies, which I'm not comfortable with. But your mother and I both believe that the true faith is that of the Good Men, and if they come to preach in a village house, we go to hear them. They've been here too."

In the evening, they celebrated Christmas Eve with the whole family by enjoying a feast of wild boar that had been given to them in exchange for a good length of Pedro's father's fine woven cloth, as was the norm. They had wine from the small tavern in the village, and they put their troubles to one side as they feasted and enjoyed each other's company.

On Christmas morning, Pedro and his family set out to go to church. It was a clear, bright day and the mountain peaks covered in snow glistened in the sun. The pure white snow against the cobalt blue of the sky lifted Pedro's heart. He loved these mountains and foothills surrounding Montaillou. The village was strangely quiet.

"Where is everyone?" said Pedro's father.

"Maybe they're all in church," said Grégoire.

But as they progressed down the steep and icy track through the village to the bottom of the hill where it opened out and flattened near the meadow and the church, they saw a group of their neighbours. It looked as if the whole village was there. Angry voices could be heard, everyone talking at once, some shouting, their faces serious, and many of the women were crying. As Pedro and his family approached the group, one or two stopped talking and looked at them.

"What on earth's the matter?" said Pedro's father.

"It's terrible," said one. "Arnaud Lizier is dead."

"They found him this morning outside the château," said another. "Murdered... his throat cut."

Pedro and his father looked at each other.

"We'll go on to church," said his mother, gathering the younger children to her. "Arnaud, Guillemette, come with me."

Pedro and his other brothers stayed with their father to find out more. Everyone spoke at once, and some were incoherent with rage or distress. They pieced together that the body of Arnaud Lizier had been discovered early that morning by one of the servants at the château. Bernard Clergue the Bailiff had been informed. He went up to look at the body and had said he would deal with it.

"This is Bernard Clergue's work," Fabrisse Rives whispered in Pedro's ear. "It's a warning to the Liziers, who had recently denounced the priest and his family for having too much power over the villagers."

Pedro turned to look at Fabrisse. He remembered what his father had told him about her daughter.

"This village is controlled by the Clergue family, and the Belots and the Benets are all in it together. They try to control the rest of us…" Fabrisse looked around.

The crowd was quietening. The priest himself had come into view. He was making his way to the church to celebrate Mass. His neat figure in priest's robes moved towards them with a confident stride, and a little smile played on his lips. He stopped and spoke when he was beside the group. People looked down and shuffled their feet.

"A terrible thing has happened in our village during the night of Christmas," he said, now looking grave. "And we will find the culprits. But our Lord would not want it to prevent us from celebrating Mass. My brother is attending to it. So, come down to church with me now." He looked around at the people then looked at Pedro and hesitated a moment as if about to speak. Pedro looked back steadily, then Father Clergue resumed looking at the crowd until his eye fell on someone else.

"Ah, Madame Maurs." He smiled. "I'm pleased to see you here; I've not seen you in church for a little while."

Madame Maurs straightened her back and held her head up high. "You'll not see me in church again," she said. "Not until we have a new priest, one who is honest and true, unlike you, Pierre Clergue." She spat on the ground and walked away, her head held high.

There was a shocked silence, and everyone looked at Father Clergue. His face was grim as he stood for a moment, watching the retreating back of Madame Maurs. He looked at the villagers.

"What's the matter with you all?" he said. "It's time for Mass."

Everyone slowly followed Father Clergue to the church. Many people were whispering together as they walked. Pedro and his family exchanged glances but remained silent.

When they returned home after Mass, his mother took the younger children inside. Pedro's father, Pedro, Jean and Grégoire lingered outside the front door.

"Good for Madame Maurs," said Grégoire rather too loudly.

"Hush, Grégoire," said his father. "You'll get us all in trouble. Sadly, I think Madame Maurs might regret saying that."

"I hope not," said Pedro. "What can the priest do?"

"He's not averse to violence. As you've just witnessed," said his father. "He gets someone to do it for him."

The following day, Pedro was walking through the village with Grégoire when Bernard Belot appeared from the side of his house.

"Well, if it isn't Pedro Maury," he said. "I heard you'd come back; you were at church yesterday. In fact, I've heard a lot about you recently, Pedro." He came up close to Pedro and whispered into his ear. "I heard what happened at Arques, and that you're a marked man. You staying here in Montaillou makes life dangerous for us. You are no longer welcome."

Pedro stepped back. "I should be welcomed by you, Bernard, you who follows the Good Men."

"Not if it puts the rest of us in danger," said Bernard, giving Pedro a look that chilled him.

Pedro could hardly breathe as he tried to stay calm. Losing control would only put him and his family in danger. "I shall leave soon enough," said Pedro.

"The sooner the better," said Bernard.

Grégoire tugged on Pedro's tunic. "Come on, Pedro, let's go home."

"How could he say that?" said Pedro when they were out of earshot of Bernard. "All I did for Raymond and Ricard, and no thanks from them, now this from Bernard Belot."

"I know," said Grégoire. "Let's go home and tell Father."

Pedro tried to clear his mind and think as they made their way home. Bernard was saying what Ricard had said. That because of his association with Ricard and Raymond and the other Cathars in Arques, he was a marked man and anyone who associated with him was vulnerable too. Perhaps Bernard was right; he should leave Montaillou quickly.

When they returned home, Pedro and Grégoire told their father and Jean what Bernard had said. Jean shuffled about uncomfortably.

"Well… Pedro," he said. "I hate to say this, but I've been thinking – you must realise the Inquisition will be watching you now. And we know what they're capable of – I think Bernard is right, and…" Jean cleared his throat. "Our household could suffer too."

"I thought I would have been welcomed by the Cathars in the village," said Pedro. He couldn't stop the tears that welled up in his eyes. "But I'll have to leave now, I can see that."

"It would probably be for the best," said Father, sighing. "But there's no hurry, you can stay for a few more days. Keep out of Bernard Belot's way then there's no trouble."

"I'll leave now," said Pedro, wiping away his tears.

His mother appeared at that moment, wiping her hands on a cloth. She looked at them. "What is it?"

"I must leave, Mother," said Pedro. "My presence puts you in danger."

"How is that?" said his mother.

"I'm a marked man after what happened in Arques."

"He doesn't need to leave now, does he?" She appealed to his father, whose expression told her that yes, he did.

"But where will you go?" said Mother through tears. "We've only just got you back and you're off again."

"Don't worry, I have a friend in Ax who will always welcome me," said Pedro.

"I don't want you to feel you can't come here again," said Mother. "All this furore over the people of Arques will soon be forgotten, but until then you must come secretly."

"Be careful," said Jean.

"Look after yourself," said Mother.

Pedro collected his bundle of belongings together. All of them had tears in their eyes as they embraced him and kissed him in turn. As he went through the door, his father came after him.

"I nearly forgot," he said. "There's work in Ax if you want it. Our neighbour tells me that his cousin, Barthélemy Bourrel, is taking on shepherds."

PART 2

1306–1316

CHAPTER 9

Guy Belibaste

Raymond de Toulouse continued to care for Guy in the safe house at Rabastens. Guy progressed from sitting up in bed to standing, from walking around the room to eating meals with the others in the house, and eventually to walking outside. Although his chest was much improved after a few weeks and breathing was no longer painful, he still had the remains of a cough and was breathless after walking only a short distance. Raymond said he must cultivate patience. Philippe d'Aylarac visited Guy whenever he was free, and they sat together and talked.

Guy learned that he was in the safe house that Raymond de Toulouse, Philippe d'Aylarac and Pierre Authier called home, although it was often shared with other Perfects and their shepherd guides as they rested after travelling to a *consolamentum*.

Guy was physically much improved, but he was unable to stop retracing in his mind the events at Cubières. At night, he was tortured by dreams of a terrifying devil, huge and strong, who was trying to force his way through to him and he was fighting it off. He knew he must kill this demon in the dream. His wife and children, his two brothers and his father featured in his dreams as well as Barthélemy, the dead shepherd, who seemed to be trying to speak to him. In the dreams, Guy couldn't hear what he said, and as Barthélemy, bleeding and misshapen, approached him, Guy woke up trembling and sweating.

He felt too ashamed and guilty to talk to Philippe about it, even though Philippe encouraged him to speak about what was on his mind. But recently, Philippe had started to read passages from Saint John's Gospel to Guy and one passage stayed with Guy: "For God sent not his Son to condemn the world; but that the world through him might be saved. He that believeth in Him is not condemned."

"Philippe," he said. "That passage, about not condemning – it makes me think – I have something on my mind. It's not easy to speak of."

"Because you fear condemnation?" said Philippe.

"Yes," said Guy. "I'm tortured by dreams and thoughts of the past, you know, about what happened at Cubières, how I had to leave my family… and what I did… I worry sometimes that it wasn't an accident… I think it was, but…" He began to sob. It was quiet, painful sobbing. Philippe sat still and waited.

"I'm sorry," said Guy.

"There's no need to be sorry," said Philippe. "You've lost a great deal, and you need to grieve – talking may help."

"I miss my family and I dream that they're searching for me. I wake up crying," said Guy. "But worst of all is that I killed the shepherd. I killed him; I can't get over that. I'm having terrifying nightmares… a huge devil is trying to force its way through to me. I'm fighting it off. I must kill it. Barthélemy the dead shepherd comes to me too; he's trying to speak to me… he's bleeding and misshapen… I wake up sweating and trembling."

"You didn't intend to kill him. It was an accident – a cruel accident – God knows that. Everyone who knows you knows that.

You must stop punishing yourself – instead you should pray to God to give you strength to bear it," said Philippe.

He trusted Philippe, but there was something… a voice in his mind that told him something he already knew but didn't want to know, or was it rather that it was something he was not sure about? It was such a muddle in his mind. He knew he was angry that day, angry with his father for sending him to confront the shepherd, angry with himself for being weak and unable to change his life, and angry with the shepherd, but was he so angry that he wanted at that moment to kill him… that's what the voice said to him. "You wanted to kill him," said the voice. He might have thought so, but did he mean it? Did he really mean to kill him or was it just one of those things that people think in a moment of rage? He didn't know the answer.

As Guy relived with Philippe what happened that day, his state of mind that morning as he left the Perfects with his father, how he approached the shepherds and what they had done, and how it all escalated into the confrontation with Barthélemy, that fateful moment when the shepherd fell back and changed Guy's life for ever, he started to talk about the voice and his doubts. Philippe simply listened. And as Guy grew stronger, he worried less about this and was more able to put to one side this doubt. He knew it was an accident.

One day, Philippe told Guy they had received news of his case from Cubières. Guy had been found guilty in his absence because of the testimony of the two shepherds who were witnesses. Guy could never return to Cubières. This unleashed another torrent of grief about the loss of his family. He had hoped that someday he might be reunited with them. He would never give up that hope entirely. But he was beginning to understand something that Philippe had said to him – that God had given him a second chance – a chance to make another life for himself. He remembered he had briefly stopped to pray that morning on his way to confront the shepherds. Perhaps this was God answering his prayers. As Philippe commented, "God moves in mysterious ways." How would his life unfold now?

When Guy had been in the house at Rabastens for six months, he thought less about the past and more about his future. He questioned Philippe about the faith of the Good Men, and he asked Philippe to teach him their beliefs.

One morning after walking all night from a *consolamentum*, Philippe visited Guy in his room to tell him that Guillaume Authier was staying in the house, and that Guy could meet him that evening after the Perfect had rested, if Guy wished. To meet Guillaume Authier as well as Pierre Authier would be a rare privilege. Guy spent much of that day praying and thinking about what he might say to Guillaume Authier. Before meeting the Perfect, Guy went to speak with Philippe. Guy wanted to ask Guillaume Authier to make him an official Believer.

Later, Guy and Philippe went together to join both Authier brothers, who were sitting at the table in the simply furnished room. Guillaume resembled his brother in looks, and his kindly, easy manner was the same. Both men had that aura that everyone noticed, a kind of dignity, a specialness. People described it differently: some said it was holiness; others said it was an aura of goodness. The two were talking but stopped when Guy and Philippe entered. Guy and Philippe performed the *melioramentum*. Pierre introduced Guy to his brother. Their fish supper was served to them by the housekeeper. Guy could not stop his mind wandering and glimpsed for a moment a vision of a juicy wild boar steak. He tried to concentrate on what the Good Men were saying. He heard something that interested him.

"It's the key to continuation of the faith," Guillaume Authier was saying. "We must prepare more Perfects to lead the Believers."

"And there is money still in the coffers," said Pierre.

"Which helps," said Guillaume. "But it's a slow process."

"And not many are prepared to give up homes, farms, wives and families," said Pierre.

"No, that's the most difficult thing of all." Guillaume looked down and there was a silence, during which they all paid attention to their fish. That was exactly what the Authier brothers had done – left everything behind by choice as Guy had been forced to do.

"In the old days, when the numbers of Believers were much greater, there were houses full of women Perfects, women whose children were grown and whose husbands had died." Pierre shook his head. "But that was then, and those days have gone; these are different times, and we must take different measures."

When they had finished eating, Guillaume turned to Guy.

"Philippe has passed on your request, Guy," he said. "And the answer is yes."

Guy, overwhelmed, was lost for words. Guillaume stood up. His eyes sparkled.

"In fact, I'm surprised this hasn't been done before; it's very remiss of my brother and Philippe not to have suggested it to you, and as you have asked for me to do it, I'm happy to oblige." He turned to Philippe. "If you all agree, we can do it here and now?"

"Yes, why not?" said Philippe.

"Yes, of course," said Guy as he cleared his throat and found his voice.

"Let's move to sit near the fire," said Guillaume. "You sit next to me, Guy."

Philippe and Pierre sat facing them on the opposite bench.

"Before I formally bring you into the faith, I must say that I believe that God has brought you here, Guy." Guillaume took hold of Guy's hand and looked seriously at him. His blue eyes looking into Guy's eyes seemed to search into the depths of Guy's soul. "I know you have trodden a rocky pathway and that there have been many pitfalls along the way." Guy nodded. "But Philippe tells me you have spent many hours with him and that you understand what it means to become a Believer. You know, of course, how much we are hated by the Roman church and that by doing this, you could face many dangers in pursuance of your faith."

"I know," said Guy. "I have thought about this and I am ready to commit."

"Will you do what you can to bring others to our faith?"

"I will."

"Are you ready to put to one side all that the Roman church has taught you and open your heart to the beliefs of our faith?"

"I am, and I believe that God has shown me this way, through bringing me to this house," said Guy.

"You have come to be made a Believer of your own free will?"

"Yes, God has guided me here, but I have made up my own mind about becoming a Believer."

"How do you see your future, Guy?"

"Well, I have an idea, but I don't think I'm…" He stopped, unable to say the words.

"What is it, Guy?"

"Well, I've spent the last few months recovering from my illness, during that time I've thought a lot about what happened at Cubières. And I've prayed and asked God for forgiveness and I've asked Him to show me the way… and now an idea keeps coming into my mind…"

"What is this idea?" Guillaume smiled encouragement.

There was a small silence; Guy took a deep breath. "What I keep coming back to is… that I want to be a Perfect."

"Ah," said Guillaume. "I see."

"But I know I'm not worthy of that," said Guy.

"None of us is worthy: we're human, we're men," said Guillaume. "We don't claim to be able to change bread and wine into the body and blood of Christ, like the Roman priests. It is through leading pure lives that we hope to do God's work."

"But I have killed a man." Guy could not look at the Perfect.

"God forgives our sins if we pray for forgiveness and renounce our evil ways," said Guillaume. "And the best way to make reparation is to serve God."

"That is what I want to do," said Guy.

"It's not an easy path," said Guillaume. "It requires dedication and hard work for at least a year and not everyone is able to attain it."

"I want it very much," said Guy. "I want to succeed at this; I've never wanted anything so much as this."

"That's a good start, but first things first, Guy – you asked if I could make you a Believer."

"Yes."

"There is a small ceremony, the *convanenza*, and to clarify – so you know exactly what this means for you, Guy – you are then accepted as a Believer, and if you are ill and it's thought you may die, you can receive the *consolamentum* from a Perfect, providing your soul is still in your body."

Guy nodded to confirm what he knew and what he wanted.

"So, Guy, will you kneel and repeat after me… Good Christians, God's blessing and yours…"

Guy knelt and repeated Guillaume's words. As he spoke, a shaft of sunlight from the setting sun beamed directly into the room. He felt the warmth of the sun as it enveloped him. He breathed deeply and took it in to his body. He felt strengthened. Now, he could look forward to the time when his sins would be forgiven, and he would enter Heaven. For the first time in a long time, joy pervaded his heart. He was a Believer.

After this experience, Guy began to take a more active role in the house. He cooked and helped with household chores. He had more energy, dwelt less often on the past and talked regularly with Philippe about the faith.

"I know what your hopes for the future are, Guy," said Philippe after one of these talks. He smiled. "To become a Perfect."

"I know I'm a long way from becoming a Perfect," said Guy as he felt his neck and face flush. "Perhaps I was premature…"

"Why do you say that?" said Philippe.

"Because of… my history."

"Your history? You're referring to the death of the shepherd?" Guy nodded, and Philippe went on. "That need not stop you, at least from the point of view of myself and the other Perfects; you could be at the beginning of your journey, if you so wish." Philippe smiled. "It is a long journey, so we don't always know where it will lead. But wherever it takes you, Guy, you must forgive yourself as God forgives those who ask him for forgiveness. Raymond de Toulouse and I have talked at length about this with Guillaume and Pierre Authier, and we will help you as much as we can."

Guy was at a loss for words. He was still unable to believe this might be possible. He sat in silence, letting Philippe's words surround him and settle into his mind.

"Think and pray some more, Guy," said Philippe. "And when you are ready, we can speak again. If you do wish to continue, we could start by reading the Gospels. Saint John's Gospel is the important one for us, but you would need to know them all. I would be your mentor and teacher; you could learn the basic tenets of our faith."

"I do want to pursue this," said Guy. "But… I… well… I have doubts about my ability…"

"We all have doubts frequently," said Philippe. "But I notice you have already become more active in helping to run the house – I wonder, perhaps you could come with us when we go to give the *consolamentum*? You are physically recovered from your illness, you could manage the walking, and if we had any close by to start with, you could build up to going further afield…"

"I'd like that," said Guy.

It was two weeks later when Philippe came to tell Guy that he and Raymond de Toulouse were going that evening to give the *consolamentum* to a young shepherd boy who lived near Montaillou with his parents.

"This is a young boy; I won't tell you his name or the name of his parents – the less you know, the better," said Philippe. "But we have had word that this shepherd boy wishes to receive the *consolamentum*. His parents were against it; they're frightened of it getting out and the Inquisition coming for them. But they relented when he begged them and told them he knew was dying. It's a sad case – the boy is only seventeen."

The three of them set off early evening after resting in the afternoon. They did not need a shepherd guide as they all knew the route to Montaillou. Guy had not managed to rest much as he was plagued with guilt and worry about his suitability to be a Perfect. How could they think he was suitable? He was weak; he lacked learning to the level of the Perfects he had met. He did not read Latin; he only knew the prayers he had been taught as a child. He liked studying and reading up to a point, but how much he could understand and retain, he was unsure. Did *they*, the Perfects, only agree to him becoming a Perfect because they were in desperate need of more? Were they prepared to lower their standards?

They walked in silence through the early part of the night, arriving at Montaillou before dawn. They were met at the outskirts of the village by a shepherd who took them to the house where they were expected. It was a small, poor house and they entered the one room, where the dying boy was sleeping. The boy's mother showed them to her son's bedside. His father did not want to meet them or be present at the blessing, so he had nothing to tell the Inquisition if they arrested and interrogated him. Guy looked at the boy, who was lying on a makeshift straw bed and covered with a grubby blanket. His eyes were closed. Raymond de Toulouse knelt on the floor next to the boy and took his hand.

"We're here to give you the blessing," said Raymond. "Can you hear me?"

The boy opened his eyes, looked at the men around him and tried to speak. He was racked with a coughing fit which shook his whole body. His mother handed him a cloth and he spat bright red blood into it.

"Yes, I hear you," he managed to say.

"I'm going to ask you some questions about your faith," said Raymond. "Take your time; there's no hurry."

The boy answered in a whisper. Philippe read from Saint John's Gospel. He placed his copy of the Gospel on the boy's head and then held it there whilst Raymond put his hands on it and said the Lord's Prayer. The boy's mother began to cry. Guy felt tears welling up. He brushed them away.

"Thank you, God bless you," the boy whispered, hardly audible. He sank back onto the straw and closed his eyes.

As the Perfects began to leave the mother tried to give them some stale bread for their journey.

"Keep it for yourself," said Philippe. "We have food with us."

Once outside, they went a little way into the village, where they were due to stay in a Believer's home.

"That was one of the saddest we have done," said Philippe, wiping his tears away. "That poor family, and the boy, so young."

They walked in silence towards the house where they were to rest.

After more weeks of study, teaching and accompanying the Perfects as they travelled from deathbed to deathbed, Guy was asked by Philippe if he understood how the Good Men differed from the Roman priests. "Apart from their different beliefs," he added.

"There is no church and no sacrament, apart from the *consolamentum*," said Guy.

"That's true, but we are not priests like Roman priests; in fact, we are not priests at all. We do not claim to be intermediaries with God; we are spiritual teachers and guides. We are just men, but men who lead our lives according to the rules that govern our lives as Perfects. If we break these rules, we are no longer Perfects, and if we perform the *consolamentum* in this state, it will not be effective."

"I hadn't thought of it like that," said Guy.

"It is a great responsibility," said Philippe, "and anyone who takes it on must be strong enough to carry it."

"I know I shall find it difficult at times," said Guy. "I'm not the strongest of men. I will miss the comfort of a woman. I miss my wife greatly."

"Always remember: God will help you if you ask Him," said Philippe. "Because now Raymond, Pierre and Guillaume Authier, and I think you are ready to put yourself to the test of living as a Perfect. This time is the *abstinentia*. It will be for a year or so. You will live as a Perfect, eat only fish, vegetables and fruits, and pray as we do. Are you ready for this, Guy?"

"I… I think so," said Guy.

"Are you ready to pray several times a day, fast regularly, sometimes for long periods of time?"

"With God's help, I am ready."

Guy saw how receiving the *consolamentum* comforted and helped both those who received it and their loved ones. His own body grew stronger as he walked and climbed the mountains. His mind was fortified by prayers, and by the example and strong presence of Philippe and the other Good Men, who were his spiritual guides. Guy never saw Philippe deviate from the rules of austerity required of him. Guy was tempted by thoughts of his wife, her body and her touch, which caused him to pleasure himself. He struggled to keep these thoughts from entering his mind. He prayed with Philippe that he might conquer this.

"If I find those kinds of thoughts coming into my mind," Philippe said. "I do two things. One is I do something that requires great physical effort – like chopping logs – and the other is I pray whilst I'm doing it. That usually helps me."

It was early in 1306 when Guillaume Authier told Guy that the opinion of as many Perfects as possible had been sought. They agreed that Guy was ready to become a Perfect. Guillaume Authier would conduct the ceremony that would change Guy into a Perfect. It would take place in the house at Rabastens, and Guillaume would be assisted by Pierre Authier and Philippe d'Aylarac.

"The time has come when your life will change," said Guillaume. "You will receive the spiritual baptism of the *consolamentum*, like we give to the dying, but yours will take place here, with the Holy Prayer, the Lord's Prayer and the imposition of the hands of as many of the Perfects as we can gather together. This laying on of hands has been passed down from Perfect to Perfect since the time of the Apostles until the present day. It will have a profound effect upon you, Guy."

"It's what I've been preparing for," said Guy. "I only hope I'm ready."

"Although we think you are ready for this, you know, you will at times have doubts; it's only natural. All of us at times have our doubts and struggles; it's such a big undertaking to change your life in this way. I'm only sorry that the ceremony will be small – it used to be a grand occasion, but the times we live in mean we cannot risk drawing attention to ourselves. But it will be a beautiful ceremony nevertheless and there will be many there to support you. Remember, this is God's will."

The night before the ceremony, Guy knelt beside his bed. It was the early hours of the morning and he couldn't sleep. His mind was in turmoil, tortured with doubts, misgivings and guilt. Thoughts of Estelle and his children intruded into the prayers he was saying. How he still missed them, his children growing up without him knowing them, without them knowing him – it was wrong. But most of all, despite the support of the Perfects, he felt unworthy and uncertain about undertaking the ceremony the following day. He had managed to live with the discipline of the Perfect's way of life for a year, but he doubted his ability to discipline himself in future. Would he be strong enough to carry the burden of responsibility? Would he be able to resist temptation if there was no-one to watch and support him? Oh Lord, I am a weak and hopeless man; give me the strength to resist temptation.

The responsibility to others was great. If he lapsed or broke the rules, he let not only himself down but, worst of all, he would let down the people who looked to him at the end of their lives to help them achieve salvation. In this case, it was only by going through another ceremony to make him a Perfect that he could legitimately perform valid *consolamentum* again. And then… he came back to the same old worry, the fact that he had killed a man. Had he meant to do it or was it just an accident? Should he wake Philippe and ask him for guidance? No, he had talked about these things with Philippe and Pierre so often before and they had always reassured him – all of them had doubts and difficult moments because they are men; he must remember that and stop torturing himself. If the Perfects have faith in him and it is God's will, then he will do his best.

On the morning of the ceremony, he waited in a side room with Philippe. He wore a simple everyday tunic that would be replaced by a Perfect's blue tunic during the ceremony. Aware of the enormity of what he was about to undertake, he felt overwhelmed by concerns. Would he remember the correct answers to the questions that Guillaume Authier would ask him? Or would his mind go blank as it often did under pressure? Most of all, after the ceremony, that same old worry; would he be able to maintain his promises? He realised he was shaking. He put out a hand and Philippe, seeing this, faced him and placed his hands on Guy's shoulders.

"Guy, I have faith in you," said Philippe. "Remember, God will always help you; He has called you to work for Him and this is the moment you have been working towards. This ceremony will transform and strengthen you. So, come now, it is time. We must go; they are waiting for us."

Philippe led the way to the largest room in the house, where the ceremony would take place. This room at the top of the house was normally kept as a dormitory for visitors. It was away from any prying eyes that might be peering in from outside. Before they entered, Philippe took hold of Guy's hand, kissed him on his cheeks and smiled.

"God is with you, my friend." Philippe opened the door.

Guy stood at the threshold and gasped. His first impression was of a brightly lit room. The sweet aroma of beeswax candles filled the air. The beds and chests had been moved to the edges of the room to make space in the centre for a small group to assemble. The tiled floor gleamed in the candlelight; the high windows and the woodwork shone with cleanliness.

As his eyes grew accustomed to the brightness, Guy saw the Perfects – Jacques Authier, Prades Tavernier, Martin Frances, Amiel de Perles – and… he could hardly believe it, his brother… his brother Bernard was there too. And there was Pierre Montanier, a shepherd who acted as a guide to the Perfects, and another man he didn't recognise, also dressed as a shepherd. The Perfects wore their plain blue or green tunics. There was a woman at the back – it was Sybille Baille, dear Sybille, whose home he had stayed in with Philippe as he accompanied Philippe on his journeys.

Philippe took his arm and guided him to stand before Guillaume Authier. Philippe stood on one side of him and Pierre Authier on the other. He looked up at Guillaume Authier. Their eyes met. Guy searched Guillaume's face. Guillaume gave him a small smile of encouragement before he spoke.

"Guillaume Belibaste, known as Guy, we are here to witness you making a commitment to God, to others, and to yourself, to live as a Perfect according to the vows you will take today. Are you, Guy, ready to undertake this task, to which God has brought you?"

"I am," said Guy. He studied Guillaume Authier's face, whose lips twitched a tiny smile at this response. It was enough to bolster his confidence. He straightened his back and held his head up high. Yes, he was ready.

"Lord, bless us and have mercy upon us, let it be done unto us according to Thy word. May God forgive you your sins." Guillaume Authier repeated these words three times, and everyone responded by saying the Pater Noster.

"In the beginning was the word, and the word was with God, and the word was God… may the Father, the Son and the Holy Ghost forgive all your sins." Guillaume Authier read from Saint John's Gospel. He handed the book to his brother, who placed it on a table and covered it with a cloth.

Guillaume Authier took Guy through the Pater Noster, phrase by phrase. As the only prayer that Christ himself taught, this was a significant prayer for the Perfects and their Believers.

"Are you ready to renounce the cross by which you were christened and accept instead the baptism of the spirit?" said Guillaume Authier.

"I am."

"Are you ready to undertake to deny yourself all luxuries, to renounce meat, milk and eggs, to travel together with Believers and other Perfects, and never to allow the fear of death to stop you from performing your duties and obligations as a Perfect?"

"I am."

It was the moment when Guy was required to prostrate himself face downwards on the floor. He knelt, then lay. The polished, clay tiles felt cool and solid beneath him. The fresh aroma of the recently scrubbed floor rose into his nostrils as his nose squashed against the tiles. Guillaume Authier placed a copy of the Gospel of Saint John upon his head and called upon God to give the blessing of the Holy Spirit to him, Guy, the new Perfect. The other Perfects surrounded Guy and knelt beside him to lay their hands on his head and shoulders. He felt deeply moved as he lay there, the weight and the warmth of the Perfects' hands touching him and each other.

The strength of the Perfects came through their touch. He prayed silently that the strength he felt from them would help him to live as a Perfect. Tears were running down his cheeks as he was raised up by Pierre Authier.

Guy stood before Guillaume Authier. Philippe helped him to remove his brown tunic and replace it with a new blue one. Guillaume Authier kissed him and handed Guy his copy of the Gospels. Philippe embraced and kissed him, followed by the others, who crowded around him to kiss and congratulate him. Guy was now a Perfect.

CHAPTER 10

Pedro Maury

Pedro arrived in Ax early in the afternoon. All was quiet in the lane approaching Sybille's house. The shutters were all closed at this time of day. Each tall stone house, which rambled into its neighbour in a haphazard way, had tall double front doors concealing a private courtyard only glimpsed if a door happened to open as you passed by. Over Pedro's head, there was an ice blue bolt of sky, faded by the dazzling white rays of the sun, which shone brightly even at this early point in the year. He stood before Sybille's front door and pulled the bell. He was impatient to see her. He smiled, anticipating the joy he would feel when he saw her. It seemed a long time before he heard footsteps approaching the door. And there she was. He gazed at her beautiful, strong face.

"Pedro," she said, smiling. Her dark hair had half fallen, as usual, out of her crooked head-dress and lay in disarray on her shoulders. She glanced up and down the lane. "Come in." She closed the doors and, taking hold of his hand, led him into the courtyard. "How are you? I've been worried about you, I've heard rumours…"

They moved together and embraced. He pushed her gently back against the side wall of the courtyard. They kissed. She pulled away.

"Stop..." she said, a hand gently pushing on his chest. "There are people here..."

"Let's go to your room," said Pedro. "No-one will find us there."

"I shouldn't." She smiled.

"But you will." He laughed.

"Only for a short while," she said.

"It won't take long," he said.

She shook her head and laughed. "You're wicked."

He grabbed her hand. They crept through the house, up the stairs into the attic where her room was situated. "We're like naughty children."

As soon as they were in her room, he kissed her again, a luscious, soft and sweet kiss. Her body was warm against his. Although he had been here many times over the last two years, he was still surprised that this warm and generous woman desired him as much as he desired her. He kissed her neck and nuzzled his face there, breathing in her scent. His hands moved over her body, caressing her breasts and buttocks. Her hands travelled down his back, round to his groin to fondle his erection.

"I think you're ready," she said, laughing again.

"Umm," he said. "Are you?"

She took his hand and, lifting her garments, she placed it between her legs. "Tell me..." she said. "What do you think...?"

"I think..." he said, as he pulled away slightly and began to pull his tunic over his head, "you are."

She laughed and pulled at her clothing. They looked at each other standing naked.

"You're beautiful," he said.

"And you," she said, her eyes sliding to his erection, "are magnificent."

Afterwards, they lay for a little while together.

"I have been wondering when I would see you," she said. "Rumours have been flying around about the Believers in Arques… how are you? And I've been expecting that you would turn up as usual with two of the Good Men. Speaking of whom, I must go back down to my guests,;they'll be wondering where I am."

"Who's here?"

"Philippe d'Aylarac, Guy Belibaste and Pierre Montanier, their guide," she said. "Pierre Montanier is just passing through; the Perfects will stay a while longer." She sat up. "Are you coming to meet them?"

"Let me rest for a while," he said. "I'm very tired, and there's a lot to tell. Oh, and by the way, will you delouse me later?"

Sybille left promising to delouse him. She nearly always undertook this job for him when he stayed with her. He lay in her bed and looked around at the familiar room. There was a large chest at the foot of the bed and sheepskins on the floor. He loved the simplicity of it and this bed was surely the most comfortable bed he had ever slept in. He closed his eyes. The last few months in Arques had taken their toll on him. The physical work of caring for the livestock and the mental torment of constant vigilance, watching to see who was walking or riding over the horizon to arrest him, had been exhausting. Thank God he could stay here with Sybille and recuperate for a few days before he looked for work.

Later he went down to the kitchen. There he found the two Perfects sitting at the table. Sybille was preparing vegetables. He noticed river trout lying on a marble slab. Pedro bowed his head, knelt before the Perfects and greeted them in the Believers' way with the *melioramentum*. The Good Men embraced him and kissed him in turn.

"Are you staying here tonight?" said Philippe.

"Yes," said Pedro. "And you?"

"We will stay a night or two," said Philippe. "We need to rest; we've had a long journey. Do you know Guy Belibaste?"

"We've never met," said Pedro. He turned to Guy. "I've been to your father's house, and I met him and your brothers. I've been working for my cousin, Raymond Maulen, and Ricard Peyre at Arques, for the last few years – it was through them that I met your family."

"How are things at Arques?" said Philippe.

"All went very well for some time, but then... well, there were... some difficulties and I'm no longer working there."

Sybille looked up.

"What happened?" said Philippe.

"You've not heard?" said Pedro.

"There have been rumours, but we weren't sure of the truth of them," said Philippe, glancing at Guy.

"It all started a few weeks back when Gérard Peyre was arrested and taken to prison..."

He tried to be fair to Raymond and Ricard and the others as he told the story – after all, he understood why they had done what they did, but when he got to the part where they told him to go, or they would be obliged to arrest him, he broke down – they had been so close – how things had changed.

"This is not an easy path to follow," said Philippe, "especially when your friends and family no longer welcome you."

"And when you know to visit them would be too dangerous for everyone," said Guy.

"I'm not welcome in Montaillou either," said Pedro. "My family want to see me, but I'll make it dangerous for them if I go there openly."

"Yes," said Philippe. "Both of you, Pedro and Guy, have been chosen by God and that means many sacrifices."

Pedro saw pain and sadness in Guy's face. What had happened to him? What had his journey been? The three of them spent the next three days together at Sybille's and over that time they told each other of their journeys. Guy jumped around in the narrative, which sounded muddled and confused at times. Philippe helped him clarify and over the three days Pedro heard the full story. Philippe said that they were both fugitives. Pedro and Guy looked at each other across the table. Pedro put out his hands and clasped Guy's outstretched hands.

"We're brothers," said Pedro. "We must look out for each other."

Guy nodded, tears in his eyes.

"The Inquisition will be watching you," said Philippe.

Pedro shivered. Perhaps Philippe was right. "Never underestimate the Inquisition" – his father's words rang in his ears again. But still he found it difficult to believe that the Inquisition would be interested in him.

Pedro stayed at Sybille's until the new year. He sat at the bedroom window one morning as Sybille deloused him. She stood behind him and combed through his shoulder-length hair with a small, fine comb.

"I said I'd do this earlier," she said. "But it's been so busy."

"I know," he said. "Ouch, be careful."

"It needs trimming."

"Mmm."

There was a small silence. "Sybille, I think… it is time…"

She stopped combing his hair. "I know," she said. "You're ready to leave."

"How do you know?" He smiled.

"Because I know you have to. The sheep, the mountains, escorting the Good Men – these things are your life."

"You are my life too." He stood and turned, put his arms round her waist, and laid his head on her shoulder.

"I know," she said. "We both have work we must do, passions we must follow. Neither of us follows convention; our arrangement suits us both."

"I'll be back as soon as I can," he said, hugging her.

Pedro was taken on by a stockbreeder, Barthélemy Bourrel, who farmed near Ax. He was immediately sent south over the mountains to Aragon with another shepherd to join the ones who were minding the flock that Bourrel kept in Tortosa. Pedro and the other shepherds would return with the flock, including all the new lambs the following spring at Easter. Pedro was buoyed up with excitement about this. This was what he'd dreamed of, the chance to explore new ground. He would be away from the jurisdiction of the Carcassonne Inquisition, and it would allow time for the dust to settle over the Cathars of Arques. Barthélemy Bourrel had no connections with the Good Men, and neither did any of his shepherds, as far as Pedro knew. He reasoned that by going away for a while, the Inquisition would forget about him – if they had ever given him any thought at all. His commitment to the Good Men would lie fallow over the months he was in Aragon.

The walk over the snow-covered mountain passes would be tough. He could take only what he could carry in a small bundle. That did not concern him. He had very few possessions: a change of clothing and his woollen cloak was all he needed. The freezing weather conditions meant he would wear most of his clothes to keep warm. In honour of the occasion, he allowed himself a new pair of boots, which cost a great deal of money. They were of the finest leather, lined in fleece and were perfect for walking and climbing over the mountains. He had to keep his feet warm and comfortable; it was the only expense he had. Despite the cold and the steep mountain pathways, the journey was uneventful. They had each taken food supplies, and they slept in barns and shepherd's huts. It was a welcome relief for him to concentrate on the physical immediacy of crossing the mountains to Aragon. They arrived tired but exhilarated by the mountain air and the beauty of the landscape. The shepherds welcomed them as extra hands.

And so, Pedro's winter passed with no signs of Good Men anywhere. The ewes began to lamb at Christmas, and by Easter all the sheep and lambs were ready to make the journey back over the mountains to Ax. It was a flock of several hundred sheep with many shepherds that made the journey back over the mountains to Ax. It was conveniently near to Sybille's home. It couldn't be better.

In June, Pedro's employer sent him to the fair at Laroque-d'Olmes, to purchase some rams. It was the feast of Saint Cyr and Sainte Julitte, Friday 16th June. Pedro's sister Guillemette, now married to Bertrand Piquier, was living there, and Pedro planned to visit her. Although younger, Guillemette was the sister nearest in age to Pedro. He had always looked after her. It would be good to see her married and settled. He arrived in Laroque-d'Olmes the evening before the sheep sales began and went straight to the tavern in the centre of the town to ask if they knew where Bertrand and Guillemette lived. He found the small house easily at the edge of the town. He knocked on the door and Guillemette opened it. She had a petite, trim figure and her young, pretty face showed surprise and pleasure when she saw Pedro. But was that also sadness that passed over her face momentarily? It happened so quickly, he could not tell.

"I am so happy to see you," she said, beckoning him inside. They entered straight into the only room, which served as a living room and kitchen. Guillemette stood at the table in the centre of the room, and as he looked at her and before she spoke a word, she sank down onto a bench, her face collapsing and tears falling down her cheeks.

"Guillemette," said Pedro. "What on earth is the matter?"

He went to put his arm round her. Her small body was shaking as she leaned into him and sobbed. He held her gently whilst she gained some control. She looked at him.

"I'm sorry, Pedro," she said.

"What for?" he said. "You're upset – tell me what's upset you."

"Look." She pulled up the sleeve of her tunic. Her arm was covered in bruises.

"How did that happen?" said Pedro. She looked down.

"Bertrand?" he said. She nodded, her head still down.

"When did he do that?"

"He does it often," she said. "My whole body is covered in bruises."

Pedro took a deep breath in. "Guillemette—"

She interrupted him. "I have to leave him – help me, please help me get away." She wiped away her tears with the edge of her tunic.

"I will, I'll take you away from him," said Pedro without any idea of how he could do that. "You can't stay here."

"If you can't help me, I'll find a way myself," she said. "I'm so desperate, I've even thought of walking the streets to raise money to get away from him."

"Guillemette, you must never think like that; I will take you away," said Pedro. "Look at me." He lifted her chin up. "It's not your fault; he's a bad husband."

"I know, but the longer I stay, the worse I feel. I'm so ashamed. I must be doing something wrong."

"Shall I come and stay here tonight? He can't refuse you that if I just turn up, surely?"

"No, I think that will be all right…" She hesitated. "Pedro, do you know where the Good Men are?"

"The Good Men?"

"Yes, I met Pierre and Jacques Authier in Montaillou," she said. "They came to our parents' house before I was wed. They seemed so gentle and good. I think… I think I would like to find out more, become a Believer and work with them."

"I'll have to see what I can find out, don't worry. I'll get you away from here, one way or another."

He put his arms around her. Poor Guillemette; he must help. He left with the promise of returning in the evening. He was so furious with Bertrand that it was difficult to think straight. It was not an uncommon occurrence, men hitting their womenfolk. But his own father had never done so, and he could not condone it. Guillemette was not yet twenty – still a child. Whatever she had done, she did not deserve to be beaten like that. He must take her away from Bertrand Piquier. The pungent aroma of sheep suddenly engulfed him. He'd arrived at the market. The animals were bleating loudly at the indignity of being penned up so close together. The shouts of pedlars selling food and trinkets competed with the voices of farmers and shepherds greeting each other, shouting and laughing. He leant on the fence looking at the sheep. Where could he take Guillemette? And where would he find the Good Men? Who could he safely ask in Laroque-d'Olmes? Maybe he would bump into one of the shepherds he knew to be a Believer and they could help.

He felt a tap on his shoulder. He turned and was taken aback to see Philippe d'Aylarac and Guy Belibaste standing behind him as if he had conjured them up by sorcery. They wore brown tunics and looked like the farmers and shepherds that were mingling together at the fair. This was God's work. He almost blurted this out to Philippe and Guy, and he remembered just in time not to perform the *melioramentum* but to give them a normal greeting as if they were shepherds he had met by chance.

"Let's take a walk." Philippe spoke quietly. "Perhaps down by the river?"

Pedro gave as careless a nod as he could, and they made their way through the crowd of people. They soon arrived at the riverbank, which was quiet and shaded by trees. They walked in silence until they reached a place where a path led off the main track.

"There's a secluded spot down there," said Philippe.

They followed the pathway through some bushes until they reached a clearing where they stood still and glanced around. There was silence; they would hear the crunching of leaves and sticks underfoot if anyone approached. Pedro remembered the *melioramentum*. He bowed his head. Philippe put his hand up.

"No need for that now," he said. "We must be careful in case someone should come upon us. Let's sit here."

"What are you doing here?" said Pedro as they seated themselves on a fallen tree trunk.

"We had some work to do nearby," said Philippe. "We always travel together."

"This is God's doing," said Pedro.

"How so?" said Philippe.

Pedro told them about Guillemette and her wish to leave her brutal husband and to be with the Good Men. They looked at each other.

"It's a terrible shame that your father didn't arrange a marriage for Guillemette with someone who had the understanding of good," said Guy. "Instead of marrying her to this Bertrand, who mistreats her."

"I'm sure he thought he had found her a good husband," said Pedro.

"Never mind that now," said Philippe. "It is as it is. She needs us to help her and we will. She's on the wrong path and we will put her on the right path. As she wishes to be with us, we must think about where she could go; perhaps she could be placed with some Believers at whose house she could serve."

"That would be the answer to her prayers," said Pedro. "But I'm concerned that it's wrong to take a woman from her husband, who has been married in the eyes of God."

"It is a sin, but I will absolve you of that sin because Believers must protect other Believers from evil, and as you know, Pedro, marriage performed in the Roman Catholic church is not a long-lasting thing, or even a good thing, but the other marriage which is performed by the son of God is good and long-lasting," said Philippe.

"So, what can we do?" said Pedro. "I'm going back tonight to stay with her, but her husband will be there all evening," said Pedro. "And in the morning, I must go early to market to buy rams for my employer, but I can meet you after that."

"Let's meet here tomorrow after you have bought the sheep," said Philippe.

That evening, Pedro made his way to Guillemette's home. This was going to be an ordeal. He must contain his angry feelings and act as if everything was normal. Bertrand Piquier deserved a beating, a taste of his own treatment. It was not Pedro's way to use violence, but talking to Piquier would do no good either and might only make things worse. No, the only answer was to help Guillemette get away. Perhaps the two Perfects would arrive at a solution, because the next day he must return to work with the rams.

Bertrand Piquier's mother and younger brother were at the house when Pedro arrived. Bertrand's mother was a thin, unsmiling woman. Her eyes were black pellets in her sour face. Her younger son was a smaller version of Bertrand, not yet fully grown but with a supercilious expression on his face. Pedro's attempts to make polite conversation with Bertrand's mother, whilst Guillemette cooked and served a meal for them, were stilted. He desperately wanted to tell Bertrand's mother that her son was a violent bully, but instead he talked about the rams he hoped to buy the next day. Whenever he glanced at Bertrand, he wanted to stand up, challenge him about hitting Guillemette and punch him in the face. Violence only begets violence, he told himself – but it did little good. He could hardly eat his meal as his contained rage ate away at him. Bertrand drank a great deal of wine throughout the meal. His eyes were on Guillemette the whole time, watching her every move. She was nervous, and when she accidentally spilled some water on the table, he shouted at her.

"Clumsy bitch!" He looked at Pedro. "I've got a job to do with her, to teach her to be a good wife."

"Guillemette's a good girl," said Pedro.

"You think so, do you?" said Bertrand. "She's got some strange ideas, I can tell you; it comes of living up there in Montaillou, amongst those crazy heretics!" He grabbed Guillemette's arm. She looked terrified.

"Leave her alone!" Pedro stood up.

"Don't you know," said Bertrand, standing up close to Pedro and pushing Guillemette away, "never to interfere between husband and wife? It's none of your business." With his face in front of Pedro's face, he jabbed his finger into Pedro's chest.

Pedro clenched his fists; his whole body was taut. How he wanted to give Piquier what he deserved, but he took some deep breaths and sat down. He remained silent for the rest of the evening. It was torture to sit seething inside as Bertrand constantly criticised Guillemette throughout the meal. Bertrand's mother and brother sat there seemingly oblivious to it all. Pedro was shocked at the way they ignored this ill treatment of Guillemette. What a relief when they finally left, and they could all go to bed.

There were only two small rooms upstairs and it was not long before Pedro heard banging and screams as Bertrand beat Guillemette in the room next door. He was desperate to intervene and stop Bertrand, but he sat on his makeshift, sheepskin bed, holding himself back. It would only provoke Bertrand more if he tried to stop him, so he sat and listened, his head in his hands. He prayed for help and called on all his resources to be patient. Suddenly he could stand it no longer. He stood and walked out of his room and into the next room. As Pedro entered, Bertrand stopped, his arm raised above his head. He looked at Pedro. Guillemette was cowering on her knees on the floor, her hands and arms protecting her face and head, sobbing. Bertrand's face was contorted into an ugly rictus of drunken shock and rage. Pedro moved to stand in front of Bertrand to shield Guillemette, who had fallen silent.

Pedro was taller than Bertrand by over a head's height. He looked down at Bertrand, who swayed, his eyelids flickering beneath Pedro's gaze. Pedro pushed him and Bertrand fell back onto his bed. Pedro turned to Guillemette.

"Come with me; sleep in my room tonight."

As they left the room, Pedro glanced back to Bertrand, who was lying on his back with his eyes closed and his mouth open.

Pedro gave Guillemette his sheepskin rug to sleep on and he curled up on his cloak and tried to sleep. The tiled floor was hard and uncomfortable, and Guillemette woke up, crying and screaming a couple of times. He comforted her, telling her he had met the Good Men and they would help.

"Tomorrow we will have a plan," he told her. "You just have to behave as normal tomorrow morning, and I will come to find you later in the day."

He rose early the next morning, having hardly slept. He reassured Guillemette as he left that he would return, and told her to stay out of Bertrand's way. Worry about Guillemette was at the forefront of his mind, but first he must go to the market. The sheep he wanted to buy came up for auction mid-morning. By the time he had bought the rams and arranged to leave them in a pen at the market until he was free to collect them later, it was nearly midday. He made his way to the riverbank where, on the way to the clearing, he caught up with the two Good Men ambling along. He told them what had happened the previous night.

"That confirms it; there is no doubt in my mind," said Philippe. "She cannot stay there."

"We don't want her living without a proper home and job, becoming a whore for anyone who wants her," said Guy.

They continued along the riverbank until they came to a field, where Pedro was startled to see Guillemette working. She was behind a row of trees, raking the hay. She was alone.

"God is indeed helping us, Philippe, Guy," said Pedro. "Look, Guillemette is here." He pointed and took the two Perfects over to meet her. Guillemette saw them and came across to the low wall bordering the track. "Guillemette, look, here are the Good Men to help you," said Pedro. She bowed her head. "No, none of that, people may see us," said Pedro urgently.

"Leave her with us, Pedro," said Philippe. "We want to talk with her and find out what she wants. And we have an idea of how we may help her."

Pedro went back to the fair, where he met some of the other shepherds who were going to the tavern to eat. They asked him to join them, and he agreed. It was a good cover story if anyone wanted to check his movements on that day. After lunch, he went to find Philippe and Guy. On the way he found Guillemette, still in the same field, raking hay. She told him to go and find Philippe and Guy in the clearing, and to do as they asked. She said she must go home for the moment, but she was happy because they had come up with an escape plan.

Philippe and Guy were sitting on the tree trunk in the clearing, where they had talked the day before. Their plan was for Pedro to take Guillemette to Rabastens, where she could live with them as their housekeeper in the Cathar safe house there.

"You want me to take her to Rabastens?" said Pedro. "I thought she would go with you. It's quite a long way; it will take about three or four days to walk there, and I should take the sheep to my employer."

"You'll have to arrange for someone else to take the sheep. You can do that, can't you? We have some work to attend to first, then we'll follow you," said Guy.

"I suppose I can find another shepherd to take them. But I'm not sure if I can or if indeed I should be the one to take her," said Pedro. "Suppose her husband and his family pursue us, what then?"

"They won't come after you, they won't know you've taken her, but if they do, tell them you're going on a pilgrimage," said Philippe. "You must do this, Pedro – your sister is under the power of a wicked man and if you help her escape you will have your reward in Heaven."

"I don't know the way to Rabastens," said Pedro, "and I don't know anyone there, or which house to take her to."

"You will go to Mirepoix first, then to Bayville and then to Caraman, then you will ask the way to Rabastens. You should lodge there for a day or two before Saint John's Day. On Saint John's Day whilst Mass is said in the great church, leave your sister in the lodging house and come to the great church. There you will find me, or Guy, or his brother, Bernard, or some other trusted person there on my behalf to welcome your sister. Wait for us to meet you outside the church, between morning and midday on 24th June," said Philippe, in such a firm way that Pedro felt he could not argue with him. "And now Guy will preach a small sermon for us."

"Once there were two Believers next to a stream. One of them fell asleep. The other stayed awake, and he saw something that resembled a lizard, which came out of the mouth of the sleeper and suddenly it crossed the stream on a plank or a stem that was stretched from one side of the stream to the other. There was a head of an emaciated donkey there, into which the thing went and then came out of, running through the holes of the head. Then it came back via the plank to the mouth of the sleeper..."

Pedro found his thoughts wandering... It was going to be difficult to find a shepherd to take the sheep to Barthélemy Bourrel for him. Most of the shepherds would have left the fair by now. If, on top of that, Pedro was several days late returning to his job with no proper explanation, then he could lose his job altogether... but that might not be such a bad thing. He would find another job easily enough, and he didn't seem to have any choice now in the matter of Guillemette; she was his sister, after all, and he couldn't argue with the Perfects any more about it. They must have something important to do – another *consolamentum* – that's what they seemed to spend most of their time doing as far as he could tell, and the timing of those *consolamentum* was crucial. He listened again to Guy.

"The soul of a man always stays in his body until the body dies, but the spirit of the man went in and out, as they had seen this lizard leave the mouth of the sleeper, enter the donkey's head and go back into the mouth of the sleeper. Since they had seen this, they could believe it."

This was the first of Guy's many sermons Pedro listened to, or, rather, tried to listen to – and it wouldn't be the last time he found his mind wandering onto other things. When Guy stopped talking, none of them could think of anything to say, so they went back to the town centre and the fair, which was closing. There were some shepherds and farmers still there. Pedro asked around and soon found a shepherd he knew who was willing to take the rams to Barthélemy Bourrel.

Pedro, Philippe and Guy stayed in the tavern in the centre of Laroque-d'Olmes that evening. The place was full of shepherds and farmers, and the three of them blended in. But the Good Men had some conger eel, which they wanted to cook in a pot separate from everyone else's, as the other pots contained meat. It looked as if there was going to be a scene as the landlady told them not to make unnecessary expense by using a separate pot. Guy told the landlady they would pay her well to use the separate pot. She looked at them as if they were mad, but she accepted the money and kept quiet. Philippe blessed the bread quietly with his back turned towards the other people in the tavern and no-one appeared to notice.

The following day, Pedro took leave of the Good Men and went to tell Guillemette that he would take her to Rabastens the next day. She was alone in the house and she hugged him with delight.

"Oh, thank you, thank you," she said, and started crying again.

He held her in his arms, hoping he was doing the right thing. They agreed to meet at the cemetery on the outskirts of the town. Pedro had planned to stay at the tavern for another night, but he was restless. Suppose Bertrand discovered their scheming and the Good Men's involvement, and beat Guillemette even more? Bertrand might hunt him down or go to the Inquisition in Carcassonne. Bertrand had hinted that he knew of Guillemette's interest in the Good Men. His parents should know of all this too. In fact, he could go to Montaillou after he had taken Guillemette to Rabastens. Or he could go now. The rams were taken care of; he wasn't taking Guillemette away until tomorrow. He was a speedy walker. There was enough time to visit his parents, return to Laroque and catch a few hours' sleep.

He walked the five leagues to his parents' house in two hours. It would take most people twice as long. He arrived just as darkness fell. The village was quiet, and no-one saw him as he slipped into his parents' house through the back door. They were distraught when they heard about Bertrand Piquier.

"We thought he would be a good husband," said his father. "Aunt Mersende knows the family…"

"Poor Guillemette," said his mother. "She could come back here and live with us."

"She wants to help the Good Men, and they're happy to take her," said Pedro. "Best to leave the arrangements as they are. If it doesn't work out, she can always come back here."

"She will be safe with them," said his father.

Pedro was back in Laroque-d'Olmes by the early hours of the morning. The tavern was closed and locked up. He went to the clearing near the riverbank, where he slept soundly wrapped up in his cloak on a bed of dry leaves. The next morning, he waited for Guillemette at the cemetery as they had arranged. He half expected a mob, out for his blood led by Bertrand to appear, but Guillemette arrived unaccompanied. She carried a large bundle.

"Guillemette, whatever have you got there?" said Pedro.

"It's my wedding dress and the bedlinen I brought as my dowry when I married," she said.

"We'll be travelling for three or four days at least," he said. "And this bundle will slow us down and make us conspicuous – can't you leave it somewhere?"

Guillemette began to cry. He softened. Poor Guillemette; she'd had a difficult time. They set off with the bundle carried by Pedro. They saw only a few farmers working in the fields and women going about their business in the villages they passed through. Pedro wished many times over that they had left the bundle behind as some people remarked on it and asked where they were going. Pedro told them they were on a pilgrimage and changed the destination each time or that they were delivering some linens to newlywed relatives. He would have to pray for forgiveness for all these lies. They walked into the early hours of each morning, rested briefly under hedges, in shepherd's huts or in barns, and rose early to resume their journey. They arrived at Rabastens the evening before the Nativity of Saint John. They stayed in a lodging house near the church. Pedro told the widow who lived there that they had come to celebrate the Nativity of Saint John and would meet a relative tomorrow. She seemed satisfied and asked no further questions. The next morning, they found Bernard Belibaste, the brother of Guy, outside the church.

"Guy and Philippe had to go to Ax urgently," he said. "I'll take you to their house."

Bernard took them to the safe house, which was quiet. Pedro saw Guillemette to the safe house and left her with Bernard after some refreshments. As he took his leave of Bernard and Guillemette, Bernard reassured him that Philippe and Guy would take good care of her.

"As if she were their sister," he said.

"And I promise to do everything I can to deserve their love and esteem," said Guillemette. "Pedro, will you visit me soon?"

Pedro embraced her, said he would do his best to visit her and took his leave, feeling relieved that she was safely here. He was sure there would be no ill treatment from the Perfects. He could return to his job with a lighter heart.

When Pedro arrived back at his workplace, he found he had no job. He was not surprised. In fact, he saw it as an opportunity to visit Sybille. She had previously reminded him to be extra careful when he visited her, as the news about the events in Arques and his status as a fugitive had spread around Ax. It seemed a long time ago since all that had happened. But he rested in a copse of bushes off the main track, leaning against the trunk of a large sweet chestnut tree as he waited for dusk to fall, before going to Sybille's. It was time for a change and Sybille may know where a shepherd was needed. When darkness fell, he covered himself with his cloak and hood and made his way through the quiet town and into the maze of lanes and passages where Sybille lived.

Sybille's eldest son, Bernard, opened the door when Pedro knocked. Bernard was on his way out. He left Pedro to find his own way into the living room upstairs, where Sybille was preparing food. Sybille lifted her head as he came through the door.

"Pedro," she exclaimed.

Philippe d'Aylarac and Guy Belibaste were sitting at the table with Sybille's youngest son, Arnaud, sitting between them. They were all eating slices of bread. Pedro took off his hood and cloak, and bowed his head low. Philippe put his hand up.

"No need for that," he said, flicking his eyes over to Arnaud.

"Ah yes," said Pedro, understanding. He turned to Sybille's son. "So, we meet again, Naudy. Has your father sent you back here? Has he had enough of you?"

Pedro ruffled Arnaud's hair and grinned at him. Arnaud rearranged his hair and grinned back. It was their playful routine; they always did it when they met. Sybille came over and embraced Pedro. She left floury marks on his tunic.

"You've arrived at the right moment," she said. "I was thinking about you and wondering if you'd be free to accompany Philippe and Guy to Rabastens in the next day or two."

"This is fate – and God's work, of course," said Pedro, glancing at the Perfects. "I was thinking of going to Montaillou to see my family before I look for work." He stopped himself from articulating the thought that it was a good cover story if one was needed.

"Aren't you working for Bourrel any more?" said Sybille.

"No, I went to the fair at Laroque-d'Olmes, where I met Guy and Philippe, then I took my sister up to Rabastens and I was late back – Bourrel employed another shepherd whilst I was gone. So, I need to find work soon."

"There was someone here a few days ago," said Sybille. "A shepherd; he was saying a stockbreeder called Pierre Andre in Planèzes is taking on shepherds."

"That's not so far from my home in Cubières," said Guy. "I know the Andre family; they aren't Believers." He put his hand up to his mouth; he'd forgotten about Naudy.

"I could try there," said Pedro. "If I'm needed for… other work, well, anyone who wants me can seek me out."

"Or," said Philippe, "you could go south."

"No, this is fate and God's will," said Pedro. "I will go to Rabastens with you, then to Planèzes, and we can stay in Montaillou en route."

Guy and Philippe exchanged glances.

"It's far out of your way to Rabastens. We could go alone," said Philippe. "We have each other."

"As long as you're happy to go to Montaillou first, which is a detour for you, I will go with you to Rabastens."

"There's no hurry for us to return," said Philippe. "We need to rest here for a night or two and then go to Montaillou. It would be good to see your family."

"That suits me," said Pedro.

This time, Guy and Philippe wanted to travel during daylight hours. But when the day dawned, it was raining lightly, but a heavy, grey sky accompanied by ominous, rumblings of thunder heralded a storm. Rather than wait for it to clear, the Perfects decided it would be safer to travel in bad weather as fewer people would be outdoors unless it was necessary. They would be covered by their cloaks against the weather and that would disguise them too. Guy told Pedro they were tired of moving around on the mountains at night;

they had both fallen and injured themselves, and it took them some time to recover and rest after a long night's trek.

As they left Ax, a great clap of thunder resounded overhead, and a bolt of lightning zigzagged terrifyingly close. The rain came down in sheets. They gathered their cloaks around them and plodded on. They hardly spoke and the Perfects didn't preach, which they often did when walking. The water was running down the mountain tracks in streams, and their boots and cloaks became sodden. It took all their strength and concentration just to keep going and remain upright, slipping and sliding as they were through the mud. When they arrived at the village of Sorgeat, there was no-one about; the weather kept everyone indoors. They stopped for a moment, sheltering in the lea of a barn. They decided to walk as far as possible without stopping to avoid meeting people. It would normally take three to four hours to walk from Ax to Montaillou, but with the conditions as they were it would take another hour or two longer. The storm followed them for most of the morning and into the afternoon. When they reached the top of the escarpment of Lasitardor, not far from Montaillou, they stopped to catch their breath. Thunder still rumbled deep and long overhead, but it was moving away. The lightning eased off and thankfully the rain stopped, and the sun shone down on them. When they reached a place where some scrubby bushes grew near some large boulders, they rested and took off their damp cloaks.

"I'll be glad when we're there," said Guy.

"There's a wood above Montaillou where we can rest and dry off," said Pedro. "We can wait there until it's dark before going to my parents' house."

It was late afternoon when they reached the shelter of the wood near Montaillou. They moved deep into the fir trees until they found a place that was dry. They took off their boots and tunics and hung all their sodden clothes over low tree branches. The dense closeness of the trees meant that the rain had hardly penetrated, and the ground was dry. They dared not make a fire and risk drawing attention to themselves, but they sat on the pine needles under a tall spreading tree whilst they ate the trout pâté, bread and wine that Sybille had given them. Philippe blessed the bread without getting up in case anyone suddenly appeared. They lay down and rested, staying in the wood until dusk fell and little bats silently fluttered out from the trees.

They made their way from the wood to the village of Montaillou, walking along the grassy slope, enfolded in the darkness. The air was fresh and the smell of wood smoke hung in the air. There was no-one to be seen.

Pedro's parents' house was on the edge of the square in the centre of the village. They welcomed him and the Perfects. They were used to these nocturnal arrivals and could usually cobble together a meal. Fortunately, there was plenty of river trout for the Perfects that Grégoire had caught earlier that day, and lamb for everyone else, all eaten with turnips. They finished the meal with cheese, and preserved plums and figs.

"How is life in Montaillou at the moment?" said Philippe when they had finished eating and the younger members of the family had gone to bed.

"I have plenty of weaving to do," said Father. "I concentrate on that and try not to get involved in the religious tensions in the village."

"I hear that feelings run high at times between the two groups, the Believers and the Romans," said Philippe.

"It's not easy," said Father. "You have to appear to belong to the Roman church, attending Mass, crossing yourself, genuflecting, saying the prayers and all that, but really believing in something else entirely. You never quite know who to trust, who believes in what. Some bad things have happened…" he sighed. "Terrible things… Madame Maurs was found by her sons to have had her tongue ripped out. Everyone thought it was because she openly challenged

Pierre Clergue, calling him a two-faced bastard. That's been... very disturbing."

The two Perfects looked at each other. "How is Madame Maurs?" said Philippe.

"Not well," said Mother. "We're frightened of visiting her in case we're punished for that. I see her sons sometimes in the village. It's difficult."

"It's never easy following the path of truth and justice," said Philippe.

Before they turned in for the night, Pedro told his father of his plan to go to Planèzes after going to Rabastens with the Perfects the next day. His father asked him if he thought the Fenouillèdes was a safe place to go. Pedro replied that he believed he should follow his fate, and that, as far as he knew, his prospective new employer had no connections with the Good Men. He would be out of harm's way up there.

Pedro was employed by a farmer called Pierre Andre. In all, he stayed there for nearly three years. The farm was on the river Agly, but the animals were moved around regularly to different pastures. The years Pedro spent in the Fenouillèdes were remarkable only by the relative absence of involvement with the Good Men. He was asked to take the Good Men on night-time journeys occasionally as they visited deathbeds, and he heard snippets of Cathar news from shepherds or other travellers passing through. He stayed overnight occasionally with his parents, who brought him up to date with news from the village. It was during one of these visits, early in 1307, that his parents told him that the Inquisition had appointed a new Inquisitor at Carcassonne. His name was Geoffroy d'Ablis and he had joined up with Bernard Gui, the Inquisitor from Toulouse. The Inquisition were not giving up; in fact, they were doubling their efforts.

CHAPTER 11

Guy Belibaste

The safe house in Rabastens was now the place Guy called home. He worked as a Perfect with Philippe d'Aylarac. Raymond de Toulouse was often away as his healing abilities were much in demand. Much of Guy and Philippe's time was spent on the move, traversing the mountain tracks as they travelled to perform the *consolamentum*. They were treated well by the families of those they consoled, given the best of food and goods that people could afford in gratitude for performing the ritual for their loved ones. Guy found the life hard; they walked long distances in the dark and he did not have as much stamina as Philippe. He was always relieved when they had more than a few days of respite back in the house at Rabastens. He missed his wife and he often longed for a slice of roasted wild boar or a wedge of cheese. But it had worked out well with Guillemette Maury keeping house for them. Philippe and Guy agreed that she was a good housekeeper, a little argumentative at times, answering back when she should keep quiet, but both had grown fond of her.

The house, outside the village, was usually quiet. Guillemette looked after the house: cooking, cleaning, washing clothes and bedlinen. The villagers accepted the story she and the Perfects had agreed that the men who lived there were her uncles and that they travelled to work on other farms when help was needed. The occasional visitors were explained as friends and relatives who were passing through, or who came to tell the uncles when they were needed for work. Guillemette was relieved to be away from her violent husband, and happy to be with the Good Men.

In the spring of 1307, Guillemette had been in Rabastens for several months. Early one morning as she and the two Good Men lay sleeping, a group of men, riding good-looking horses, picked their way along the main track to the house. Apart from the slow clip-clop of the horses' hooves, birdsong was the only sound as they approached. The horsemen did not speak, but through signing, waving his hands and changing his facial expression, the man in charge directed the others to dismount and tie up the horses in a small glade of trees opposite the front of the house, and sent men – *you three that way; you three the other way* – round the back. He took two others with him to the front door. They banged on the door and hollered.

Guy awoke. God in Heaven, what was the matter? Banging and shouting. He heard his name.

"Guy Belibaste, Philippe d'Aylarac, open up! Open up!"

Bang, bang, bang! What on earth…? Then he knew. His heart knocked as loudly as the banging on the front door as he leapt out of bed, pulled on his tunic and flew down the stairs, where Philippe and Guillemette were already standing together. Philippe had his fingers on his lips, signalling to Guillemette to keep quiet. She put her hand over her mouth to stifle a sob. Guy put his arm around her shoulders; she was shaking. He exchanged a helpless glance with Philippe. What can you do when the Inquisition come knocking at your door?

"The back door," said Philippe. "It's our only chance."

"We could hide," whispered Guy.

"They'll soon break down the door," said Philippe. "They'd find us in no time; no, we must run out from the back and hide in the wood."

The banging and shouting grew louder. Guy ran back up the stairs into his room, pulled on the rest of his clothes, crammed his feet into his boots and picked up his cloak. He noticed his purse next to the bed and grabbed it. Philippe ran to collect things from his room. Guy's heart was thundering in his chest and his mouth was dry as he ran to meet Guillemette and Philippe at the back door. They were all dressed and wrapped in their cloaks. Guillemette was sobbing. Philippe put his arm around her shoulders now.

"Hush, Guillemette, they will hear us," he said. "We must leave silently and run to the wood in the hollow behind the house, can you do that?"

She nodded. Philippe and Guy looked at each other and nodded. Philippe began to pull back the iron bar that locked the door. It scraped and rattled as he slid it. He hesitated. The banging and shouting at the front door continued.

"Just pull it back, Philippe, for God's sake," said Guy. "They can't hear us… all the noise they're making."

Philippe slid the iron bar out of its position and opened the door a little. He put his head out, pushed the door wide open and signalled for Guy and Guillemette to follow him. Guy took hold of Guillemette's hand. They crept out of the doorway and broke into a run as they left the building.

They came at them from both sides of the house, six of them, huge and strong like great wild beasts. They grabbed at Guy, Philippe and Guillemette, forcing their arms up behind their backs. They were laughing.

"You really thought you could get away?" said one of them as he spat out a globule of mucus. He yanked Guy's arm higher.

"Get off!" Guy struggled, shaking with shock and pain.

"Move."

Two of the men pulled, pushed and shoved each of them forward into a stumbling, screaming, struggling bunch of arms and legs. Guillemette screamed. Philippe and Guy roared with pain and frustration. Their captors yelled at them. Guillemette fell and was dragged up.

As they were taken around the side of the house to the front, they saw more men on the track and several horses tethered in the clump of trees facing the house. The men wore green and red tunics with insignia upon them. The Bishop's insignia. They all carried knives tucked into their leather belts. With their shaved heads and sculpted beards, they looked hard men capable of anything. One of them, his tunic light grey with red insignia on it, looked at Guillemette. His black eyes glinted as they moved over her, up and down. He smiled, sidled up to her and lifted her chin with his finger.

"Now then, who have we here?" he said.

Guillemette sobbed. He slapped her face. It knocked her sideways and she screamed.

"Answer me," he shouted in her face.

"Guillemette Maury," she sobbed.

"You're a pretty little thing," he said. "I think you can come with me." His smile revealed the bad teeth that festered at the front of his mouth. "We're going to Carcassonne, to the Wall."

"No, oh no, please no, Philippe, Guy, help me," screamed Guillemette.

He hit her again and she collapsed onto her knees. He pushed her over with his booted foot. She lay on the ground sobbing.

"Tie their hands behind their backs and hobble those two together at the ankles, that'll calm them down."

Philippe and Guy struggled and shouted, "Leave her, let her go."

"You lot," said the one in the light grey and red tunic, pointing at five of the men, "walk with them – I'll go ahead on horseback with these three, we'll lead the spare horses. The little maid is coming with me, get up." He pulled Guillemette up by her arm. She stood trembling with her head bowed. She looked so small and vulnerable.

"Leave her," Philippe shouted out again. "Let her go, you don't need her; she's only our housekeeper."

The man walked up to Philippe and, in a low, threatening tone with his face up close to Philippe's, spoke. "Another word out of you, you fucking heretic, and you'll see what I need her for, because I'll show you and these others will help me." He lifted his tunic and grinned as he grabbed at his crotch.

Philippe turned away, sickened.

"Understood?" said the man. He turned as if to go, then turned back. "Oh, and so you don't forget…" He punched Philippe in the jaw.

Philippe's knees buckled and he started to sink down. He was wrenched up. Guy felt the blow as if he himself had been hit. He reeled back in shock. Philippe was the strong one. Guy couldn't bear to see him hurt and vulnerable.

"We'll see you in Carcassonne."

He walked off towards the group of horses tethered in the trees. He dragged Guillemette with him, barking out orders as he went. The men tied Guillemette's hands behind her back and threw her over one of the horses' necks like a sack of kittens. The one giving orders mounted his horse and set off with the others behind him. The sharp stink of hot horse flesh drifted into Guy's nostrils.

Philippe and Guy were pushed along by the other men. They had their legs bound together as if they were about to run in a three-legged race. Philippe's head and face were swollen and bleeding, and he struggled to remain upright and walk. Tethered to Guy, Philippe was an immense weight dragging Guy down. Guy breathed in. Now it was his turn to help Philippe.

"Don't give up, Philippe, we'll think of something," said Guy.

"Stop that whispering," shouted one of the men, and gave Guy a shove in the back.

Every step of the way, the weight of Philippe threatened to drag Guy to the ground. His shoulders and back were straining, and with Philippe hanging on to his arm, he felt as if his arm could be pulled out of its socket at any moment. Philippe was barely conscious. He stumbled and shambled beside Guy. Philippe fell, and fell again, pulling Guy down with him. Each time they were jerked up by the guards. Guy's mind raced, frantic with worry about both Guillemette and Philippe. Poor Guillemette, what terrible things had happened to her already, now, this... the thought of what was happening to her... bile rose in his throat. He stopped and retched... he couldn't do this... it was too much to walk with Philippe tethered to him... pulling him down. His mind fogged over with pain and weakness... what could he do? These guards were muscular and sinewy... to try anything physical, tied up as they were and with Philippe injured and on the verge of collapse, was impossible. He remembered his purse. But he had only a small amount of money, not enough to bribe them all. He was weak and helpless; he had no chance of doing anything, of influencing their guards, of changing the situation, until they reached Carcassonne. And then what? Perhaps he could bribe a gaoler, or help might come from the outside. That thought comforted him. News of their arrests would soon reach their supporters, who would work to help them... he must pray... for strength and guidance... and for what they might have yet to bear, and for Guillemette. He concentrated his mind on surviving each moment, each step of the ordeal and the suffering they were experiencing. One step at a time. Dear God. He prayed and put his trust in God.

And he found within himself a small reserve of strength. He spoke to Philippe, telling him not to worry, that they would soon be there, that their ordeal would soon be over and then they could rest. He promised to look after him and he urged Philippe to pray. God, give me strength to survive this and strength to help Philippe. And for Guillemette, God, help poor Guillemette... and send the Good Men out there to help us all.

CHAPTER 12

Pedro Maury

It was September 1307, late in the evening. Pedro was in the pastures in the valley below Planèzes. The other shepherds were sleeping in the barn. He was head shepherd and, after checking the sheep fold was secure, he sat beside the fire watching the glowing embers, enjoying the peace and the night sky. Pedro had been waiting for the last two nights for two visitors, and on this third night, he waited again. A soft breeze swept over the embers of the fire and momentarily fanned up some small flames. Would his visitors arrive that night? Or had something happened to prevent them?

He heard a noise coming from behind the barn, the rustle of leaves. He stood up and looked over. It was impossible to see anything as he moved away from the firelight; there was no moonlight. Was that his name he'd heard whispered?

"Pedro." There it was again.

"Who's there?" He moved towards the barn.

"It's me, Pierre Montanier." The shepherd appeared from behind the bushes at the side of the barn. An old friend and a Believer.

"Are you alone?" said Pedro.

"No," he said. "Are you?"

"Yes, the other shepherds are asleep in the barn."

"Good," he said. "I've brought Guy and Philippe. They were captured in a dawn raid on the house at Rabastens a few days ago and taken to the Wall. We got them out, but Philippe is injured. They hid all day behind a waterfall near Carcassonne. We've made slow progress; they're in a bad way." He spoke to the bush. "You can come out now – Pedro will look after you. I must go. You're in safe hands." He gave Pedro a nod and faded away into the darkness.

Two men emerged from the bushes. One of them staggered and was supported by the other. As he moved to help him, Pedro saw Philippe's face was swollen with an open wound on one side. Philippe leant heavily on Pedro's arm as they walked to the fire. Philippe shivered and Pedro realised Philippe's clothes were wet through.

"Come and sit here." Pedro threw a handful of sticks on the embers and flames leapt up. "You can warm up beside the fire. Take your damp clothes off; they'll dry out overnight. I'll find something to cover you."

In the store, a small hut beside the barn, there were some old woollen cloaks and a couple of blankets. Pedro rigged up an arrangement of fencing poles and ropes for them to drape their clothes over near to the fire. They wrapped the ragged blankets Pedro gave them around themselves. It was only then that Pedro thought to perform the *melioramentum*.

"No-one must know we're here," said Guy, looking around.

"Don't worry, the others are asleep in the barn. You can dry your clothes, eat, drink and rest overnight in the storehouse. I'll find some sheepskins for you to lie on; there's enough room in there," said Pedro. "And I should look at that wound on your face, Philippe. I'll clean it and put some herbal salve on it – we use it on the animals, but it works for men too."

As they ate and drank and warmed themselves, they told Pedro what had happened.

"I prayed, I was desperately trying to think of how we could escape as we walked towards Carcassonne," said Guy. "I couldn't think of anything. I felt so helpless; all I could do was to pray. That journey with Philippe injured, and no hope of escape – well, I thought we'd reached the end. Once in the Wall, I kept thinking that the next time we saw the outside world would be when we were walked towards a Roman bonfire. But I should have had more faith in God. A guard came to our cell in the early hours of the morning. He told us to follow him, and we went through a labyrinth of passages and tunnels – slipping past cells where some poor souls screamed and ranted as we passed – until we came to a small door. The guard had a key. He pushed us out. We emerged from the back side of the Wall into the darkness. Pierre Montanier was waiting. He took us to a stream. He told us to hide behind a small waterfall during daylight hours and promised to come back when darkness fell the following night. We waited the rest of that night and all the following day. It was cold and damp with no space to move; we had no food. Thankfully, Pierre turned up as he promised. He told us that the guard had been bribed. We walked through part of the following night; we were both too weak and tired to walk far. It's been a long journey of walking as far as we could, then sleeping for a few hours. But we made it."

"My God, what an ordeal," said Pedro. He threw some more wood on the fire. "Where will you go from here?"

"We must go south," said Guy. "We've had a lucky escape this time, but next time, well…"

Pedro nodded; that seemed the best plan. They sat in silence for a few minutes watching the flames dancing. Pedro stood.

"I'll clean your wound," he said, and went to the storeroom. As Pedro attended to him, Philippe said that some Believers had already gone south to Aragon, and he thought more would follow.

"We will find somewhere safe to rest and recuperate for a while," said Philippe. "There are people to help us in Aragon, but I'm afraid I shall have to take it slowly."

"Rest now, I'll wake you before first light and take you to the river crossing."

He remembered after they retired that there was someone he must ask them about.

The next morning, he woke them early as promised. They had slept well and, dressed in their dry clothes, they both reported feeling better. Pedro inspected Philippe's wound.

"It looks a little less swollen and inflamed," he said. "I'll give you some salve to take with you, and some food."

He took them in the cool, quiet of the morning to the Agly river ford, between Rasiguères and Tournefort. It was nearby, just half an hour's walk.

"This is the place," he said. "There is only a trickle of water so it's easy to cross over. I wish you well."

He performed the *melioramentum*. They thanked him for his help and blessed him.

"Come with us," said Guy, catching hold of Pedro's hands. "Come now, leave everything behind."

Philippe looked at Guy in surprise.

"It's not time for me to leave yet," said Pedro. "I will leave when God calls me, and I will know when that is."

"It's growing more dangerous by the minute," said Guy.

"Leave him," said Philippe. "We must be on our way."

"Before you go, tell me, where is Guillemette?" said Pedro.

They glanced at each other and back to him. He searched their faces and a wave of despair surged through him. They told him what had happened. He walked back to his sheep, hardly daring to think what might have happened to Guillemette. He had no idea how he could help her. The person to ask was Sybille. Her network of contacts might find a way.

It was still dark and quiet when he arrived back at the pastures. He stoked the fire and sat down watching the flames flicker and the fire roar into life. He put his head in his hands. Poor Guillemette.

He thought he had taken her to a safe place. How he wished he had taken her somewhere else. But it was what she wanted, and what they had all thought was for the best. His parents would be heartbroken. He felt his own heart breaking; tears coursed down his face. His little sister who had done no wrong in this world, to be treated so cruelly; why would God allow such things to happen to her? Would he ever see her again?

In late spring the following year, Pierre Andre sent a child up to the pastures with a message for Pedro to go urgently to his house. This was strange; it was coming up to cheese-making time and all hands were needed. It must be important. Was someone ill? Or taken by the Inquisition? A family member? His parents? He prayed it was not them, but what else could it be?

There were two men waiting for him with his employer at the door of the farmhouse. They wore well-cut tunics decorated with insignia. As he approached, he heard his employer speak.

"Here he is – Pedro Maury."

"Pedro Maury," said one of the men, "we're here on behalf of the Public Prosecutor to issue you with a summons to appear before the Public Prosecutor on the 14th of April, in the main square of Saint-Paul-de-Fenouillet." He handed a parchment to Pedro.

"What's all this, Pedro?" said Pierre Andre.

"I really don't know." Pedro looked at the two men who had brought the summons. They shrugged their shoulders.

"We just deliver the summons; you must turn up or you will be in more trouble."

Pedro looked at Pierre Andre.

"I don't know what this is all about," said Pedro, "but it looks like I've no choice in the matter, I'll have to go. I'll put my trust in God and hope that my fate is to return here."

"The 14th of April is a few days hence," said Pierre Andre. "So, as I have to let you go, you could do a job for me at the same time."

"If I can. What is it?"

"To take a load of salt to Bernard Torte in Ax; after that you can go to Saint-Paul-de-Fenouillet, deal with the matter there and then return to work."

"Are you sure?" said Pedro. "It will take me two to three days to walk to Ax then back up to Saint-Paul; I'll be gone for nearly a week."

"I know, but I should have sent that salt before. We've got a good lot of shepherds now; they'll manage without you."

"I'll do that. I'm glad to be of use," said Pedro. This was true, but if he made good time with the load of salt, he would also have time to visit Sybille. If anyone knew anything about this summons, it would be Sybille.

He searched his mind as he walked to Ax, with a mule carrying the load of salt. What could they be charging him with? He'd accompanied many Perfects as they journeyed to dying Believers to perform a *consolamentum*, but they usually travelled by night and avoided being seen. Any Believers who were involved knew this. Had one of them betrayed him? One of their own? Under pressure and fear of torture, many would betray others to save themselves. Helping Guy Belibaste and Philippe d'Aylarac was the most recent time he had helped the Perfects, but that was in autumn the previous year. He hadn't been asked since. It was possible that this could be connected to them, their escape from the Wall and their subsequent disappearance. Word would have spread around. The Carcassonne Inquisition and the Toulouse Inquisition had joined forces; their campaign was gaining ground. But then again it could be that they had nothing on him – it was difficult to believe they might be interested in him. Perhaps they wanted to ask him about Guy and Philippe or other Perfects. That could be it.

It occurred to him that at that moment he could change course, walk over the mountains to Aragon, away from the Inquisition, find the other Believers and start a new life. But now was not the time…

maybe in the future, but not yet. He could not leave Sybille. How he loved her. Her lovely face, the warm scent of her, her thick hair falling down her back – everything about her uplifted his heart. She was still in Ax, carrying on with her work, believing in what she did; she was an example to them all. It was possible that Sybille might know something about this summons. In any case he just wanted to see her.

He dropped off the mule with the load of salt, exchanged pleasantries with Mr Torte, who wondered why his friend and Pedro's employer, Pierre Andre, would send his head shepherd at a busy time with a load of salt to Ax – and what he should do with the mule? Pedro talked vaguely about a family emergency; he was needed. He would collect the mule on the way back. But now he must hurry. Sybille would be busy preparing food at this time of day. She'd have pulled her head-dress off and her hair would be loose around her shoulders. He would remove it anyway if she hadn't. He'd run his fingers through her silky hair perfumed with the lavender soap the Perfects gave her as a gift. He covered himself with his cloak; no-one must recognise him as he moved along the lane towards her house. It was late afternoon, warm, shady and quiet. He rang the bell and smiled when he heard footsteps approaching the door.

"Oh, Pedro, I didn't expect to see you at this time of the year," said Sybille, looking up and down the lane. "I'm happy to see you, though. Come in."

"I must talk with you," he said as they stood for a moment while she closed and locked the door.

"In the kitchen?" she said.

"Yes."

He put his arms around her from behind as soon as they entered the room and inhaled the complex perfume arising from her – hair, cooking and the undertone of her femininity. He pulled away and sat down at the table. She brought bread and water then sat opposite, looking at him. Her eyes were warm and full of concern.

"Has something happened?" she said.

"Is there anyone else here?" he said.

"I'm expecting visitors later this evening, but there's no-one here at the moment."

He explained about the summons. "Do you know anything about this?"

"No," said Sybille. "But I can try to find out what this is about and then see if anything can be done to stop it, or more likely at this stage to try to find people to speak for you so you can deny the charge, whatever it is."

"I will deny the charge," said Pedro. "I will lie, and then I will pray for forgiveness."

"Are you sure that Planèzes is the best place for you?" said Sybille. "You could easily go south and avoid the summons all together. There are a few Believers there already."

"I know… but… I'm not sure, besides there are still plenty of Believers living in the Sabarthès, particularly in Montaillou," he said. "And there's you. I'm not the only one."

"That's true," said Sybille. "But you are the one who has been summoned; it means the Inquisition are watching you."

"Or someone has betrayed me," said Pedro. He hesitated. "I believe that God has shown me my fate, which is to help the Good Men wherever I'm needed. And I want to be close to you, Sybille." He leaned across the table, took her hands in his and kissed them all over. She laughed and shook her head at him.

"Well, that makes two of us," she said. "We're on the same pathway." They sat holding hands across the table for a long moment, until Sybille said she must prepare the meal.

"By the way, how's Naudy?" he said.

"He's gone back to live with his father in Tarascon," she said, "where there's none of this kind of talk."

"You must miss him," said Pedro.

"I do," she said. "I miss all my children when they're not here. They will come to visit soon, I hope."

Pedro lodged in a house on the square in Saint-Paul-de-Fenouillet, the night before he was due to appear before the Public Prosecutor. He lay on the bed in the small room he had rented, studying the wooden ceiling. It was ancient and there were gaps between the slats where he could see the roof tiles. Some of the tiles were missing. He hoped it wouldn't rain heavily during the night, but the signs were that the sunny spring weather would continue. He could, of course, find somewhere else to stay, with a watertight roof. Or he could leave Saint-Paul-de-Fenouillet altogether; there was still time. Was he being stubborn by refusing to avoid the Prosecutor? He trusted that God was with him and to stay was his fate. In the future, perhaps, he would go south; maybe Sybille would go too, if the community of Believers and Perfects was growing down there... the time might come... but for now, he knew she would have done her best to help him. And if she hadn't been able to mobilise help for his case tomorrow, she would have found a way to tell him. He knelt to pray for strength to face whatever God had in store for him.

The following morning, he stepped out into the square. There were workshops and houses all squashed close together around the small space. The rich smell of a hog roasting on a spit nearby wafted over to him. A couple of stalls were selling bread and cheese. On the far side of the square was a podium. Behind and beyond the buildings were the ubiquitous mountains, perpetually witnessing the lives of the people who were milling around in the square. These were local people, ordinary working folk. He made his way through the crowd, which was gravitating towards the podium. He suddenly felt suffocated, as he was elbowed and pushed along by the crowd of chattering, laughing people. These people were hoping for a spectacle. God, he hoped he would not be it.

He gave himself a shake. Stop. Stop worrying. He was here to face this now. His height meant he could see above the heads of the people. He looked around wondering where he should be. Two men were arranging tables and benches on the podium. He moved through the crowd towards them. The men were settling themselves at the small table at one side and arranging parchments. He walked up the steps to the podium.

"Yes?" said one of the men as he approached.

"I'm Pedro Maury."

The man unfurled a parchment scroll. His finger traced the writing. "Ah yes, Pedro Maury, you're up first, they'll be here… they're coming…" The parchment furled itself back with a crisp whisper. The other man moved to Pedro's side and took hold of his arm.

"Stand here."

The crowd quietened as three men, dressed in fine brocade tunics, climbed the steps and arranged themselves at the larger table in the centre. Pedro shivered. *God help me… and forgive me…*

He stared at the three men. The one in the middle, who must be the Public Prosecutor, was banging on the table with a small wooden hammer. The crowd's residual movement and murmuring ceased. All eyes were on the men on the podium. The Prosecutor was a short, stout man. He looked familiar as he introduced himself and the proceedings. *Sweet Jesus, it was him…* Maître Girard – the very same Maître Girard who had attended the dinner at the Belibastes' farmhouse. Pedro looked at the men sitting on either side of the Prosecutor, who was now speaking to the crowd, introducing himself and the proceedings to the people. On one side was the Lord of Saint-Paul, Othon de Corbel, and on the other was Arnaud de n'Ayglina, the Bailiff of the town. These were also men he knew. They were drinking acquaintances from the taverns of Saint-Paul-de-Fenouillet. The guard spoke in his ear.

"You're up now."

Pedro walked the few paces with the guard to stand before the three men. They gave no hint of recognition; all three looked serious and severe. *God, help me… give me strength.* The Prosecutor was speaking again. He heard his name.

"Pedro Maury, you have been summoned to appear before me on charges of aiding two heretics. I believe that you, Pedro Maury, were alone in the pastures with your sheep last September, when two heretics came to you by previous arrangement. One was from Cubières, whose surname was Belibaste, and the other was from Coustaussa, named d'Aylarac. These two heretics had escaped from the Wall, the prison of Monsignor, the Inquisitor of Carcassonne, and went to you for food and shelter. You are charged with helping them in this way." He leaned forward in his seat. "What do you say to this charge?"

"Not guilty, my Lord Prosecutor," said Pedro. "I was not there."

The Lord of Saint-Paul, Othon de Corbel, addressed the Prosecutor.

"My Lord Prosecutor, Pedro Maury was in the vineyards with myself and several others at that time. I can confirm that what he says is the truth."

"And I can corroborate this," said Arnaud de n'Ayglina.

Some voices from the crowd joined in: "I was there too"; "I saw him there."

The Public Prosecutor looked around at the crowd and then directly at Pedro. "Pedro Maury," he said, "in that case with these witnesses saying you were elsewhere, I need more time to find out the facts. I will set another day for you to appear here again, Pedro Maury; in the meantime do not leave the County of Foix."

"I will stand surety for him," said Arnaud de n'Ayglina.

Thanks be to God, thought Pedro, for hearing my prayers… for protecting me. God had taken care of him when he needed it. It was not over yet, but he was sure now that the charges against him would be dropped.

He was sent a summons to appear a month later and, during the month of waiting, his confidence began to seep away. As he worked, his thoughts returned to the same subject. Why had Othon and

Arnaud lied for him? Were they Believers themselves or had they been bribed? His previous contacts with them had always been in a group of people in one or other of the local taverns, not a situation where such dangerous topics as the Good Men could be discussed. The fact that they had spoken only at the last minute and not before the Prosecutor opened the proceedings made him think they had recent information about him, which they had acted upon. It was likely that, at the last minute, Sybille had mobilised the network of Believers to help him. In that case, he need not worry. But he did worry as other possibilities came to him. He was still working with Pierre Andre and some of the same shepherds. If any of them came to hear of this, they could testify that he *had* been on the pastures at that time. He needed to invent a story to explain to them what the summons was about. More lies.

He worried too that Othon and Arnaud could change their stories or change their minds about lying for him. Lying was a serious offence. But they had already lied, so that was unlikely, or was it? Or someone other than the shepherds might come forward to say where he was. He thought about the night at the Belibastes' when the Prosecutor was the honoured guest. The Good Men had been there too. Should he now, given this second chance, go to Aragon? He was tying himself in knots with thinking so much, but there was no-one to confide in except Sybille… he wanted to speak with Sybille, but another absence from work for a few days, especially when it was possible that he was being watched by spies, was not a good idea. The shepherds began to ask him if he was ill – he was quiet, preoccupied, not his usual self. He told them he had been charged with starting a fight in one of the taverns at Saint-Paul. But the Bailiff and the Lord had spoken on his behalf, so the case had been postponed. Even though he wasn't guilty, and he was sure the outcome would be good, he couldn't help but worry, he told them. He hated all this lying. The month passed with these concerns alternating with moments of confidence that he had been given another chance, that everything would turn out well. If he was cleared of the charges, this could mean that he was no longer suspected of helping the Good Men, and the Inquisition would no longer be interested in him. If he disappeared to Aragon, he would look guilty. So, he stayed.

Pedro returned to Saint-Paul-de-Fenouillet to appear before the Prosecutor the following month. He stayed the night before in the same lodgings. He had a restless night and a disturbing nightmare in which the Prosecutor had met him at an inn and taken him to a secret place to meet the Good Men, which had turned out to be a prison. He woke in the night sweating and terrified. The same questions plagued him over and over. Had he done the right thing coming back here? Should he have taken this second chance to go to Aragon? He rose early and went out into the square. The morning air smelled fresh. He meandered around looking at all the shops and workshops, which were still closed. The man with the hog roast arrived and began to set up his spit and fire. He nodded to Pedro, who stopped and leant against a house wall. He looked up at the mountains above and behind the buildings. The sun was rising in the cloudless sky. The snow on the mountain tops and crevices had almost disappeared. It would all be gone in the next week or two. He gave thanks to God who had brought him here, guided him to stay and face this. He lingered a while, watching as the square came to life with people opening their shops, bumping into their neighbours, passing the time of day. He roused himself and went back to eat breakfast and pay the woman whose house he had lodged in.

It was time. He had to see this through. The square was busy as he made his way over to the podium feeling calm, trusting in God and his fate. Everything was the same as before. The Prosecutor, flanked by the Lord and Bailiff of the town, went through the formalities. Pedro was called first. The Prosecutor announced that his investigations had led him to discover that it was someone else, not Pedro, who helped the heretics. Then the Prosecutor added a warning: "The whole of the area and Montaillou is full of heretics. This year we will find them all and we will remove them from the county."

A warm rush of relief flooded through him. Thank God. He had trusted in God, prayed to God and God had heard him. He was free! He must go and tell Sybille. It was several leagues to Ax, but he could cover the ground in two days, although most people would need three. He had questions about what her part had been in this. The Prosecutor's words were beginning to sink into his mind. He puzzled over them as he walked the leagues to Ax. Was the Public Prosecutor a Believer himself? Or was he taking the opportunity to profess himself on the side of the Inquisition, as a cover? Was he giving Pedro a personal warning? Whatever it was, he had let him go and Pedro had no wish to stir anything up. It was a close brush with the Inquisition, but God had protected him.

He found Sybille in a quiet house again with no visitors expected for a day or so. She whisked him indoors, delighted to see him.

"It's so good to be here," he said, blinking away tears as he hugged her.

"I trust all went well," she said as they mounted the stairs. She led him to her bedroom.

"Yes, yes, yes," he said. He picked her up and swung her round. "Dear Sybille, how I love you." He pulled her towards him, feeling he couldn't get enough of her; he would never let her go. He removed her head-dress and put his hands under her kirtle. Her skin was soft and warm, and the scent of her enticed him as he pulled off each item of her clothing. She helped him tug off his own clothes. He sat on the bed and he tugged at his boots. She grabbed each boot in turn, pulled them off and collapsed beside him, laughing. They lay side by side, caressing each other's bodies, gradually slowing their movements and fondling each other gently. She moved onto her back and parted her legs for him. He gently pushed inside her. They moved together. Afterwards, Sybille lay with her head on his chest, his arm around her body.

"I'm so happy to be free," he said. "God protected me."

"Tell me what happened."

He told her the story and asked her what she had done to help him.

"I just put the word out," she said. "It's best I say no more."

He nodded and kissed her. "I'm hungry, have you got anything to eat?"

"Of course." She laughed.

Later they sat together in the living room, eating lamb with vegetables.

"It's good to eat meat," she said. "I eat so much fish here with the Perfects."

"These are excellent chops." He finished his mouthful, took a sip of wine and told her what the Prosecutor had said at the end. "Do you think he's a Believer?"

"He could be; if so, he's covering himself and maybe giving you a warning. They knew about you, and Guy and Philippe. They knew who to arrest, didn't they? Someone talked. They have methods… and they have spies." She looked at Pedro, her face drawn and worried-looking.

"You know they took my sister, Guillemette," said Pedro. "When they arrested Guy and Philippe. I don't know what's happened to her. She's probably in the Wall."

"I haven't heard any news about her."

"She was separated from Philippe and Guy."

"I'll ask my contacts again, see if I can find any news of her," said Sybille.

"I don't suppose there'll be much help to get her out; she's not as important as Philippe and Guy. Poor Guillemette, she's had a terrible time with a husband who beat her, and now she's been arrested. She's so young, Sybille, and she's done nothing wrong. Why isn't God protecting her?"

"The Believers will get her out if they can," she said. It sounded hollow and they both knew that Guillemette was probably lost.

"I should have been able to protect her," he said. "I haven't told my parents she was taken. Perhaps I should have done, then maybe someone from Montaillou could have helped."

"You did what you thought was for the best; don't give up hope."

"I'll keep praying – that's all I can do."

"I have some good news," she said. "Guy and Philippe have arrived safely in Aragon. I'm not sure where they are."

"They wanted me to go with them. I'm glad they're safe, but I'm not ready to leave," he said. "There is still work to do here. And I won't leave you."

"I shall never leave," she said. "But you should think about it."

In late September of 1308, Pedro was up on the high pastures when Martin Fort, a shepherd from Montaillou who was a Believer, came up with flour and other supplies for the shepherds. He followed Pedro into the storeroom and, making sure the other shepherds were busy mending fences, began speaking quietly, telling Pedro that earlier in the month, on the day of the Nativity of the Blessed Virgin Mary, all the men and women of Montaillou aged fourteen and over had been arrested for heresy.

"What?" said Pedro. "Everyone? Are you sure?"

"That's what I heard," said Martin. "The soldiers came on horseback led by Jacques de Polignac, the Master of the Wall. Pierre Clergue, the priest, met them. It seems he was expecting them. He took them around the village and showed them the Cathar houses."

"Pierre Clergue – he was supposed to be their protector. It doesn't make any sense," said Pedro. "But if this is true, this means my family, my parents, my brothers… they will all have been arrested."

"Some were questioned and let go there and then," said Martin. "Some were given dates to attend at Carcassonne for interrogation and some were detained in the dungeon of the château. I don't know any more details except that Pierre Clergue helped Jacques de Polignac by taking him to the homes of Cathars, despite not long ago openly entertaining Pierre Authier at his home and everyone knowing his father was consoled by a Perfect before he died."

"But why? Why would he do that?" said Pedro. "Unless… of course, it was to save himself."

"That's what they're saying – that he had to change sides or be arrested himself on charges of heresy. He betrayed everyone in Montaillou." Martin Fort looked hard at Pedro. "They're closing in; I'd leave this place if I were you."

"I think interrogating the people of Montaillou will keep them busy; they won't be making any more arrests for a while," said Pedro.

"You aren't afraid that now they've started making arrests, they'll soon be making more? Don't you realise that those people they've arrested will talk about you?" said Martin, shaking his head. "I'm leaving the area – I've family in the south. You really should be careful, Pedro."

The thought of his parents being flung into a cell was unbearable. Even the walk to Carcassonne would have been an extreme hardship for them. They were growing older; how would they withstand the harsh conditions in the Wall? The place had a terrible reputation. Prisoners could be chained and on bread and water rations… it was said there were instruments of torture in the dungeons… it was a filthy, vermin-infested hell hole.

"I must find out what's happened," said Pedro. "I'll go to Montaillou."

"Don't do that, you'll be playing right into the hands of the Inquisition."

"You're right. I'll go to my brother, Jean, in Rasiguères. He may know more."

What had happened to the rest of his family, his brothers and sister – were any of them at home with their parents when the Inquisition came? And Arnaud, his youngest brother, who was only fourteen, was he captured or let go? Pedro told one of the shepherds to tell their employer that he had to leave on urgent family business.

Rasiguères was only a short distance from Planèze, and he was there in less than half an hour. The farmer said Jean had left for Montaillou the day before. He was expected back soon. The farmer and his wife were kind and told Pedro he could stay in their barn if he needed to. He thought it best not to mention what had happened in Montaillou. Pedro made himself useful about the farm, cleaning the sheep pen whilst he waited. Images of his parents being arrested and dragged away kept coming into his mind. And of the Wall itself, a huge stone fortress with hundreds of cells where people were kept indefinitely… and usually died of starvation and disease… He tried to concentrate on the task in hand, but those images would disappear only to return later. He was greatly relieved when Jean arrived later that day with their youngest brother Arnaud. Pedro embraced them both. They were sad and quiet.

"I'm so relieved to see you both," he said.

"Arnaud," said Jean. "Go up to the farmhouse and ask for some bread and water."

Arnaud wandered off reluctantly. Pedro watched him go; his slight boyish figure looked so vulnerable. It must have been terrifying for him to witness his parents being arrested with the other villagers.

"Poor Arnie," said Jean. "He saw our parents arrested and taken to Carcassonne; he was alone in the house when I arrived not knowing what to do. No-one else was at home when the soldiers came, and they left him there by himself. We must leave here, Pedro, and take Arnie away with us. Montaillou was desolate, so many people taken – others kept in the dungeon of the château – and the soldiers torched Guillaume Fort's house." He shook his head; there were tears in his eyes. "All betrayed by Pierre Clergue."

"We should do something," said Pedro.

"There is nothing we can do," said Jean.

"There must be something," said Pedro. "We must find a way to get them out of the Wall, along with Guillemette. We should speak to a Perfect—"

"Pedro," Jean sighed. "We know no-one on the inside of the prison; we have no way of influencing anyone there. If we try to do anything, we may make matters worse. We must have faith in God and faith that others will work on our behalf. The best thing we can do is to go away from here and take Arnie with us," said Jean. "I spoke to some of those left behind in Montaillou. Some are going to Aragon. I heard that Aunt Gaillarde and Aunt Mersende are selling up in Ax and going to Aragon. I think we should get away from here too. There's a stockbreeder in Puigcerdà; the Maurs brothers told me before about someone they worked for previously. It's very remote, high up in the mountains. We should go, Pedro, and take Arnie with us – we can look after him there." He put his arm on Pedro's. "Our parents will be questioned and released, I'm sure. The Inquisition will want information about the Perfects from them – that's who they're really after."

Pedro nodded reluctantly. Jean was right: there was nothing they could do; any intervention from them could cause more trouble. They must look after Arnie and leave others to work for their parents' release. Jean wanted to leave urgently, but Pedro wanted to postpone their departure for a couple of days. He wanted to speak to Sybille. She may have further information and… he was not sure about going to Puigcerdà … he must talk to Sybille before he decided. Jean was reluctant to delay their journey but agreed that the Inquisition had plenty to keep them occupied with the people they had taken for questioning. A couple of days wouldn't make any difference. If Pedro left immediately, he could walk through the night and arrive the next morning. He could stay the following night at Sybille's, catch up with sleep and return the day after. Jean agreed to wait for him.

His mind was in turmoil as he walked. Images of his parents, of his brother Arnaud and of Guillaume Fort's house burning plagued him as he journeyed. And what to do next? Those Believers left free should surely work to help those who had been taken by the Inquisition. But then if he was a marked man, wanted by the Inquisition, he would have to spend his life ducking and diving, trying to stay safe. He hoped to persuade Sybille to flee south with him. But she would want to stay; she would never leave her home unless forced to. Perhaps Jean was right: he should go with Jean and Arnaud, somewhere out of the way until this latest wave of persecution had blown over. Talking with Sybille would help him decide the best way forward.

But when he arrived at Ax, he found the town centre in chaos. There were crowds of people everywhere. He looked over the heads of the crowd as he elbowed his way through towards the lane that led to Sybille's house. There were two soldiers blocking the lane. He heard the soldiers' shouts as people were trying to pass them.

"What's your business here? Do you live here? Where do you live? Go home. You can't enter here." A cold stone of fear sank his heart. He turned to the man next to him.

"What's happening?"

"They've arrested a woman for heresy."

"Which woman?" The man looked at him, puzzled. The words had stuck to the side of Pedro's mouth – he had to lick his lips, clear his throat and repeat them.

"Oh, Sybille Sicre, I heard," said the man.

Sybille Sicre. Sybille Baille. He must find another way in. He pushed his way through the crowd. Up the street and round a corner there was another entrance to Sybille's lane. He saw immediately that this place was also guarded by two soldiers. Wasn't there a path to Sybille's around the back of all these buildings? One that not many knew about? He pushed through, round the corner, round another corner. There were fewer people in this part of town, but there were two more soldiers guarding the narrow alleyway to Sybille's house. He approached the soldiers.

"What's happening?"

"A heretic woman has been arrested," said one of the soldiers. "What's your business?"

"Where have they taken her?"

"To Carcassonne, to the Wall, I expect." The soldier stared at Pedro. "Did you know her?"

Pedro backed away. He must be careful. He turned and ran back towards the crowd, where he pushed his way to the middle of the mass of people. He heard someone shout.

"Show's over, go home!"

The crowd began to thin and disperse. He set off running. He ran around the centre, but as the crowd thinned, he noticed people were staring at him. What was he doing? Where was he going? He stopped. He hadn't gone far; he was at the thermal pool. He sat on the stone wall edging the pool. He must not draw attention to himself. It would not help Sybille if he was arrested. The best thing was to leave. That was all he knew. The state of numbness he was in meant he could neither think nor feel. He walked until it was dark, when he found a secluded spot under a hedge and slept for a few hours.

The next morning, he woke feeling hungry and thirsty. He stopped in the nearest village where a few women were gathered at the water pump – he drank and asked where he could find food. A woman offered to give him some bread and cheese, which he devoured sitting on a low wall near her house. He must return to Rasiguères.

He arrived late at night and went into the barn where he found Jean and Arnaud sleeping. He moved carefully so as not to wake them. He made himself comfortable on the hay and slept. When he woke, Jean and Arnaud were still sleeping. He went outside to wait for them to wake. The sun rose over the mountains in the distance. It was a fine day; they would make good progress. It was the only thing to do now.

He said little to Jean and Arnaud, except to explain that the person he wanted to see was no longer there. He was very aware of Arnaud having been through enough. He did not want to worry or frighten him further. They had a difficult journey ahead of them and they needed to concentrate on that. He prayed for strength to get through this journey, although there was a seed of doubt in his mind. Did praying help? He thought not. It seemed as if everything happened in a random fashion; there was no sense to it. He could not think any more about anything. He still felt numb.

It took four days of hard walking, climbing and scrambling at times over the mountains. Pedro left Jean to take charge of the journey, finding shepherd's huts and barns for them to sleep in, asking for milk, bread and cheese off the shepherds and farmers they met in the valleys. At the end of the fourth day, they reached Puigcerdà, high up in the mountains, where Jean had a contact. Jean had been told where to go and they found the entrance of what looked to be a large estate.

"This could be it," said Jean, as a man appeared from the small gatehouse. Jean whispered to Arnaud, "I want you to keep quiet, Arnie, let me and Pedro do the talking."

"Good evening," said the man, casting his eyes over them. "Can I help you?"

The man wore a brown tunic, made of high-quality wool cloth, and he looked neat and clean, with his small beard and short dark hair.

"Good evening," said Jean. "We're looking for Raymond Boursier, the steward of the Lady Brunissende de Cervello."

"Well, you've found him." He looked at them with a relaxed and friendly smile. "What do you want with me?"

"I've been given your name by Martin Maurs from Montaillou – we're shepherds looking for work," said Jean.

"Ah yes, Martin Maurs," he said. "He's a good shepherd." He looked at Arnaud. "Is he a shepherd?"

"He's our younger brother and we've brought him with us because our parents have died," said Jean. "He can work; he's a strong young man."

Arnaud turned his head sharply to look at Jean when he heard this, but he kept quiet. Raymond Boursier looked Arnaud up and down.

"I can employ you two, and I will employ him too if he proves his worth. I'll take you up to meet the Lady; she likes to meet everyone who works here."

They walked up the track and as they rounded a bend a château came into view. It was built on the plateau of a hill and was partly hidden by trees. Pedro caught a glimpse of barns and other farm buildings behind the château. They approached an archway which led into a courtyard. A tall, slim woman came out of the great high doors leading into the château. She was wearing a plain kirtle with a tabard over it. Her long black hair was tied back; she wore no head-dress. She smiled at them and came over.

"We have visitors, I see, Raymond," she said. Her voice was deep and melodious, and when she looked at him, Pedro noticed that her eyes were large and very dark. Her Roman nose and high cheekbones were strong and aristocratic-looking. Pedro realised he was staring at her. He dragged his eyes away, embarrassed.

"Yes, my Lady, they've been sent here by Martin Maurs, a shepherd who has worked here in the past. As we need some extra hands now, I've taken them on," said Raymond.

So, this was the Lady Brunissende, not quite what he expected but he liked the look of her. After Raymond had introduced them to her, he took them to one of the barns where they were to sleep with the other shepherds and farmworkers. The Lady Brunissende de Cervello, who the steward told them was a widow, was the owner of this estate. Raymond told them she liked to work with her animals and alongside her workers on the land. It was a beautiful spot, high up in the mountains. It was remote from the Carcassonne Inquisition, and Montaillou. It seemed a good place to stay and work for a while.

CHAPTER 13

Guy Belibaste

Guy and Philippe watched Pedro walk away as they stood at the top of the riverbank.

"I wonder when we'll see him again," said Philippe.

"He should have come with us," said Guy. "It's too dangerous for him here."

"He must do what he feels is right," said Philippe. "But it is difficult to leave him behind especially with that terrible news about Guillemette. I wish we could have told him some other way, some other time."

"We could have done with him to help us on this journey; he knows these mountain passes. I'm going to have to take it slowly, I'm very tired, and you're injured; he would have been very useful to us," said Guy.

"We will take it slowly, Guy. Don't worry, there's no rush. To reach the boundary up in the mountains could take us twice as long as usual, four, five or even six days, but what does it matter?"

"It will not be an easy walk over the Albères Mountains," said Guy. "And the weather will be against us up there, and as long as we're on this side of the border we're vulnerable."

"So, the sooner we start, the better... we must cross this river first."

They clambered down the riverbank and forded the river. The water was low, barely a trickle at that time of year, before the late autumn rains. They were still dry when they reached the other side. They orientated themselves by the sun as it rose in the east. Their journey would take them in a south-easterly direction towards the mountain passes. The first part of the journey was flat enough to be easy walking, but there were a few villages, hamlets and farmsteads with people in them and around them, none of whom they should trust.

"We're going to have to balance being near villages and settlements so we can find food and shelter, and trying to avoid people who may ask questions," said Philippe.

"We should travel at night as far as possible to avoid being seen," said Guy.

"And the sun is still hot in the afternoon; we'd do well to avoid that."

They plodded on through the bleached and scrubby countryside. The sun rose in a cobalt sky and, after a couple of hours' walking, they sought shade under a sweet chestnut tree at the side of the road. They drank from a clear rushing stream. Both men closed their eyes and rested. Guy suddenly awoke with a shout from a dream, a donkey clip-clopping towards him with a sinister-looking man dressed in black with a hood over his head.

"What it is?" said Philippe, jerked alert by Guy's shout.

Guy pointed. An old man dressed in shabby clothes and leading a donkey stood before them on the track. "I think I disturbed you, I'm sorry for that," he said. "Are you in trouble? That's a nasty wound on your face. How did that happen?"

"We're avoiding the sun for a little while."

"Where are you going?"

"We're off to visit some relatives in Aragon; we've quite a long journey ahead of us," said Guy.

"Did you have an accident?" said the man.

"Well…" said Philippe.

"Yes, he was in an accident," said Guy.

"Really?" said the man. "What kind of accident?"

"I think we need to get going again, Guy," said Philippe.

"Is there anything I can help you with?" said the man.

"No, we've got everything we need," said Guy as he and Philippe struggled to get to their feet.

"Perhaps new knees would help," Philippe said. They all laughed.

Thankfully, the man was going in the opposite direction to the one they were taking. He stood and watched them as they shambled away from him.

"That was difficult," said Philippe as they moved out of sight and earshot of the man. "We're going to have to invent new names and stories for ourselves. We'll be compelled to ask for help with food and shelter. And whoever we meet will want to know who we are, where we've come from, where we're going and why."

"And how you became injured," said Guy.

"Quite," said Philippe.

"That man must have heard you call me Guy," said Guy. "So, from now on I'm Pierre and you're Bernard. That's one problem solved. We just need to remember."

"And we must give no hint of our meat- and cheese-free diet."

"Let's stick to the visiting relatives story," said Guy. "And why are we visiting relatives? And what kind of accident caused the wound on your face?"

"Hmm," said Philippe. "We must pray for forgiveness too."

For the next three days and nights, they walked over the plains and river valleys until they reached the ascent into the mountains. On and on, sometimes trudging through mud and rain, their progress was even slower than they had anticipated. They rested at midday and during the afternoon in dry spots under hedges and trees, then journeyed again in the evening and into the darkness of the night until they were exhausted, when they slept until early morning.

They stayed in barns and sheds, sleeping on hay and straw accompanied by cats and rats, stray chickens, and dogs. They gratefully took the offers of the bread and vegetables they were given; they received meat and cheese with good grace only to dispose of it later. They avoided any talk of the raid on Montaillou, even between themselves, although by then it had been broadcast widely, and one or two of the shepherds they met had heard and wanted to indulge in gossip about it. Philippe and Guy faked no knowledge of it and changed the subject. They perfected their stories, which answered all the questions the farmers and their wives wanted to ask.

It was a great relief to reach the mountains, although their progress became even slower. The air was cooler, and the gentle rain of the plains turned into torrents. There were fewer people to ask questions, but fewer to help with food and shelter. When they finally reached the summit in the mountains, where they believed they would leave behind the County of Foix and cross the border into the region of Catalonia in the Kingdom of Aragon, it was a moment of pure joy. They stopped and embraced each another.

"No more looking over our shoulders," said Guy.

"We've managed it," said Philippe. "But we must still be vigilant – there could be spies on this side too."

"And walking downhill is bad for my knees," said Guy. "I will be glad when we reach Torroella."

"Now we've crossed the border, we can rest and recover our strength for a few days in Torroella," said Philippe.

"We need new clothes too; these stink."

Pierre Montanier had advised them to go first to Torroella, a stopping-off place for Cathars leaving the County of Foix. There was a discreet hostelry there, where no questions were asked and where people were looked after well. When they arrived in Torroella, they found the hostel easily. It was tucked away in a backstreet and it seemed safe as a temporary refuge. They had enough money to stay there for a few weeks to recuperate after their ordeal. It had everything they could need. It was clean and the innkeeper was pleasant but asked no questions. It was good to sleep in the same bed each night, to eat at the same table at regular mealtimes and to walk the same streets every day. After two weeks of rest, good food and gentler weather, Philippe was feeling stronger.

"I'm feeling lucky to have survived this," said Philippe. "My injuries, that time spent hiding behind the waterfall and the walk over the mountains could have seen the end of me. I think God has saved me for a purpose."

"I believe you're right," said Guy. "God will reveal his purpose to us soon enough, I'm sure."

The innkeeper told them one evening that two new people had arrived. "They're very tired so they've gone to bed early. Two women – they have the same accent as you."

"What are their names?" said Guy.

"I didn't ask," said the innkeeper.

"Of course," said Philippe, flashing Guy a disapproving look.

Philippe and Guy went downstairs the next morning, curious as to who these newcomers were. As they entered the room, they saw two women sitting at the table eating bread and eggs. They had a strong resemblance to each other. Both were of slim build and in their late twenties. They were attractive with even features, although the older one had strong features and the younger had a softer, rounder look to her. They both looked up when Philippe and Guy entered the room, and their faces broke into warm smiles, revealing well-preserved teeth. The women turned to each other and started to speak at the same time as Philippe spoke. They all broke into laughter. Philippe and the older-looking woman moved together and embraced. She knelt before him.

"Bless us, Good Christians."

"God's blessing and ours," said Philippe. Both women knelt

to perform the *melioramentum*. Philippe turned to Guy, who was watching with surprise.

"This is Blanche and Mondine Marty from Junac," he said. "And this is Guy Belibaste, also a Perfect." As the women stood up, Philippe kissed each of them.

"This is God's gift to us, you're Heaven sent," said Blanche, the older of the two.

"This is *good*," said Mondine. "In every way."

"Let's all sit together and eat; I'll bless the bread," said Philippe.

He lifted the cloth off the bread, draped it over his shoulder and blessed it. They all sat down and ate breakfast.

"So, you're from Junac?" said Guy, as he helped himself to bread.

"I've stayed at their father's house many times," said Philippe. "Their family supported Guillaume and Pierre Authier whilst they were in Lombardy and when they came back. By the way," Philippe looked around and lowered his voice, "I'm Bernard and this is Pierre to the innkeeper and people hereabouts, just first names here."

Guy had heard of this family. They were a prosperous family of farmers. They were well known in the community of Believers. But there was much to catch up on. The family were no longer prospering. Their mother Fabrisse, and their eldest sister, Bonnefemme, died some time ago; both were consoled by Guillaume Authier. Their father died more recently and their brother, Arnaud, was ordained as a Perfect, only to be captured soon after and burned at the stake. Their property had been confiscated by the Inquisition. Mondine's husband had also been taken and imprisoned in the Wall. He hadn't been heard of since and they think perhaps he had died. Blanche had also been taken for questioning, an ordeal after which they had left to come south. Mondine had not been summoned.

"So many losses," said Philippe, as they listened to their story. "It's so hard to bear, and then to come down here to start again – this is no easy thing."

"There wasn't much choice," said Blanche. "I was summoned

by the Inquisition and interrogated by Geoffroy d'Ablis, but I soon realised he was not very clever." She laughed. "So, I played him for a fool."

"What do you mean?" said Philippe.

"I was terrified at first with my family being such prominent Cathars. I thought my time had come and that I would end up in the Wall, or worse. But I had thought a lot about how I might play the situation so I could escape sentencing. I knew I must pretend not to know anything about my family being Cathars, and I thought I could do that by pretending to be a bit slow," said Blanche. She touched her head. "You know, not all there, and I put on this voice and spoke like a child." Blanche demonstrated her voice, which sounded like a young girl. She made them laugh. "So I spoke like this, in this voice, and said I wanted to confess my terrible sins and begged for mercy – as I said that, I threw myself on the floor and grabbed him round his legs. He said in a gentle voice that I mustn't be afraid – I said I had done something terrible that he would have to punish me for, and when he asked me what it was, I said I hadn't gone to church for three Sundays in a row and I listened to someone who said the sacrament at the altar wasn't the body and blood of Christ. I pretended to weep and clung on to his legs begging for mercy. He patted me gently and said, 'My child, there is no need to fear me, I won't harm you; for that sin you need only say some prayers and you will be absolved.' And so it went on, every time he asked me a question, I answered in the same manner and he treated me with great care. In the end, he let me go with just a few penances for the terrible sins I had committed. I didn't tell him anything of what I know or the real sins I had committed."

As soon as she arrived home, Blanche said she and Mondine decided to leave for Aragon to avoid Mondine being questioned.

How wonderful to laugh with Blanche and Mondine. What a relief to be able to relax with people who believed in the same forbidden faith. Mondine had heard this story before and would hear it again many more times, but she would always laugh. It became a favourite tale to recount whenever a few of the Believers were gathered; it always uplifted everyone's spirits. When they had recovered from laughing, Blanche told them that as they were leaving, they heard that ten members of the Authier family had died, some in prison, but Pierre, Guillaume and Jacques Authier had been burned alive, one by one. Pierre Authier was the last one; he was burned at Toulouse. Some of the other Perfects had died in prison. Their own brother was one of them. It had all happened so quickly. They thought there were no more left alive.

"We only just got out in time, Philippe," said Guy.

"We may have to return; we may be needed," said Philippe. "And I will go if I'm needed." They all looked at him. "If there's no-one else, and if as you say there are no Perfects left now in the County of Foix, then we're all here in the south, Raymond de Toulouse, Guy and myself."

"I think that must be so," said Blanche quietly. They sat in silence for a long moment until Blanche spoke. "But the exiles here will need you; there are enough Believers here to keep the faith alive and they need Perfects."

"Guy can stay here. I will go wherever God sends me," said Philippe.

"We'll worry about that when the time comes," said Guy. "*If* the time comes – anyway, where will you go next?" He looked at Blanche and Mondine. "Have you any contacts down here?"

"We'll go first to Lleida where the Servels are living. We know them of old; they are a family of Believers who provide shelter for others coming south, who have... who have also left everything behind," said Mondine. Her voice shook and tears rolled down her cheeks.

Guy put his hand on her arm. "It's very hard," he said. "For anyone to leave so much behind, family, home, possessions – and then to have to find the strength to start again, it takes a lot of courage. I know.

And the journey is long and tough; you have done very well to survive all of that. We must pray to God to give us the strength we need to continue on our pathway, which we believe is the right pathway, and we must trust in God and never lose our faith."

Mondine nodded and wiped her eyes with her hands. Guy leant towards her and put his arm round her shoulder. She leant into him. He noticed the musky feminine scent of her and felt the warmth of her small body. He gave her shoulder a little squeeze. She looked up at him and smiled.

"I heard that Raymond Issaurat and Bérenger Servel took off their tunics with the yellow crosses on them when they crossed over the border. Raymond flung his over a bush and Bérenger hid his behind a rock," said Blanche with a laugh.

"It's a good feeling to cross the border to safety," said Philippe.

"Where will you go next?" said Mondine.

"We must find work soon – so wherever there is a chance of that," said Philippe. "And to wherever we are needed."

A few days later, Guy and Philippe received a visitor. It was Jean Maury, Pedro's brother. Jean's face was drawn and serious. He asked Philippe to walk out with him as there was something he wished to discuss. When they returned, Philippe asked Jean to wait whilst he went to fetch Blanche, Mondine and Guy. They all sat around the table. The mood was sombre after the friendly greetings. Philippe glanced at Jean.

"I shall come straight to the point," said Philippe. "Jean here has been asked to find a Perfect for a man who lives in the Donezan area, just north of Cerdagne. This man believes he is dying and wishes to receive the *consolamentum*. So, as there are no Perfects there, Jean came to find me."

"I asked the Believers in Montaillou; they said this was the first place to look and where I may find a Perfect…" said Jean. His words tailed off as he looked at them all.

"Raymond de Toulouse is somewhere in Aragon too, but we

don't know where he is," said Philippe. "So, I shall go. Jean will guide me." He cleared his throat.

Blanche, Mondine and Guy looked from one to the other.

"You can't go," said Guy. "It's too dangerous." His voice sounded as if someone had grabbed him by the throat.

"God has called me," said Philippe. "And I must go; I have been expecting this."

"Surely it can wait until things are more settled," said Blanche.

"Blanche, you know as well as I do that these things cannot wait," said Philippe. "It's no use any of you trying to persuade me otherwise: I'm going. We shall leave tomorrow at first light. I think you, Guy, should go with Blanche and Mondine to the Servels in Lleida. When I return, I shall come and find you there."

Guy sat there helpless and terrified. Hot tears sprang into his eyes. Philippe must not go; he must stop him. How would he manage without Philippe? He looked at Philippe. He saw the determination and resignation in his face and knew that Philippe would go, and that he could not stop him, but he couldn't resist another attempt. He was terrified of what could happen to Philippe and terrified of being left alone.

"Philippe," he said, but a sob rose from deep in his chest and stopped him from speaking. Guy took a deep breath and brushed away the tears from his cheeks. "I see you are set on going, so I'll not try to persuade you to stay; instead I will pray for you constantly, and, as you are doing God's work, He will protect you." Another deep breath. "There is just one thing I ask of you… as you are going… and if you can find a way… I would be grateful if you could send a message to my wife and children, tell them to come down here and find me. I want to teach my son the ways of the Good Men."

Mondine, sitting next to him, patted his arm.

"I'll do my best," said Philippe.

CHAPTER 14

Pedro Maury

When Pedro and his brothers began working in Puigcerdà, they had thought of it as a temporary arrangement, and for Jean and Arnaud it was. After a few weeks, they both felt it was safe enough for them to return home to Montaillou. Jean came back to Puigcerdà on occasions and worked as a shepherd, but Arnaud stayed on in Montaillou. He had been learning to weave at his father's side for the previous year and he wanted to continue weaving. His brother Grégoire was in Montaillou, also working as a weaver. Their sister Raymonde had married and moved away, as had his brother, Guillaume. But as the time passed for Pedro and he was still in Puigcerdà, one year, two years, he knew it was unlikely he would go back to his old life in the Fenouillèdes. During this time, his grief for Sybille occupied his thoughts and feelings every day. Some days more than others. At times, his pain was so profound it felt unbearable. But as he faced it and experienced the hurt, it slowly strengthened him. He worked long hours as that too gave him respite from his grief. He could lose himself as he worked with the animals, so alive and warm, their simple faces, the feel of their woolly coats, their need to be looked after, the routine of their daily lives – it gave purpose and meaning to his life, which seemed at times so trivial and pointless compared to these terrible losses.

He was governed, as always, by the seasonal movement of the sheep. In the autumn he took the sheep south into the pastures at Flix, near Tortosa, in the Kingdom of Aragon, where they spent the winter. At Easter, they returned north to the mountain pastures for the summer. He was head of many shepherds who kept hundreds of sheep in one great flock. They were comrades sharing the work, managing the animals and their communal life. They worked together, they cooked together, they ate together and they went to sleep together. There was a rhythm to their shared existence, with lambing at Christmas and in the new year, shearing in spring, and cheese-making, when the lambs were weaned, in May. Shepherds came and went, his brother Jean, the Maurs brothers from Montaillou, and the other villages of the Sabarthès, as well as local men and the occasional Saracen.

The heresy was rarely spoken of and it was only through the visits of shepherds from Montaillou that Pedro heard news of events in the County of Foix. The news was often sad. His mother died in the Wall. He was filled with grief again. He thought of her life and death. She had always been a loving mother despite the many struggles in her life: too many children, too much work, too little money – and to die in such a terrible place, when she could have had a few years of reprieve, perhaps with one of his sisters looking after her during her last years. It seemed so unfair, so wrong. He raged against God and questioned his faith again and again. Who could be so cruel as to allow this to happen to his mother, who had never done anyone harm? Why did God play with people like this? It occurred to him that perhaps there was no God. It was the only way he could make any sense of anything.

Their father had been allowed home after two years in the Wall, and although Pedro longed to see him, he knew it would be unsafe.

He would probably never see his father again; not many survived the Wall without bearing the scars of imprisonment, poor diet and lack of fresh air and exercise, and the loss of loved ones. His father deserved to have been looked after in his later years by his children too: to work less, to enjoy his grandchildren and to die when God sent for him. Those questions again – is this what God wants? Or is this life and what happens in it is merely random? Or does God play with us, and we just take our chances alongside everyone else? That seemed a reasonable way of thinking about it.

When Jean returned to Puigcerdà, he brought the expected bad news. Their father had been broken by his stay in the Wall, and Jean said, sadly, that he did not have long on this earth. Arnaud and Grégoire were looking after him well. Jean brought many tales of the suffering of the people of Montaillou, of incarceration, of health ruined and of death. Several families had been destroyed as their family members were arrested and kept in prison. Some had had their property confiscated, their houses and land taken. Many had died in the Wall. Only the Clergues, by living, it would seem, without morals or conscience, changing from Catholic to Cathar and back again whenever there was danger from one or the other, seemed to manage to keep themselves safe. They were calling Pierre Clergue the little bishop now, Jean said. He did whatever he wished, he slept with whichever woman he desired and he took whatever else he wanted.

Pedro was desolate when he heard that the Authier brothers had been burned alive. The wise old Good Men had gone. What terrible wrongs had been perpetrated in the name of God. The arrests of other Perfects followed, one after another. Prades Tavernier, Amiel de Perles, Arnaud Marty, Raymond Faure, Martin Frances, all arrested, interrogated, imprisoned and burned alive.

During these years, Pedro grew to know and respect the Lady Brunissende. Although a wealthy and aristocratic lady with her own farm and livestock, she treated everyone with respect, down to the lowliest peasant. She worked on the farm herself and knew all her animals. There developed a closeness, a warmth of feeling, between her and Pedro. They were comfortable with each other. She regularly invited him to eat at her table, and it was a refreshing change for him away from all the sad news. She was kind and tolerant with him during this time, even though he could only tell her a small part of what the matter was with him. She was warm and attractive too with her black hair and eyes. He had the same feeling of being at home with her that he had had with Sybille, and over time they became close friends. She welcomed him into her life, her home and her bed. Their shared passion and interest was their work and their animals. Pedro never spoke of the heresy with her; he didn't want to incriminate her, although he suspected she guessed more than she said. That's how it had to be.

They heard sad news of the Martys, a family from Junac, who were prominent Cathars. Their family had been broken and split up. Their father was said to have died naturally of old age, but there was a rumour going round that he was murdered by the Inquisition. One of the sons, Arnaud, was a Perfect and he had been burned alive. Their two daughters, Blanche and Mondine Marty, had fled to Aragon and were thought to be staying with the Servel family in Lleida, who welcomed displaced people from the County of Foix. Philippe d'Aylarac had returned to the County of Foix to perform a *consolamentum*. He had been arrested and burned alive. It was hard to accept that Philippe – kind, patient Philippe – was dead. He was angry with Philippe for putting himself in danger like that. But that was Philippe; he would do that, risk his own life for others. His beliefs were so strong; they came above everything else. Pedro became preoccupied with thoughts of Philippe and Guy – where was Guy now? And how would he manage without Philippe? Philippe was always the stronger of the two. Would Guy stay on the right pathway without him, and would he keep his Perfect's vows? Without Philippe to support and guide him, Guy would not find his Perfect's life easy. Jean had heard that Guy may be with Blanche and Mondine Marty somewhere in Aragon. Pedro thought about Guillemette, his little sister of whom he had had no news. Was she alive or dead? Or was she still in the Wall? He thought of his parents, broken by all of this, and wondered, again and again, had it all been worth it? Was this what God wanted? Was there a God? And how would any of them know?

By 1312, Guy and Raymond de Toulouse were thought to be the only Perfects left. Pedro heard that both were in Aragon, moving around to keep safe and finding work where they could. Guy was not skilled at any job, so finding work and staying hidden would not be so easy for him. He hoped that Guy had found friends amongst the Believers who lived in the south.

In January 1313, Pedro was on the pastures in the valley outside of the village of Flix, where he was spending the winter with the sheep. One afternoon as he leant on the fence surrounding the sheep pen, checking a couple of ewes that were due to lamb, a shepherd arrived. He came to tell Pedro that he had met a man of Pedro's kinship in the centre of Flix, and that this man wished to see Pedro. The man had not given his name but had said he would wait for Pedro on the riverbank in Flix the following day. This must be Guy. After all this time, it would be good to see him again.

The next morning dawned cold and crisp; a watery sun hung in the ice blue sky. Huge birds of prey circled above him, and Pedro held his cloak tightly around him as he made the short walk to the centre of Flix, a small, quiet village. All was taken care of on the pastures below him; many of the ewes were in the barn waiting for their lambs. Some had already given birth. He walked briskly through the pasture, up the hillside and along the track into the village. The river flowed on the opposite side of the village. He made his way down through the quietness to the riverbank. He saw immediately the lone figure of a man walking there. There was no-one else about. The man waved. As Pedro drew closer, he looked carefully; this wasn't Guy, but there was something familiar about him, his pleasant, open face and gentle manner as they moved towards each other. The man was carrying a bag. He came up to Pedro.

"Are you Pedro Maury?" he said.

"Who are you?" said Pedro.

"Do you know Pierre Belibaste?"

"No," said Pedro. "I know of no Pierre Belibaste."

"There is a Pierre Belibaste in Tortosa, who knows you and who is looking for you; he has sent me to find you."

"I know of no Pierre Belibaste, but I know the brothers, Bernard, Raymond and Guy Belibaste, and their father, Guillaume – at least I did know them; I went to their home in Cubières, but I have not seen any of them for a long time," said Pedro.

"Ah, then I must tell you that Guy Belibaste sometimes calls himself Pierre since he came to Aragon."

"I see," said Pedro cautiously. "And who are you?"

"My name is Raymond de Toulouse," he said, "and I give you God's blessing and mine."

"Ah yes, I remember now..." said Pedro. "I accompanied you and Philippe d'Aylarac one time..." Pedro was about to perform the *melioramentum* when Raymond put up his hand.

"We must be careful and find somewhere more private – you never know who's watching," he said. "I'm working as a pedlar selling combs and small household articles." He patted his bag. "I remember you too, although it's been quite some time."

"Of course," said Pedro. "Maybe we should give ourselves a cover story. I know where we can go. There's a Saracen who worked with me – he lives in the village. I'd like to see him anyway, so we'll go there, see if they want any of your goods, I'll tell them you came to the pastures and I know you from the old days. Then we can leave and find a quiet place to talk."

Mofferet and his mother welcomed them and offered them refreshments, dried figs and raisins, vegetables, bread and wine. They told Mofferet and his mother that they knew each other from working together in the past. Raymond opened his bag of haberdashery and spices. Mofferet's mother was delighted and bought some needles and spices. As soon as they could politely leave after the meal, Raymond and Pedro made their excuses and left to walk beside the river. Raymond told Pedro that Guy had been moving around quite a bit and was now in Tortosa, with the two sisters, Blanche and Mondine Marty, and another man, Raymond Issaurat from Larnac, who was also a Believer. Mondine Marty was a widow; her husband, Raymond Piquier, had been taken by the Inquisition and was thought to have died in the Wall.

"How is Guy?"

"Guy is getting by," said Raymond. "He works at whatever job he can find to earn money. He wants to see you."

"Tell him to come and see me and I will give him some work, if I can. I would like to see him again. It's been too long."

Pedro gave Raymond de Toulouse two Jacquins shillings when they parted. Raymond said he would tell Guy where Pedro was.

It was just before Easter when Pedro and the other shepherds moved the sheep up to the summer pastures. As they tramped through the fresh grass, Pedro noticed a figure in the distance coming over the hill. The other shepherds took their belongings and the tools to the barn while Pedro squinted at the approaching man. There was something familiar in his shape and gait. As the figure came closer, Pedro recognised him. It was Guy. How good it was to see him. They moved towards each other and embraced. They stood back to appraise each other. Guy looked older, with wrinkles around his mouth and eyes. The last few years cannot have been easy for him.

"You look well," said Guy. There was a small silence.

"How are you, Guy?" said Pedro.

"Ups and downs, you know. You heard about Philippe?" Guy sighed. "I told him not to go." He peered into the distance, his mouth set in a thin line.

"Can you stay a while?"

"Yes, if… if you could find me some work… for a week or two. Where are the others?"

Pedro looked around. The other shepherds were clustered round the barn. One of them was staring in their direction. "I'll tell the others we're related – you're my cousin."

"Well, so we are cousins." Guy smiled. "I'll try to remember."

Pedro narrowed his eyes. Try? For God's sake, Guy, this was no game they were playing. And Guy knew that as well as Pedro did.

Guy stayed for the next two weeks, and if anyone suspected the two men were not related, they kept it to themselves. On Easter Saturday, Guy left, saying he must be in Tortosa on Easter Sunday. Pedro gave him two Barcelona shillings from his own money as well as payment for the work he had done.

Later that year, Pedro's brother Jean arrived at the pastures with news from Montaillou. The arrests had stopped, although the interrogations had not. People were still being summoned to appear before an Inquisitor at Carcassonne. After one interrogation, they could be sent home with another date when they were required to make the long journey, which for most of them was on foot, back to Carcassonne to be interrogated again. Anyone who was old or frail, or suffering a disability, had great difficulty in making the journey. Few owned donkeys or horses or could afford to hire one. But the Inquisition had what they wanted, the Perfects, so there was a strange kind of peace in the sad place that Jean said Montaillou had become. A villager named Guillaume Fort had been burned alive as he would not recant his heretical beliefs. Several villagers wore the yellow crosses as punishment, walking as if the crosses sewn onto their clothing were a great weight. Many families were depleted as their members languished in prison. No-one survived the Wall for long. On his way back, Jean had by chance met a shepherd from Cubières, who told him that Guy's wife and children had died from a feverish illness that had that swept through the region. Jean thought that Guy did not know of these events.

It was the following spring of 1314 when Guy next turned up at the pastures bringing with him Raymond de Toulouse and another Believer, Raymond Issaurat, who was known for acting as a guide to those fleeing from the Inquisition in the north to Aragon. The three were searching for work for a day or two, so Pedro put them to erecting fences. This job would take them all day and into the evening, and it meant they ate later than the other shepherds, and so avoided any awkward questions about who they were and where they were from. After the day's work, they sat round the fire and ate a meal together. Pedro asked where they were going next.

"I'm going to the Servels' at Lleida. They're established there now," said Raymond de Toulouse. "I hope to stay with them a while."

"I'm going back to Tortosa," said Guy. "Blanche, Mondine and I will stay there for a while then we may go to a little place called Prades, off the beaten track and where we will be safer." He sighed deeply. "I'm still hoping to bring my wife and children here from Cubières. My wife could help keep house and I want to bring my son up as a Believer and begin his preparation as a Perfect. We desperately need to prepare new Perfects."

There was a moment of terrible silence as Pedro felt the great weight of the knowledge he carried about Guy's family. The others were all looking at him. It must be written all over his face.

"Guy," said Pedro.

"What is it?" His voice was low and quiet.

"They… Estelle and your children… they can't join you, Guy," said Pedro. He swallowed as he struggled to find the right words.

"Your wife and children... I'm so sorry to tell you... they are no longer on this earth."

Guy was sitting cross-legged next to Pedro. His head dropped onto his chest. A log on the fire broke up, flared and illuminated him for a moment. Pedro saw his shoulders shake as he wept, silently at first, until he broke into sobs. He leant his head on Pedro's shoulder and the still night air was filled with the sound of his pain.

CHAPTER 15

Guy Belibaste

The following morning, Guy left with Raymond de Toulouse and Raymond Issaurat. The journey to Tortosa was made in near silence. The sad news cast a heavy pall over the three men. Raymond de Toulouse started to say how sad he was at the loss of Guy's wife, but Guy cut him off.

"Leave me be."

All Guy could think of was Estelle and the children, and the other life he had before... if only he could have seen them one more time... to explain and to have them with him in Aragon, by his side. All along he had hoped that his wife and children would follow the faith. Maybe his son would have become a Perfect...

Now the stark, cruel reality was that none of that could ever happen. Of course, he knew his son may not have wanted to be a Perfect, just as he himself had not wanted to be a farmer. The hope could have been a vain one, but it had sustained him through these last years. He had loved his wife and children, even while he hated his life as a farmer. He had memories of Estelle when they first married... when the children were born... another life... another time... so much had happened since. And his wife... well, that could never have been possible because there was Mondine to consider. His life was in Aragon now. He must attend to the living.

On reaching the outskirts of Tortosa, Guy bade farewell to the two Raymonds. He went in search of Blanche and Mondine, who were waiting for him at the tavern in Tortosa. They greeted him warmly. It reminded him that he was surrounded by friends and supporters. But he was restless, unable to settle. It was time to put into action an idea they had of moving to the quieter village of Prades. After resting just one night in Tortosa and hearing his sad news, Blanche and Mondine understood that he wanted to move on. They collected their few belongings together to begin the journey to Prades by foot.

Guy stomped along, preoccupied with his thoughts as they made their way in the warm sunshine. His old life had gone. A new life was beckoning on the horizon – albeit one that did not sit comfortably with his vows as a Perfect. He was weak; he could not function well without the close friendship and support of another human being. Philippe was gone. Mondine was becoming closer. He felt deeply guilty about this, but he could not find it within himself to change anything. This situation, irreconcilable as it was with his life as a Perfect, was to torture him constantly. The first step, which he had agreed with Mondine, was to face Blanche with a plausible story. He could not reveal the whole truth. A little bending of the truth would be a step in the right direction. He must speak to her before they set up home together. He was terrified of speaking to Blanche about this; she was a strong, outspoken woman and any hint of... she would say what she thought, and that may influence Mondine. He took a deep breath and caught up with Blanche and Mondine, who were walking in front of him. He positioned himself between them.

"Blanche," he said. "There's something I've been meaning to talk to you about. It's an idea I've spoken to Mondine about, and she agrees, so... as we are setting up in a new place, a new home for us all... I think we should take care to divert suspicion away from me as a single man – and therefore possibly a Perfect, you know, in case of spies from the Inquisition." Blanche threw him a glance. He continued. "So, with that in mind, I propose that Mondine and I should appear as if we are a married couple to the outside world. That way, anyone searching for Guillaume Belibaste, the Perfect, the single man, will not even consider me as a possibility."

"Really?" said Blanche. "You think you could do that?"

"Yes, why not?" said Guy.

"What will the other Believers think?" said Blanche. "Do you think they will accept that?"

"They will know that we are not man and wife – I will explain to them – and they will understand why we should do this," said Guy. "Just think, Blanche, anyone coming down here nosing around and asking questions is going to be looking for a single man. A married couple whose sister lives with them is not going to interest any spies sent by the Inquisition."

"Umm," said Blanche. She stopped in her tracks. "What about you, Mondine? What do you think?"

Mondine stood still. She looked at Guy. Guy took hold of Mondine's arm. Mondine glanced at her sister and looked down. Her face flushed deep pink under Blanche's gaze. She mumbled something.

"Mondine," said Blanche. "I can't hear you. What's the matter? Look at me."

Mondine looked at Guy, avoided her sister's eyes, looked down and didn't speak.

"You thought it was a good idea when we spoke of it, didn't you?" said Guy.

"Yes," said Mondine. Her voice was hardly audible.

"Did you? Are you quite sure of that?" said Blanche, as she set off walking again, leaving Guy and Mondine behind.

They made the rest of the journey in silence. Blanche marched on ahead. When they arrived in Prades, Guy asked them to sit beside the fountain in the centre whilst he went to find a place where they could lodge for a few nights until they found somewhere of their own.

"What's going on, Mondine?" said Blanche, looking at Mondine.

"Nothing," said Mondine. "Please, Blanche, everything will be fine."

"Hmm," huffed Blanche.

Guy appeared, saying he had found two rooms in a good lodging for them. The landlady met them.

"These are the rooms – next to each other," she said. "One for you and your wife, and the other for your sister-in-law here."

"What?" said Blanche.

"Thank you, Madame," said Guy, nodding at the landlady, then staring hard at Blanche with the unspoken message "don't you dare speak" written on his face. "We'll settle ourselves in now."

"If you need anything, I'll be downstairs." The landlady left them. As soon as she had gone, Blanche turned to Guy.

"What's this? We should all sleep in one room together, or I should share a room with Mondine. You must think I'm a fool. If you sleep in the same room together you will behave as man and wife." Blanche poked at Guy's chest with her finger. "And you, Master Belibaste, are supposed to be a Perfect, who does not touch women in that way."

"I can assure you that will not happen," said Guy. "We must start here as we intend to carry on. We're doing this so that anyone who comes nosing round these parts will assume we're man and wife."

"There is only one bed in there," said Blanche, who had opened the bedroom door and was peering into the room. "So how do think you can avoid touching her in any kind of way?"

"We will wear our undergarments so our skin will not touch,

and our flesh will not be weak," said Guy. "We will do our utmost not to touch."

Blanche shrugged her shoulders. Her mouth was set in a firm line. "Well, I'm not happy with this at all, but I'm tired – I'm going to bed," she said. "Good night." She left them.

Guy looked at Mondine and took her hand. "Don't worry about her," he said. "She'll get used to the idea."

"Blanche is furious," said Mondine when they were in their room and sitting on the bed together. "Do you think she suspects?"

"No-one must know anything; it's imperative we keep it from everyone. To the outside world, we're man and wife; to the Believers, you're my housekeeper," said Guy. "Blanche will have to learn to accept it."

"How am I going to explain it when I start to show?" said Mondine. She pulled her kirtle tight across her abdomen. "See, there's already a little bump."

"We'll think about that later. All sorts of things might happen – let's not concern ourselves with that yet."

"I suppose so."

"Come, Mondine, we'll think of something; let's go to bed now," said Guy. He moved towards Mondine and kissed her gently. She put her arms around him. He moved his hands over her body and slowly began to unfasten her kirtle.

Guy slowly surfaced. He was curled around Mondine's warm body. He stretched a little and put his arm round her; this was so comfortable. She was still half asleep with her back to him. But when she felt him move, she turned over to face him. He caressed her soft body, her breasts and her buttocks, and kissed her gently on her mouth. She murmured a little as he moved his hand down between her legs. She was relaxed, warm and responsive. He touched her where he knew she liked it. She murmured again.

"Is that good?" he whispered.

"Mmm."

He moved his body towards hers, and she opened her legs and bent her knees. He threw off the covers as he moved into position between her legs to enter her. Just as he entered her, the door to their room burst open. It was Blanche.

"Oh, Madame," she said. "I knew it, I've caught you at it."

"Get out, Blanche," shouted Guy. "It's not what you think."

Blanche left, slamming the door shut. Guy flopped onto his back and Mondine lay still. They turned to look at each other and Mondine put a hand over her mouth. She stifled a giggle. Guy could not control himself as a giggle bubbled up from his chest. They could not stop – it was hysterical, and they gave themselves up to it, rolling around on the bed, until Mondine finally turned away from Guy and managed to control herself. A final hiccup of laughter burst from her then she was silent for a minute.

"What now?" she said, turning to face him. Her eyes were shining from laughing. "This is not funny at all, you know; I can't face her."

"I don't know, I need time to think. For now we'll say she imagined it… I don't want her telling the other Believers," said Guy. "They'll… well, I don't know what they'd do."

"They won't do anything. They all love you and will believe you; a Perfect never lies."

"Don't… don't say that…" said Guy. "I don't need reminding how bad this is. The fact that we're… together …"

Guy lay still on his back for a few seconds. There was no rush. He turned to Mondine.

"We'll have to get out of this bed soon and face Blanche, but I think that first we should finish what we started." He put his arm across Mondine. She giggled. She sounded hysterical. Afterwards they emerged from their room and joined Blanche, who was by herself downstairs eating bread and preserves for breakfast. As soon as they entered the room, she started on them.

"You are a misbegotten bitch, Madame. I knew it; I knew what was really going on," she said.

"Hush, Blanche, for God's sake, you will compromise the cause of our Holy church," said Guy.

"Me, me compromise our Holy church!" screamed Blanche. "No, sir, it's you who have done that!"

"Blanche, please," said Mondine. "Please don't shout."

"You are mistaken, Madame, nothing has happened." Guy took Mondine's arm and led her to the door. "We're not stopping here to listen to this. Come, Mondine, we'll leave this dried-up old cowherder alone."

"Good riddance," Blanche shouted after them.

"I think we'll change our plans. I'm not staying here; we'll go to Tortosa," he said, as they went to their room. "Raymond de Toulouse went there. He'll help us to get settled. Don't worry about Blanche – she'll be able to find us if she wants to."

"It will take us two days, maybe more," said Mondine. "I'm so tired at the moment, I can't walk far." She burst into tears. "I don't like leaving Blanche all alone."

He put his arms around her. "Don't cry," he said. "I'll look after you, we'll find somewhere safe to stay and, as for Blanche, she can look after herself."

"But where will she go?" said Mondine.

"Let Blanche alone for the time being – she'll soon come round and find us, I'm sure," said Guy. "Don't worry, we'll take it slowly."

They made slow progress. Mondine was tearful and worried about Blanche. They stayed at an inn for one night and in a farmer's barn another. They arrived in Prades three days later, where they found lodgings in a quiet tavern. Mondine rested at the inn whilst Guy searched for Raymond de Toulouse. Guy didn't know what name Raymond was using, so his search was hampered. After two days of meandering around the lanes and streets of the village, Guy met

Raymond by chance at the market. Raymond agreed to help Guy find a place to live, and to start a small business making cards for the wool trade. Raymond appeared to accept that Mondine was Guy's housekeeper, and that they wished to appear as a married couple to the rest of the world. Guy wondered at times if he should be honest with Raymond, but he couldn't bring himself to face the consequences of that. Raymond moved on after a few days and they heard nothing from Blanche. Mondine found a job at the inn, helping the landlady with household chores. Their money was running out, but Guy's heart was not in the business, and it was hard to make ends meet. He'd broken his Perfect's vows, badly so, and he had no idea what to do about it. Apart from receiving the *consolamentum* all over again, there was nothing else he could do. And how he would ever arrange to do that, he could not think. It would mean abandoning Mondine, and that was out of the question, unless she came with him and he kept her just as his housekeeper, but that was not something he wanted to consider. It seemed impossible unless he could find a way to go to Lombardy. And at that moment, travelling all the way back there, through country infested with the Inquisition out for his blood, was not a viable proposition for him. He prayed constantly for forgiveness and understanding as he struggled with these thoughts. He did not want to burden Mondine with this. And Mondine, although she knew that he had broken his vows, wanted to support him. He told her he wanted to look after her. He had no wish to leave her. He would keep up the pretence that all was well, for everyone, including himself. But there was no outlet for his worries, no-one with whom he could talk, and, preoccupied as he was with these concerns, he was moody and irritable. But he could see no way out of his dilemma until something changed and he had no idea what that might be.

To supplement his income, from time to time, Guy worked as a farm labourer and shepherd. In February 1314 he went to find Pedro, who was at that time with the sheep on the nearby pastures of Tortosa.

CHAPTER 16

Pedro Maury

"I can find you some work, but we'll have to say you're a relative again, from say… Laroque-d'Olmes?" said Pedro. "The Maurs brothers are here, and they know you, but they can be trusted."

"I shan't stay long," said Guy. "I'm thinking of going to Lombardy with Mondine – you could come with us, Pedro."

"Lombardy? Whatever for? What's prompted this?"

"Well, for one thing to escape this constant looking over my shoulder, I can't settle anywhere I'm so on edge all the time and, well, this is rather delicate… Mondine has confided in me. She is with child."

"Oh, I see," said Pedro. "Who's the father?"

"Some passing pedlar apparently, but I think if we go to Lombardy, we could all start anew, I've told her I'll look after her – she's very ashamed. But you could come with us, Pedro, we'd be away from the Inquisition. Why don't you sell up and we three can leave together?"

"No, Guy, I don't want to do that, my work is here. I'm a shepherd. A shepherd I've always been and a shepherd I shall remain for the rest of my life. I don't want to go to Lombardy."

"I might even go further south," said Guy. "I'm really not sure what to do for the best, and there's another thing – Mondine and I have had an upset with Blanche and, well... we've parted company."

"What about?" said Pedro.

"Well... it's rather complicated," said Guy. "Wherever I go, Mondine is coming with me as my housekeeper; Blanche will have to manage on her own. I haven't got enough money to keep her too. Perhaps Mondine and I could go to Morella."

"Go close to some Believers who would welcome you," said Pedro.

Pedro's brother Jean appeared on the pastures shortly after Guy's arrival with a message for Guy. The Perfect Raymond de Toulouse was seriously ill; he was lodging in La Granadella, where he had been recently working with Jean. Jean, sad and quiet, said Raymond was dying and he needed Guy to give him the *consolamentum*. Jean's arrival was timely. Pedro's employer had been asking the shepherds questions about Guy. Did any of the other shepherds know him? Where was he from? He'd seen Guy praying and had made a comment to Pedro about his relative Guy being of the wrong religion. It was time for Guy to leave. Pedro would go with them. He wanted to see Raymond de Toulouse. They left that same day. They would only manage five leagues or so each day at Guy's speed. Guy had never liked walking long distances and he seemed to be slower than ever these days. It would take them two to three days.

"I can't keep up with you and Jean, Pedro," said Guy between breaths, as they marched along the track towards La Granadella.

"You don't get enough exercise, you old heretic. It's living with Mondine that does it; she waits on you far too much."

"Mondine's my housekeeper. Isn't it about time you had a woman in your life?"

"I have."

"I don't mean one of those you visit from time to time, I mean a wife."

"I can't afford to marry – anyway, I'm always on the move."

"Leave him alone," said Jean to Guy.

Pedro stopped and waited whilst Guy caught his breath. They stood together and looked back at the route they had taken. Guy's slow pace was of concern. Guy had wanted to stop for longer, but Pedro pushed and pulled, and jollied Guy along. Pedro was losing patience. Was it Guy's innate laziness, or was there some reason he didn't want to see Raymond? Guy owed Raymond this last service at the very least.

They made the journey in two days, arriving late at night to the house where Raymond and Jean had been lodging for some time. Jean said they were kindly folk, not interested in religion much, more concerned about Raymond, whom they had become fond of and whom they had cared for in Jean's absence. Jean reassured Guy that they would not interfere or ask too many questions about their visit. He had told them Guy and Pedro were relatives of Raymond's.

The owner of the house, Mersende, showed them into Raymond's room, where he lay in bed. The room reeked of a decaying body that was decomposing from within. The stench of death. Raymond looked like death. He was thin and gaunt, his yellowed skin stretched over his cheekbones. His eyes were dark and sunk deep into his skull. But he seemed lucid and was able to converse a little. They were in time.

"I am relieved to see you," he said. "My time is near. God has been good enough to grant me my last wish."

Raymond's mouth was dry, and his voice came out in a husky whisper. Mersende brought a damp cloth and a bowl of water to moisten his lips and mouth. He took a small sip of water. He looked at her gratefully.

"Is there anything else you need?" she said.

Raymond shook his head.

"Well then, I'll leave you," she said. She handed Pedro the cloth and water as she left. "Here, you can moisten his lips with this."

"I can't swallow," said Raymond, his voice hardly audible.

"Don't try to talk, Raymond," said Pedro, going to hold his hand. "Guy is here to give you the blessing."

Pedro and Jean stood to one side, watching as Guy performed the ritual. First, he asked Raymond about his beliefs and Raymond responded in his hoarse whisper. Guy placed his copy of the New Testament on Raymond's head and rested his hands on it. Guy spoke again to Raymond, and Raymond whispered back to him. This was repeated several times over until Guy, tears in his eyes, moved back.

"Now I can go in peace," Raymond whispered. "I am truly thankful for your blessing. God bless you all."

Pedro looked at him sadly; it was clear he didn't have long for this world. The three of them sat on the floor to watch and wait. The landlady, Mersende, knocked on the door and came in saying she had food for them, and she would bring sheepskins and blankets for the night.

"That's all I have," she said, bringing in an armful of bedding for them.

"That's enough for us," said Pedro. "We appreciate your help."

"He's a good man," she said.

They divided the time up between them. Pedro took the middle part of the night. Raymond continued to sleep. His breathing was steady and quiet; he hardly stirred. Mersende was right: Raymond had been a good man. And he had been a support to Guy, helping him when he could. The same old concerns about Guy coping with less and less support worried Pedro until it was time for Guy to take over the watch. Pedro lay on the floor and closed his eyes. He was exhausted.

It was early morning when he woke. Guy was sitting beside Raymond. He looked up when he saw Pedro stirring.

"He's gone," he said.

"When?" Pedro rose and walked over to the bed.

"Not long since, an hour or so; he never woke up, just peacefully faded away."

Jean woke up and joined them as they all stood still with heads bowed, and Guy prayed. Pedro arranged with Mersende for Raymond's body to be interred and gave her some money to cover the costs. Mersende told them that Raymond had said he was just waiting to see them before he could let himself go and be relieved of his suffering. They were a sombre group as they set off on their journey home.

"You're the only one left now, Guy," said Pedro.

"I know," he said. "And I wish I wasn't – I'm not fit for the job. Why God has chosen me to be the last of the Perfects, when there were so many more suitable men than me, I cannot understand, because I tell you, Pedro, I am not worthy of it."

They walked in silence back to their lives.

PART 3

1317–1324

CHAPTER 17

Pedro Maury

Guy appeared regularly on the pastures at Tortosa looking for work. On one of these visits, Pedro had agreed with him that they would buy six sheep together. Pedro bought the sheep as Guy had no money. Pedro gave Guy a further five sol to help with expenses.

"I'll take my three sheep when I leave," said Guy.

"That's not the arrangement," said Pedro. "I will look after these sheep here, you can pay me for them whenever you can, and when we shear them and sell the wool, you can have a part of the profit after I have taken out my share and payment for looking after them – that's more than fair."

"I thought the cost of them and the five sol you gave me were given to me for the love of God; you Believers are all supposed to contribute towards my expenses and upkeep," said Guy. "But people are slow to put their hands in their pockets. I don't have enough to live on, so I'll take mine now."

"No, you will not," said Pedro. "I'm trying to help you, Guy, and you are trying to take advantage of me."

"What's the difference?" said Guy.

"I'm not being made a fool of – anyway, I've changed my mind now and the deal's off," said Pedro. "And you should be off too. I've had enough of you, be off with you!"

It would be another year before they met again.

In 1319, Pedro spent the winter months in Tortosa. When he first arrived, he went as usual to collect flour from the woman who owned the mill. He had known Na Franqueta for many years.

"Pedro Maury," she said when she saw him. "A woman and two men of your kinship were in here a few weeks back; they asked after you."

"Who are they?" said Pedro.

"Well now, you know I don't deal in names. I only know you shepherds from long acquaintance, but if you want to see for yourself, you'll find them in Horta."

Pedro went straight back to the pastures and told Martin Maurs to take over as head shepherd as he was taking time off to go to Horta, to find his relatives. It was only three or four leagues away; he would be there in a couple of hours. When he arrived in Horta, he questioned the locals, who sent him to some lodgings, where a woman and her two sons were staying. There in the lodging house, Pedro found his Aunt Gaillarde, and her two sons, Andre and Pons, from Ax. Aunt Gaillarde had been married to his father's cousin Julien. She was a widow of a few years. Aunt Gaillarde had aged well. She had put on a little weight, but her round, jolly face was unlined. She only had the two sons, and her husband had done well with stockbreeding and farming. Her life had been relatively easy.

"Aunt Gaillarde," said Pedro. "It's been a long time, but you're looking well, and you have two fine boys here." The boys were good-looking youths in their late teens. They inclined their heads self-consciously as Pedro mentioned them.

"You've just come in time," said Aunt Gaillarde after they exchanged kisses and embraces. "We've been resting here for long enough. It was quite a journey from Ax, and we couldn't bring much with us. But we're off to San Mateo tomorrow as we heard it's a better place to earn a living." She lowered her voice to a whisper. "I've got a bit of money from when we sold up. It was getting too dangerous there and I wanted to be near the Perfect. He's in Morella now."

"Ah yes," said Pedro. "The Perfect. I haven't seen him in a while."

"I heard he was in Morella with Mondine Marty and her daughter – we'll seek them out when we're established in San Mateo."

"What will you do there?"

"Why, we'll buy some land, and farm and breed sheep as we've always done. I've got these two strong lads to help me." She smiled at her boys. "We can take care of ourselves; you've got to look after yourself first, I always say."

Pedro stayed overnight with them in their lodgings, and they ate a meal together. The two boys softened a little as the evening wore on, telling Pedro they were missing their home and wondering what life would be like in Aragon. Aunt Gaillarde told Pedro that her sister Mersende had also come down here with her daughter Jeanne, and Jeanne's husband, Bernard.

"But," she whispered again, "she's trouble, that one."

"Who is? Mersende?"

"No, no, not Mersende, it's Jeanne."

"What's the problem?"

"She's mad, shouting and hitting her mother, calling her names – she's called her an old heretic cowherder! She'll land us all in trouble if we don't find a way to shut her up," said Aunt Gaillarde.

"Was she like that before they came down here?" Pedro didn't remember hearing anything like that before about Jeanne. They were only distantly related, but he had met her when they were children.

"No, that's just it. She doesn't want to be here. Her mother brought her down here under false pretences. I don't know what she told her – promised her something, I expect, to get her to leave her home. But it's not turned out well. Thank God they're in Beceite, and off the beaten track."

The following day, Pedro left with a promise to visit them as soon as he could.

It was three months before Pedro found time to visit Aunt Gaillarde again. After asking around in San Mateo, he found her on the outskirts, where she had bought a farmhouse and some land.

"Welcome to our new home," she said. "I'm glad you've come – let me show you around the place."

Aunt Gaillarde's farm was in good condition. There was a workshop for combing wool in a room in her house, and a pretty, shady courtyard surrounded by rooms.

"Andre and Pons like it here; they're working hard to make a success of it," she said.

"This is a lovely place, Aunt Gaillarde," said Pedro. "I think you'll prosper here."

"I need to start building up my flock of sheep now that we're settled in here… you don't know anyone who wants to lease their sheep out, do you?"

"You could look after some of mine," said Pedro. "I could lease you about one hundred and fifty animals, say for about five years. That should get you started."

Aunt Gaillarde embraced Pedro warmly. "That's a generous offer, I appreciate it. I can contribute to the cost of looking after them."

"We'll split the profits and losses between us," he said. "I'm always pleased to help any member of my family if I can."

It was a brief visit to San Mateo and when he returned to his flock, the shepherd Pierre Montanier arrived with the news that a new Bishop had been appointed in Pamiers. His name was Jacques Fournier. He had set up his own Episcopal Inquisition and had issued a proclamation.

"It's about you and Guy Belibaste," said Pierre Montanier. "You're both officially wanted by the Inquisition on suspicion of heresy. Anyone who can inform the Bishop as to your whereabouts, or who can take you to him, will receive a handsome reward."

"His jurisdiction doesn't extend to Aragon," said Pedro.

"He has spies working for him; he will find a way – believe me, he's known for his ruthlessness and determination. You and Guy must take extra care."

"I'll tell Guy when I see him – he comes to me for work occasionally – but it won't make much difference to me; I shall carry on as usual. I'll go back north with the sheep in the summer – I feel safe enough in Puigcerdà, where I spend the summers working for the Lady Brunissende. I go to San Mateo as often as I can to see my family then, but in the winter months, I'm not so far from them, as I bring all the sheep – I work for two or three employers – down to overwinter in Aragon."

"All of us Believers are in danger, but capturing and burning the last Perfect would be a great symbolic victory for Bishop Fournier," said Pierre Montanier.

"I'll do what I can," said Pedro.

But the following summer, Pedro's time was taken up with other things. He had found Brunissende in poor health when he took the sheep back in the spring. She looked thin and had a hacking cough – the worst cough he'd ever heard. He felt the terrible pain of her illness each time she had a coughing bout. She was pale, the colour had leeched out of her lovely strong face and she was covered with bruises for which there was no explanation. She was weak and spent her days lying in bed. The cough had started some weeks back and the weakness and bruises had followed soon after. A physician had attended her and given her medicinal herbal preparations. But nothing had improved. The smell of death hung over her; it was the same odour that had permeated Raymond de Toulouse's room. Brunissende was fading away. Her son and his wife were running the farm. She asked Pedro to stay with her, and he sat next to her bed, holding her hand for a long time each day.

"I want you to help Bérenger with the farm," she whispered, her voice weak and husky.

"I'll stay as long as he needs me," said Pedro. "There's nothing for you to worry about."

"I want you to have some of my sheep," she said. "You've been the best of friends; there's money for you as well."

"Hush," he said. "Don't speak of these things – you must rest."

The end of Brunissende's life came quietly towards the end of summer. Her son, Bérenger, and Pedro were with her when she died. Bérenger asked Pedro to stay for a while to help with the farm, whilst he dealt with the lawyers about his inheritance. Pedro found, as he had done before, that work helped him to get through the sad days of mourning. Although he had learned that mourning never really goes away, he learned to face it and live with it. The patterns and rhythms of life on the farm, the land, the animals, the crops, none of this stood still. There was always work. In the autumn, when it was time to take the animals south again, Pedro told Bérenger that he wished to carry on with his life as it had always been, and it was time to take the animals south for the winter.

"You can stay here as long as you want, Pedro," said Bérenger. "There's always work here for you. Come back whenever you wish."

"I appreciate your kindness. I'm going to take the sheep down to the plains, I'll take Raymond Boursier's sheep along with Brunissende's... yours, and when the shepherds and the sheep are settled there, I must go to see my aunt in San Mateo. I will return next spring with the animals."

"You will always be welcome."

It was November before Pedro was able to leave the sheep. Two of the shepherds had decided to go and work elsewhere, and he had to find replacements for them. As soon as he could leave the sheep in good hands, he went to San Mateo to see Aunt Gaillarde.

"Where have you been?" she greeted him. "We've all been worried that the Inquisition had taken you. Have you heard about Bishop Fournier?"

Yes, he'd heard about the Bishop, but he'd had things to attend to, he explained; he didn't tell her about Brunissende, as it was none of her business. Aunt Gaillarde and her sons seemed to be thriving, but not so the sheep he had leased to her – most of them had died. She told Pedro that some of the wool had been taken by Guy Belibaste, back to Morella. Guy hadn't paid her for it yet, so she had no money for Pedro. The small amount of money from the wool that she had taken was used to buy more lambs. She blamed Guy, saying he was tight-fisted.

"I'll go and see him, but I don't suppose I'll get any money out of him," said Pedro.

"Will you go and see Mersende at Beceite as well?" she said. "Jeanne's still causing problems there, hitting her mother and threatening to expose them as heretics."

"Can't her husband deal with her?"

"No-one knows what to do with her; I think she might be better off if someone pushed her down a cliff and left her to die," said Gaillarde.

"Don't say things like that, Aunt Gaillarde, even as a joke. I won't be party to any violence."

Had Gaillarde just said what she really wished would happen? And had she told him the whole truth of the matter of the sheep? Probably not. Irritated and out of patience with Gaillarde and Guy, Pedro wanted to leave them behind. But he should go to see Guy, find out what had happened to the sheep and make sure Guy was managing well enough. How petty and trivial it all seemed after the loss of Brunissende.

Guy, he thought, as he strode out towards Morella, was always trying to pull a fast one, to get something more out of people. The

Believers tended to turn a blind eye to it because of his position as their Perfect. He seemed incapable of being any different. Guy's human weaknesses always got the better of him. But Pedro had some sympathy and understanding of Guy's position, which was fraught with danger. He sighed. Despite what Guy did, Pedro would support him.

Morella was about three leagues from San Mateo. The town built on a rock with a Saracen castle on its peak was surrounded by huge ramparts. It was an impressive sight as he approached. After asking around, Pedro found Guy living in a rented house in the area where other cobblers, weavers and card-makers lived. He had set up another card-making business and lived there with Mondine and her little daughter, Guillemette. Pedro was pleased to see him, despite their differences. Pedro greeted Guy with the *melioramentum*. Guy kissed and embraced him warmly.

At suppertime, Guy blessed the bread and gave a piece to each of them. Mondine, little Guillemette and Pedro ate the blessed bread with mutton Pedro had brought, and Guy ate salt fish. After dinner, they were visited by some neighbours, so there was no opportunity to discuss anything to do with the Believers. The following morning, Pedro told Guy he was going to Beceite, to see Aunt Mersende and her family.

"Will you call in and see us again soon?" said Guy.

"I'm not sure," said Pedro. "You might as well know, I'm not pleased with you, as I know you took that wool from Aunt Gaillarde and didn't pay for it."

"That was to keep me going," he said. "You're all supposed to contribute to my upkeep; I can't earn enough – you know I have to pay Mondine for her housekeeping."

"You're getting a reputation for miserliness; people don't like that."

"It's not easy trying to earn a living here," he said. "Pedro, come and see me on your way back; we could talk more. I haven't seen much of you for a long time."

"I don't know," said Pedro. "I came to tell you that the new Bishop has offered a reward for information that leads to the arrest of you and me, so now I've told you I will leave. But you must take extra care."

"I think I'm safe enough with Mondine and Guillemette with me. That's why I keep them here – no-one is looking for a man with a family."

Pedro walked briskly as he made his way to Beceite. It was a day's journey, and it gave him time to think about the difficulties they had in their small community of Believers. There were so few of them and they were spread out. Aunt Gaillarde and her two boys in San Mateo. Aunt Mersende with Jeanne and her husband in Beceite. The Servels in Lleida. So different to the early years of the century, when there were Perfects and Believers all over the area around Ax and beyond. Could Guy prepare more Perfects? It was unlikely that Guy had the skills and knowledge of the Authier brothers, who had spent nearly four years in Lombardy learning about their faith. Guy struggled just to get by and that sometimes brought out the worst in him. Despite that, the small community of Cathars did still seem to revere him. Could they support him more? Most of them had lost a great deal in support of their faith, and their continuing reverence of Guy was tied up with that. Aunt Gaillarde was the most comfortably off, but she had been let down by Guy and would be unlikely to give him much more.

He soon found Aunt Mersende in Beceite. She was outside her house, cleaning out the chicken coop. He hadn't seen her for years, but he would have recognised her anywhere; she was very like her sister, Aunt Gaillarde, and she too had aged well. She stopped her work and watched him as he approached.

"Aunt Mersende," he said, grinning. "How are you?"

She looked hard at him. "I can't believe it. Pedro Maury. I'd heard you may visit." She moved towards him and threw her arms around him. "It's a long time since I saw you, how are you?" She stood back, smiling. "You're like your father but taller and broader… you'll stay a night or two? You must – I want you to see how Jeanne is, and see if you've any ideas about what to do with her. She's no better; in fact, I think she's worse. I'm at my wits' end with her."

They sat together on the low wall outside Aunt Mersende's house, and she told him the story.

"I thought it would be easier when Jeanne and Bernard moved into a small house of their own, and it was at first, but now she's reverted back, just the same as she was before. She comes round here often and threatens me. She's my daughter, but I can see she's lost her senses; the move has upset her so much and she's blaming me for bringing her here. She drinks all the wine she can get her hands on and that makes her worse. I'm really worried that she will denounce me to the Inquisition, along with the other Believers down here," said Mersende.

"What do you think we should do?" said Pedro.

"I have no idea; I wish she'd go away from here. I told her husband to take her back north, but they've nothing to go back to and hardly any money, so that's not possible," said Aunt Mersende. "See what you think when you meet her, Pedro."

Bernard and Jeanne appeared later that evening just before Aunt Mersende served the meal. Jeanne was a huge woman. She was nearly as tall as Pedro, and bulky, with a bush of wild black hair framing her big, bad-tempered-looking face. Pedro understood why people might be frightened of her. His confidence ebbed away when he was faced with the reality of Cousin Jeanne.

"Your cousin is here," said Aunt Mersende when Jeanne walked in.

"My cousin? Who's that? I didn't know he was my cousin; you never told me that." Jeanne spoke loudly with an irritated note in her voice.

"It's a long time since we met," said Pedro, trying to smooth things over. "We were children; we knew each other then as cousins."

"No, I don't know you," she shouted, her voice rising. "I said I don't, and I don't."

"Calm down, Jeanne," Bernard said. "Come and sit at the table. Don't worry about Pedro, he's a friend." Bernard looked small and inconspicuous beside his wife.

Jeanne sat down, throwing Pedro a filthy look. Aunt Mersende brought the food in, said grace and they began to eat. Should he speak and risk saying the wrong thing? Or should he sit quietly and hope Jeanne became better-natured as the meal went on? He noticed she was helping herself to the wine that he had brought with him.

"Do you like the wine, Jeanne?" he said.

"What are you trying to say?" Jeanne replied. "She's always telling me not to drink wine; she says I drink too much."

"No, that's not what I meant, Jeanne—"

"You're all the same," said Jeanne. "You're no better than that old heretic there, my mother. She made me leave Ax; she deserves to burn."

"Mon dieu, Jeanne, that's no way to speak to your mother," said Pedro, shocked. "She was trying to do the best for you, bringing you here."

"You're no better," said Jeanne. "In fact, I believe you're worse – you're a fully qualified heretic, from what I've heard."

Jeanne stood up and picked up a pillow that was lying on the bench beside her. She started to hit her mother about the head with it. Bernard ran round the table, shouting at Jeanne.

"For God's sake, Jeanne, leave your mother alone, you stupid bitch," said Bernard, grabbing Jeanne by the arm. They struggled together but Bernard was no match for his wife. Finally, he hit her hard on her face and this subdued her. She looked dazed as he took her away.

"My God," said Pedro. "She's really angry. You're right, she's a problem, very volatile."

"She was a good Believer before we came here," said Aunt Mersende, who had tears in her eyes. "I think she misses her life in Ax, but I don't know what to do with her; someone needs to take her away from here."

"Look," said Pedro. "I'll talk to the others about it and to the Perfect and see if we can come up with a solution."

"I hope you can," she said.

The following morning, Bernard appeared at the house just as Pedro was about to leave.

"I'm glad I caught you before you left," he said. "You can see what Jeanne is like; she's got a demon in her, and she's worse than ever when she drinks wine, even crazier than usual – we must do something, otherwise she'll jeopardise the whole Church of God. She's already been to San Mateo, so she knows what's going on and who's there…"

Pedro went back to Morella to see Guy and told him about Jeanne. Guy said he had met her while he was in Horta during the grape-picking season a few weeks before. She was there with Aunt Mersende, as well as Aunt Gaillarde and her two sons. They all stayed in the same place together and were going to press the grapes the next morning when Jeanne, as soon as she saw Guy, rounded on him, calling him "a bad man" and saying she'd "set the ghosts and devils of the dead onto him". She terrified him so much that he ran off without his shoes for two leagues and left behind some of his belongings. The picture of Guy running away without his shoes and clothes made Pedro laugh, and Guy smiled too.

"But this is a serious matter," said Guy. "It's obvious an evil spirit has entered into Jeanne. She must be kept well away from me in future."

"But what can we do to help her mother and husband?"

"Go and see your Aunt Gaillarde, ask her and the other Believers what they think should be done," he said. "But stay the night here first."

After the evening meal, Guy started to preach.

"I'll tell you about Saul, who persecuted the Church and devastated it, and how the Son of God spoke to him and converted him. The Son of God changed Saul's name to Paul, and he became a good Believer and converted others. Having previously been very wicked, he later became good and Holy. However, at the beginning, the others did not trust him, dreading his past wickedness, then as time passed and they got to know him, they saw he was a good Believer." He stopped. "But I don't think Jeanne is like Saint-Paul, because, as her mother has told us, before she came to this region, she was a good Believer and well mannered. After she came here, and her mother showed her the Believers here, she became wicked and terrified us all. It will be good to deliberate on what needs to be done about it; either someone takes her far away from us, or even back to Ax, where she was happy. It's necessary to cut down the bad tree because it gives bad fruit, and I don't want her brought here, because I'm afraid that one of these days she will denounce me and everyone else."

As Pedro left the next day, Guy said he thought Jeanne should be taken to some distant town and left there, and that those who take her should leave her slyly, without her knowing.

"But she knows all the places where the Believers are, and she would come back to them and be even worse," said Pedro. "At least Beceite is fairly remote from all the main places that people frequent; it's well out of the way and no-one is likely to take too much notice of her ranting and raving – that is, of course, as long as none of Fournier's spies go there."

"Umm," said Guy. "I hope you're right, but we still need a solution to this problem… you and the others should deliberate amongst yourselves about it."

In fact, no-one knew what to do about Jeanne. Aunt Gaillarde suggested that someone should kill Jeanne by throwing her down a ravine or poisoning her, but no-one wanted to do that. Everyone was frightened of her because she was so big and strong. Pedro, irritated with them, told them he couldn't agree to the death of anyone – after all, he said, it's possible she could change in time. He offered to take Jeanne back to Ax, at his own expense, but they did not want him to go to Ax as it was too dangerous. The following year, Jeanne's husband was killed outright in an accident. A tree he was cutting down fell on him and killed him. It seemed to divert Jeanne's attention away from the Believers she hated so much. But this was only a temporary improvement.

Pedro's life followed its established pattern: in the mountains in the summer with the sheep, and in the south in the winter with them. How he missed Brunissende, particularly in the summer months, the time he used to spend with her, when they often worked side by side on the farm attending to the animals and enjoying the companionable quietness as they laboured in harmony. It had been as if there was unspoken communication between them; they had hardly needed to speak. At the end of the day, they would enjoy a simple meal together, often cooked by one or the other of them.

In the winter months, Pedro visited his two aunts, and also Guy and Mondine, as often as he could. He aimed to help Aunt Mersende and Jeanne to live calmly. The only way to contain Jeanne and her madness was to keep her in Beceite and out of the way. The times he enjoyed most were when he, Guy and Mondine visited Aunt Gaillarde and her sons in San Mateo, and they all ate a meal together. Guy often preached on these occasions. It was not easy to understand what he was trying to say when he preached to them all. Pedro was never sure that Guy had the Cathar legends and the Bible stories accurate. Despite this and everything else, everyone still seemed to revere him as their Perfect.

In November 1319, Pedro went to see Aunt Gaillarde and her family in San Mateo. She couldn't wait to tell Pedro the latest news.

"Oh, Pedro, you've come at last, I've been waiting for you," she said as she ushered him into the large living room. "There is someone you know amongst us here," she said, as she brought out a wineskin and put a loaf of bread on the table. Her eyes danced as she grinned at him.

"It's about four or five weeks or so ago… I was in the village square asking if anyone had corn to grind, when a young man came out of the cobbler's shop on the corner of the square. He waited until I was near him and he asked me where I was from. I was cautious, you can't be too careful these days, so I said Saverdun. He said, but you speak like someone from Montaillou or Ax, the Sabarthès. So, I asked him who he was. He replied that he was Arnaud Baille, son of Sybille Baille; he also sometimes calls himself Arnaud Sicre, his father's name – he uses the names interchangeably."

"Arnaud? Sybille's son?" said Pedro. "Here in San Mateo? Are you quite sure?"

"I think so," said Aunt Gaillarde. "I told him we must stay in touch and see each other on Sundays or holidays, when we're not working, and he said he hoped we could get to know each other. I told Guy, and he and Pons went with me to see Arnaud in the cobbler's. Arnaud was working alone when we went in, and I told him that Guy and Pons had come to meet him. He said it was an honour to meet them. Guy hardly spoke and stared at him for a long time; it was uncomfortable but, well, he does look as if he could be Sybille's son – there's a resemblance around the chin and mouth, and he's about the right age…" Aunt Gaillarde didn't finish her sentence.

"What's the matter? You don't sound too sure," said Pedro.

"Well, Guy just blurted out, 'I remember you as a little boy when I used to stay at your mother's house; you may remember me, Guy Belibaste' – I expected Arnaud to get down on his knees and perform the *melioramentum*, but he didn't."

"Were other people present?"

"No, but it is a public place, of course; anyone could have walked in," said Aunt Gaillarde. "And he has lived for a long time with his father, who was staunchly Roman and very much against the Good Men."

"What did he do?"

"He said he had the understanding of good and that he'd met the Authiers at his mother's house." She looked at Pedro. "He's been here to my house since and he brought fish for Guy when he's been here, but he has never performed the *melioramentum*."

"What does Guy think?"

"He's suspicious, but we're in it up to our necks now: Arnaud visits regularly; he's been to see Guy in Morella and taken fish there. He's made himself at home; he's like one of the family: he eats with us, he brings bread and cheese – he's even stayed over and slept in the same bed with Guy – so, well, the fact is, we can't help feeling quite at ease with him now…"

"But you're still unsure?"

Aunt Gaillarde nodded, her face worried. "I'm sure when I'm with him, but afterwards…"

"I should meet him."

"Well, he's coming here tonight, so you can see for yourself."

Arnaud arrived that evening with fish to share. Aunt Gaillarde took Arnaud in to meet Pedro, who stood to greet him. The two men looked at each other for a long moment. Arnaud appeared to Pedro just as he might have expected Sybille's grown-up son to look. He was tall like her and had her strong features.

"Pedro, I'm Naudy," he said. He grinned just like he always used to. "I remember that's what you all called me then. I remember you visiting my mother's house in Ax; I've never forgotten those times."

"Naudy! It really is you – I thought so." Pedro moved towards him and embraced him. "I remember those times too."

"It's all gone now," said Arnaud, shaking his head. "The Inquisition took it all, my mother's house and all her possessions.

Our family were split up, that's why I'm here: I'm trying to find my brother, Bernard. Jacques, the eldest, is safe and well. But I've been searching for Bernard the past two years. I knew there were some exiles down here, but I'd no idea where they were. My prayers were finally answered when I found your aunt."

"Your mother was the best and most dedicated of all the faithful. I wish she was still with us… the only comfort is that she is in Heaven now," said Pedro.

Aunt Gaillarde entered the room with a platter that had some small slices of bread and pâté on it. She poured out the wine.

Arnaud shook his head and looked sad. "There are not many Believers left. But it must be God's will that I'm here. And to find Guy Belibaste, the very last of the Perfects, the only one left, it's a miracle!"

"Yes, he's all we have. I know Guy very well, and he's my friend, but he does have his… difficulties… he doesn't find it easy… being a Perfect."

"But he's the only one now."

"That's true, and we must hope and pray for the future; who knows what God has in store for us?"

"We must put our trust in God," said Arnaud. "Although there have been times when my faith has been sorely tested, since I've been left with nothing. I loved my mother's house with its quiet courtyard. And my relatives are all gone or lost to me, but a shepherd told me that my sister, and maybe my brother, are with my Aunt Alazaïs in the Pallars. I want to join them. I thought they might be here when I found you all, but…"

"If you find them, you must bring them here," said Pedro. "We all need to be together, near others of the same faith and to be close to the Perfect, so we can receive the *consolamentum* when we die. You mustn't worry about having no money here; we share what we can, well, some of us do."

"I'd like to stay here for a while; I'm weary of searching for the moment," said Arnaud. "And I need to work and earn some money, then when I have enough, I can start my search again."

"And Christmas is coming, and the weather isn't good for travelling – besides, I want you to make me a new pair of shoes," said Pedro, laughing.

Arnaud left in the New Year to visit all the Believers in Aragon to see if they could help him with his search for his family. He had asked Pedro and Aunt Mersende all the details of where people lived. He promised to be back soon.

It was late in the day when Pedro arrived in Morella.

"Good to see you," said Guy, clapping Pedro on the shoulder when he opened the door.

Mondine came forward to greet Pedro, wiping her hands on her tabard. "Supper won't be long," she said.

"Is there time for a stroll?" said Guy. Mondine nodded. Guy grabbed hold of Pedro's arm. "Come, Pedro."

They walked through the narrow cobbled streets of Morella. Small houses clung together on each side, some set up and opened as stalls, in the process of closing and shuttering for the day. The owners called out as Pedro and Guy passed.

"Good evening!"

"Nice evening for a stroll."

As soon as they were away from the centre of the town, Guy grabbed Pedro's arm again.

"So, what do you think?" he said.

"What about?" said Pedro.

"Our friend Arnaud Baille, or Arnaud Sicre – is it him?"

"It's him all right, I've no doubt about that; he remembers how we called him Naudy, when he was a boy at his mother's house."

"Yes, I think it's him, but what concerns me is why he didn't perform the *melioramentum* when we met?"

"Yes, it is strange," said Pedro. "But it could be because he didn't spend that much time with the Good Men as a boy. He was brought up mainly by his father, who was a staunch Roman, and now there are no Perfects, he's never learned it."

"Perhaps you're right," said Guy.

"I'll teach him – he should know it," said Pedro.

They walked on in silence for a while.

"When I didn't see you for some time, I was worried about you too," said Guy.

"Well, I'm here now."

"Where were you? What were you up to?" said Guy.

"Busy. Working."

"With a woman? Or maybe you've become a spy for Bishop Fournier?"

"Don't be crazy, you know I would never betray my fellow Believers."

"It was a woman then."

Pedro was silent; he had no intention of telling Guy about Brunissende.

"You know, Pedro, you should stop whoring around and settle down."

Pedro said nothing. Hearing Guy speak of Sybille and Brunissende in those terms made him angry.

"You shouldn't go into the mountain pastures in the summer," said Guy. "It's too dangerous now – suppose you were taken ill and died there, and there was no-one to console you? What then? We all worry about you when you're gone for a long time."

"If I'm destined not to be consoled at the end then so be it; if not, I shall continue to follow the path that is shown to me," said Pedro.

"I think you should find a good woman to marry, one who has the understanding of good."

"Guy," said Pedro. "I'm going back. I don't want to talk about this, let me be."

Pedro turned round and walked back to the house. Guy followed behind him. They ate together but there was little conversation. Mondine and her little girl, Guillemette, took one look at the two men and kept quiet. Pedro could not put his finger on it, but there was something wrong. Was it that Guy was worried about Naudy? In any case, Pedro suggested to Guy that they should go to San Mateo the following morning, so they could see how things were there and talk with Aunt Gaillarde.

The journey to San Mateo took the best part of a day due to Guy's slow pace. Pedro tried to be patient as he listened to Guy's problems with earning money. Guy stopped suddenly beside an outcrop of rocks.

"Wait a minute, Pedro, I have a stone in my shoe." Guy leant against a rock and took off one of his well-worn shoes and shook it. "That should do it." He remained leaning on the rock and looked at Pedro.

"You know, Pedro, it really is time for you to marry," he said. "You would be happier with a good woman to look after you, and it would be someone to talk with you about the heresy. She would comfort you and give you pleasure and—"

"Not that again," said Pedro. "I've told you there are many good reasons why I don't marry; my work takes me away, I can't afford to keep a wife and, anyway, I don't know of anyone suitable. I can't understand why you're so interested in this."

"Umm," said Guy, giving Pedro a look that he couldn't fathom.

"Umm?" said Pedro. "What do you mean by that?"

"Well," said Guy. "This is rather delicate."

"Delicate?" said Pedro. "Guy, what are you talking about?"

"Well, it's Mondine."

"What about Mondine?" Pedro was exasperated.

"Hush, Pedro, keep your voice down." Guy looked around although there was no-one about.

"For God's sake, Guy, tell me, what is it?"

"Well, I'm trying to tell you – it's Mondine, she loves you."

Pedro, dumbfounded, stared at Guy. Guy looked away.

"What?" said Pedro. "Mondine loves me? I've not seen anything in Mondine's behaviour to make me think that, Guy… What is this?"

"You could do a lot worse, you know," said Guy. "She's a good woman, she keeps house well and she is one of us."

"That's true, but it never occurred to me—"

"She's loved you for a long time, and you like her, don't you?"

"Yes, she's a nice woman, but—"

"But what? I could marry you two when we get back; I promised her I'd tell you about this before we arrive back and then you could sleep with her tonight."

"No, no, that's too quick, I can't do that; besides, she's married to Bernard Piquier, isn't she?"

"We don't know what's happened to him; he's probably dead by now. Anyway he's not going to come down here after you, is he?" said Guy.

"No, I suppose not."

"Well then – she loves you, you like her. We needn't go to San Mateo. We could just turn round and I could marry you tonight when we get back. Then, she would be here for you whenever you come back here. You could still work as a shepherd and everyone would be happy." As Guy said this, his face did not look at all happy. In fact, he looked miserable.

"Are you sure you're all right? Guy?" said Pedro. "You don't look… pleased at all."

"I'm perfectly well… when we get home, we'll arrange it with Mondine." Guy looked down.

They turned and walked back in silence. Pedro wondered about Guy's suggestion. Could this be his destiny after all? Maybe it was not such a bad idea. First, he should wait to see what Mondine had to say about it. When they arrived back at his home, Guy began to shout for Mondine.

"Mondine! Where are you? Mondine? Mondine!" He turned to Pedro. "She must be upstairs – let's get her down here and see what she has to say for herself."

He went to the bottom of the stairs and called to Mondine again. Mondine appeared and came down the stairs. She was blushing and didn't look at Pedro. He saw that she understood what this was about. They had talked beforehand, as Guy had said. She was embarrassed about it. Pedro felt sorry for her.

"I've been telling Pedro what we discussed," said Guy. His face was scarlet. His voice was thin and husky. He had to clear his throat several times. Mondine's face flushed an even deeper red than Guy's.

"This can be simply done amongst Believers; I can start it off for you and if you both agree to the marriage then there are no other commitments required of you. So, neither of you have any objection to this?"

Pedro looked at Mondine. She glanced at him. They caught each other's eyes.

"Are you sure you want to do this, Mondine?" said Pedro; his voice was gentle.

"Yes," she said in a small voice.

"No objection, Pedro?" said Guy.

What should he do? He should say, no, wait, but he couldn't find it within himself to do that; he hadn't the heart to say no. He shook his head. No, no objection. Mondine made a small gesture with her head, barely discernible.

"Mondine, come here," said Guy. "One on either side of me. Pedro, here, give me your hands."

Guy took hold of their hands, which he placed one on top of the other. He looked at each of them sternly as he assumed a deeply resonant tone of voice. He chanted like a priest as he said the words.

"Pedro, do you wish to marry and care for this woman, Mondine?"

Pedro could only nod again.

He asked Mondine the same question and she too nodded. "Well then, I now pronounce you man and wife."

Mondine and Pedro looked at one another and exchanged shy glances. What had he done? He stepped forward and gave Mondine a kiss on her cheek. Guy turned away.

"Carry on, Mondine." Guy shooed her off. She disappeared outside, returning later carrying water in a leather bucket.

"Sit down, Pedro, let's have some wine," he said. "Let's think about Arnaud some more. I know he *is* Arnaud, but is he genuine? By that I mean, does he really embrace our faith? And how can we know one way or another? We must think of a way to trick him…"

Guy gabbled on about Arnaud and drank a lot of wine. Pedro hardly spoke – what was happening here? And what had he got himself into? There was an undercurrent of feeling that he didn't understand. They sat down to eat, Mondine and little Guillemette, Guy and Pedro. By this time Guy was drunk, and he picked at his food and swayed over the table at times. It was a strange, awkward, silent meal. When Mondine took Guillemette upstairs to bed, Guy moved to sit by the fire. He didn't speak again. He sat there brooding and dozing. Mondine was a long time upstairs with Guillemette, and when she came down, she disappeared into the back part of the house, staying there for what seemed an inordinate amount of time. Pedro went to find her.

"Mondine," he said. "Is everything all right? I mean, are you all right?"

Tears welled up in her eyes and she shook her head. "I can't say," she said.

Pedro went over to her and put his arm around her shoulder. "Is this to do with Guy?" he said, and she nodded. "You must tell me, Mondine – it's this marriage, isn't it?"

"Yes," she said, and wiped her eyes with a cloth she was holding. "I'll tell you, but don't tell Guy – oh, it's just too bad, but I just can't do what he wants…"

"Let's go upstairs and sit down quietly and you can tell me what's going on."

"I don't want to wake Guillemette up," said Mondine. "She's asleep in my room."

"Look," said Pedro, pointing through the door to Guy, "he's drunk, he's fast asleep – we'll go in and sit at the table and you can tell me quietly what the matter is."

They tiptoed into the room where Guy was snoring loudly by the fire and moved to sit at the table. Mondine placed her hands together on the table as they faced each other.

"I'm expecting another child," she whispered. "So... well... to divert suspicion away from himself, Guy said I should marry you, sleep with you and then claim the child is yours... that's it..."

Pedro took a deep breath. He knew Guy to be capable of deceit, but now he was treating them as if they were merely objects he could move around to save his own skin. He was playing with their lives and denying the child that Mondine was carrying the knowledge of its true father. It was breathtaking.

"But, Pedro, it's wrong, I can't go through with it." Mondine started to cry. "You do understand, don't you?"

"Yes, I do, and don't worry, I don't expect you to go through with it, but we could give him a taste of his own medicine."

"What do you mean?" she said.

"There are two rooms upstairs, aren't there? We'll go up together: you sleep with Guillemette as usual; I'll sleep in Guy's room. He's out for the count, so he'll stay down here tonight. But we won't tell him; we'll let him think we slept together and that we did... well, what he wanted..."

"Let him think it happened and see how he likes it." She laughed and put her hand over her mouth to stifle it. Guy stirred and moved, then settled. They both put their hands over their mouths as they crept up the stairs to their separate rooms.

In the morning, Pedro found Guy sitting at the kitchen table with his head in his hands, looking miserable.

"What is the matter? Is something wrong?" said Pedro.

"I can't say," said Guy. "I think I must fast for a few days, leave me be."

"You had too much wine last night," said Pedro. "That's what's wrong with you."

"Leave me be, I told you," said Guy. "If you want to be helpful, you can go out and get some food for us; we need some food for the day."

It was raining hard, but Pedro went out and called in at a tavern. He stayed out for a couple of hours, hoping this would give Guy time to recover himself. But when he returned later with mutton and conger eel, Guy seemed no better. Pedro gave the food to Mondine to prepare and then sat down with Guy.

"Guy," said Pedro. "Are you feeling unwell?"

Guy shook his head and grunted.

"I've brought some food for us," said Pedro.

"I'm not hungry," said Guy.

"You must eat, I've brought conger eel for you."

"I must fast for three days and three nights," said Guy.

"As you wish."

They sat in silence until Mondine brought in the cooked food. Guy did join them at the table and even picked at the conger eel, but no-one spoke. Even little Guillemette sat quietly, looking at the adults' serious faces and picking up the atmosphere. When they had finished the meal, Guy stood and announced that he would fast for three days and nights. He would spend his time working in the outbuildings at the back of the house, and not to disturb him. When he'd gone, Mondine and Pedro looked at each other.

"We must tell him soon," said Pedro. "It's not fair to torture him like this, although this is not good – in more ways than one."

"I know," she said. "He's broken his Perfect's vows… but one more night," she said. "Really, he deserves it." She grinned.

"One more night." He laughed. "I'm enjoying this too much."

"So am I," she said.

Pedro and Mondine talked, ate and amused Guillemette with stories of the brave knights of old and their beautiful ladies. Guillemette's little face was full of wonder. Guy came into the house to warm himself by the fire on a few occasions. In the evening, although he had said he would fast, he sat beside the fire drinking and fell asleep. Pedro and Mondine went upstairs and left Guy downstairs. The following day Pedro went out in the morning to buy more food. When he returned at midday, he heard raised voices. It was Mondine's voice he heard first.

"I thought you people shouldn't curse and swear…" She stopped talking when Pedro entered the house. Guy looked stricken with despair. Mondine walked away and left them.

"Don't pay any attention to women's whims and fancies," said Pedro, beginning to feel they had pushed Guy far enough and wanting to make him feel better. "I never do."

"It's for their whims and fancies that I've worked," he said. "She's been insolent to me. I can't stay here any longer." He started to collect his tools together and put them in a basket.

"No, Guy," said Pedro. "You must stay and sort this out; it would be foolish to leave now. Besides, it's very cold outside and beginning to snow."

Guy stopped and sat down on the bench beside the fire. He put his head in his hands.

"Look, I'll prepare some food for us, then I'll take Guillemette out, and you and Mondine must discuss this," said Pedro.

Guillemette sat at the table with Pedro as he sliced up some cold meat and bread. Mondine sat at the table too but they were quiet now. This had to be faced soon.

"Come and eat something, Guy," Pedro said.

Guy shook his head. Mondine picked at her food. Guillemette and Pedro tucked in and, in between mouthfuls, they made faces at each other. Guillemette giggled but, sensing the heavy atmosphere, put her hand over her mouth.

"Would you like to come out with me, Guillemette?" said Pedro, feeling sorry for the little girl. "It's snowing and very cold, but you can come if you wrap up warm."

"Yes, yes! I've never been out in snow before. Can we take the sledge?" She looked at Guy and Mondine. "Oh, please, you promised."

Guy and Mondine looked at each other and Guy nodded. "There is one somewhere in one of the outbuildings out back," said Guy. "We were speaking about it a few days ago."

"Come, Guillemette, wrap up warm – we'll go and find that sledge." Pedro turned to Guy as Mondine muffled Guillemette up in her wool cloak and hood, and her sheepskin boots. "We'll be back in good time for dinner this evening."

Guillemette and Pedro picked their way carefully down the steep and icy cobbled streets of Morella. It was snowing thickly, and the ground was covered. They found a spot just outside the village which had a perfect slope. It was lively with children and adults laughing and screaming as they tumbled around on makeshift sledges and threw snowballs at one another. Pedro and Guillemette stayed until the sky became dark and heavy. They were cold and hungry as they plodded home. He thought he'd kept her out too long but she seemed happy as he pulled her on the sledge, slipping and sliding up the tracks of Morella until they arrived back at Guy's house.

Mondine was sitting at the table preparing vegetables. Guy was sitting beside the fire. The atmosphere had changed. They both seemed comfortable, their faces now relaxed. Mondine blushed when she saw Pedro but gave him a small smile. Guy stood and picked up Guillemette.

"Did you have a nice time sledging, Chérie?" he kissed her cheek. "Your cheeks are frozen – come and sit by the fire with me, whilst Maman prepares our meal."

He gave Pedro a little smile. It was a placatory smile, a "sorry, can we be friends?" smile. Pedro gave Guy a "yes, I suppose so" look back.

"Take off your cloak and sit here, Pedro," he said. They all sat near the fire, Guillemette on Guy's knee, and they talked together about sledging and how many times she fell off but never once hurt herself. Guy glanced in Pedro's direction once or twice, and as Pedro's body thawed out in front of the blazing fire, his mind thawed out as well. He could never stay angry with Guy for long. Guy and little Guillemette made a delightful picture of a loving father and daughter.

They sat down to eat together, and Guy blessed the bread in the heretical way with the cloth half on his shoulder and half holding the bread. The recent events weren't mentioned; they spoke of the weather, about Arnaud Baille and about Pedro's plans for the year ahead. That night, Guy asked Pedro to share his bed for the night, saying that he wished to pray with him. Pedro wished that he hadn't agreed as Guy was up and down praying many times during the night.

In the morning, Pedro prepared to leave. He thought it would be autumn before he returned. Guy offered to walk a little way with him. They made their way through the town; the cobbled track was still icy, and they needed to concentrate on staying upright. When they were clear of the houses and buildings, Guy stopped.

"I'm going back home now, Pedro, but I want to say that… well… I deeply regret this recent… what I've said and done."

"What is it that you regret?" said Pedro.

"That I gave you my companion Mondine as your wife. I acted wrongly, and if you wish, I will release you on behalf of God from the promises you made to Mondine, when you married her."

"I see," said Pedro, studying his face. "If Mondine wishes to be released from the marriage, then I'm willing for you to dissolve it."

"I'll talk to Mondine about it, and I will release you both, but… I want you to promise me that if I do, you will no longer behave with her as if she is your wife? You understand me, don't you?"

"Yes, I understand, and I promise," said Pedro. "In fact, I didn't behave with her like a husband anyway, so the child she is carrying is yours for sure."

Guy looked into Pedro's eyes. "That's what she said; I was wondering what you would say."

"It's true, she couldn't do that to you… and neither could I."

"But you let me think so—"

"Yes, it's only what you deserved, but you must let it go now, Guy, enjoy your family. Your secret is safe with me, although I'm sure it won't stay secret for long."

"I know the Believers all think I'm less than I should be," he said. "And it's true, I am. I've done some bad things and broken my vows in more ways than one. I'll have to find a way to go through the ceremony to absolve me of my sins so I can be the Perfect I'm supposed to be again."

"Maybe one day."

"And Pedro, I have another request," said Guy. "Mondine and I talked a lot yesterday and another thing we regret is the disagreement with Blanche, Mondine's sister. Will you go into the mountains to Prades, to find her and bring her to us?"

"Are you sure you won't regret this as well?" said Pedro. "You told me she was a difficult and argumentative woman."

"Even so, we want her to be near us. In these terrible times, we should stay together."

"I'll go as soon as I can. I'm going to Castelldans now to work with Jean. I have to earn my living."

"Go when you can," said Guy. "The last I heard was that she's in the house of a notary there called Pierre Fontana, and she calls herself Condors now."

"I don't know why I should do any more favours for you, Guy, but I'll do this for Mondine, if that's what she wants," said Pedro.

"It is for Mondine. She wants her sister with her."

"Pray, Guy, pray," said Pedro as he left. "For God's sake – and for your own sake, pray."

Guy nodded and kept his head bowed. Pedro couldn't help but feel sorry for him.

It was early spring when Pedro went to Prades, where he found Blanche in the main square. She resembled her sister so much that he was confident about going up to the woman he saw in the marketplace, where busy trading was in progress, and asking her if she was indeed Condors, formerly Blanche.

"And who are you?" she asked sharply, looking at him with a glint of suspicion in her eyes.

"I've been sent by Guy and your sister Mondine," said Pedro. "They want to see you."

"Oh, my Lord," she said. "After all this time – it's two or three years since I saw them – how are they?"

"They're well and living in Morella. They sent me to say they would like to put the past behind them. They would like you to go there, if you wish. They will be pleased to see you."

She looked at him with tears in her eyes. "I would like to see them, yes, I would," she said. "Who did you say you were?"

"I'm Pedro Maury. I'm a shepherd, originally from Montaillou."

She embraced him with such warmth and firmness that he was taken aback. He was so used to being caught between the Believers and their disagreements that it was good to feel this straightforward joy that she clearly felt.

"I'm so happy to see you," she said. "Come, let's find somewhere to sit and talk where we won't be overheard."

They talked for a while. He told her about the other Believers in Aragon. Blanche was eager to see Mondine again and Pedro offered to come back to take her to Morella before Christmas.

On All Saint's Eve, Pedro went to San Mateo to see Aunt Gaillarde.

"We've not seen you in a long time," she said. "How are you? Where've you been? I heard all about your marriage – Mondine told me."

"Let's not discuss that, please, Aunt Gaillarde."

She looked disappointed. "Very well, but you need to know that Mondine had a baby boy in June." She looked knowingly at him. "That tells you all you need to know. Guy used you. You need to watch out for him in future – do you know what he told my sons? That he was wary of you staying with him and Mondine in case you wanted to… well… you know, with Mondine." Aunt Gaillarde gestured, a circle with her left finger and thumb, her right index finger poking in and out through the hole.

"I would never do that," said Pedro. "I know he can be weak at times, but I've forgiven him, so you must too, Aunt Gaillarde."

"Hmm," said Aunt Gaillarde. "I suppose you're right, but look out for yourself in future."

"I will," said Pedro. "Now, tell me about Arnaud Baille. When did you last see him?"

"He was here for a few weeks in the summer. He worked, earned some money and went off again to search for his aunt. He's coming back sometime around Saint Andrew's Day, end of November."

"I'll try and come then, I'd like to see him," he said.

Pedro's visit to Morella was brief. All seemed calm there and both children were thriving. The baby was a lovely boy with his plump limbs and toothless grin. There was a definite resemblance to Guillemette in him; they were brother and sister for sure. Pedro stayed one night to let them know he had found Blanche and would be bringing her to them in time for Christmas. Mondine and Guy were delighted.

It was mid November when Pedro brought Blanche to Morella. He told her Mondine had two children now. The little boy had been born since they'd last met. She glanced at him.

"I don't suppose you know why I fell out with Guy and

Mondine?" she said. "It was because I went into the room they were sharing and found them... well, to speak frankly... they were... fornicating. I saw them."

"Are you quite sure? Couldn't you have been mistaken?" said Pedro, wishing this conversation wasn't happening. He felt such a fool for allowing himself to be used by Guy. He should have known better.

"No, I'm not mistaken. I know what's what and I know what I saw. Do you want me to describe it in detail?" she said.

"No, Blanche, just forget it now. We must pray for Guy to be stronger in future; we must support him. You want to be able to get on with them when you're living with them, don't you?"

"Well, yes," she said.

"Well then, best to let bygones be bygones and look to the future, don't you think so?"

She sighed and agreed. They walked in silence for a while until Pedro spoke.

"You know, there is hope for the future: my brother Jean has been talking with Guy about going to Lombardy one day and becoming a Perfect himself."

"That's good to hear," she said. "We must pray for help to bear our burdens and be able to forgive."

"Mondine needs you – her life is not always easy."

"Yes, I'm sure you're right." She looked at him and smiled. "Now tell me about Arnaud Baille."

They passed the time talking about Arnaud Baille, and Blanche was in good spirits when they arrived at Morella. It was a joyful and tearful reunion with Mondine and Guy. They had prepared a celebratory meal, and Blanche made a big fuss of the children, her niece and nephew.

In the morning, Guy and Pedro left to go to San Mateo, where Arnaud Baille was expected to be back.

"I wonder if he's found his relatives," said Pedro.

"Umm," said Guy. "I'm still wondering whether to trust him and why he has never performed the *melioramentum* – it concerns me – and you know he calls himself Arnaud Sicre most of the time? It's his father's name and that makes me think he's on his father's side."

"Don't worry, I'll teach him the *melioramentum*. Let's see what he has to say for himself this time," said Pedro. "Try not to be concerned, Guy – we're well away from Bishop Fournier down here."

They found Arnaud Baille ensconced in Aunt Gaillarde's house. Arnaud had arrived earlier that day and was talking in an animated way. Aunt Gaillarde and her sons, Pons and Andre, were sitting on benches with him in front of the fire. They were hanging on his every word.

"My aunt is suffering from a heart condition and wishes for two things only at the end of her life," Arnaud was saying. "One is that she would like very much to receive a Perfect in her home. The other is that she wishes that my sister, Jacquemette, become betrothed to a Believer. My aunt is a devout Believer."

Aunt Gaillarde jumped up when Guy and Pedro entered, and she and her sons performed the *melioramentum* to Guy. Guy embraced and kissed them all. They looked to be happy, clearly enjoying the company of Arnaud and his stories. Arnaud looked on as the ritual was performed with Guy, but he didn't join in.

"Sit down," said Aunt Gaillarde, pointing to the bench. "Let me get you some wine. Arnaud is telling us all about his aunt."

"I take it you found her, then?" said Guy stiffly.

"Yes, she does live in the Pallars, as I was told. She took some finding, but I persevered, and it paid off. My sister, Jacquemette, is there with her; she looks after her – my aunt has painful joints and feet; she can hardly walk."

"The poor thing," said Gaillarde. "It's a good job she has your sister there to look after her."

"What about your brother – was he there too?" said Andre.

"No, sadly he wasn't – no-one knows for sure where he is, but he was last heard of in Valencia. I'm thinking I might go there after Christmas and see if I can find him," said Arnaud.

"I could go with you, if you wish," said Pedro.

"It would be good to have some company," said Arnaud.

A small silence prevailed during which Pedro noticed Guy looking intently at Arnaud, who shifted about under his gaze.

"I have some more news for you," said Arnaud brightly. "It's about Father Pierre Clergue – do you remember him, the priest at Montaillou? I've heard he's been arrested by Bishop Fournier, and he's under house arrest in the Abbey of Saint-Antonin, just outside Pamiers."

"Arrested for what?" said Guy.

"For heresy," said Arnaud. Arnaud's eyes glinted in the firelight.

"Oh, my Lord," said Aunt Gaillarde. "A priest of the Roman church arrested for heresy! He's a two-faced devil, that one… if he talks, we're all done for. He knows all about those of us who left the County of Foix. If he tells the Bishop, they'll send someone after us." A tear ran down her cheek. She sniffed and brushed it away.

"He doesn't know where we are," said Pedro. "He will talk about those he knows in Foix, not us. Let's not concern ourselves over Pierre Clergue. I hope he gets what he deserves; he and his family have been playing games with the lives of the people of Montaillou for too long. The Bishop will be much more interested in him than us – after all, he's a priest of the Roman church."

"Well said," said Pons. "Let's not let this spoil our Christmas celebrations."

"Speaking of Christmas," said Arnaud. "I haven't had chance to tell you yet – my aunt is quite well off, she's not short of money, and she gave me some coins so I can treat you, Guy, to a special Christmas this year."

Arnaud reached in the woven bag he had at his feet and brought out a leather purse. "This is full of the ange coins she gave me for you and for my return journey."

"And I will contribute to our Christmas as well, Guy, so that you don't have any extra expenses," said Pedro.

"That's much better news," said Guy, smiling at last. "It will be good to have your company at Christmas."

Guy stayed over for one night in San Mateo and, as the evening progressed, he became more relaxed. Pedro shared his bed that night.

"Are you still worried about Arnaud?" Pedro asked him as they prepared for bed.

"I'm still not sure, Pedro," he said, shaking his head. "I'm still not sure. Something's not right."

"I think we're going to have a good Christmas, Guy, so let's just enjoy the time we have together, you, Mondine and the children – Arnaud and I will join you on Christmas Eve, and we'll not let any of these worries about Arnaud interfere with Christmas."

"Yes, that pleases me – and he does seem genuine – it's just… well, I just… I can't get rid of this feeling of not being able to trust him fully because he doesn't perform the *melioramentum*. It's as if he doesn't understand it at all – he seems to pay no attention when people perform the ritual."

"Well, Guy, life is not easy for any of us down here away from our families and the places we love; we all hate the feeling of having to always look around and watch our backs in case someone's watching, but after all, he's Sybille's son… he knows how close I was to his mother, don't forget that."

"Yes, I know you're right, it's because I know it's me – I'm the one they want most of all. To capture the last Perfect – me – and burn me alive, would be a great symbolic moment for the Inquisition. I'm under no illusions." He sighed deeply.

"Let's pray together and ask God to look after us," said Pedro. They knelt together.

The next morning as Guy and Pedro sat down to eat breakfast with Aunt Gaillarde, her sons and Arnaud, Aunt Gaillarde was full of smiles.

"I've been thinking," she said. "I couldn't get to sleep, I was so excited when this idea occurred to me…"

Guy and Pedro looked at her.

"Well," she said. "As Jacquemette is ready to be betrothed, and as Arnaud's aunt wants her to marry a Believer, I think that Andre, my eldest here, would be the ideal choice of husband – what do you think?"

Pedro looked at Guy and Arnaud, then at the two boys. Arnaud and Andre had clearly been told about this and were nodding in agreement.

"If it's what Andre wants, then why not?" said Pedro.

"Why not indeed," said Aunt Gaillarde. "It's a match made in Heaven: two Believers, bringing together two families of Believers, and Arnaud hinted that there may be quite a substantial dowry involved."

"Well, if she's anything like her mother, Sybille, Jacquemette will be a good woman, and you will be a lucky man, Andre," said Pedro.

Pedro and Arnaud met at Aunt Gaillarde's two days before Christmas, as they had arranged. They walked together to Morella on Christmas Eve. A pale sun shone in the cloudless sky and it was unseasonably mild.

"I think we're going to have a good Christmas, Pedro," said Arnaud.

"I hope so," said Pedro. "Life is not easy for Guy."

"No, I suppose not, always on the lookout for spies," said Arnaud.

"He worries about you," said Pedro.

"Me? Why on earth would he worry about me?"

"It's the fact that you don't perform the *melioramentum*, Arnaud."

"I had no idea that was worrying him," Arnaud said, frowning. "I've seen the others kneeling and kissing him when they meet him, of course, but I thought that was only for those who have been formally accepted into the faith. I didn't realise that everyone should do it. You see, I spent most of my time with my father, and although I saw my mother sometimes and we talked about the faith, I think she thought I was too young to worry about the formalities of it all."

"I understand that's how it was, but it would be a nice surprise for Guy if you performed it when we go to his house today. It would help to set his mind at rest."

"In that case, you'd better tell me what to do," Arnaud said in a bright voice.

"Well, you've seen it often enough, but I'll go through it step by step with you."

Arnaud performed the ritual without hesitation later that day when they arrived in Morella. They were greeted warmly by Guy, Mondine and Blanche, who ushered them towards the fireside and gave them wine. Guy looked pleased when Arnaud performed the *melioramentum*, and Blanche too appeared comfortable and settled. There was no hint of any tension between any of them. Arnaud played with the children, tickling the baby and making shapes with his hands to amuse little Guillemette, until both children were taken off to bed.

Arnaud then related the story of his aunt to Blanche and Mondine and explained that Aunt Gaillarde was keen to make a match between her eldest son Andre and Arnaud's sister Jacquemette, who would have a large dowry to bring to the marriage.

"Aunt Alazaïs has also given me money to go and search for my brother, Bernard, who we think might be in Valencia," he said. "And Pedro has offered to go with me."

"Is there any news of the Inquisition? I wonder about friends and relatives I've left behind," said Blanche.

"Bishop Fournier has Gaillard de Pomiès assisting him as well as Geoffroy d'Ablis," he said.

"That old devil, d'Ablis, why has he lived so long?" said Blanche, and she told the story of her interrogation by him. Everyone laughed, particularly Arnaud, who had never heard it before. Arnaud asked her to repeat what she had said to Gaillard de Pomiès.

As the evening progressed, Blanche and Mondine served a festive meal. There was fish for Guy and wild boar for everyone else, served with vegetables. There were preserved fruits afterwards and cheese, and wine. After this, Guy began to preach.

"The prophet, Isaiah, tells the story of a Good Man who started to have doubts about the faith because there was disagreement amongst them. He decided to read to find out if he had a good or bad faith. He read the books for three days and nights without growing weary…

The meal, the wine, the fire and the sermon, which went on for a long time, made everyone sleepy, and when Guy's sermon was over, they all went to bed. Guy, Arnaud and Pedro shared a bed.

On Christmas Eve and on Christmas morning, none of them wanted to go to the Roman church in Morella. No-one wanted to genuflect and cross themselves, and smile at the priest. Pedro hoped none of their neighbours would notice and think it remarkable that no-one from this household attended church. After eating up the remains of the previous day's feast at midday, Pedro suggested a walk. It was partly to avoid another of Guy's sermons. Arnaud and Guy went with him. It was cold but the sun was shining, and they strode out in good spirits. Guy told Arnaud he thought it was a good decision to search for his brother.

"We should approach as many Believers as we can; we must stay close and all help each another. I'm pleased that you are thinking of marrying your sister to Andre – he's a hardworking young man. When Believers marry, they can support each other. They can receive the Good Men in their homes and hear their preaching, and…" Guy stopped and looked at Arnaud. "I have been thinking, as I am the only Perfect now left, as far as we know, I am prepared to make the journey to see your aunt and to join the young couple in marriage."

"Are you sure that's wise?" said Pedro.

"None of us can be sure of anything in this life," said Guy. "But I think… I feel God is calling me to do this, so I should go…"

"My aunt and I wondered if you would feel able to make the journey. My aunt will willingly serve you and welcome you into her home," said Arnaud. "The money she has given me will pay for a horse to take you, if you want one. My aunt suggested making the journey to the Pallars during Lent. We will all be eating fish, and no-one will think anything of it. After that we can go to Valencia to search for my brother."

"I believe that Raymond Issaurat may be in Valencia too," said Guy. "You could make discreet enquiries about him when you're there."

They began to plan for the journey. Lent, in March, was only a few weeks hence. Pedro had to leave to go back to his sheep, and Arnaud, Andre and Guy agreed to make the arrangements.

When Pedro arrived at the pastures, the shepherds told him that his brother Jean was lying in the barn, ill with a fever. Pedro went to look at him. Jean was burning hot and glassy-eyed. Pedro gave him a sip of water from his leather pouch.

"Jean, how long have you been like this?"

"A few days," he said in a hoarse voice. "I'm getting worse – my chest is tight. I can hardly breathe. I'm weak."

"You need to be at Aunt Gaillarde's, where you can be looked after," said Pedro. "I'll find a donkey for hire so I can take you there, could you manage that?"

Jean nodded and licked his dry lips. Pedro found a donkey for hire through one of the shepherds. They weren't far from San Mateo and they made the journey slowly. Pedro helped Jean to sit on the donkey, but Jean was weak and limp, and unable to sit upright and maintain his balance on the animal. Pedro walked beside the donkey holding Jean in position to prevent him from slipping off. Jean was burning with fever. Progress was slow. It was a great relief when they arrived at Aunt Gaillarde's house. By this time, Jean was talking in a loud voice and not making any sense. Pedro managed with the help of Andre and Pons to get Jean off the donkey, support him into one of the rooms off the courtyard of Aunt Gaillarde's house, take off his clothes and put Jean in a clean bed. Aunt Gaillarde and Pedro stood looking at Jean, concerned by his flushed face, his shallow, rasping breathing, and his restless tossing and turning.

"I think he needs to see Guy," said Aunt Gaillarde.

"I think you're right," said Pedro. "I'll see if I can make him understand, see if I can get any sense out of him – it's up to him, I think."

"I'll go and fetch some water," said Aunt Gaillarde.

Jean's eyes were closed. Pedro put his hand on Jean's forehead and Jean opened his eyes, which looked bloodshot and wild.

"What are you doing?" shouted Jean. "Don't touch me, leave me alone."

Aunt Gaillarde came back into the room with a pitcher of water. "What's the matter?" she said. "What's he shouting about?"

"He's feverish," said Pedro in a whisper. "He's not in his right mind." He turned to Jean and knelt beside the bed. "Jean, it's Pedro." Jean opened his eyes again and looked at Pedro. "Jean, you're looking very ill and weak; I think the time has come for you to put your affairs in order... and to do what a Believer has to do at this time," said Pedro.

"I'll put my affairs in order, but I'll not have our Saint Pierre here. No matter what, I don't want to be received or made a heretic by him." His voice was rising as he spoke, and he tried to move himself up.

Pedro turned to look at Aunt Gaillarde. "Our Saint Pierre?" said Pedro, frowning. "Who do you think he means?"

"I think he means our Perfect. Guy called himself Pierre Belibaste when he first came down here," said Aunt Gaillarde. "But if he's speaking like that, I think he's possessed by the Devil." She moved closer to Jean. "You should let the Perfect come."

"Don't talk to me about that. I'll get you all arrested and you'll go to Hell," said Jean, his voice becoming louder.

"Stop it, stop talking like that," said Aunt Gaillarde.

"Come away, Aunt Gaillarde, let him be," said Pedro. "He's got a fever; he doesn't know what he's saying." Pedro was still kneeling beside Jean. He took Jean's hand between both of his hands. "Jean, hush, listen – it's up to you; it's your decision. I don't mind what you do; you must do as you wish. I'm going to sponge you down and give you some herbs, which will help to cool the fever. Then you can rest."

Aunt Gaillarde opened her mouth to speak again but Pedro got up and ushered her out of the room.

"Leave him, Aunt Gaillarde," he said.

"If he carries on talking like that, he'll get us all arrested," she said when they were in the courtyard. "It would be better to send him out of this world, rather than have him put us all in danger."

"I'll not tolerate any of that kind of talk; I will never agree to the death of my brother under any circumstances, nor to the death of anyone else, for that matter, and if I found out that you had done anything to hasten his death, I will devour you with my teeth if I can't get revenge on you otherwise. Besides, you would go to Hell for that." Pedro stopped. "I remember you wanted to murder Jeanne, Mersende's daughter – you wanted to give her some medicinal red arsenic or throw her into a ravine. It's not the answer to any of our problems. I'm going to stay for a few days; I'll care for him myself. When I'm sure he's recovering, I'll leave him with you. Now, will you bring some water and a cloth so I can sponge him down and a beaker so I can get him to drink?"

Gaillarde quietened immediately at this. Pedro looked at Jean. He was sweating and red-faced. He wondered whether he should send for Guy but was reluctant to do anything that may provoke Jean to another outburst. He knew how to care for Jean, cooling him with sponges soaked in cold water, making sure Jean drank as much as possible, washing him, changing the linen. He'd seen it done many times before in his family. He had Aunt Gaillarde's help, such as it was; he would nurse Jean through this.

After Jean's fever broke a few days later and Jean, although weak, was better and able to think more clearly, there was no need to send for Guy. Jean stayed with Aunt Gaillarde for a few weeks, until he was fit enough to join Pedro at the pastures. He didn't remember much about his illness and Pedro never told him what he had said. Jean, Pedro and Andre worked together on the same pastures until the beginning of Lent, when Andre and Pedro left to go to Morella to meet Arnaud Baille and Guy to prepare for their journey to the Pallars.

CHAPTER 18

Guy Belibaste

The business of Pedro and Mondine's marriage tormented Guy. There was little respite. The guilt was unbearable. How badly he'd used those whom he loved and who loved him, behaving as if he could hide the truth both from God and the other Believers. He was blessed with Mondine as his partner and Pedro as his friend. He could have lost them both. But his actions had been borne out of desperation. His life was impossible, a constant struggle with his wish to live as Mondine's husband – *properly* live with her, sleep together as man and wife, and be open about the situation with everyone – and how he knew he should live his life as a Perfect. When he gave into temptation and was intimate with her, he was overwhelmed by hatred of himself and remorse. He lurched between thinking that he'd broken his vows anyway, so what did it matter if he behaved as a husband with her one more time, and the hope that if he abstained from gratifying his urges and fasted and prayed, that God would forgive him much more readily. All this circled round and round in his mind. He thought he would go mad. Sometimes he wished he could go completely mad, then he would know nothing of this.

Then there was the *consolamentum* he had given the Perfect Raymond de Toulouse. Raymond, kind, patient Raymond, who had nursed him through his illness and injuries in his calm, gentle way – and he, Guy, had repaid him by giving him a *consolamentum* which would be invalid in the eyes of God. Was God powerful and forgiving enough to save Raymond's soul? After all, Raymond had done nothing wrong; it was he, Guy, who should be punished. And then there was the death of Barthélemy, the shepherd. Had he meant to kill him? Perhaps it could have all been sorted out calmly. But his anger that day about everything all came together, his resentment at being sent on that fateful journey. His frustration at not being able to live the life he wished. Then he came back to knowing it was an accident. At his lowest point, he would consider the best way to kill himself. Maybe throw himself down a ravine up in the mountains? But the death could be slow and painful if he didn't die immediately. Eat a poisonous plant? He didn't know much about plants and he might make himself ill but not die. Could he hang himself? He would mess up the knot and injure himself. He was such a hopeless coward that he could not even kill himself.

He prayed. Would God show him the way? He found a shred of hope within himself, which he could build upon. This involved planning for a future where he could make the long Inquisition-infested journey to Lombardy and undergo another *consolamentum* ceremony with the Perfects there. He would then devote his life to spreading the faith and die a happy man. God would answer his prayers and show him the way. It felt as if God was showing him the way already, through Arnaud Sicre/Baille and Arnaud's aunt's request for a Perfect. It was a way he could cross the border. And after visiting Arnaud's aunt in the Pallars, he could make his way to Lombardy. Perhaps Pedro would come with him to Lombardy. He would need someone to help him, to keep him on the right pathway. How weak and hopeless he was, so ill-suited to the path he had chosen, to the path which God had shown him.

Then there were the terrible nagging doubts about Arnaud, and his story of his aunt and sister. He didn't trust Arnaud Sicre/Baille one bit. Arnaud, who didn't perform the *melioramentum*. Arnaud, who should have known to perform the *melioramentum* if he was a Believer. Pedro was blind to Arnaud because he had loved Arnaud's mother. Pedro didn't believe that Arnaud would betray them, didn't think Arnaud would betray his mother's friends. Pedro didn't care about money and property himself, but Guy knew that others did, and he suspected that Arnaud did. Quite what money was involved, he wasn't sure, but he guessed the Inquisition would pay well for the services of spies. The Church was wealthy; money from Rome must be funding the campaign against the Cathars. And he, Guy, was the last of the Perfects; he would be a great prize – whoever turned him in would be rewarded substantially. Yet, despite these concerns, he was drawn to going with Arnaud across the border. God was calling him to make this journey: he had to go; this was his chance for atonement. Yes, he would go, but he would do all he could to protect himself.

CHAPTER 19

Pedro Maury

It was late afternoon when they arrived in Morella. As soon as they entered the house, Guy took hold of Pedro's arm and, ignoring Andre and Arnaud, who were about to perform the *melioramentum*, asked Pedro to walk out with him. This left the others gathered inside, open-mouthed, and Pedro protesting. Guy ignored this and continued to guide Pedro outside and down the lane away from his house. The houses and workshops on each side were quiet, closed early as it was Saturday. Guy stopped when they rounded a bend and glanced back.

"Guy, what are you doing?" said Pedro, irritated. "Let go of my arm. What about the others?"

"I'm very worried about going over the border," said Guy, looking around. "I've got a very bad feeling about it, so much so that I've been to see my neighbour, Galia."

"Your neighbour?" said Pedro. "What about?"

"He's a soothsayer; I asked him if the journey would go well. He performed a spell to find out," said Guy.

"I can't believe you would do that, Guy, you're a Cathar Perfect, for Heaven's sake. Whatever were you thinking?"

"I've been in such a state – I had to do something," said Guy. "Galia took one of my shoes and measured from the hearth to the door of my house with it. He said that if the whole shoe or most of it, on the last measure was outside the door of the house, this meant that if I went on this journey, I would not come back, but if more than half of the shoe or the whole shoe remained inside, I would return. But most of the shoe was outside. I'm so very afraid." His eyes gleamed wildly in his haggard face as he stared at Pedro.

"Guy, for Jesus's sake, you know that spells and witchcraft are worthless; they're just superstitions that old women cling on to, but you, you're a Perfect – you should know better. I shouldn't have to tell you that what you need to do is to pray to God for guidance."

"I do pray, but still I don't know the answer," said Guy. "I believe God is calling me to do this journey, but I feel so much foreboding about it."

Pedro studied Guy's face. There were deep lines around Guy's eyes and mouth, and dark circles under his eyes. He looked as if he hadn't slept in a long time. He was thinner. Pedro sighed. Guy was not strong enough to live up to his responsibilities and the expectations of the Believers. After all, Guy was just a man, like himself, and everyone else.

"Look, Guy," said Pedro. "If you don't have the heart for this journey then you mustn't go."

"I have promised Arnaud I will, and if God, my Father, has asked for me, and I believe he has, then it is time for me to go to him," he said. "So, I will go, Pedro, I must go. And I have reasons of my own for going over the border."

"What do you mean?"

"I'm thinking of going on to Lombardy. But let's just leave it at that, Pedro."

Pedro sighed again. If Guy was taken by the Inquisition when they crossed over the border to Foix, there would only be one outcome. And Lombardy would be out of the question. But if Guy was determined to go, he would do his best to support and protect him.

Later that evening, Pedro and Guy helped Arnaud and Andre put together a marriage contract. It was simple. Arnaud's aunt would give a dowry to her niece, Jacquemette, of 100 Barcelona shillings, a new set of clothes and two mules to carry their belongings. They sealed this arrangement by oath and Guy officiated. After this, they dined together with Blanche and Mondine. Guy blessed the bread, which he gave to them solemnly. They took it and ate with serious faces. Guy was silent and unsmiling throughout the meal, but Arnaud and Andre began to talk about the journey, how long it would take, where they would stop overnight, about Jacquemette, and the forthcoming marriage, how the marriage would be good for the Cathar community down here, and how they needed more people of the faith, and more Perfects. Blanche and Mondine were quieter. Pedro suspected that they, like him, were worried about Guy's sombre mood and him making this journey.

The four men slept in one room together that night. Guy was up and down praying many times. It disturbed the others, but they were up early the next day to start their long walk. Guy kissed Mondine and the children tenderly as they said goodbye. He had a tear in his eye as he lingered with his arm around Mondine. Pedro took Guy's arm.

"Come, Guy, we must leave now – let's not delay any longer," he said gently. "We'll be back in no time and they will all be fine – Blanche is here to help."

They were a subdued group when they set out, but it was a fine sunny day and, after walking through one of the gateways in the stone walls of Morella, and leaving the goodbyes behind, Andre and Arnaud were soon talking and laughing again. They made their way past the cultivated terraces of vines outside the town. Guy remained quiet and preoccupied. Pedro walked alongside him. Their journey was to take them through a changing landscape. At times it was flat and scrubby; at other times there were wooded foothills, and then there were the rocky outcrops of mountains to negotiate. Streams, waterfalls and rivers fell down rocks and meandered through the valleys and plains. Their first stop was to be Beceite, where they hoped to see Aunt Mersende.

It was the end of March, a good time to travel as the weather was mild, not too hot and unlikely to rain. As the sun rose at midday, they stopped to eat their bread, cheese and trout pâté in the shade at the edge of a wood. They drank from a stream at the side of the track. After he'd eaten, Pedro leant back against a tree trunk.

"I think we should stay at the tavern in Beceite," said Pedro. "We don't want to bump into mad Jeanne when we go to Aunt Mersende's."

"I must stay away from her at all costs," said Guy. "She is completely out of her mind."

"It's better if I don't meet her," said Arnaud. "I visited Aunt Mersende before once – mad Jeanne wasn't there, but I've heard everything about her."

"Andre and I could go to see Aunt Mersende," said Pedro, "whilst you, Guy and Arnaud, arrange for us to stay and dine at the tavern. I'll make sure Aunt Mersende gets Jeanne out of the way so you can go later, Guy. Aunt Mersende will want to see you."

They made good progress and arrived at Beceite late in the afternoon. The village nestled on the banks of the River Matarranya beneath massive limestone mountains that surrounded it to the north and east. The tavern lay on the other side of the village to where Aunt Mersende lived. Guy and Arnaud went on ahead to the tavern whilst Andre and Pedro made their way to her house.

"We'll not stay long," Pedro said to Andre. "We'll say we're just passing through, that we're going to see about buying some sheep at Ascó. If I can, I'll catch Aunt Mersende by herself, and tell her to expect me and Guy later this evening and that she should get Jeanne out of the way." Andre nodded agreement.

Jeanne was inside the house with her mother when they arrived. She looked at them suspiciously, but she listened to their story about passing through without comment, then went outside saying she must bring in the washing. As soon as she disappeared, Pedro whispered to Aunt Mersende.

"Aunt Mersende, you must get rid of Jeanne tonight, tell her you're ill or whatever excuse you think best... then Guy and I will come back later. He's at the tavern with Arnaud Baille."

Mersende opened her eyes wide with surprise but nodded her assent. Jeanne came back inside, and they passed the time talking about the fictional sheep they might buy at Ascó, and eating the bread and drinking the water that Aunt Mersende gave them. Jeanne behaved politely enough, although Pedro felt her watching him as she folded the laundry she'd brought in. He was on edge the whole time they were there. Lying was hard work. He was worried he might say the wrong thing and he wasn't in the right frame of mind for small talk. So, as soon as they felt enough time had passed, they made their escape back to the tavern, and joined Arnaud and Guy. The tavern was small and quiet. It smelled strongly of an unidentifiable but rancid aroma. There were two men eating and a gathering of four others sitting at one side, drinking. It was unlikely that anyone would recognise Guy. He had never been to Beceite before, so they could relax for an hour or two. But Guy was quiet. He regularly glanced furtively around the room. Guy, please stop, thought Pedro. If these people had no suspicions at first, they would now because of Guy's behaviour.

"If that smell is the food, it doesn't smell too good," said Andre.

"We've no choice, there's nowhere else to go," said Pedro. "We'll have to try it."

The landlord said it was fish stew made from local sources. But it was hard to identify what kind of fish was in the grey mush that appeared in front of them. They picked and poked and tasted.

"It's tasteless," said Andre, who usually enjoyed his food.

"You and I don't need to eat this," said Guy to Pedro. "Mersende will have something for us."

"That's true, but we must make a show of eating, so we seem as if we're staying here. We'll go to Aunt Mersende's when it's dark. We'll say we're going for a stroll, if anyone asks. The more careful we are about who sees where we go and who we know, the better," said Pedro. Was he being over-cautious? Possibly, but he would take no risks.

When darkness fell, Guy and Pedro left to walk over to Aunt Mersende's house. She performed the *melioramentum* to Guy and welcomed them in. Jeanne was not there. Aunt Mersende told them, as she offered them wine, that Jeanne often stayed out – she thought there might be a man. They took the wine, not wishing to offend her. Pedro was tired. He saw Guy and Aunt Mersende had plenty to say to each other, so he left them talking and went to bed.

The next morning, Pedro rose early and ate an early breakfast of stale bread and goat's milk with Aunt Mersende. She told him she had talked with Guy until the cock crowed. And she was very afraid for Guy making this journey. She thought it was the wrong thing to do.

"Someone should have gone on ahead to see if the reason behind the journey is true or false. I've heard of these journeys before, which have ended badly for the Perfects. They're lured to a place where someone is waiting to arrest them. I beg you, Pedro, persuade him not to go," she said.

"I have spoken to him about this, and he has the same concerns, but he's made up his mind. He says if God, his Father, wants him, then he will go. Aunt Mersende, he must make up his own mind. I shan't try to persuade him to do otherwise," said Pedro. "But I will speak to Arnaud about these worries that we all have."

"I must also tell you…" Mersende hesitated.

"What?" He looked at her sharply.

"It's Jeanne…"

"What about her?"

"She's got in with a bad lot," said Aunt Mersende. She looked sheepish and avoided his eyes. "They're a band of wandering rogues and vagabonds; they live by stealing sheep or anything they can get their hands on. They know a man in the village that Jeanne drinks with. They've told Jeanne that they're searching for some heretics living in Aragon… that there are bounties on the heads of two of them and… when they find them, they'll take them to the Inquisition."

"Christ in Heaven," said Pedro. "Lord above. Do not tell her about our journey, for God's sake – last night, they could have come into the tavern… you should have said… Aunt Mersende, how could you? We were in real danger last night and so were you."

"I was too terrified," said Mersende. "I *am* terrified. I don't know what to do for the best. Perhaps I should move somewhere else. I threatened to kill her if she even thought about divulging what she knew, because I'm one of them, her own mother." Mersende began to cry.

"Did you tell Guy?"

"I nearly did but thought better of it."

"Thank God for that," said Pedro. "He's got enough on his plate without that to worry about as well." He sighed deeply. "For God's sake, watch Jeanne, keep her happy and do not provoke her."

"I'll do my best," said Mersende.

Guy appeared at the breakfast table, looking tired and drawn. Pedro watched him as he picked at the bread. This already dangerous journey had just become even more so.

They met Andre and Arnaud outside the tavern after breakfast. They said the landlord had been asking where they were.

"Don't worry, we told him you'd decided to go on ahead overnight to see some relatives in the next village," said Arnaud. "I'm not sure he was convinced, but he'd didn't ask any more questions."

Pedro looked at Guy. "The sooner we get out of here, the better," he said.

There was an awkward silence as Andre and Arnaud looked from Pedro to Guy.

"How was Aunt Mersende?" said Andre.

"Arnaud," said Guy. His voice was weak. "I hope you're taking us to a good place."

"Guy, you know where we are going," said Arnaud.

"I hope so," said Guy, looking with suspicion at Arnaud.

"We're going to Ascó today," said Pedro brightly, trying to overcome the despair which had gripped him since the conversation with Mersende earlier. "It's another long day's walk, so we'd best get going. Guy, you're tired. You talked to Aunt Mersende all night. She's full of doom and gloom. She's enough to put the fear of God into anyone. Let's get away from here."

Pedro set off at a cracking pace. The fury he felt with Aunt Mersende was hard to contain. The others were almost running to keep up with him. How could she have neglected to warn them the previous night about Jeanne? Why did she keep Guy up so long knowing he had a long journey ahead of him? It was difficult to think clearly when he was so angry. But gradually he calmed as they strode out. The snow-topped mountains surrounded them, the sun was bright and warm, and an idea about how he could put Arnaud to the test began to take shape in his mind. He allowed it to grow and decided it was probably the best he could come up with. He stopped and looked around for the others. Arnaud and Andre were close behind him, but Guy trailed behind.

"You two go on ahead – I'll wait for Guy and help him along."

"I'm so slow. I'm holding you all up," said Guy as he caught up with Pedro. "I just can't go any faster this morning."

"Let's sit on these rocks and rest for a moment," said Pedro. They watched the other two walk on ahead and out of earshot.

"I know you're worried about this journey and about Arnaud," said Pedro.

Guy sighed. "I keep asking myself why I am doing this. All I know is that I feel this is something I must do, that God is calling me, and that keeps me moving on." He hesitated and took a deep breath. "I have in my heart a hope that I can redeem myself for all my failures, so I must keep going."

"How do you imagine you could do that?" said Pedro.

"I can't say," said Guy.

They walked on in silence again until Pedro said he thought they should try and put Arnaud to the test.

"And I've got an idea of how we can do that," he said. "It's not the most original idea, but I can't think of anything else… and there isn't much time."

After Pedro told Guy about his idea to expose Arnaud, Guy stepped out with a longer stride and a firmer step. They walked on through a rocky woodland as they approached Ascó from the south. The village looked like it was part of the rocky landscape, as if it had always been there. They found Andre and Arnaud waiting near a vineyard on the riverbank, where wine was for sale.

"This looks a good place to buy some wine for this evening," said Arnaud.

Pedro put his head around the open door of the large wayside shed. Steps led down into the cool, dark cavernous space that housed the barrels of wine.

"You all go on to the inn. I'll buy the wine," he said. "I'll join you there."

"We'll arrange for a room and some food," said Guy. "I hope we have a better meal tonight. The food Aunt Mersende gave us was stale."

Andre and Arnaud left with Guy. Pedro arrived at the inn shortly after. A good smell of cooking greeted him. He looked around. The floors of the small space were swept and clean, and a handful of tables and benches were arranged around the room. The landlord nodded at him genially as he entered. A few men in working clothes were already seated and eating their food with relish. Guy and Arnaud were settling themselves at a corner table opposite Andre. Pedro squashed himself between the tables and other diners, greeting them and excusing himself as he went. He held up the two wineskins he'd just purchased as he approached the others.

"I don't think we'll drink all that," said Guy.

"We should celebrate – we're well on our way to the Pallars," said Pedro, pouring some wine into Arnaud's goblet. "Try this, Arnaud, tell me what you think."

Arnaud savoured the wine, rolling it round his mouth. "That's good," he said. "It's strong but smooth."

"Do you like it?"

"Umm, I do." Arnaud smiled and held out his goblet for more.

"Straight from the barrel," said Pedro. "Good health and here's to a safe journey!" He held his goblet up high.

The others joined in although Guy's face was serious, and he looked around at their fellow diners suspiciously as he had done at Beceite. Pedro took charge of the wineskins. Guy watched him as he filled up Arnaud's glass and gave himself and the others smaller amounts. Andre and Arnaud, chatting and laughing together, appeared not to notice. Guy shot glances around the room from time to time and remained quiet, saying he was very tired and wanted an early night. They ate trout pâté on bread and then large pieces of fresh fish with bread and vegetables.

"Arnaud, wait until you see the Servels' daughter in a few days' time," said Andre. "She's very pretty – you might start thinking about marriage yourself when you see her."

"I might be thinking of shomething. I'm not sure it'll be marriage," said Arnaud, slurring his words.

"Better watch out," said Andre. "That's how it starts."

"I'll tell you what I'm ready for," said Arnaud. "Shome more of that delicious wine." He hiccupped. He pushed his fish around his platter with a piece of bread but had trouble putting it neatly into his mouth. He slurped some more wine. Andre looked at him.

"He's drunk," he said, laughing. "Arnaud is drunk."

"He does seem a bit drunk," said Pedro. "Enjoying the wine, Arnaud? Have some more." He poured more wine for Arnaud, who took another large swig of it. He looked round at them grinning and slid gracefully down from the bench onto the stone floor.

"I can't believe he's so drunk so quickly," said Andre. "He looks flat out."

"He does," said Pedro. "I think I'd better take him up to bed."

Guy helped Pedro get Arnaud on his feet, as the other diners and drinkers laughed and shouted out.

"That was quick! Hasn't he had a drink before?"

Arnaud seemed to come round a bit. He swayed but managed to support himself by holding on to the table. He started to lift his tunic and undo his clothing.

"He's going to pee," said Guy. "Take him outside."

"I'll help you," said Andre, standing up.

A man from the next table stood. "Need a hand?" He grinned.

"No, thanks, I can manage," said Pedro. "Look, he's walking now."

"You stay here," said Guy to Andre.

Andre sat down. Arnaud and Pedro stumbled out of the door. Arnaud's arm was around Pedro's neck and Pedro had his arm around Arnaud's back. They made their way outside and into a small opening leading into an alleyway adjacent to the inn. Arnaud peed there and leant back against the wall, looking at Pedro.

"Is that better?" said Pedro. Arnaud nodded slowly. "Good. Listen, Arnaud, I've been thinking, I've got an idea – this is an opportunity for me and you; why don't we take that old heretic in there back to Pamiers, and get paid for him by the Inquisition? We'd get a lot of money for him – we could share it out between us, and we could each live comfortably off it. He only spouts a load of old nonsense anyway."

Arnaud seemed to regain his senses. He looked at Pedro, narrowing his eyes. "Am I hearing you right? Everything is going round and round, but if you said what I think you said, well, I could never do that; I'd never betray him," he slurred. "And I'd never shtand by and watch you betray him either – that's outrageoushsh." Swaying as he spoke, he poked Pedro in the chest with his finger. "Pedro Maury, that's outrageoushsh."

"That's good, Arnaud, very good. Now, forget I said it, let's get you back in there."

Pedro put his arm round Arnaud, and they staggered back into the tavern.

"Give me a hand, will you, Guy, I think we should put him to bed. You stay here, Andre, we can manage him, and we'll be back down to finish off the wine."

They guided Arnaud up the stairs; he was cooperative and easy to manage with them supporting him. They put him on the bed. His eyes closed. Pedro shook him but he didn't respond.

"Help me undress him," said Pedro. "He's completely out of it; we won't hear from him until the morning." Together, they undressed Arnaud and covered him with a blanket, and Pedro told Guy what had happened. "I tested him out," said Pedro. "There's nothing to worry about. He's not going to betray us; he was upset when I suggested that we could hand you over to the Inquisition and get some money for you. He was really outraged by it."

"I'm not surprised he was outraged," said Guy, looking offended. "I only hope you're right."

"Let's leave him to sleep it off. Forget about him for a while, and don't say a word to Andre."

That night, Andre shared a bed with Arnaud, and Pedro slept with Guy. They were all in the same room. Guy rose several times during the night to pray, disturbing Pedro, although Arnaud and Andre slept deeply. The next morning, Arnaud moaned that he had a headache.

"I'm not surprised, you were drunk pretty quickly," said Andre.

"Do you remember anything of last night?" Pedro grinned at Arnaud.

"Not much," said Arnaud. "That wine was strong, wasn't it? I remember coming to bed, taking my clothes off… then I must have passed out; I was completely out, but I don't feel so good this morning."

"There's no rush this morning; it will only take us an hour or two to reach Flix," said Pedro. "We'll have an early lunch there with Pons Ortola, a friend of mine. But no talk of the Good Men, remember. You'll like Pons and his wife. I hope they've not forgotten about us."

"We should have some more good fish there," said Guy. "It's noted for its fishing because the village is surrounded by a bend in the river."

It was a pleasant short walk along the riverbank to Flix, which lay in green pastures and a horseshoe-shaped curve in the river. It was a fine dry day and a comfortable temperature for walking. They reached Flix in good time for lunch. Pedro's friend had remembered. They spent a pleasant couple of hours with the couple. The simple lunch was set up at the back of the village house which overlooked the river. The fish was excellent and, with no talk of the Good Men, they all relaxed. It set them up for the next stage of the journey to Sarroca, where they would stay the night. Pons Ortola gave them bread, cheese and fish for their journey.

Sarroca was due north. It would take them the rest of the day to walk there. It was early evening when they saw the rocky hill with a castle on the top, which told them they were almost there.

"We should look for shelter for the night," said Pedro. He was worried about Guy's overtly furtive behaviour whenever they stayed in public places. "A barn or shepherd's hut would be safest for us."

They soon came upon a barn on the outskirts of Sarroca. The door was open. The sharp, earthy smell of hay enveloped them as they entered. There was no-one about to ask if they could stay, so they arranged themselves on bales of hay and ate the supper that Pons Ortola had given them. They slept well on their hay beds covered by their cloaks and woke refreshed. Even Guy seemed brighter.

It was only a morning's walk to their next destination of Lleida. The plan was to arrive around midday and to spend the rest of the day and night with Esperte Servels. They all looked forward to staying at this Cathar household with someone they felt at ease with. Lleida was a busy town and Esperte Servels and her daughter, Mathène, who was about eighteen, lived on the outskirts. Esperte and Mathène were excited to see them and welcomed them with warm smiles. They performed the *melioramentum* to Guy, and he blessed them. A delicious smell of cooking pervaded the air.

"It's very good to be here amongst other Believers," said Guy. "And something smells good."

The women had prepared a feast of fish for them. It tasted very good and was beautifully served on bread trenchers. They brought out some local wine which they said was of a special vintage year, especially for Guy and the others. The four men relished the home-cooked food and attention. Esperte was grieving for the loss of her husband, who had died not long before. He was unconsoled as his death had been sudden. She was clearly glad of the company and the opportunity to talk with Guy about this. It also served as a diversion from Guy's worries. Guy was at his best when one of the Believers needed him in this way. Andre and Arnaud enjoyed an evening of flirting with Mathène, who was lively as well as pretty. They all slept well that night.

The next morning, Mathène and Esperte waved goodbye with many good wishes for their journey and hopes for future visits from their Perfect. The men left early as it was a long day's walk to their next planned stopping place, Agramunt. They were all refreshed. Even Guy seemed to be in better spirits.

It was quiet and still as they strode out in the cool air of the morning. The track they followed had a hedge of thorny bushes on one side, marking the boundary of a farmer's land. As they passed along this hedgerow, there was a rustling and chattering noise. A magpie flapped out in front of them and landed on the track. It strutted across the path in front of them. Guy stopped, his eyes wide as he watched the bird, which flew up and perched in a tree only to swoop down and strut across the path again. Then, chattering loudly and looking at them, it strutted back across the path for a third time. Guy's face turned white. His eyes widened. He sank to his knees, saying, "Holy Spirit, help us."

Pedro ran up to the offending magpie and chased it off. "Be off with you, you damned bird." He turned to Guy. "It's just a bird; such things are superstitious nonsense, a matter for old women." His voice was overly cheerful.

"It's an omen, it's telling us… it's crossed our path three times," said Guy, looking up. "I hope to God that you are being honest with us, Arnaud, because I have a very bad feeling about this." He fixed Arnaud with his staring eyes.

"Of course, Guy, there's nothing to worry about," said Arnaud in a bright but strangled voice. He cleared his throat and his eyes slid away. "You mustn't take any notice of a silly bird."

Guy looked so serious and terrified that Pedro gently held on to his arm and helped him up on his feet. He gestured to Arnaud and Andre to move on.

"You can turn back now, Guy, if you wish to. There's still time to change your mind. But we're not so far from Tírvia now, so time is running out. What do you want to do?"

"I must go on," said Guy. "God, my Father, is calling me." He embraced Pedro with tears in his eyes and took a deep breath. "Help me to go on, Pedro."

Pedro stood before Guy and put his arms on Guy's shoulders. He looked into his eyes, saying, "Of course I will, Guy, I will do my best for you. I'll walk beside you."

"Our Father which art in Heaven…" said Guy, as they set off again, Guy reciting the Lord's prayer and Pedro walking beside him.

They stopped at the small village of Pons for lunch and bought bread, sausages and cheese to take with them. The afternoon seemed endless as they progressed towards Trago, where there was a stream to ford. They stood on the steep bank and stared at the flowing water. It looked deep. Arnaud suggested that Pedro, as the tallest of them, should go into the water first to test the depth. Pedro took off his boots and handed them to Andre. He hoisted up his clothes as far as he could and stepped in. He shivered. The water was cold but not freezing. It had a pleasant silky feel to it, and he soon became accustomed to the temperature. His feet found their footing on the smooth pebbles which made up the bed of the stream. He planted each foot carefully, finding a firm place. The bottom became sandy, and his feet sank in as the water came up to his shoulders. He turned his head and looked back at them on the bank, making a face of false horror and fear. They laughed, half nervously, but trusting he was safe. He was in the middle at the deepest point. The flow was lazy, and the stream not very wide, and he made it easily to the other side in a few strides.

"I can carry you all over on my back," he shouted to them. "Not all at once, mind."

Guy was the first. He was the smallest. After a wobble in the deepest part when Pedro nearly lost his footing, Guy dropped off Pedro's back onto the bank at the other side, damp but safe.

"You ate too much of that damned fish last night," said Pedro.

It was good to see Guy laugh at this. He sat in the sun on the bank and watched as Pedro went back for the others. Andre was next and waved to Guy from Pedro's back. When the three of them were on the far side, they made a pretence of leaving Arnaud behind on the other bank by waving goodbye to Arnaud, who laughed and shook his head at them. When they were all safely on the far bank, they sat for a while and laughed at this escapade, and at Pedro, who was soaking wet through. The sun shone warmly on them and they rested and dried out quickly. The adventure in the stream energised them and they made good progress. They were determined to reach Agramunt that evening.

It was dark when they came across a shepherd's hut, which had bundles of straw and hay piled in a corner. The hut wasn't very big, but they were able to fashion makeshift beds from the hay for each of them and there was enough room for them to lie alongside each other. Covered by their cloaks, they were comfortable for the night. But Guy was up and down throughout the night, praying and walking outside. Pedro woke once or twice and noticed it. Arnaud and Andre slept through it.

Pedro was up early the next morning. Andre and Arnaud were still asleep, but he found Guy already up and sitting on a rock a little distance from the hut. He saw as he drew near that Guy looked exhausted. His skin was grey and the lines on his face seemed to be etched deeper than ever. Pedro sighed. He sat down next to Guy.

"You look tired, Guy," he said. "Did you not sleep well last night?"

"I just cannot shake off this feeling of foreboding," said Guy, shaking his head.

"But after that drunken evening the other night, there can't be anything to worry about. Surely we can trust Arnaud now."

"You might think so," said Guy. "I'm not so sure."

"Arnaud's like a member of the family; he's like a brother or a cousin to Andre."

"You were close to his mother," said Guy. "And that means you don't see him as I do. You see him as a little boy sitting at the kitchen table in Sybille's kitchen; it colours your judgement."

"Andre likes him," said Pedro. "He's spent so much time with Aunt Gaillarde and those boys – surely that can't have all been false."

"I don't trust him; I know he's done the *melioramentum* since you taught him, and he's done it with good grace, but this story about the rich aunt worries me. Someone should have gone beforehand to confirm his story." Guy looked at Pedro. "You know, Pedro, I am so tired, tired of all the worry over this journey, tired of having to play the game that Mondine isn't my wife to the Believers, and that she is my wife to the folk of Morella. I try not to behave with her as if she is my wife, but there are times… I can't resist temptation… sometimes I forget who I should be deceiving and about what. I'm not like the Authier brothers, learned and well read, and well versed in the New Testament, with all that dignity and goodness they had about them, and that strong sense of the rightfulness of being a Perfect."

Pedro watched an iridescent green beetle walk slowly past them.

"It didn't do them much good, did it?" said Pedro. "All that learning, it didn't stop them from burning on a Roman bonfire. Remember, God has chosen you to be the last Perfect. Accept this responsibility with good grace and take heart that you're doing God's work. Let's go on, we're nearly at our journey's end; it will soon be over."

"Do you know what's worst of all? I'm letting everyone down. I'm so tired of it all. I should go to Lombardy and undergo another ceremony to change me into the Perfect that I should be. You know the *consolamentum* I performed for Raymond de Toulouse was not valid? I've broken my vows so many times; I'm not fit to call myself a Perfect. I'm only glad I've not been required to perform any more *consolamenta* since, but it could happen any day. We're all vulnerable; any one of us could become ill and close to death."

"Is that why you agreed to come on this journey?" said Pedro. "To carry on to Lombardy and undergo another ceremony?"

Guy nodded. "I owe it to the Believers of our community. I know they put up with me because I'm all they've got. Each time they perform the *melioramentum* to me, the shame of my situation washes over me." He sighed and shook his head. "There is so much more I regret… I'm so tired… of… everything… So, I must press on and hope that I can undergo the ceremony again and become once again a true Good Man."

"We'll be at Tírvia tonight. If you're continuing with this journey, we can decide what to do after the visit to Arnaud's aunt. Otherwise let's take this a step at a time. Look, Andre and Arnaud are coming out now. Let's go forward in good spirits."

They stood up. Pedro patted Guy on the back and greeted the others as they approached.

"Is everything good?" said Arnaud, looking at Guy and Pedro.

"Guy's a little tired," said Pedro. "I think we'll all be glad to arrive at Tírvia – it's been a long journey. Let's see if we can find a farmer to sell us some bread and milk, I'm hungry."

They were all subdued as they progressed quietly along the track. Guy's misery infected them all. After a while, Guy began to preach.

"The sea will swell and take up the whole earth and the sky will come down so there will be no moon or stars. Then fire will come and consume the sea, then the sea will come back and put out the fire, the fire will come again, and this cycle will go on eternally. This will be the pit of Hell, where all the bad souls and demons and Satan will be thrown into this pit of Hell and remain there for ever. This world will be Hell. But the Son of God and all who have the 'understanding of Good', the Good Men and the Believers, will be in the Kingdom of the Father, where they will share the good without any evil. They will want for nothing other than what they have, and they will forget everything they have seen and had in this world."

Despite the message of hope for them as Believers, this sermon seemed to increase the feeling of despondency that hung over them. They plodded on. Pedro wondered if Guy's fears were linked to his feelings of guilt about his broken vows. It was as though Guy felt he deserved to be punished. Surely God would see that Guy had been thrust into a situation that was beyond him, and possibly beyond most men. The Perfects usually lived and worked together – that way they could support each other. They were less likely to break their vows if they had others to talk to and pray with. He thought in all honesty that Guy should probably not have been made a Perfect. But he was, and they were making this journey for what it was worth, and they would soon see what was waiting for them. If, as Guy suspected, Arnaud was a spy, they could all be in danger. Pedro still found this hard to believe; he could not reconcile Guy's view of Arnaud with that little boy who had sat at his mother's table a few years ago. He also took the view that his fate was in God's hands. Still, he shivered at the thought of capture, interrogation, torture and imprisonment, but surely it wouldn't come to that?

He looked back at Guy, who was walking as if his limbs were lead weights. His head hung down. Pedro stopped and waited for Guy.

"Let's rest for a moment," said Pedro. "This part of the journey seems to have taken us a long time. It will be late when we arrive at Tírvia. Why don't we try to find somewhere to sleep outside Tírvia? That way we can proceed to the village tomorrow morning and be refreshed when we meet Arnaud's sister, who will be there to greet us."

Shortly after they had walked through the quiet village of Castelbo, they came upon a farmer, who told them they weren't far from Tírvia. It was about an hour or so further up the track. He agreed to let them sleep in his barn. His wife would bring them some food. There amongst the hay and in the company of a tabby cat and her kittens, they bedded down. The soft sounds of the kittens suckling their mother lulled them to sleep. But it was another restless night as Guy was up and down many times to pray, and Arnaud was up early and whispered as he left that he was going for a stroll. The other three closed their eyes.

The sound of the barn door scraping on the stone floor woke Pedro. The door was being pushed open. The pale light of dawn was streaming in. He sat up and saw the others stirring and shielding their eyes. As the great door opened, all of them within the barn saw, framed in the doorway, not the farmer nor his wife, nor Andre's future bride and her aunt, but a group of men. Arnaud, Andre, Guy and Pedro scrambled to their feet. Arnaud walked the few paces away from his travelling companions to stand with the men. The oldest, a sturdy, strong-looking man with grey hair and beard, nodded to Arnaud.

"I'm the Bailiff of Tírvia; these are my men." He looked at Pedro, Guy and Andre, clustered together. "Guy Belibaste, Pedro Maury and Andre Maury, you're to come with me to Tírvia, where I shall formally arrest you on charges of heresy." He looked at Arnaud beside him. Arnaud nodded.

"Arrested?" Andre looked at Guy and Pedro, bewilderment on his face. "What's happening?"

"We've been betrayed," said Guy. "And you know who has betrayed us." He looked at Arnaud. "How could you?"

The Bailiff gestured to his men. "Get hold of them. Two to each man."

"I can't believe this," said Andre, struggling as two guards held his arms. "Tell them to stop. Arnaud… Arnaud."

"Be quiet," said the Bailiff. "Move along."

"Arnaud," said Andre. "What have you done?"

"Silence," said the Bailiff.

They were taken through the countryside to Tírvia. Pedro and Guy walked quietly, knowing that dissent was useless. Andre's protests and struggles soon died out. As they reached the village, a few women who were carrying pots on cushions on their heads, going for water, and men carrying tools on their way to the fields stopped to stare and speculate about these men the Bailiff was taking to his house.

It was the village manor house and the front door opened into a large hall furnished with one long table surrounded by benches. They were taken in. They watched as the Bailiff opened a great chest which lay to one side of the door. There was a loud clanging noise as he rattled and pulled out shackles and chains. He sorted through them until he had what he wanted. He turned to Arnaud.

"Which one is the Perfect?"

Arnaud pointed to Guy. "This one – he's the Perfect. The prize."

A shiver ran through Pedro's body.

"I'm shackling you to your betrayer," said the Bailiff, approaching Guy and signalling to Arnaud, come here. Clink, clank. The chains rattled as he put the shackles on Guy's ankle and wrists. "It's the usual way, betrayer and betrayed."

Arnaud nodded. Guy shouted and struggled. "Don't tie him to me. I don't want him near me – he's betrayed me."

"Arnaud, stop this now," said Pedro.

"This is how we do it," said the Bailiff, signalling for another man to help him. "You might as well accept it." Clunk. Arnaud and Guy were shackled at the ankles with a short chain as Andre watched, stunned.

"I knew it; I knew all along you were a Judas, you bastard son of a viper. I should have taken notice of my intuition," shouted Guy.

"Guy, it has to be you," said Arnaud, as iron cuffs snapped onto his wrists. "You in return for my mother's house and my family's possessions."

"Don't mention your mother," said Guy. "You're not fit to mention her name – what would she think of this?"

Pedro and Andre were standing to one side, as the Bailiff and his men checked the chains and shackles. Arnaud looked over and caught Pedro's eye then Andre's. A look of shame passed over Arnaud's face. He turned away and spoke to the Bailiff.

"There's no need to retain those two. I hired them to assist me. Let them go," he said. He looked at Andre and Pedro. "Go, you two, go, what are you waiting for?"

Andre and Pedro glanced at each other and back at Guy.

"Go," said Guy. "There's nothing you can do for me. Here, take this." Guy tried to point at something with his shackled hand. Pedro went to him. "There are two Jacquins shillings in that pocket," he said. "Take them for your expenses. Now, go, go…" He called as they moved away. "And look after Blanche and Mondine and…" Guy's voice broke. "And the children."

"I will, I promise," said Pedro. He caught hold of Andre's arm. "Come, Andre."

Pedro and Andre strode out, leaving Guy and Arnaud shackled together, watching them as they walked.

CHAPTER 20

Guy Belibaste

Guy felt the animal heat and strength of Arnaud's body shackled so close to him that their flesh and bones could be one. Arnaud's breath was on his cheek, Arnaud's smell – stale sweat – was mingling with Guy's. Blood was pulsing through Arnaud's body as it pulsed through his own. Arnaud, who had wormed his way into their lives, who had lived with them as a friend and who had been treated like family, but who had betrayed them. Arnaud, who knew about every one of the Believers in Aragon, where they lived, what they believed in, could betray them all. Pedro would do his best to save them… and with Andre to help… but would they have enough time before the Inquisition…?

"Walk in step," shouted one of the guards.

But walking in step with his betrayer felt impossible. This man was taking him to his certain death. But somehow, as they limped and staggered along, Arnaud pulled and pushed Guy into his rhythm, and, despite his feelings, Guy fell in with Arnaud's stride. Guy smiled grimly; they'd all been dancing to his tune anyway – why stop now? Arnaud was taller than Guy, his stride longer, and Guy stumbled and fell regularly, pulling Arnaud down with him. They were helped up by the guards, Guy roughly, Arnaud assisted with more respect. Guy was so tired, so weary, he could hardly go on, but a glimmer of relief flickered in his mind. Now he could give up the struggle that had worn him out. There would be no need to try so hard, he could give himself up to God, put himself in God's hands. He prayed silently for forgiveness for all his sins.

Arnaud, beside him, was full of vigour. "Guy, for God's sake, concentrate," he said. "Stop, now, wait, no, no, move the leg that's tied to mine, now, together."

But Guy wasn't ready; he couldn't do it. He collapsed in a heap, pulling Arnaud with him.

"I can't – I just can't walk with you."

"You've no choice in the matter; you might as well get on with it." Arnaud yanked the chain. Guy yelped with pain.

"Get up, move," shouted the guard.

Up again, they staggered along, one pulling, the other stumbling, but slowly, slowly, they again achieved a rhythm of sorts. Dear Lord, is this Your will? Guy prayed. *Dear Lord, give me strength to face what lies ahead.* His life sacrificed for Arnaud's mother's house. That was what lay ahead.

It was his own fault, caused by his inability to keep himself as pure as a Perfect should be. God knew what he had done and had decided it had to stop; it could not continue. God was asking for him. He'd known this for some time, but he had not known what to do about it, how to stop living the lie. He was no longer a real Perfect; in fact, if he was honest – and now was the time to be honest if ever there was such a time – he had never felt that he was a real Perfect. He had always had the feeling that the Authier brothers only allowed him to become a Perfect out of desperation. They had needed more Perfects. So, this was the time of reckoning; it was only what he deserved. He stumbled along, shackled to Arnaud. They lost the rhythm many times and were jerked into acknowledging each other. The chains round his legs were heavy. The shackles rubbed against his ankles; painful sores were developing. This was his final test. It was his chance to make up for his past failings. God had given him another chance, a chance to make a good ending. He vowed before God as he shambled along, that as his end approached, he would not renounce his faith, nor would he betray the Believers. Dear God, give me strength to face what I must endure to achieve absolution and eternal life.

The next stop was at a village where there was a fortress with a tower. Here they were to stop and rest. Flanked above and below by the guards, Arnaud and Guy were taken up several flights of steep, spiral stone steps, still dragging the chains. Either of them could fall and drag the other down, breaking their bones. The steps went on and on, round and round. Guy was sick and dizzy; his legs ached dreadfully. Finally, at the top, they were guided into a room. The door was shut and locked behind them, leaving them alone.

The room was small, barely two paces square, and there was no furniture. There was a tall window open to the elements, with a metal rail across it halfway up the opening. Framed by this opening, the countryside, wooded mountain slopes and river valleys stretched out for leagues before them. A soft breeze wafted into the small space. They stood, still chained together, and looked at each other.

"I thought they might have unchained me to let me go with them for refreshment," said Arnaud.

"Umm," said Guy. "They want me alive and as you are chained to me, there's more chance of that. Otherwise, I could throw myself out there." He nodded towards the opening.

"Let's sit down and lean against this wall," said Arnaud, trying to suppress a shiver. "We should rest."

They shuffled and rearranged themselves so they were sitting on the floor leaning against the wall. They both stared into the distance through the window opening.

"I might as well tell you," said Guy. "I've decided to fast from now on, and that way I may die before they get round to burning me alive."

"Oh, Guy," said Arnaud, turning to Guy, his face suddenly full of sorrow. "I wish I could help you. I was thinking as we walked, what a terrible thing I have done. I should not have done this. I've done it for worldly goods and possessions, which will be of no use to me in the hereafter. Now I see the error of my ways and I need God to forgive me." He gave a little sob.

"Hmm, that's all very well, but I can't trust anything you say, Arnaud, not after what you have done."

"I mean it, Guy, I was carried away with the idea of regaining my mother's house and goods, but now, faced with you, chained together as we are, you who have been my friend, and the realisation of what it will mean for you, I see I must repent and do what I can to save you."

"If you have finally discovered your moral conscience enough to repent and you really do mean that, Arnaud," said Guy, "I have an idea."

"What is it?" said Arnaud in a small voice.

"Well, I don't care about this earthly body of mine, which was created by the Devil and belongs only to the worms. God the Father is interested only in our souls, Arnaud."

"What's your idea?" said Arnaud, his voice now a hoarse whisper.

"This is a desperate situation we're in, but if you want God to forgive you, I could console you, God will forgive you your sins, and we can jump off this tower together and plunge to our deaths. If we do this now, our souls will ascend to Heaven, where beautiful angels with golden crowns will surround us and take us to meet the Heavenly Father."

"God won't forgive you taking your own life… and mine…" Arnaud swallowed, "in that way."

"In our faith, the only true faith, it is acceptable." Guy made a move to get up. He yanked the chains that bound them together.

"No, no, sweet Jesus, Christ above, Holy Mary, I'm not jumping off this tower with you," said Arnaud as he pulled Guy back with a strong jerk of the chain. "There's no need for… such… such drastic measures. Stop fasting and I will help you to escape – that way you can carry on the work of the Good Men and we will both be saved," said Arnaud. "Or you could recant, that might help."

"I could stop fasting, but I'll never recant, never, never, never. If I don't escape from this situation, I will go to my death upholding my true beliefs."

"Lean back against the wall here, Guy, for God's sake. Try to be calm, and I promise you that I will find a way to help you."

Guy sighed. "If God wants me now, I shall go to him with good grace; I will pray for forgiveness for my sins and I will remain true to my faith."

"Well then, there is nothing more to say for the moment – let's sit here and rest."

They manoeuvred themselves so they could sit more comfortably on the cold, stone floor and leant against the stone wall. They sat together quietly.

CHAPTER 21

Pedro Maury

Andre was looking back over his shoulder as Pedro grabbed his arm and pulled him along.

"Quick," said Pedro.

"Arnaud... Arnaud..." Andre shook his head. "He was like a brother to me."

"Andre, don't look back." Pedro gave Andre's arm a little shake. "We must go before the Bailiff changes his mind – we must go and warn the Believers."

"Surely the Inquisition have no power in Aragon?"

"They can enlist the help of local Bailiffs – and they have spies – as we well know."

Pedro strode out at great speed. Andre moved alongside him, almost running now.

"How could he?" Andre said.

"He let us go, Andre. He's got what he wants – Guy, the last Perfect. Now we have a chance to save the others. They will have to leave their homes and find another place to live. We must help them."

"He knows about all of us," said Andre. "But surely, now he's let us go, he'll not betray my mother; she was so good to him…"

"We can't take that chance," said Pedro. "We have to go to all of them. We'll go to Lleida, to the Servels' first, and then to Beceite, to Aunt Mersende and Jeanne. Then you must go and warn your mother, and I'll go to Morella to tell Mondine and Blanche… we'll manage with as little sleep as possible."

"My mother's got animals and a big property, I don't know how she can just leave it…"

"I know," said Pedro. "But think of those women on their own, the Servels, Mondine and Blanche, and the two children, Aunt Mersende and mad Jeanne, how will they fare? They've no money and no men to help them, and mad Jeanne, well, I wouldn't like to have to try and persuade her to move. At least your mother's got money and you two boys to help her."

"Arnaud must have been laughing at us the whole time. I feel such a fool for being taken in like that."

"I trusted him too; we should have listened to Guy. I was sure that because he knew me when he was a child, and he knew I loved his mother, that he would never do anything like this," said Pedro. "But now we must aim to walk twice as far as usual each day. That way we will reach everyone in about four days."

"I suppose we should be grateful that he let us go," said Andre. "But I don't know if I can keep that pace up – your journeys are quicker than anyone else's. Seven leagues in a day is a lot for me."

"We have to try," said Pedro. "Let's aim for Lleida and the Servels' first. We'll stop overnight and sleep for a few hours somewhere."

"We'll have to eat," said Andre. "We've nothing with us."

"Don't worry, we'll stop and find food wherever we can. I've got money; we won't go hungry."

They pushed on and on southwards, buying food wherever there was a village with an inn, or knocking on a farmhouse door where farmers shared whatever they had. Pedro allowed no slacking of their pace, and they marched until they were dropping. They rested for a few hours overnight at Àger, having covered about fifteen leagues that day. They fell asleep in a rough shepherd's hut in a field and were on the road again at first light. They reached Lleida and the Servels' house by late afternoon. Esperte couldn't take in the news at first; she sat in stunned silence, her face like a mask, then she got up and went outside without a word. Mathène's pretty face crumpled up and tears flowed down her cheeks. Pedro suggested he should help Mathène to prepare some food. Andre went outside to find Esperte. After a while, they came in, Andre with his arm around Esperte. They sat down to eat together.

"It's hard to believe Arnaud would betray Guy," said Esperte. "He seemed so much like one of us."

"He was so friendly with us all – it's hard to take in," said Andre.

"But now everyone must act to protect themselves," said Pedro. "You know that don't you, Esperte?"

"I see it's the only way," she said. "But another move, leaving things behind – it's not an easy thing, but… we have no choice, I suppose. Perhaps we could go to Juncosa – we were there before, and we know people there. What do you think, Mathène?"

Mathène nodded, her face pale, her eyes filled with tears.

Andre and Pedro left them making their preparations to pack. It was another two days of walking to Beceite. They hardly spoke. They stopped only to eat the bread and cheese Esperte had given them. They slept when the sun was high in the sky for four or five hours at a time in shady, quiet places under trees and hedgerows. They drank from clear mountain streams and walked in the dark of night to arrive at Beceite in the early hours of the morning, startling Aunt Mersende as she peeped through the shutters to see who was throwing pebbles at them. She came out immediately with a worried face. When she heard the news, she began to weep.

"This is the end for us," she wailed. "Who will be our Perfect now?"

"Listen, Aunt Mersende," said Pedro. "First, you must move from here with Jeanne – I'll come back and help you when I can, but I have to go to Morella now to warn Blanche and Mondine. Andre is going to San Mateo to tell his family and to help them sell up and move on. There is no time to waste, do you understand?"

"How can I do that with no-one to help me?" wailed Aunt Mersende. "I don't know where Jeanne is; she's hardly ever here these days. But… then again, perhaps I'll be better off alone. She would only cause me trouble – you know how the move affected her last time. Maybe that is the best thing. I'll go by myself and I won't tell Jeanne where I'm going."

Pedro and Andre exchanged glances. "I'll help you," said Pedro.

"I haven't any money – Jeanne steals from me," said Aunt Mersende.

"Listen, Aunt Mersende, Andre and I will have a short rest here, then I must go and warn Blanche and Mondine, and Andre will go and tell his mother," repeated Pedro patiently. "Then I'll come back here and bring some money to help you. I don't have enough money with me to give you any now. In the meantime, sell whatever you can't take with you and, if Jeanne returns, try to make her understand."

Andre and Pedro set off in the early hours of the next morning on their separate journeys. It was with a heavy heart Pedro made his way along the familiar route to Morella. He was dreading having to tell Blanche and Mondine about Guy. Especially Mondine, the mother of his two children, who loved him most of all.

It was early evening when he passed through the town gates. A small market was in progress. He walked up the lane where Blanche and Mondine lived. Blanche came out of the house with a basket on her arm. She stopped when she saw him. She put the basket down and clasped her face in her hands.

"Pedro," she said. "What's happened?"

"Where's Mondine?" said Pedro.

"She's inside with the children."

"Let's go in."

Mondine was sitting at the table, eating bread with little Guillemette. Mondine stood up and moved towards Pedro when he entered with Blanche. She searched their faces, from one to the other, with frightened eyes. Her complexion paled.

"Pedro," she said. Her voice faltered. "What are you doing here? Where's Guy?"

"Mondine…" said Pedro. "I'm afraid… I'm sorry to have to tell you… there is no easy way to say this: Arnaud Baille betrayed us."

"I knew it!" said Blanche, putting her hands up to her face. "Guy didn't trust that man."

"Where is he?" said Mondine.

"They took him." He put his arms around her to comfort her. She wept silently on his shoulder.

Blanche looked at Pedro over Mondine's back and pointed towards little Guillemette, who was still sitting at the table looking with big eyes at her mother. The baby was asleep in a large wooden cradle beside the fireplace.

"Where's Guy?" said Guillemette.

"He's gone over the border with Arnaud, Chérie," said Blanche. "Some men have taken him to meet the Bishop… but… perhaps… we'll see him soon, I'm sure."

"Why is Maman crying?" said Guillemette.

"She's missing Guy. She wants him to be here with us," said Blanche.

"So do I," said Guillemette.

Pedro looked at little Guillemette. This beautiful, innocent child had now to be dragged away from everything that was familiar to her. The future of this little family was going to be hard. He couldn't bear to think about that. The pain of his shattering heart threatened to overwhelm him. His legs, then his whole body felt weak, and he leant back against the nearest wall.

Mondine wiped away her tears, held his arm and guided him to sit at the table. Blanche brought water and bread for him. He sipped the water and nibbled the bread. He felt a little better for it and began to wonder how he could explain to little Guillemette without frightening her too much that Mondine and Blanche must take her and her baby brother away from here. He swallowed hard.

"Guy has sent a message to you all," he said. "He says it's time for you to move away from here, so it will be easier for Maman and Blanche to look after you whilst he's away." He felt tears rising as he spoke this half-truth, but he stopped, took a few deep breaths and managed to control the flood of tears that threatened. He cleared his throat.

Guillemette stared at him and Mondine nodded. "I think that will be for the best," she said.

"And the sooner the better, I should think," said Blanche.

"Yes," said Pedro. "That's right, Blanche, if you sell everything that you can't take with you now... I'll accompany you. Andre has gone to tell Aunt Gaillarde the same thing – we've already seen Aunt Mersende and the Servels; they're all packing up and moving on. I'll go back and help Aunt Mersende and Jeanne."

"I'll go into the village – I think I know someone who'll buy Guy's tools and perhaps his other things, then we can decide what to take with us. I'll need to find some work soon enough," said Blanche. "We could go to Valderrobres; I worked there once before, and I know a few people..." She glanced at him. He nodded.

He was grateful to these two women. They did not need him to spell out to them why they had to move. It flashed into his mind as he sat there, with Blanche and Mondine planning their move, that perhaps he would take a boat from Peniscola to Majorca, and see if he could settle there, away from it all. But first, he must help Blanche and Mondine. It took them all evening and most of the next day to sort out all their household goods, and Guy's tools and equipment from the outbuildings. Fortunately, a neighbour knew someone who would buy most of their household goods as well as Guy's tools.

They went to bed early to prepare themselves for an early start in the morning. The walk from Morella to Valderrobres normally took a day, but with the children and their belongings, the women would make slow progress. Pedro walked with them, carrying children and bundles of clothing and food. It was late at night when they arrived in the village. The inn had a room for them. The innkeeper, a kindly old man, promised he would help them to find somewhere more permanent in the morning. Pedro took their bags and bundles to their room. They followed behind. He looked around the room.

"This looks clean and comfortable," he said. "And I must say goodbye for now," he said. Mondine began to cry. He put his arms round her. "I will come back as soon as I can…"

"We'll manage well enough," said Blanche in a cheery voice. "Come, Mondine, the children need to sleep – let's concentrate on them. I'm sure things will look brighter in the morning… we'll find somewhere to stay for a while… and Pedro will come and find us…" She looked suddenly sad and spread her palms out in a helpless gesture.

"I will come back soon," he said. "I must find my brother Jean to warn him… and then… I'm not sure exactly when…"

He stifled a sob, closed his eyes and took a deep breath. There was so much he had to do before he could rest. He moved towards the door, summoned up some strength and turned to face them. "I will be back."

He must check that Andre had persuaded his mother and brother to move on. Then he must find where his brother Jean was grazing his sheep. He walked for several more hours, catching a few hours' sleep under a dry, secluded hedgerow in the afternoon, arriving at San Mateo in the evening.

Aunt Gaillarde was angry with Arnaud Baille, and angry with Guy and Pedro for trusting Arnaud.

"I'd rather the lot of you died than our Perfect," she said. She was angry with herself too for trusting him. She did, however, understand the need to move and, with the help of Pons and Andre, was busy with her plans. Pedro left them, saying he was going to walk through the night and find Jean on the pastures. As he left, Aunt Gaillarde ran after him.

"Pedro, I must tell you…" She looked shamefaced and seemed to be struggling to speak.

"What is it, Aunt Gaillarde?" he said with a sigh. "Tell me, don't be afraid." It was an effort to stay calm.

"I think I may have mentioned to Arnaud Baille about Jean, your brother Jean and his hopes of becoming a Perfect." She started to cry.

"Oh, Aunt Gaillarde," he said in desperation. He saw how frightened she looked. Her eyes were downcast. Patience, he told himself, they were all trying to do their best. "Don't worry, Aunt Gaillarde," he said. "It's just as well you told me. I'll think about it and I'll arrange something…"

If Arnaud told the Inquisition this, they would search for Jean. What could be done to disprove anything that Arnaud might have told the Inquisition about Jean's wish to become a Perfect? Whatever it was, it needed to be done in as public a way as possible, so everyone knew it wasn't true. But how? Pedro's mind was so full of Blanche and Mondine, the Servels, Aunt Gaillarde, Aunt Mersende, mad Jeanne and, most of all, Arnaud, and what he had done, that it was difficult to think. And he was weary. He looked for a place to lay his head for a few hours. There was no point in waking Jean and any other shepherds until dawn. He found a shepherd's hut and made a bed for himself on the straw he found there. He needed a long, long sleep. But he could only allow himself that when everyone had been taken care of, and that included Jean.

He woke at first light. He knew the grazing areas surrounding San Mateo well and he quickly found a group of shepherds who told him where Jean was working. Jean spotted Pedro's familiar tall figure walking towards him and waved as Pedro approached him.

"What's the news?" said Jean as they embraced. "I've been worrying about you all."

"There is a lot to tell you…" said Pedro. "Let's find a shady spot to sit."

They moved to lean against a large rock jutting up through the turf. Pedro told Jean all that had happened. Jean, shocked and disbelieving at first, was then angry with Arnaud and distressed about Guy. He saw the need to protect himself and the other Believers.

"I'm going back to Beceite now," said Pedro. "Then I've arranged to meet Blanche and Mondine again in Valderrobres, and make sure they're safe. Then I might go to Majorca. Why don't you sell your sheep and come with me, Jean? You'd be safe there and we could start a new life."

"No," said Jean. "I'll stay in Aragon and keep an eye on the Believers – as far as I can. If I move around, the Inquisition won't find me. I need to think about how to show the world I have no intention of becoming a Perfect. Perhaps I'll get married."

"Good idea," said Pedro. "We can think about that. Now, I need to sell my sheep. If I tell your landowner we've had a family crisis, do you think he'll buy them?"

The landowner agreed to buy Pedro's sheep for seven hundred Barcelona shillings. Pedro said goodbye to Jean. He promised to come back as soon as he could. He turned to see Jean watching as he walked away. He waved. But his heart was heavy.

There was no time to delay any longer. He walked at speed. He could make it back to Beceite that day to give Aunt Mersende some money and help her to move. He would grab a couple of hours of sleep in the afternoon somewhere quiet and shady.

He found a calmer Aunt Mersende in Beceite. Mad Jeanne had not returned home; she seemed to have thrown her lot in with the band of villains. Aunt Mersende thought she'd manage better alone. She planned to move to Alcañiz, where she'd heard there might be work. It would take three or four days to walk there. She had no money and only a few belongings. Pedro told her of his plan to go to Majorca. He gave her two hundred Barcelona shillings, promising to seek her out when he came back.

Then he pressed on back to find Blanche and Mondine in Valderrobres. It was only an hour's walk away. He went to the inn. The innkeeper had found lodgings for them. There was a widow who owned a large farmhouse on the edge of the village. She would be glad of the company. The women were pleased to see him, grateful for his help but subdued and sad. They would manage well enough: they had some money from selling Guy's tools and they intended to move around, following the harvests for seasonal work. The needs of the children would keep them going. He told them he was going to Majorca. He didn't know for how long. He wanted to leave Aragon behind. He'd done what he could for them all. He was desperate to rest and be alone.

CHAPTER 22

Guy Belibaste

The guards' leather boots slapped on the stone steps leading up to the tower. They shouted to each other. The words were indiscernible. The door swung open.

"Up, get up," shouted one, grabbing hold of Guy's arm. "We're taking the shackles off until you're downstairs." He poked Guy in his chest. "You can walk free – for the moment." He sneered. "Ha."

The guards pulled Guy and Arnaud up and removed the chains. Arnaud shook his limbs and grinned. "That's better," he said.

They descended the spiral stone staircase in single file. Two guards then Arnaud, two guards then Guy, two guards behind. What a relief to be unshackled. How easily they manoeuvred their way downstairs. But Guy was still their prisoner, and he harboured no hopes of escaping.

At the bottom, a guard grabbed Guy. "Don't get any ideas," said the guard as he chained Guy's arms together.

The guards surrounded Guy. They were explaining to Arnaud that it was easier this way, they would chain Guy at night so everyone could sleep and they would arrive at Pamiers sooner. Ah,

Pamiers, that was where they were going. He'd thought as much. The Episcopal Palace of the Bishop/Inquisitor, Jacques Fournier was there. This Bishop was the most feared of all the Inquisitors, known for his ruthlessness and rigour.

The group set off at a smart pace: Guy surrounded by guards, Arnaud on the periphery. It would take several days to reach Pamiers. He would take each day as it came. It would give him time to prepare for what was to come. There was a lot to think about. He had always known it would end like this. He blamed himself, lazy and weak-willed as he was. Now, God had called him, and he would go where God wished him to go. Dear God, help me to bear what lies ahead. Imprisonment… interrogation… possible torture… further imprisonment… and finally, burning. It wasn't that he wasn't terrified of all of this – he was. Most of all, he was terrified of the fire, the flames licking the sacrificial garments from his flesh, the scorching heat on his skin, the pain, then – oblivion. It was said the smoke quickly rendered the person tied to the stake senseless, mercifully ending their suffering. It would all soon be over. No more hiding, no more running, no more pretence and lies. This was his fate and his punishment, but also his chance to atone for his sins. *Whatever happened he would not denounce his beliefs.* And through this, he would achieve salvation. What he had lacked in life, he was determined to make reparation for in death. As for this final journey, he would avoid Arnaud, avoid discussion with any of these men. He would think about what was to come and how he might fortify himself. He would pray for help and forgiveness, and for Mondine and Blanche, and his dear children. A tear fell down his cheek as he thought of them – so many regrets… He looked up to the mountains which surrounded him and the white scudding clouds in the deep blue sky. *I will lift up mine eyes unto the hills from whence cometh my aid.* Almighty God was with him. Lord give me strength as I walk towards my fate and guide me through the ordeals to come. Amen.

It took them six days to reach Pamiers. The late spring weather was fine with a light breeze. It was a comfortable temperature for travelling. They slept where they could in the mountains, in barns and shepherd's huts. Guy, chained to a tree or a firm post, meant they all slept well, tired from their exertions. It was a relief to reach the lower reaches of the mountains, where there were villages, and more chance of replenishing food supplies and finding a bed for the night. Guy gave up any idea of fasting and ate the bread and water given to him by the guards. He refused the occasional meat and cheese that was offered to him, and he became weak and lightheaded – his back, legs and knees ached continuously, and the sores on his ankles were painful and weeping. By the time he reached Pamiers, late at night, he was barely aware of anything. They moved through the dark and quiet streets. The guards, one each side of him, held him upright. He could not stand alone. They were in a narrow lane between high buildings. He shook his head; his mind was slow and foggy. The guards dragged him through a square towards a tall terracotta building. There were gates before him, guards talking, then he was handed over and grasped by two more guards. They made their dragging, stumbling way through an open area, then steps and more steps; the skin on his shins was scraped as he gave up trying to climb the stairs. A door was opened; he was pushed through. He fell to the ground and closed his eyes.

He woke to the sound of a key turning in the lock and the door opening. Sunlight was streaming in through a high opening. He checked his body. He was stiff and sore everywhere. He slowly pushed himself up into a sitting position. A man, who looked to be in his fifties, stood before him. This man wore neat, clean, peasant clothes and his face had an amiable expression on it. Guy felt foolish sitting on the floor before this man and attempted to stand. He fell back. The man helped him up.

"Sit down over here," said the man, pointing towards a corner of the room where there was a straw mattress. "I'll help you." Guy and the man staggered across the space and Guy collapsed onto the mattress. Guy manoeuvred himself to look at the man standing next to him.

"Who are you?" he said.

"I'm Jean Belmas, a guard. I've brought you some bread and water."

"Where am I?" said Guy.

"In the Episcopal Palace."

"Pamiers?" said Guy.

"Yes, Pamiers and the Bishop…"

"What?" said Guy.

"The Bishop will see you now."

Guy steadied himself with his hands against the wall and slowly attempted to pull himself to his feet. His head swam; his legs trembled and gave way. He slid back down onto the straw.

"I'll help you," said Jean Belmas. "But first, have a drink and a bite of bread – you'll be all the stronger for it."

Jean went out of the open door and brought in the water and bread. Jean could leave the door open without fear of Guy making a run for it. The water tasted sweet and fresh. He bit into the hunk of bread that Jean handed to him on a platter. It was hard but edible and he pulled great chunks off it, swilling it down with water, suddenly hungry and thirsty. Almost immediately he felt a little stronger, his head clearer. He allowed Jean to help him as he stood. Jean held his arm as he steadied himself and they set off carefully through the grand palace. Jean Belmas kept up a stream of reassuring chatter. Guy had no idea what he said but it propelled him through the staircases, halls and corridors towards the place where he was to meet Bishop Fournier.

They were in a huge hall with many doors leading off it. Jean guided Guy towards a great carved door. Jean knocked on the door with a stick. Guy had not noticed the stick before. It must have been to hit him with if he attempted to escape. He smiled at the thought of this unlikely event. The door was opened by a monk and Guy was passed over. The monk was rougher than Jean Belmas. He pushed Guy towards a great table, behind which some men were seated. Guy's impression was of a room full of people. A wave of dizziness hit him. He grabbed hold of the chair in front of him and swayed. His legs gave way.

"He's too weak to stand," said the man directly facing him who was wearing a mitre and heavily embroidered garments. "Help him to sit."

Guy sank into the chair slowly – so painful, but what a relief to sit. A dense mist dropped like a curtain in his mind. He tried to concentrate. This was a Bishop in front of him. Shouldn't he kneel or stand before a Bishop?

"You are Guillaume Belibaste, known also as Guy Belibaste?" said the Bishop.

Guy stared at him. "I'm sorry…"

"Are you Guillaume Belibaste, also known as Guy Belibaste?"

"Oh… yes." The mist cleared a little.

"By the grace of God, I am Bishop Jacques Fournier, and this is…" Bishop Fournier was introducing the four men that flanked him. Guy looked around; perhaps there were only those four after all. Two monks, Brothers something or other, and two clerks. Their names went over his head, but this Bishop was Jacques Fournier. *That* Bishop. Known for his rigour. Behind the Bishop, Guy noticed a great crucifix on the wall facing him. Christ's body, life-size and painted in grisly detail, wounds spilling blood, the crown of thorns causing blood to drip down his face. The nails in his hands and feet, also dripping blood. The Crucifixion. A slow and painful death, probably a worse fate than being burned alive.

"Guy Belibaste, you are brought here before me on charges of heresy and blasphemy. I have information from several witnesses who have sworn under oath and given evidence to that effect. I require you to take an oath before I question you."

The Bishop's eyes bored into him. The fog in Guy's head swirled. There was a long silence as the curtain of mist swirled again then slowly rose to reveal his mind now clear.

"Guilty," said Guy. "I'm guilty."

The four men and the Bishop reeled in unison as if Guy had shot and pierced each one of them simultaneously with an arrow. They stared at him with shocked expressions, ten eyes boring into him. He was calm. He knew what he was doing. He'd had time to think on the journey. He would tell them whatever they wished to know about himself, but he would lie about his friends and the Believers who had formed the community in Aragon. It had been a dilemma. A Perfect does not lie. But he had committed so many worse sins that lying about the supporters and Believers would be a minor sin compared to the others he had committed. He'd not tussled with this dilemma for long. God would understand; his decision was the lesser of two evils. He simply could not betray the Believers. It was not in him to do that. He would deny all knowledge of their beliefs and of their whereabouts. That part was at least true. He expected that Pedro and Andre would have helped them all to move to pastures new. The Bishop could do what he wanted with him – he'd heard rumours of torture – but whatever they did to him, he confirmed to himself that he would never betray the Believers. And he would never recant his beliefs.

"You are required to take an oath that you will tell the truth, the entire truth, pure and simple, both about others, whether living or dead, and about all questions concerning your faith. Repeat after me."

This had been another dilemma. Perfects did not swear oaths. It would be a sticking point if he would not say it, so, with the same logic as before, he had already decided that he would swear an oath. A minor sin to save the Believers. God knew what was in his heart and mind, and he continued to pray for guidance and forgiveness for what he had to do. So, he repeated each phrase as Bishop Fournier spoke them.

"I, Guillaume Belibaste, also known as Guy, appearing before you, Reverend Father in Christ, my Lord Jacques, by the grace of God, Bishop of Pamiers, promise that I will tell the entire truth, pure and simple, about myself and others, whether living or dead, and about all questions concerning the Holy Roman church." God forgive me, he added silently.

The Bishop questioned him for only a few minutes more. Had he ever met Guillaume or Pierre Authier? Or Prades Tavernier? Or Philippe d'Aylarac? Or Raymond de Toulouse?

The Bishop waited. Eventually the Bishop began again.

"We have information that you lived in Rabastens with Philippe d'Aylarac and Raymond de Toulouse, that you accompanied them to give the deathbed ritual to dying Believers."

Memories of those overnight journeys with Philippe slid into Guy's mind. The men and women they consoled. The many times they stayed in Montaillou with Pedro's family, who made them so welcome.

"I must press you to answer my questions, otherwise we will help you to answer them." The Bishop's tone was threatening. "Where did you stay on these journeys?"

"In Montaillou." It slipped out of Guy's mouth.

"In whose house?"

Guy lay his head on the table. What had he nearly said? He could not trust himself to speak. He would feign delirium. He must avoid betrayal of any living person or families whose loved ones had received the *consolamentum*. They could not force him to speak, whatever they did to him. He groaned. He heard the Bishop speaking but the words were confusing. Something about the Clergue family and the Maury family.

Then it was over. Bishop Fournier crossed himself as he spoke.

"*In Nominee Patris et Filii et Spiritus Sancti, Amen.*"

Guy must also cross himself. Another dilemma he'd solved beforehand. He forced himself to sit up enough to cross himself.

And he said to himself the words that Guillaume Authier had told him to say. *This is my nose. This is my stomach. This is my left side, and this is my right.*

Guy was kept in the attic for two weeks. The sores on his ankles were painful and weeping. Jean Belmas washed and bandaged them every day but the fetid stench from them grew stronger. And Guy grew weaker. He was helped to eat and drink the bread and water rations by Jean Belmas. He moved in and out of awareness, conscious only of the food and water being given to him and the changing of the light, which came through an opening high in the wall; sometimes it was light, sometimes dark when Jean came to him.

Bishop Fournier came to the attic, bringing an entourage of men. They stood around Guy's bed. It was difficult to connect the Bishop's words. "Your end is near… Believers in Aragon… Pedro Maury… the Perfects?"

Guy lay on his pallet bed with his eyes closed. Finally, he heard: "Repent… heretical beliefs… burned at the stake."

He licked his lips and managed to reply in his strange, muffled voice. "I will not repent."

The sentence was announced in public, the usual procedure, but Guy was not fit to attend. He was visited in his room by one of the clerks, who told him the news. As Guy would not repent his Cathar beliefs, he was sentenced to be burned at the stake. He was to be returned to the place where he was born, Villerouge-Termenès, and under the jurisdiction of the Archbishop of Narbonne, his sentence would be carried out there. Guy lay on his straw bed and listened. He heard enough to understand. It was what he had expected but it felt like another blow to the core of his being. So feeble now that the world beyond his fragile body was hardly perceptible. Would he survive long enough to arrive at Villerouge-Termenès and be burned?

Guy experienced little of the journey. He was carried and placed in a covered cart; cushioned by blankets, he felt warm and comfortable. The swaying of the horse-drawn cart lulled him to sleep. Occasional jolts woke him out of his numbed slumber, but he suffered no further injury during the day-long journey. They carried him to a small cell in the dungeon of the château at Villerouge-Termenès. There was a bed of straw, and a bucket for him to relieve himself. They brought bread and water twice a day and helped him with his daily needs. His mind was clear and calm. His suffering would soon be over. They sent a priest to him every day, asking if he wished to pray or to recant. But he did not.

It was early on the morning of the day he was due to be burned, and a guard who he knew as Michel entered with bread and water.

"The Archbishop is coming this morning," said Michel. "Take this refreshment now and be ready for him."

The Archbishop, fully attired in his fine robes and regalia, seemed incongruous in Guy's squalid cell. The small space was filled with people, but it was only two monks accompanying the Bishop. Guy lay on his straw mattress covered by a dirty blanket. With effort, Guy focused his eyes to study the Archbishop. He was a small man with dark eyes. His plump face had a supercilious expression on it. The Archbishop had his hand over his nose but moved it when he spoke.

"Guy Belibaste, I am here in the presence of…"

It was difficult to follow the Archbishop. He talked for a long time. He intoned the words as if he was praying in church. Finally, he stopped. A small silence and he started again.

"You are… end is near… recant."

Something was required of Guy. He must speak but it was difficult to articulate the words. His mouth was dry. Someone put water to his lips.

"I will not recant," said Guy. He hoped they understood him.

There was silence. The Archbishop said a few more words and

left. Michel came in and said something, but Guy couldn't make it out. Michel carefully removed Guy's clothing and placed a white cotton garment over his head. Michel kissed him on his forehead.

"I shall pray for you, Guy."

The guards carried him to a place between the château and the river where the pyre was laid. The Archbishop, two monks and a handful of villagers were standing by. One of the monks held a large cross. The Archbishop was praying. Guy, calm and aware, prayed as he was carried to the pyre and tied to the stake. *Our Father, which art in Heaven...* He watched as the wood was ignited... *hallowed be Thy name...* He felt the heat from the flames as they licked ever closer. The smell of wood smoke in his nostrils. His garments caught fire. He screamed. The smoke swirled around him; it entered his mouth and nose. He screamed again, coughed, spluttered and choked...

The Testimony and Confession of Guy Belibaste Villerouge-Termenès 1321

And considering that the aforementioned Guy Belibaste, as the result of what precedes, has committed many crimes as regards heresy, seeing various heretics, hearing their preaching, and believing the aforesaid errors, worshipping the heretics and receiving and eating the bread blessed by them, and committing other acts of heresy contained in his present confession, that he became a heretic himself, undergoing a ceremony performed by other Perfects to make him a Perfect. And that he preached and received others into the heresy, that he consoled many who were dying, laying his hands on their bodies and assuring them of forgiveness for their sins. And that he denied that the Holy Roman Church was the only church of God our Father.

He declared himself guilty and ready to receive the sentence that Monsignor the Bishop and our Lords the Inquisitors wished to impose on him for these crimes that he has committed as regards heresy, and he gave up to all defences through which he could raise in right or in fact against his present confession, wanting to stand by it and persevere with it for ever, as true, lawful and containing the true facts made willingly and spontaneously not out of fear or the pressure of torture. He promised never to go back on this present confession; he would never recant or change his beliefs. He asked for no clemency.

The aforementioned Guy Belibaste, son of the late Guillaume Belibaste of Cubières, confessed, testified, abjured and swore in the aforesaid manner in the presence of the aforementioned my Lord Bishop the year, date and place as above, in the presence and to the testimony of the religious Friars Gaillard de Pomiès, Arnaud du Caria, O.P., from the monastery of Pamiers, Bernard de Taïx, monk of the monastery of Fontfroide of the order of Citeaux, Guillaume Peyre-Barthe, notary of the aforementioned my Lord Bishop as regards the Inquisition and Jean Strabaud, Notary Public of Monsignor the Bishop and particularly in the cases of the Inquisition, which has, on the order of Monsignor, carried out at the reception and was present at the public reading of everything which precedes, and has written it for the most part, even though part of this confession has been written by Master Guillaume Nadin, notary of the King and of Monsignor the Bishop as regards the Inquisition, which was not present when this public reading took place, and could not receive it as a result.

And I, Jean Jabbaud, cleric of Toulouse, have written and corrected this.

CHAPTER 23

Pedro Maury

Valderrobres to Peniscola was a distance of eight leagues. Pedro did the journey in one day. He was deeply weary, and this journey taxed him more than the recent days of helping people to pack and locate elsewhere. What a relief it was over, and all the Believers had moved on. But what next? He had no clear idea or plan. One step at a time. He walked along the harbour, boats bobbing on the water, the smell of fish and the sea. The piles of fishing nets everywhere. Seabirds wheeling and screaming.

There were frequent sailings back and forth to Majorca, and he quickly found a boat that was due to leave shortly. He paid his passage and walked along the gangplank. He searched out a place away from the other passengers; he didn't want to talk to anyone – his mind was too full of everything that had happened, and he was desperate for sleep. Below deck, it was quiet and there were benches along the sides. He found a space where he could lay his head on his small bundle of belongings, closed his eyes, experienced for a moment the gentle rocking of the boat and fell immediately asleep.

He woke to the sound of sailors' voices shouting to each other, to the bangs and bumps of the boat against the wharf and to chains rattling. They had arrived in Majorca.

He found lodgings in the port and decided to rest there for a few days. He didn't know what else to do; he couldn't think beyond his need to sleep. He slept and dreamt. The same old nightmare of being chased and trying to run and not being able to move his legs – he was stuck with an unseen monster chasing him and catching up… He was taken to Carcassonne where Arnaud Sicre sat on a high throne flanked by Dominican monks… he looked closely at their faces, one of them… no, all of them… had the face of Pierre Clergue… the priest of Montaillou… Pedro was taken and dragged towards a bonfire… he knew they would throw him onto it… his parents were watching… he screamed and struggled… he woke up, screaming, "No, no, no!", drenched in sweat, his heart racing hard. He dreamt every night during the first few nights he was there. Sometimes flames licked around him; another time he was married to Mondine and mad Jeanne was chasing him.

During the day, he wandered around the busy port and allowed his mind to roam as he watched the people, goods and animals moving onto and off the boats. He inhaled the salty, fishy smell as he watched the fishermen with the daily catch. He thought of the Perfects and their fish and vegetable diet. And of his family, of his brother Jean, of Aunt Gaillarde and her sons, of mad Jeanne and Aunt Mersende. Of Blanche and Mondine, and the children. How were these people he had grown to care so much about? And Guy? He could hardly bear to think about Guy, but images of flames came to him often, both in dreams and when awake. The pain of his losses was visceral. So many of the people he had loved and known now gone. His parents and his sister Guillemette. The women he had loved, Sybille Baille, Brunissende. And all the Perfects – the Authiers, Raymond de Toulouse, Philippe, dear Philippe… Prades Tavernier – he had met so many of them as he had accompanied them on overnight journeys. And there were many others, ruined or damaged through their part in the faith. He should pray for all these people and himself. But he didn't have the inclination. What had it all been for? Did God mean this to happen? Was this punishment because they were wrong in their beliefs? Was it the wrong path he had taken along with all the others? Is there a God? And if there is, how could he be so cruel as to play with people's lives in this way? So many questions but no answers. But one thing was certain – without any Perfects to lead them, their faith was doomed. What did the faith mean to him now?

The answer came sharply to him. It meant nothing. They had tried and failed. There was nothing left of the faith to believe in now. He had lost his faith. His belief now was that in the end it no longer mattered what people chose to worship and believe in – or if they believed in God or not. Life happened in a random fashion. There was no meaning or sense to it. Guy came to him often. Had they burned him? And had he been strong at the end or had he recanted? He wouldn't blame Guy either way. We have to do what we can and what we think is best.

After three weeks of resting and thinking, Pedro left Majorca to return to the mainland. He needed to see the people he cared about, the ones who were still alive. And he wanted to resume his life as a shepherd, although he was now a different man to the one who had set out as the hopeful young shepherd, curious about life, who left Montaillou all those years ago. Now he felt much older, much sadder but possibly a little wiser. And he was still a shepherd at heart. He needed to return to the pastures and his sheep.

At the end of April 1321, Pedro was in Tortosa. The first thing he did was to seek out his brother, Jean. Jean had been on Pedro's mind in Majorca. Jean was the main reason he had returned to Aragon. He found him easily enough after asking around. Jean was with his flock in the high pastures of the mountains for the summer. The meadows were rich and lush, and the young lambs were thriving and growing quickly. They were being weaned and the shepherds were beginning the cheese-making. Pedro gladly joined in with the routine tasks: making the cheese, looking after the animals – it helped to soothe his still-troubled mind.

He sat up late in the evenings at the campfire, talking to Jean about all that had happened and all the people they knew and loved. The threat to Jean was serious and they needed to protect him. They discussed the idea of Jean marrying and, most importantly, being seen to marry.

"Well, that's possible," said Jean. "But suppose I do find a way to go to Lombardy and become a Perfect, what about my wife then? I don't like the idea of marrying someone who doesn't understand what that means."

"You must marry someone you can be honest with and who goes into the marriage knowing it will be a marriage in name only," said Pedro. "I have thought about this and the person who comes to mind is Mathène Servels."

"I wondered about Mathène as well," said Jean. "But will she agree to it?"

"I have a feeling that she will. The family are devout Believers. I'll visit her and her mother and put the proposition to them."

During that summer, they heard from Pierre Montanier, the shepherd who had been up in the Fenouillèdes, that Guy had been burned at the stake in the village of Villerouge-Termenès, near the château. Pierre Montanier told them that Guy had not repented of his beliefs, and it was said he did not betray any of the Believers. Jean and Pedro had been waiting for this news, but to hear that it had happened grieved them deeply. But alongside their grief was a sense of pride and joy that Guy had been strong at the end. He had remained true to his beliefs and had not betrayed his followers.

In the autumn, Pedro and Jean returned with the sheep to the plains of Aragon. Working together with a team of shepherds, they moved several hundred sheep belonging to different stockbreeders from the summer pastures in the mountains. Pedro visited Mathène Servel and her mother to suggest to them that Jean should marry Mathène. They agreed, having understood what it would mean for Mathène. The marriage was to take place in January of the following year. It was to be solemnised in church and the marriage was to be recorded officially, as if Jean Maury and Mathène Servel were loyal Roman Catholics. With that arranged and taken care of, Pedro went in search of Aunt Mersende. He hadn't seen her since she moved, and he hoped she had prospered. Maybe she could even repay him some of the money he had lent her. But when he reached Alcañiz, where she had planned to go, the villagers told him that Mersende was dead and buried. She had collapsed and died suddenly just a week or so before his visit. As for Pedro's Barcelona shillings, well, no-one knew anything about that.

Pedro left Alcañiz to search for Blanche and Mondine. He was relieved to discover, when he found them in Herbés, not far from Valderrobres, that they knew already that Guy was dead. That was a relief. He had been the bearer of bad news too often. They had heard it from Raymond Issaurat, who had heard it from a shepherd, probably just before Pedro did. Blanche, Mondine and the children were safe and well, but living hand to mouth, taking work wherever they could, following the harvests. Their life was not easy. Pedro gave them all the money he had left, which was twenty-five Barcelona shillings. He would soon earn more.

In the spring of 1323, after Jean and Mathène's wedding, Pedro went to Flix, where he expected to find work. It was two years since Guy's arrest, and it seemed unlikely that the Inquisition would come after him and Jean now. As he walked through the village of Flix, he felt, for the first time in ages, burden-free. The village was quiet, it was just after midday. Most people were inside their houses. As he left the village, going down a small hill towards the pastures, he felt a tap on his shoulder.

"Pedro Maury?"

"Yes."

"I'm the Bailiff, I'm acting on behalf of Arnaud Sicre, sometimes called Baille, who works for the Inquisition. I'm arresting you on suspicion of heresy."

There were two of them. The Bailiff tied Pedro's hands together behind his back. Pedro offered no resistance. There was no point. The Bailiff told Pedro he was taking him first to Barcelona, where he would undergo preliminary questioning. Later, he would be sent to Carcassonne or Pamiers to be interrogated by the Inquisitors.

He had thought Arnaud would leave him free. Arnaud, who knew how much Pedro loved his freedom, who knew that what Pedro loved most was to be on the pastures with a flock of sheep, and to sit with the other shepherds by the campfire at night. Why now? After all, with no Perfects left, Pedro was no threat to Rome. They wanted to punish him, be seen to punish him and so tie up all the loose ends. Or perhaps the Inquisition had withheld Arnaud's reward of his mother's house until he brought him in. Could Arnaud have always known he would have to bring in Pedro and hand him to the Inquisition? Had Arnaud given him two extra years? There was time to think about what he might say. He was prepared to lie to save the Believers, who still lived their lives in Aragon and the County of Foix. And to save his own life.

The Testimony and Confession of Pierre Maury 1323

He did not say anything else that was relevant, [although] he was interrogated promptly.

And considering that the aforementioned Pierre Maury, as the result of what precedes, has committed many crimes as regards heresy, seeing various heretics, hearing their preaching and believing the aforesaid errors, worshipping the heretics and receiving and eating the bread blessed by them, and committing other acts of heresy contained in his present confession, he asked him if he repented of having been so seriously guilty in the aforesaid acts, and having sinned on so many occasions outside of the Catholic faith by believing these errors. He replied that he repents with good will and a good heart of having committed what precedes and, from what he said, he genuinely wants to surrender the belief in these errors, and from now on to keep, follow and even defend the faith which the Holy Roman Catholic Church keeps and preaches. He declared himself ready to receive and carry out the sentence or penance that Monsignor the Bishop and our Lords the Inquisitors want to impose on him for these crimes that he has committed as regards heresy, and he gave up all defences through which he could raise in right or in fact against his present confession, wanting to stand by it and persevere with it for ever, as true, lawful and containing the true facts made willingly and spontaneously not out of fear or the pressure of torture. He promised never to go back on this present confession and asked to be absolved of the sentences of excommunication which he had incurred because of these acts.

And he was absolved by the aforementioned my Lord Bishop of these sentences and reconciled and reunited with the Catholic Church, provided, however, that he wants to come back with a good heart and an unfeigned faith to the unity of the Sainte-Mère-Eglise and give up the aforesaid errors, and he has wholly confessed to the truth as regards heresy as much about him as others.

He reserved the right, however, that if something came back to him to his memory that he has not yet confessed to, he could confess to it without danger, which was granted to him by the aforementioned my Lord Bishop.

But before being absolved of the aforesaid sentences of excommunication, he abjured and swore as follows: "I, Pierre Maury, son of the late Raimond Maury of Montaillou… all my possessions."

And he concluded like this in the present case and asked that the sentence was rendered and that he was shown mercy.

The aforementioned Pierre Maury confessed, testified, abjured and swore in the aforesaid manner in the presence of the aforementioned my Lord Bishop the year, date and place as above, in the presence and to the testimony of the religious Friars Gaillard de Pomiès, Arnaud du Caria, O.P., from the monastery of Pamiers, Bernard de Taïx, monk of the monastery of Fontfroide of the order of Citeaux, Guillaume Peyre-Barthe, notary of the aforementioned my Lord Bishop as regards the Inquisition and Jean Strabaud, Notary Public of Monsignor the Bishop and particularly in the cases of the Inquisition, which has, on the order of Monsignor, carried out at the reception and was present at the public reading of everything which precedes, and has written it for the most part, even though part of this confession has been written by Master Guillaume Nadin, notary of the King and of Monsignor the Bishop as regards the Inquisition, which was not present when this public reading took place, and could not receive it as a result.

And I, Jean Jabbaud, cleric of Toulouse, have written and corrected this.

Jean Duvernoy, *Le Registre D'Inquisition De Jacques Fournier*
Translated by Amy Hargreaves

Aftermath

After long and intensive questioning (his is the longest deposition in the Jacques Fournier Register), Pierre (Pedro) Maury renounced his heretical beliefs. He was sentenced to the Wall, the notorious prison at Carcassonne. He was kept on bread and water rations but not shackled. The manner and date of Pierre's death has not been recorded.

Jean Maury was arrested with his wife, Mathène, and his mother-in-law, Esperte, shortly after his brother, Pierre Maury. Jean was sentenced with Pedro on Sunday 12th August 1324. They both received the same sentence.

The records of Guy's interrogations are not available. (His confession is a product of my imagination.) But we do know that he did not recant his Cathar beliefs and that he was burned at the stake in Villerouge-Termenès. The château at Villerouge-Termenès belonged to the Archbishops of Narbonne until the French Revolution. It was taken over and occupied by villagers until the end of the twentieth century, when the French government bought it and restored it. It is now a tourist attraction.

Arnaud Sicre/Baille was given back his mother's house and possessions as a reward for bringing the last Perfect to the Inquisition and for betraying his friend Pedro Maury to the Inquisition. He continued to work for the Inquisition in an administrative position for the rest of his life.

The graves of those consoled by Cathar Perfects were dug up. The piles of muddy bones were paraded through the streets of Pamiers on carts, then ceremoniously burned to ashes. Even dead Believers were not left to rest in peace.

Bishop Jacques Fournier had an illustrious career on the strength of his work as an Inquisitor in Pamiers. In 1327, he became a Cardinal and, in 1333, he was elected Pope Benoit XII. He built a grand Pope's Palace, which is now one of the main tourist attractions in Avignon. He died in 1342 and his remains are in the Cathedral at Avignon.

Susan E Kaberry 2021

Acknowledgements

Thanks are due to many people for encouragement and help in bringing this book to life. To all who read early drafts of the book, you know who you are. To Emma Darwin, who gave support and advice which enabled the book to develop into its present state. To Rene Weis, Professor of English at University College, London, whose book *The Yellow Cross* I bought when I visited Rennes-le-Chateau, and which inspired me to write about the Cathars. To Emmanuel Le Roy Ladurie, who first translated Bishop Fournier's records from Latin into French, and in doing so gave this story to the world. To Amy Hargreaves, who translated the records from French to English.

Finally, to David, who has lived with Pierre Maury (Pedro) and Guillaume Belibaste (Guy) for several years. He accompanied me on many excursions into the Pyrenees to discover the places where Pedro and Guy worked and lived. Together we explored Ax-les-Thermes, Pamier, Foix and Avignon, where Bishop Fournier built his magnificent palace, when he became Pope. Walking in the footsteps of the people who lived so long ago was a charged experience. It helped me to understand their lives and inspired me to try and bring them to life again in the pages of this book. To all of you, your support has meant so much to me. Thank you.

Susan E Kaberry 2021

About the Author

Susan E Kaberry lives in Manchester and spends as much time as possible in France. She began writing fiction when she retired after working in the NHS for most of her life. Her first Cathar novel was *The Chatelaine of Montaillou*, also based on Jacques Fournier's records. She also has written a memoir, *Britannia Street*, using her maiden name, Beth Cox.